Claiming What's His

Kings of Hawthorn Series

A.M. McCoy

Contents

Chapter 1 – Cora Ten Years Ago

I walked into the party just after midnight and cursed the entire night in my head. I moved through the living room first and tried to ignore the multiple people fucking in a giant orgy on a vintage Henry Bogs ornate carpet.

I clenched my fists at my sides as I avoided bodies and ignored people who called out to me as I searched for Mav. He wasn't even supposed to be here tonight, and that was what pissed me off even more than having to actually come here looking for him. He told me he was staying home, and that he wanted a quiet night alone. And then his mom called me and asked if he was staying at my house or coming home after our movie night tonight and I did what I hated the most, I lied.

I told her he was staying with me and then I'd gotten dressed and drove across town to find him at the biggest party going on tonight. We graduated three days ago, and he had been on a bender for about two months straight already, leaving me unsure if he was even going to survive long enough to go off to college with me in the fall. He needed to take a damn break from all of this, or he was going to end up like–.

I couldn't even bring myself to say his name in my head; I'd break down and start crying if I did and I had something important to do right now, so I needed to focus.

I could not cry.

I saw Tim and Josh playing pong in the kitchen with a couple of naked girls from school and forced myself to walk in. I hated this rich kid lifestyle, even though I was a rich kid.

"Hey, Cora kitty. I didn't think you were coming out tonight." Josh, one of Mav's best friends, said to me as he threw a ball across the table and directly into a cup held between a girl's tits. I didn't recognize her, though if she had clothes on, maybe I would. Maybe I wouldn't, I tried to distance myself from these people at all costs usually.

"I didn't want to come here tonight, but Marsha called me and was looking for Mav. Is he here?" I asked.

Josh glanced at me and then over at Tim.

Red flag number one.

"Uh yeah, I think I saw him earlier, he might have left though, I haven't seen him in a while." He said, unable to meet my eyes.

Red flag two.

"Be straight with me Josh. I just want to make sure he gets home safe." Unease filled my stomach as I looked between Maverick's friends while they contemplated telling me something.

Finally, Tim sighed and looked at me straight, "He went upstairs about a half-hour ago." He said nothing else, and I guess he didn't have to. I already knew what he wasn't saying.

"He wasn't alone, was he?" I asked, clenching my teeth together to keep from screaming.

He just shook his head no.

"Thanks," I said and turned towards the stairs. With every step that I took up them, I thought back to our ten-year relationship and all the good things we'd shared through each of those years. Everyone always called us crazy when they heard we'd been together since we were eight and that we were going to college together and had our whole life planned. But for us, it was easy because it was what we wanted most.

We'd been best friends since kindergarten when Maverick pushed JJ Lane off the swing set for tripping me to get to it first at recess.

After that, we were two peas in a pod. He was always a big kid, tall and wide and intimidating, with a crazy amount of money and power from his parents, which left him untouchable, even at a young age. And he'd taken me into his world and protected me ever since that. He kissed me on the cheek on that same swing set two years later and asked me to marry him. He had given me a ring pop and everything.

We made it official; we'd been inseparable since then.

Or at least, we had been until a drunk driver killed his twin brother two months ago and his world collapsed around him. I had felt us drifting apart the last few weeks and deep down, I'd known this night was coming. I'd been holding onto him longer when I had him, which had been less and less as his broken heart left him incapable of loving me the same way he used to. He kept me at arm's length like he was afraid his own pain and rage would rub off on me somehow.

My heart ached with each bedroom door that I passed, unable to make myself turn a single knob until I stood outside of the last door in the hallway and felt a tear slide over my cheek. I swiped at it quickly and looked around to make sure no one saw me standing there crying.

I didn't want anyone to witness my destruction.

I heard something from inside the room and froze, holding my breath as I tried to hear better. I pressed my ear to the door but couldn't make it out. So I quietly forced myself to turn the knob, and I opened the door by pushing it.

"I bet I'm so much better than her." A female voice said from the other side of the room. I'd recognize that voice anywhere, even before my eyes adjusted to the dim lighting in the primary bedroom of the mansion; I knew who it was.

It was Sarah, my best friend.

That couldn't be happening.

Even without seeing his face, I could tell that Maverick clenched his teeth as he replied, "Shut up."

"Admit it, I feel better on your cock than Cora does. Why else would you want to fuck me like this, all rough and needy?" Boiling rage filled my heart as I stepped into the room and saw Mav's back. He had Sarah in his arms, pinned between him and the wall with his pants down around his thighs as he thrust into her. As he fucked her, she wrapped her legs around his hips and clawed at his bare muscled back.

"I said shut up, or I'm going to find someone else to fuck." He swore. A part of my heart broke inside of my chest in a way that I'd never experienced before. It felt like a physical part of me broke.

Sarah's drunk, bleary eyes opened and focused on me over his shoulder, then a sinister smile pulled her lips back while my boyfriend of over a decade railed her into the wall. "Mmh yeah, fuck me hard. You know how I like it." She purred into his ear and he grunted. I watched in horror as he did just that. His hips jerked wildly for a few seconds before he stilled and rested his forehead against the wall while he caught his breath.

He stepped back and dropped Sarah to the ground on her own feet in a cold, uncaring way that was so uncharacteristic of him. When he pulled up his shorts and buttoned them, he saw that she still stared past him with that sick smile on her face and he turned to look over his shoulder towards the door.

The second his blue eyes locked on mine, I knew I'd never be the same.

Seeing the person you love more than your own life, destroy your heart so carelessly, just did something to your soul. The pain was no longer physical because it ran deeper than that.

"Cora." He whispered, taking a step towards me, but I shook my head as more tears fell over my lashes.

"Don't," I said back to him.

The pain on his face mirrored the expression he had as we listened to his father informing us about the death of his brother Luke in that crash. It had destroyed him that night and I recognized his pain now because I felt that it in my own heart.

"Well, it's about time she found out," Sarah said with a level of sneer I'd only ever seen her aim at her enemies.

"Shut the fuck up," Mav commanded and stepped towards me again.

As my world began crumbling around me, I turned and left the room. I didn't run, because I knew he'd chase me and it'd make a scene, which was the last thing his family needed right now. I felt him following me as I left the party, silent but close behind me, like he always did when he was protecting me from drunk losers at raging parties like this one.

I never thought I would have to protect myself from him.

People called out to us as we walked out the front door, but we ignored everyone.

"Please, just wait." He said, putting his hand on my arm as I got close to my car.

As I stopped walking, I yanked my arm away from him, feeling the sting of the burn his touch left on my skin. "Please don't touch me," I begged, on the edge of losing it.

"I'm so sorry, Cora," His sad eyes tried to get me to look at him, but I couldn't. I didn't want to remember him like this.

"Can I go now?" I asked, bringing my knuckles to my lips to keep from crying out in agony.

"Just let me explain. Let me make it better, baby. I'm so sorry. She means nothing; it was just a mistake."

"I don't want to know anything more, Mav." I said, shaking my head and backing up further, "Please, just let me go."

"Let me drive you home. I need to be with you right now. Please." He begged in a gutted voice that finally brought my eyes to his.

I shook my head. "You could have been with me earlier, Maverick! But you lied and said you wanted to be alone, but that was just the lie of a selfish cheater so he could get what he wanted, which wasn't me. I don't want to know anything else. I don't want to hear another word about what you've done or with whom. What I already know is too much, I won't survive anymore."

His eyes were wild as he frantically tried to reason with me. It was the first time I'd seen any genuine emotion in his eyes in months, and it destroyed me. "Okay. Then I won't talk, but let me be near you! Let me drive you home, you're too upset to drive. Just let me be by your side, I'll sleep on the floor and we can talk tomorrow. I can fix this if you let me. I don't even know why I did this. It's only ever been you I see, I'm sorry I deceived you, Cora, you know how fucked up I am right now! I'm just fucked!"

"I'm done Mav," I whispered and took another step back. Pain wracked my chest, and I placed my palm flat to my sternum, trying to soothe the ache there. I was so close to losing it all right here, but I couldn't.

I couldn't let anyone see me break. Valentine's didn't break in public.

"No!" He barked out, stepping towards me, and pulling me into his chest. "No, don't say that! I've been fucked in the head, and I'm spiraling and I'm sorry. You deserve so much better than this, I know that. I just didn't know how to cope, and I fucked up! Please help me, Cora. I need your help."

"I can't," I whispered as I shook my head. "I've given myself to you for ten years and in the last two months, I've watched you destroy yourself and now you've destroyed us. And I can't stick around anymore, or you'll destroy me too. I have to walk away while I still can."

"Please, baby." He begged, leaning down and resting his forehead on mine.

I pushed him away, smelling her on his skin as a sob ripped from my chest. "I love you Maverick. But I have to love myself more."

"I love you more than myself, Cora! I see that now, please just give me a chance. I did this because I was trying to protect you from me! From this pain! Ten years has to mean something to you, it has to prove to you I'm worth a second chance."

"Protect me?" I yelled, "I never want to feel like this again, Maverick." Tears poured down my face freely as I shook my head back and forth, clutching my keys like a lifeline. "And if I stay, you'll do it to me again. It's not the first time you've done it, and I'm confident she's not the only one you've done it with, either. I've only been with you. You were supposed to be my only."

"I am your only. Please don't do this." His voice was a mere whisper as tears fell from his lashes.

But I took a step back, and then another. "Not anymore. I used to feel safe in your arms, I used to only fall asleep peacefully when you held me and I ached for you when we were apart, but it was never the same for you. You never needed me like I needed you! You've never survived simply because I did, like I do with you every single day." My voice was so detached and didn't sound like me at all as I severed a part of my body off right in the middle of the street and walked away from it. "Get yourself home in one piece. Your mother won't survive burying another son."

I turned and got in my car, forcing myself to lock the door. I pulled out onto the street and away from him where he stood on the sidewalk, unmoving as he crumbled.

As I pulled away, I looked in my rearview mirror and watched him get smaller as I drove out of his life. He slumped his shoulders, and his forceful personality shattered inside him.

Just like my soul.

I was never going to be the same again.

And neither would he.

Chapter 2 – Cora
Present Day

I was going to be late.

On my very first day, I was going to be late!

"Move!" I groaned as the people ahead of me all meandered up the stairs of the subway in absolutely no hurry at all. How did people walk so fucking slow? Wasn't six A.M. in the business district of New York City supposed to be filled with people madly dashing for their jobs?

Where were all these slow people going?

I finally got above ground and ran across the street, dodging traffic like a scene in a movie. My work bag swung wildly as I ran a block through crazy amounts of people and finally saw the building I was going to.

Hawthorn Tower was pristine in the New York skyline, shining above all the other buildings around it, and I felt a smile pull at my lips for the first time in the last twenty minutes.

I looked at my watch, seven minutes to spare.

I was going to make it!

I slowed my pace and tried to catch my breath as I got to the front doors. I moved aside, changed into heels that matched my dress, and quickly fixed my hair after the wind messed it up.

As I moved away from the wall, the doorman greeted me with a smile and held the door open wide for me to enter.

Even after visiting the building twice to interview and do paperwork, I was still in awe of the expansive lobby with its polished wood and marble. I walked towards the turnstiles, slid my brand-new badge through, and smiled when the red light turned green, granting me magical access to the land of important people.

I felt so remarkable.

Ten years ago, my life had been derailed, and I was forced to watch every single one of my dreams and plans go up in flames as college at Duke slipped through my fingers.

When my father had cut me off, I'd lost all funding for college. No institution would give me a loan or a grant when my family was part of the one percent of wealthy Americans. And the fact that my family disowned me didn't matter to the banks. Even the colleges I'd gotten scholarships to turned their backs on me.

So I'd settled for working my way up through life, one shitty dead-end job after another. Or really, three or four jobs at a time because without experience or education, I worked for minimum wage, and it was impossible to live on that.

But today I was starting as a personal assistant to a top executive at a tech company. It was the break I needed to succeed finally, and I was going to work every second of every single day to get ahead because I wasn't naïve anymore to think I'd ever get another opportunity like it if I fucked it up.

I waited in the busy lobby for an elevator, joined a group of people in the compact car, and stood at the back with a stupid, excited grin on my face.

I watched as men and women in expensive clothing got off the elevator on different floors along the way to my office on the sixty-fifth floor. A man standing next to me looked over as the car emptied and left only the two of us as we bypassed the thirtieth floor.

"Are you new here?" He asked. I looked up at him and felt a pang of excitement when I saw how good-looking he was. He was probably in his thirties with black hair and dark chocolate eyes. He wore an expensive black suit and held a briefcase worth more than what I'd make in a year at my new job. The label was one I'd recognized from my past life.

"Is it that obvious?" I asked, cringing, and then smiling again.

He laughed and leaned back against the wall next to me. "I haven't seen you before. And I would remember seeing you before if you worked here."

I raised my eyebrow at him and then looked at the ticker above the door; fortieth floor. "This building is seventy floors tall, I'm sure you couldn't possibly recognize everyone that comes in through the front doors."

He shrugged his shoulder easily and smirked, "You're probably right, we can at least eliminate the male population of employees here, because I wouldn't recognize any of them. But the women I pay more attention to."

I laughed at his cringy flirting. "So, you're straight. Got it. I wasn't sure, with your choice of shoes and all." I dropped my eyes to his incredibly fashionable black shoes and tsked my tongue at them as if there was something wrong with them.

"You think my shoes make me look gay?" He asked, feigning outrage. And I laughed again at his charismatic banter.

"I wouldn't say they make you look gay, per se. I also wouldn't say I was getting straight vibes either, though." I looked back at the ticker.

Fifty-seventh floor and counting.

"Hmm." He said and then turned back to me. He held his large hand out to me, "Reid Haskins." He introduced.

I took his hand and tried to ignore the electricity that burned in my palm when he wrapped his long fingers around mine. Fingers that long could do certain things for a woman, I thought devilishly.

Down girl.

It had been way too long since I'd had sex and being stuck close to an attractive, successful man like Reid was dangerous for my health.

"Nice to meet you, Mr. Haskins," I said and tried to ignore the purr that vibrated in my chest as I said it. I hadn't meant to sound sexual, but the sudden arousal in my blood left me unable to hide it.

"You didn't tell me your name." He said, still holding my hand, and I didn't miss the way he pulled it closer to his suit jacket as he stared down into my eyes.

"I didn't?" I tilted my head to the side and hitched my hip out. Which was a mistake, because he dropped his gaze from my eyes and looked down at my body with a slow perusal. "Hmm. Weird." I said and slid my hand from his.

Right on time, the elevator doors opened at the lobby of Halo Optics and Tech.

I stepped backward from him until I was in the lobby, and he followed until he stood right inside the elevator doors. He looked past me to the office behind me and grinned.

"Halo suits you; because you're angelic." He dropped his eyes down my body again and then rubbed his thumb over his bottom lip as he shook his head. "I like a good game of cat and mouse as much as the next man. So game on, new girl."

I dropped my gaze demurely and nodded my head. "Have a nice day, Mr. Haskins." The doors to the elevator shut, but not before I heard the manly groan that came from his throat.

Damn!

I took a deep breath to calm my nerves and turned to the reception desk where a woman my age sat. She had a fashionable short black hairstyle and a full face of makeup that made her look like a beautiful, bold, pin-up girl. She was watching me with her mouth open and a raised eyebrow.

"I desperately need to know what happened in that elevator before you got out and handed him his balls." She said, leaning forward on her elbows and shaking her head.

I laughed and wiped my forehead off like I was fatigued. "I don't even know myself, to be honest with you."

She smirked and winked at me. "That's exactly how it should be." She shook her head again and fanned herself and got back to business. "How can I help you?"

"Oh right," I took my badge and clipped it to the belt of my burgundy dress, "My name is Cora Valentine, today is my first day as PA to Mr. Peterson."

"Ah! Cora! I'm Nat." She stood up and walked around to me. "You're just in time. They're looking for you, frantically almost."

My face fell, and I looked at my watch. "Am I late?"

She put her hand on my arm, "Oh no, not at all. There was a mix-up with scheduling or something and HR needs a PA to help with the CEO upstairs this afternoon, so they wanted to get you on board and up to speed as fast as possible before you're needed up there. He's..." She paused and chewed on her cheek, "Demanding and kind of a hard ass to be honest with you."

"Oh." That was all I could say.

"If you handle him like you did his CFO, Mr. Haskins, at the elevator, you'll be just fine." She said with a wink and then nodded for me to follow her.

We walked through the maze of cubicles and offices on the main floor of Halo towards a large corner office where a middle-aged gentleman sat at an impressive desk looking out over the city. He had silver hair that was perfectly styled in a fashionable wave over his fifties-styled glasses and a polka-dot bow tie. He looked so warm and approachable.

Nat knocked on the open door and walked in. "Mr. Peterson, this is Cora Valentine."

The man turned and raised his eyebrows at me and stood up, coming around the desk. "Ms. Valentine! I'm so happy to meet you, and you couldn't have picked a better day to start!" He said, he took my hand in both of his and shook it eagerly and then nodded to Nat. "Please let Sebastian know she has arrived, and we will be ready in a few minutes."

"Yes sir," Nat answered and then patted my arm on her way out.

"Please have a seat, Cora." Mr. Peterson said and held his hand out towards one chair at his desk and then walked around to his spot and faced me. "I apologize about the rush you're probably feeling, coincidentally we were approached by Jones Holding this morning to see if we had anyone with experience speaking in Mandarin and, of course, we have no one. But then Sebastian in HR remembered being impressed that you were bilingual in Mandarin on your resume in your interview." He paused for a moment as panic fell over his kind face. "You are fluent in Mandarin, correct?"

I nodded quickly, "Yes, I took four years of it in school. I may be rusty at speaking it, but I can understand it well." I left out the part about taking it in high school and not college, but it wasn't an outright lie.

Relief crossed his face, and he leaned back into his seat. "Great! Mr. Jones is incredibly particular about his translators, and he fired the one he had been using this morning and was then left up a creek because he has an acquisition meeting this afternoon for a company worth nine hundred million dollars." He paused as my eyes grew large and he nodded in agreement. "I know, that's a crazy amount of money, even for him as a billionaire. But aside from being able to speak and understand Mandarin, he needed someone with shorthand abilities to take notes on the translations. So that's your task today, are you capable of that? On day one?" He asked with pure hope on his face.

"Yes sir. I can handle that." I answered confidently.

"Perfect!" He clapped his hands together and, as if on cue, a knock sounded at the door and a small man with dark olive skin stood with an extensive file in his hands. "Sebastian! We're ready for you to come on in. Cora, this is Sebastian Wallace, head of HR for Jones Holding and Halo, there are some forms you will need to sign for payment and confidentiality."

"Okay," I said, a bit of pensive apprehension ran up my spine as Sebastian sat down next to me and started pulling packet after packet out of his file and laid it out on the desk in front of us.

"Ms. Valentine, this is your payment form for your time billed to Jones Holding. You'll automatically be paid for an eight-hour day, even if the meeting only takes twenty minutes. And if the meeting were to go longer than eight hours, you would be paid for double the time at least." He said, sliding the form over to me and showing me where to sign. I took a second and let my eyes rove over the print and froze when my eyes landed on the salary for an eight-hour shift.

"I'm sorry, there seems to be a typo here," I said and pushed it back to Sebastian with my pen pointing to the salary.

He eyed it and his eyebrows fell over his eyes sharply. "Do you have experience professionally with translating or shorthand note-taking?"

"I worked as a bilingual call center rep for a while," I answered, em-barrassingly. "Surely not anything that's up to this standard, though."

"Well, it's still professional experience, and you're right, you should be compensated more for that, I'll send that back to payroll and have that raised for you."

"Raised?" I gasped, "I pointed it out, thinking that it was far too high already."

He leaned back in his chair and smiled at me, pulling his reading glasses off the edge of his nose. "You are a breath of fresh air, Ms. Valentine." He said and shook his head, folding the packet and setting it to the side. "No, it's far too low, I'm going to get you at least two grand per meeting, don't you worry dear."

I bit my tongue to keep from arguing with him, as he seemed so sure I was worth so much more.

Two grand for one meeting? Two grand used to take me two weeks or more to make, and that was working over two jobs to do so.

Holy fuck.

I tried not to show my shock and short myself publicly as he handed me more forms, including an NDA and security form to be employed as per diem for Jones Holding.

I just tried to absorb as much as possible as he went over many policies and procedures, so I would be up to speed for the meetings this afternoon and before I knew it, it was lunchtime. I was to go up to the seventieth floor at one pm for the meeting, so I had an hour for lunch.

Mr. Peterson showed me where my normal desk was, right outside of his office, and I left my work things there and went in search of some food.

When I got to the main lobby of Halo, Nat was standing up from her desk with her purse in tow as she turned to me and smiled. "Hey! How did it go this morning?"

"Uh, well I think." I said, scratching my forehead, "I think I've absorbed so much information in the last five hours that it's all just... stuck in my head, unprocessed." I laughed and so did she.

"Are you going out for lunch?"

"Yes. Can you recommend anywhere close to that's edible? I have to be back early to go upstairs for the meeting."

"Well, you're in luck, I'm headed to a cafe around the corner and I'm feeling chatty so you can come with me, and I'll make sure I get you back in plenty of time."

"Perfect."

We rode the elevators down and walked out into the warm spring sunshine and then around the corner of the building to a cafe that smelled heavenly as soon as we were outside of the doors.

"God, it smells good here." I groaned and my stomach growled.

Nat laughed and walked up to the counter, "Any deli sandwich or salad here is phenomenal. Their protein bowls are to die for, though."

She ordered a bowl and half of a sandwich, and I ordered a salad and then we took a seat while we waited for them to be delivered.

"So Reid Haskins, huh?" Nat asked, leaning in, and wagging her eyebrows at me.

"Who?" I asked, fighting with the straw in my tea.

"The drop-dead sexy man who vowed to chase you like a mouse in the elevator this morning." She deadpanned.

"Oh yeah, I'd forgotten his name, to be honest with you." I laughed and relaxed as our food was delivered. We both dug in and ate in silence for a while before I got back to the conversation. "He was quite sexy, wasn't he?" I asked.

Her eyebrows shot to her hairline as she chewed on her sandwich. "Quite! Did you know him before that?"

"No, I talked to him only from the fortieth floor up to Halo, that's it."

"Well, apparently he didn't need that long to decide he was interested in you. His secretary called down and asked to speak with HR this morning, shortly after you got in. I'm guessing he was trying to use his power to pull strings and find out your name."

"How does that even work?" I held my fingers up to my ear like a telephone and mocked some ditzy voice. "Uh yes, ma'am I need the name of the blonde woman in the wine-colored dress that works there?"

Nat laughed and covered her face as she tried to replicate my impersonation and fell into a fit of laughter. "Please don't ever impersonate me, because I'm afraid you'll pick out all of my worst features. That was phenomenal!"

I laughed and finished eating my food and then took our trash to the garbage before we started the walk back to Hawthorn Tower, at a bit of a slower pace now that we were fed.

"I think that's exactly how that phone conversation went, by the way. If he found out your name and pursued you, would you be interested?" She asked.

"I don't know." I said honestly, "I mean, he's sexy and charming. But I don't know anything about him. Tell me what you know about him and maybe we can decide if I should."

"Ooh, I like your style." She said and slid her arm through mine and walked in step. "He's the CFO for Jones Holding and is incredibly successful at it. I hear he's like one of two friends that Mr. Jones has, so that should say something too. Uh, he's dated his way through most of the building but that's nothing new with rich successful men in this world." She rushed on the last part like she was trying to brush over it.

I laughed and shook my head. "Tell me about Mr. Jones. No one has spoken about him at all, and I'm supposed to work with him in – "I looked at my watch, "Fifteen minutes."

"Uh." She paused and looked skyward. "Sexy doesn't even come close to describing him, like when he stands next to others, they disappear completely. He's all dark and mysterious for sure. But from what I hear, he's a hard ass to work for; he demands perfection and let's be honest, it's impossible to be perfect for a man like that."

"How old is he? I guess from what I did hear today I assumed he was Mr. Peterson's age but you're describing him like he's Reid's age."

"He is. I think he's thirty, maybe a year or two younger or older but I'm not sure."

"Thirty? And a billionaire and ruler of all this?" I asked, waving my arm over the skyscraper we were walking back into.

"Yep. I only ever see him in passing as he comes and goes from the building or on page six after a public event or something, but other than that he's pretty recluse. They say he's super close with his family and a few friends from high school, and then Reid Haskins and Dexter Chase, his lawyer, and that's it."

"An enigma," I said in awe as I processed it all in my head. Hearing the name Jones brought flashbacks to a boy I loved once with the last name Jones. He had been the complete opposite of the man that Nat described. He smiled almost every second, always joking and having fun. He was the opposite of a recluse, always being outgoing and charismatic in a crowd and people naturally gravitated towards him. He was my favorite person in the world for the first eighteen years of my life until he just... wasn't.

I reached up and rubbed at the spot in my chest that ached every time I allowed myself to think about Maverick. I'd cut off contact with him that night and hadn't spoken to him once since then. I'd blocked his name from all of my social media and google searches over the years, I refused to know anything about his life because if I knew what he was like today, I'd want to be a part of his life today. And that wasn't an option for me.

So instead I forced myself to remember him that night I'd found him at that party.

I forced myself to remember the way he grunted as he came inside my best friend up against a wall like she was the best thing he'd ever had.

Okay, maybe he hadn't acted like she was anything special at all, but the version in my head made me remember it as if he was downright smitten with her.

It made it easier to keep my distance from my past.

"You alright?" Nat asked as the elevator stopped at our floor.

I shook it off and nodded to her. "Yeah sorry, I was just thinking about this afternoon."

"Understandable." She said and stopped to throw her bag in her drawer. "If I don't see you before I leave at five, we'll grab lunch tomorrow or something and you can tell me all about the enigma, deal?"

"Deal," I said and walked away towards my desk. "See you."

I stopped in the bathroom to freshen up and found myself staring at myself in the mirror for a while in awe. How had I gone from no one to someone overnight?

I admired the burgundy dress that I'd found at the high-end thrift shop with a tag still on it a few days ago. It was short sleeve and had a small v notch in the high neckline and ended right above my knee with a slit in the back. There was a matching belt with a gold buckle at the waist and gold buttons on the cap sleeves. It was professional and made me feel worthy of this new position as I wore it.

With the income I was set to get from this day alone, I could go back to the thrift store and buy some more dresses just like this one that I'd had to pass up on last week when I went looking, desperate for something to make me feel like I fit in with these people.

My black heels were sky high and honestly the most uncomfortable thing in the world, but I wore them anyway and I had to admit, with the outfit, they were perfect.

My shoulder-length blonde hair had flattened a bit over the day, but it still looked cute with some beach waves left in it. I reapplied my nude lipstick and spritzed a puff of the perfume I'd had since I was in high school on my neck and wrists. I only allowed myself to use it for special occasions, and over the last ten years, I could count those special occasions on one hand. So I reveled in using it now.

The single bottle I had managed to grab when I packed a small bag and left my parents' house as they kicked me out had cost over four hundred dollars, but it was one of the most favorite things I'd owned, so I took it.

Maybe someday I'd be able to afford it regularly and could wear it daily instead of just for special occasions.

Someday.

I walked to my desk, left my purse, grabbed my brand-new shiny tablet and notebook with a few pens and my bottle of water, and walked back to the elevator. Nat was on the phone, but she held a thumbs up to me and smiled as I walked by.

I made my way into the elevator, clipped on my new Jones security badge next to my Halo one, and took a deep breath as I rose in the building.

The elevator doors opened, and I took a second to admire the vast reception area in the heart of the building. It was all white marble and steel; the wall behind the receptionist was designed to look like the steel of the wall was visible through the marble in an industrial look and it was breathtaking.

The receptionist was a younger man with bright green glasses and a satin tie, and I smiled sweetly when he looked up at me with genuine friendliness in his eyes.

"Hello, welcome to Jones Holding. How can I help you today?"

"Hi, my name is Cora, I'm from Halo, and I'm here to help translate a meeting."

"Of course, if you just go to my right down the hallway you'll see Mr. Jones's assistant's desk and Veronica will be able to show you to the conference room."

"Thank you." I turned and walked down the long marble hallway and looked at the expensive and beautiful artwork that lined the walls as I went. The hallway opened up and a giant black onyx desk sat outside a set of massive, mirrored doors behind it.

A beautiful redhead sat at the desk and eyed me up as I walked up to her.

"Hi, my name is Cora—" I started but she held her hand up and cut me off, pointing to her ear where a headset lay in her ear.

"Yes, that will be all. Make sure it's here by five pm sharp or there will be hell to pay." She snapped and hung up. She turned her attention to me with more loathing than I ever thought would be possible from someone I'd never met before, but I just smiled through her venom.

"You may follow me." She said in place of a greeting.

She walked ahead of me, and I shamelessly let my eyes rove over her skintight black dress that landed hardly mid-thigh and admired her black stockings that had a strip of black satin up the back of each leg. They were sexy paired with the red-bottomed heels and the dress, and she wore the overall look well.

Must be bitch was the persona needed to pull off such a look though, because I knew I'd fall short if I tried.

I turned and watched our reflection as we walked by the mirrored wall behind her desk and caught a glimpse of the office behind it at the last set of panels that weren't mirrored.

A giant office sat in the corner of the building and there was a large desk area as well as multiple seating areas around the space. But what caught my attention most was the back of the man standing at the wall of windows, looking down at the city beneath him.

Mr. Jones.

He was a very large man, so tall and wide in the shoulders as he stood with his hands pressed to the window above his head where he leaned into the pane. He wore a charcoal suit and had dark brown hair that was short on the sides and styled perfectly on top in a way that made my fingers itch to run through it.

I bit my lip and turned back to follow little red-riding bitch down the hallway to an expansive conference room as I tried to focus my thoughts on the task at hand and not the sexy man in the windows. There was a black onyx table in the center of the conference room with plush chairs all around it and multiple TVs on the walls.

There were two men in the room already leaning back and chatting in the chairs and they turned and stood when I walked in after Red.

Shit.

Reid.

"Ah, hello little mouse. I see we meet again already." He said with a Cheshire cat smile on his face as he stalked towards me. Red turned and watched with a furrowed brow as Reid held his hand out to take my own.

This time instead of shaking it though, he pulled it to his lips and briefly touched them to the back of my hand as he bowed forward.

"Oh, good gravy." The other man said with a smile on his face as he shook his head. "Stop drooling on her hand, she needs to be able to take notes." He said in good humor.

Reid winked and then stepped back, letting go of my hand.

The cantankerous redhead interrupted the relaxed atmosphere, "You can have a seat—"

Reid cut her off and led me to the side of the table. "We've got it taken care of Veronica." But ignoring her was obviously a big no-no because she huffed and left the room. Reid led me to a seat next to the head of the table and pulled a chair out for me before taking the one next to me. The other man took the seat across from me after leaning across the table to shake my hand.

"I'm Dexter Chase, Mr. Jones' lawyer." He was mid-thirties, maybe forties, and he was good-looking in a boy-next-door kind of way, with blonde hair, and blue eyes. His suit was immaculate and his smile carefree without the wolfish glare to it like Reid's. He had a wedding ring on his hand, and I figured his easy-going nature probably came from wearing that.

"Mr. Chase, pleasure to meet you, I'm Cora Valentine."

"What a beautiful name for an angelic woman," Reid said from next to me. And I felt the blush cover my cheeks as I ducked my head, settling my things out on the table.

It only took two seconds to get arranged though and then I was stuck awkwardly sharing space with two incredibly good-looking men and having nothing of importance to say.

Dexter laid out his own file and tablet and leaned forward, "This meeting should only take half an hour max. We started obtaining Shen Hu's firm a year ago now, this is the final meeting to sign the paperwork and do the actual exchange of property. They will have their translator who will do most of the work, but we always make sure we have our own in-house as well to keep from having any trickery going on. So if there is any discrepancy in what their translator conveys to or from their CEO, inform us right away."

"Got it," I answered easily.

"Good." He said and picked his phone up to answer a message.

Reid leaned in and whispered to me, "So Ms. Valentine, how is your first day going?"

I took a deep breath, "I'll let you know after this meeting."

He laughed and laid his hand on my arm, "You could let me buy you dinner to celebrate the success we'll be having after this meeting is over. That would be a good way to commemorate the occasion."

I looked at him and pursed my lips, "It would be a good way to commemorate something, just not sure if I'd remember it fondly after it was all said and done or not."

Dexter laughed out loud and smacked the table and Reid leaned back in his chair in mock offense, holding his hand to his chest. Before he could respond though the adjoining door opened from Mr. Jones' office and Reid and Dexter both stood up, so I followed suit. I looked down at my dress and smoothed my hands over my skirt and took a deep breath before I looked up to meet the man who owned more than I'd even begin to understand.

But the man stood frozen in place at the end of the table with his eyes locked on me as shock outweighed the scowl on his face.

"Don't even think about it Jones, she's already going out with me tonight," Reid said with a boisterous laugh and Dexter chuckled as they watched the awkward exchange between us.

But I couldn't even breathe.

Because the enigma that ruled the multibillion-dollar company and thousands of people inside of this amazing skyscraper was the boy that had destroyed me three days after high school graduation.

"Cora." He whispered, grimacing at me as I fought to remain standing upright.

"Mav?"

Chapter 3 – Maverick

I walked through the doors to the conference room and saw Reid and Dexter laughing and charming my new translator. Typical. She must be hot for both of them to be paying her attention though, because their types were polar opposites usually. Maybe I'd steal her for myself and fuck her in my office after the meeting.

I could use a good 'bend her over my desk' kind of fuck. God knows it's been a while since the last time I did that.

When I walked in they all stood up including the blonde. And even though she was looking down at her lap, the blood still roared in my veins from only a glimpse of her profile.

Cora.

Cold shivers raced over my body as she slowly raised her turquoise blue eyes to meet mine and her perfect cupid bow lips parted as her smile fell from her face.

She was shocked speechless that I was there.

"Don't even think about it, Jones," Reid said, laying his hand on the small of her back and laughing, "She's already going out with me tonight."

Dexter laughed too, but I could hardly hear it.

"Cora." Her name falling from my lips used to be second nature to me, but it had been years since I'd spoken it out loud and it felt foreign rolling off my tongue.

"Mav?" She asked, her perfect eyebrows knitted in the center as her eyes traveled down my body and back to my eyes.

My God, she was beautiful. She was always beautiful, but now, with mature womanly features, she was breathtaking.

Haskins and Chase fell silent, looking between the two of us as we were frozen in some staring contest of disbelief.

"Uh... you two know each other?" Dexter quipped.

Cora folded first, letting her eyes drop from mine as she looked over at Dexter. A blush crawled up her neck and I got vivid flashbacks of the way her chest flushed when she orgasmed. My cock hardened in my pants, growing long and hard in seconds, as I still couldn't take my eyes off the beautiful woman in front of me. Her body was so different now than it had been all of those years ago.

She had been a three-sport athlete in school and her body had been toned and lean, leaving her skinny and knobby as a teenager, but now...

She had filled out in all the ways that made a man's mouth water. She was curvy and feminine, and she belonged on the big screen with her flawless face.

"Maverick." Dexter snapped at me, and I finally pulled my eyes off Cora and looked at him. "Did you hear me?"

I looked back over at her and noticed the way that Reid still had his hand on the small of her back as he eyed me. He was a good friend of mine; we went back to Duke, but I would rip his arm out of the socket if he kept touching her.

"Take your hand off of her, right now," I ordered him. His eyes widened and Cora stepped to the side, forcing his hand to fall from her back as she looked back up at me under her lashes.

Dexter stepped towards me with his hands up. "I'm not exactly sure what is going on, but we need to get our heads on straight here Jones, Shen Hu will be here any minute now." He could tell I was on edge, but that was only the tip of the iceberg. I was a hair trigger away from exploding in agony from merely being in her presence again.

"Come with me," I said to Cora, turning and holding my hand out towards my office door and nodding my head for her to follow.

"What about the meeting?" She asked demurely. God, I missed her submissive side. She was only ever submissive to me all those years ago, and it always made me fucking psychotically hard, even now.

"The meeting will wait. Come, Cora." I added a bite to the end of the command, and she instinctively stepped forward and followed my direction toward the office door in front of me. My eyes instantly dropped to her lush ass in the pretty purple dress she wore as she walked in ahead of me. But I needed to get my head on straight, I couldn't lust after her, not after what she did to me.

As soon as I shut the door behind us, I hit the button on the wall to mirror the walls completely, encapsulating us in privacy.

She looked around my office, and a small smile pulled at her lips. "I can't believe you've built such an empire." She wrapped her arms around herself as she took it all in. Being this close to her I caught her scent as I tried to take a calming breath, but then memories assaulted my brain. She smelled like she was seventeen again and still madly in love with me. What I wouldn't give to be back there and do it all over again.

"What are you doing here Cora? They said the translator they found was the new PA for Peterson. What the fuck are you doing as an assistant down at Halo?"

She turned and faced me at my cruel tone, and I watched as her spine stiffened. "I'm sorry if a personal assistant isn't up to your standards, but I'm doing my best."

"Why aren't you doing something more with your degree?" I snapped at her and then took another deep breath trying to settle my normally cool persona.

"My degree?" She asked as she licked her lips and put her hands on her hips.

"You were always the smartest girl in the world Cora, surely you could have aimed higher than a fucking personal assistant. You have the world at your fingertips, and this is where you peaked at?"

Reid opened the door to my office, and I turned and growled at him menacingly for his intrusion. "They're here Mav, this is too big of a deal to mess it up now."

"Not now Reid." I snapped.

"He's right. Besides, I'm not interested in standing here while you belittle me anymore." Cora said as she walked towards the door, stopping when she was nose to nose with me, staring up into my eyes. "What I have done or not done with my life is none of your damn business, Mr. Jones." She said with a sneer. She walked away towards Reid and the waiting conference room.

"Fuck!" I growled and then took a deep breath. I needed to handle the deal first and then I could worry about her after.

Over my dead fucking body was she going out with Reid after work either.

I walked into the conference room the same time our counterparts did and myself, Reid, and Dexter all shook hands with their team.

Shen Hu was a self-made millionaire with a terrible gambling problem who had spent the majority of his life running through prostitutes and as of late, bad business deals. So that brought him to me. He was selling off his namesake to pay his debts and leave himself and his multiple mistresses something to live on for the rest of their lives.

His translator was a female and she sat to his left and looked around the room with jerky glances.

Which meant she was uncomfortable. She wasn't the translator they had used last time, and neither was mine but where theirs was stiff and nervous looking, Cora was poised and confident. I admired the line of her spine where she sat in her chair as I took my seat at the head of the table next to her, aching to run my fingertips up the bumps of her spine under the sexy-as-hell dress she was wearing. I desperately wanted to tear it off of her and see exactly what her body looked like now, ten years after the last time I'd seen her naked.

Fuck.

I took my seat and started the meeting. "Alright, thank you for coming today to finalize the paperwork needed to transfer all of the properties and equities to us in exchange for the agreed-upon amount of nine hundred million,"

Shen Hu himself nodded and then spoke as his translator replied. "We look forward to finalizing this deal and building a relationship with Jones Holding."

I nodded my head and Dexter started handing out the packets of paperwork to sign and started going over the numbers and conditions. Shen Hu's right-hand man kept checking his phone, which made me uncomfortable and left me feeling slighted. What else was more important than making the deal to save his leader's ass?

I sat back in my seat while I watched their interactions and couldn't help but notice the still shifty eyes of the translator, she wouldn't meet my gaze but every time she translated something she looked to Cora.

Cora was looking at her tablet and taking notes, not looking down the table at all, but she was paying attention, I could tell.

I grabbed her notepad and pen and wrote a note on it, before passing it back to her.

The translator is nervous.

She read the note and wrote back to me. Reid and Dexter were at the other end of the table dealing with the paperwork, but I caught how Dexter looked back at us with questions in his eyes.

Cora pushed the pad back to me with her response written underneath mine.

She should be. They're lying through their teeth. You're about to get fucked.

She turned her tablet to me and showed me the screen she had pulled up. It was the stock rate for the company I was about to buy. And in the last five minutes, it had dropped an obscene amount of points in the market, and every minute longer that went by, it dropped even more.

She took the pad back and wrote on it.

They sold their stocks and tanked the company you're paying almost a billion dollars for.

"Take that paperwork!" I bellowed out as I rose, while Reid and Dexter instantly grabbed the packets that our sneaky partners had been signing.

"What's up?" Reid asked walking down to our end of the table.

"They tanked it five minutes ago," I said, grabbing the papers from him and Dexter and then ripping them up as anger vibrated through my body. "Do you think I'm stupid enough to fall for a stupid insider trading scheme?"

Shen Hu stood up and started yelling at me in Mandarin and his translator looked at the floor, unwilling to translate what he said.

I looked at Cora and she raised her eyebrow at me, "Well let's just say they didn't teach us those swear words in eleventh-grade Mandarin. But he's telling you where to shove your pompous ass."

I grabbed the phone from the table and dialed Veronica. "Get security in here now! The Shen Hu firm is to be thrown out on their asses and then clear the rest of my afternoon. We're taking them for insider trading." I slammed the phone back down and leveled a stare at the man who just tried to beat me. "By the end of the day, I will have destroyed every single thing you've ever touched. Every business, every venture, every person. Mark my fucking word!"

He started yelling again and angrily came down the side of the table on Cora's side and I grabbed her chair and pulled her behind me as I squared up with the tiny man. Security ran in and grabbed him and his team before he could do something he regretted, pulling them all screaming and yelling from the conference room and out of my office before any actual punches were thrown, but I had barely restrained myself.

A billion dollars worth of punches.

"How the fuck did you catch that?" Reid asked, looking at Cora where she still sat in her chair, looking a bit shaken, but she squared her shoulders and answered him.

"Their translator was only translating parts of what they said as you explained the paperwork. She assured them that you were buying it at one point and I just... trusted my gut I guess."

"You just saved me from making a giant mistake and looking like a fool." She looked up at me and I fought the rage that boiled inside of me, letting her quiet demeanor calm me like she always did.

She smirked a small smile at me, "Just doing as I was told to do."

Dexter shook his head and picked up the paperwork, "Give this girl a raise and promote her to COO immediately." He said as he picked up his cell phone and called his team. "We're filing insider trading charges against Shen Hu's firm immediately. Get the ball rolling, Jones wants him destroyed by dinner time." He hung up and reached his hand out for Cora to shake and she tentatively took it, "That was an invaluable catch, Ms. Valentine. I think you're going to be a great asset here."

"Oh, I don't work here. I work downstairs, I'm just filling in." She said with a soft blush to her cheeks at his compliment. I hated how that blush wanted to warm up my frozen heart.

"Not anymore you don't. You work up here now." I said, surprising myself. I picked up the phone again, connecting to Veronica and barked out more orders. "Get Sebastian in here now, we're hiring Ms. Valentine full-time."

"Excuse me," Cora said as I hung the phone up again. "You can't just dictate where I work like that. I accepted a job at Halo, not here."

"It's irrelevant Cora, I own every company in this building."

She bristled and rolled her eyes, "*You're* irrelevant. I still said no. I don't want to work up here with you and little red-riding bitch. I like it downstairs."

"Red riding bitch?" I asked with a raised eyebrow as her challenging nature lit my alpha on fire, I had always loved her feisty side when she graced me with it.

Reid sat down and tried to hide his smirk but failed and ended up laughing out loud. "Veronica could breathe fire hot enough to burn the devil. That's a pretty accurate description."

"Shut up Reid, don't you have some money to manage for me or something?" I snapped.

He laughed again and stood up. He bowed to Cora and winked at her. "I'll meet you in the lobby at five for our date Ms. Valentine."

He turned on his heel and walked out the door heading down the hallway to his office before she could respond but it didn't matter.

She wasn't going.

"I don't want to work for you." She snapped at me as soon as the door was closed behind him, locking us in the glass fishbowl together.

"Why?" I put my hands on my hips and faced her head-on.

"Because I don't want to be near you."

That hurt and I lashed back crudely. "As if I want to be near you? Please. I simply want to take a valuable employee and use you where you're most effective. And you aren't most effective to me as a personal assistant in some tech firm."

"I'm aware your only interest in me is to use me, Mr. Jones." She snapped and stood up, "That's all you've ever been good at where I'm concerned. And I'm not interested. Fire me if you want, but I'm not working up here."

"Fire you?" I placed my fists on the glass table and leaned toward her, loving the way her pupils dilated, and her nostrils flared as I got close to her. "I'm trying to better your life for you since you've clearly done a shit-ass job of making anything of yourself on your own. Take the opportunity. Working up here at my side would not only help you financially, but it would also no doubt make your father happier knowing you're doing something worth being proud of."

I let my anger get the best of me, but I forgot how her own anger rivaled mine and I never saw her tiny hand move until it cracked the side of my face. She slapped me like a girl, but it still burned my cheek. Her face was as red as her palm was and her chest heaved as she took a deep breath to calm herself down.

"You do not know me, nor do you own me Maverick. Don't forget that." She grabbed her things hastily and turned to walk out of the room. She paused at the door and looked over her shoulder at me. "Consider this my formal resignation. Effective immediately."

She walked out the door as I stood there, shocked and pissed the fuck off with my mouth hanging open.

It took me a few seconds, but my feet started moving before my brain did. I was out the door and following after her before she was even halfway down the hallway. I saw the moment she heard my steps behind her because her own sped up, but I caught her at the main lobby by the elevators.

Veronica stood up at her desk when she saw me and started talking, but I held my hand up silencing her. The elevator doors opened, and Sebastian walked out with his assistant, ready to sign Cora on as my new employee. He looked from her to me as I caught up with her, "Should I come back?" He asked.

"Yes." I snapped.

"No," Cora said a moment later. "I'm not interested in working for Mr. Jones in any facility."

"Shut up Cora." I barked and grabbed her arm, dragging her away from the elevator. "You see nothing, Sebastian. Go the fuck back to your office until I call for you again."

Manhandling an employee in front of my head of Human Resources was probably not my wisest move but I was never levelheaded around her before, and it seemed that only got worse over the years.

"Get off of me Maverick!" She snapped, but I ignored her and dragged her into my office past a glaring Veronica.

When I slammed the door shut behind us I pushed her against it and crashed my mouth down on hers, silencing her demands.

She stilled instantly underneath me as my lips desperately tried to coax hers open, but only for a moment, because a second later her lips went soft under mine and moved with them in time. I had meant only to silence her, but now that I was tasting her for the first time in ten years, I couldn't force myself to stop. I put one hand on the side of her face, and she leaned into it, I tilted her how I wanted and deepened the kiss.

I ran my tongue against her lips, and she moaned and opened to me and the second my tongue touched hers, I felt like I was home for the first time in a decade.

My other hand dropped to her hip and pulled her against my body as I pushed her back into the door harder. I groaned and pulled my lips from hers and kissed her ear and neck, licking and biting my way down her throat and back up.

"Wait." She panted.

I slid my hand down her leg until my fingers felt the smooth skin of her thigh. "I can't." I pulled her dress up as I ran my fingers up the inside of her thigh and she pressed her head back into the door when my fingers pressed against her panties. I brought my lips back to hers and kissed her harder as she sucked on my tongue while I pulled her panties to the side and slid my fingers through her wet lower lips. Now it was my turn to moan.

I wedged my knee between her legs and spread them as I pushed a finger deep inside of her silky pussy. "Fuck, you're still so fucking tight." I groaned against her lips.

"Maverick." She panted. "We can't."

"Yes, we can. And we are." I ordered as I felt her trying to pull away from me. I needed this. I had spent years pinning after her, missing her and needing her and now that she was here, I couldn't stop. Even if I hated her.

I pulled my fingers from her tight pussy and wrapped them around her panties and pulled them hard, ripping them off of her body, causing her to gasp. I threw them to the side and put my forehead to hers as I fought to control the need inside of me. "Tell me you want me," I demanded.

"I –" She paused and gasped as I ran my finger over her bare clit and rubbed it. "We can't- Oh God." She moaned as I found the pressure and rhythm that she loved. It may have been ten years since I'd last had her, but my body had memorized hers long ago and never forgot.

I opened my eyes and watched her face as she wrapped her arms around my neck and hung onto me as I played with her body. Her eyes were closed, and her mouth was open, and I pushed two fingers deep inside of her as I rubbed her clit with my thumb.

"Tell me," I demanded.

"I want you." She panted. And that was all I needed from her; those words snapped any bit of restraint I had. I dropped to my knees in front of her and lifted her leg over my shoulder and stared into her eyes as I leaned in and licked her clit with my tongue. Her taste exploded on my tastebuds, and I groaned.

"I missed the way your pussy tastes," I said, sucking on her as her back bowed off the door, pressing her pussy against my tongue harder. I fucked her with my fingers as I flicked and sucked on her clit and she moaned, running her fingers through my hair, and holding onto it like a handle as she rode my face.

"Just like that Mav. Don't stop." She begged. "Please don't stop."

"Never. Let me hear you come." I ordered her, "I want to hear you moan."

"Yes." She gasped and moaned as her pussy clenched down hard on my fingers and her clit throbbed in my mouth. She came like a butterfly flying from its cocoon. She was breathtaking as her body tensed and relaxed while her orgasm rolled through her. I fought to keep myself on my knees long after her orgasm settled, and she sagged into the door. I licked her clean and nibbled on her inner thigh as I kissed over every inch of skin bare to me. "Holy fuck." She panted.

I smiled against her bare pubic bone and then stood up, wiping my face on my hand before kissing her like a man possessed. She clung to me as I drank from her lips and ground my cock into her exposed pussy. "I need to fuck you," I said and picked her up, wrapping her thighs around my hips as I carried her over to the couch. I sat down on the couch, and she straddled me with reservation in her eyes. I could feel her trying to reason with her brain to convince herself not to do this, but I couldn't let that happen.

I found the zipper on her dress, pulled it open, and then slid the fabric down until her large breasts were bare to me in a sexy-as-hell black lace bra. "Your tits are so much bigger now," I said and leaned forward, kissing each on the top of her cleavage as I reached around her and undid it and tore it off her body.

"Oh God." She gasped as I leaned forward and sucked one of her perfect nipples into my mouth, biting it and flicking it with my tongue before sucking on it hard. "Yes." She rocked her hips as she cradled my head to her chest and scraped her nails across my scalp.

"Just like that Cora. You remember what I like." I praised and she moaned. She loved to be praised when I was inside of her years ago and turned out that she was no different now.

Always my perfect little vixen, begging and purring for more from me.

"Fuck me, Maverick." She demanded and I lifted my hips, pressing my hard-on against her pussy and she started grinding her clit against it.

"Take my cock out baby."

She reached between us and undid my belt and slacks and I helped her push them and my boxers down past my knees until my hard cock laid against my stomach between us. Her eyes rounded as she looked at me. "How is it possible that you got even bigger?"

I laughed and stroked my cock as her hungry eyes watched. I grabbed her hand and wrapped it around me under my hand and used her hand to stroke me. Stars exploded in my sight as she bit her lip and watched her tiny hand trying to wrap around me. "I want you to ride me like you've spent the last ten years missing me. Ride me like it's the only thing you've dreamed about for a fucking decade."

She raised herself and I fisted my cock beneath her and watched while her tight body spread open around my thick cock as she lowered herself over the head of me. Her eyes fluttered shut and she rose back up and then took more of me inside of her.

It was like heaven wrapped around my cock as she wiggled side to side to accommodate my size. She rested both hands on my shoulders and started riding me, taking me from tip to root and bouncing up and down on me.

"Good girl, baby." I scooched to the edge of the couch, lifted my hips with each thrust, and bottomed out inside of her body.

She threw her head back and rode me with vigor as her tits swayed in front of my mouth and I took a bite. She screamed and covered her mouth with her hand before I pulled it away and held both of her hands behind her back and pulled her to lay flush against my chest as I started fucking her hard from underneath.

"Oh my God Maverick." She moaned and bit my neck.

"I want my whole fucking office to know you're in here taking my cock Cora. Don't hold back and stay quiet now."

"Yes." She moaned loudly as the sound of my thighs slapping hers vibrated into the room.

"That's my girl." I groaned and fucked her harder. I pushed her hair back from her face and held it in a tight fist at the back of her head and held her back by it as I fucked her. Her eyes rolled and her body tightened like a vice around my cock as she started coming. "Good girl. Fucking come on my cock. You're such a good girl."

She tightened so much I couldn't hold back anymore. Her pussy milked my cock, draining my balls as I exploded deep inside of her body, coming more than I ever had before. I roared her name out loud as I felt my hot come pool deep inside of her pussy.

My hips kept thrusting, long after I came as I let go of her hair and her head slumped forward against my shoulder. I loosened my grip on her wrists, brought them both forward, and kissed the red marks I'd left on each arm before laying them against my chest between us.

She sat up after catching her breath and stood up, letting me slowly slide from her body. She stood at my feet, and I watched as my come dripped from her pussy onto the carpet between her spread legs. Her eyes rounded and she tried to pull her dress down to cover herself up, but I wasn't having it.

I grabbed the hem of her dress and pulled it back up over her hips and used my thumbs to spread her pussy open, rubbing my come over her pussy lips and clit. "Do you have any idea how sexy that is for me?"

"No." She answered softly, biting her lip as she stood with her legs spread and her tits still bare, with her dress bunched around her hips. "Tell me why you like it."

I leaned forward and drew one of her nipples into my mouth and sucked on it hard, dragging a moan from her lips. "Because my come is marking you as mine."

"Yours?" She asked, her eyebrows kitting over her eyes.

"Yes. Mine." I said, kissing one nipple and then the other, "These are mine too."

She backed up and my hands and lips fell from her body as she scowled at me. She pulled her dress down over her hips and closed her legs. She crossed her arms over her body and looked for her bra that I'd thrown across the room. "I'm not yours."

She grabbed her bra and shoved her arms through it angrily.

"My come dripping from your pussy says otherwise." I bit out angrily.

She scoffed at me and zipped her dress back up.

I pulled my pants back up and stood up as she looked around for her panties, but I saw them lying on the floor by the door before she did, and I hurried across the room. I grabbed them off the floor as she reached for them and smiled sinisterly at her. "Looking for these?"

"Give them to me."

"Why? They're not going to keep my come from running down your legs all day Cora, I ripped them off of you, remember." I held them up and showed her the ripped band and her eyes squinted in anger.

"Give them to me."

"No, I think I'll keep them as a souvenir," I said and slid them into my pants pocket.

"You are such a spoiled brat, you know that?" She bit out and walked over to my private bathroom and slammed the door shut in my face.

That enraged me and I walked across the room and shoved it open. She was sitting on the toilet peeing and glared at me. "Do you mind?" She snapped.

"Not a bit." I leaned my shoulder against the doorframe and watched as she shot daggers at me from her eyes and stood up, wiping herself clean of my come, and then pulled her dress back down. She flushed the toilet and washed her hands while I stood there silently watching her, reeling from the last hour of having her back in my life.

Being inside of her had calmed me in a way I hadn't felt in a decade, but now that she was being defiant again, I was getting riled back up like I hadn't just blown my load five minutes ago.

"Are you done throwing a fit?" I asked.

She squinted her eyes at me again and walked past me, shoving her shoulder into my arm as she passed. "Yes, I'm done, because I'm leaving."

I sighed and grabbed her arm a few steps away and pulled her back to me. "We need to discuss this," I said, pointing between the two of us.

"This?" She asked, raising her eyebrow at me. "All that needs to be done now is I need to go to the pharmacy and buy a Plan B pill and get an appointment with my GYN to be tested for whatever STDs you have exposed me to. Oh yeah, and I need to find another job while I do all of that. Thank you very much for all of those things."

"I didn't hear you complaining when you were begging me to fuck you!" I bit out.

"Temporary lapse in judgment. It won't happen again." She fired back.

"Bull shit. We both know you'll be begging me for more of my come before the day's through."

"Ugh!" She screeched and ripped her arm out of my hand as she grabbed her things off the floor by the door. "I can't believe I let this happen. You're still the same self-centered spoiled monster you were ten years ago. I was stupid to think that you could have grown up a bit in that time."

"Me?" I yelled. "What about you? I'm trying to take care of you and you're acting like a bitch!"

"Fuck you!" She yelled back, pointing her finger at me. "You don't want to take care of me, you want to control me. And you hate that I won't let you. I don't want whatever stupid job you wanted to make me do up here. And I don't want whatever title you think you could give me to make my family proud of who I am. Because I stopped caring about what you and my family thought about me when I left your ass all those years ago after I found you fucking my best friend!"

She grabbed for the door handle, but I was already on her and slammed the door back shut from the few inches she had gotten it open.

"Don't walk away from me when I'm talking to you, Cora."

"Fuck you Maverick. Leave me alone!"

"No!"

"Why?"

"Because you obviously have failed to take care of yourself over the years and I won't stand by while my ex, slums it as some chump's personal bitch in my own building."

"I don't want anything from you! All I want is for you to leave me alone!" She brought her knee up to my crotch and I doubled over in agony as nausea rolled through my system.

She pushed me aside and walked out the door with her spine straight and escaped into the elevator. Veronica glared after her and then turned to me where I leaned on the door watching her walk away from me again and hated the way it made my skin crawl with a desperate need to drag her back to me.

"Not a word," I ordered my assistant and slammed the door shut.

Fucking infuriating Cora.

Chapter 4- Cora

My hands shook as I rode the elevator down to my floor. Or rather my old floor.

Damnit!

I really wanted this job. I really needed it!

When the elevator doors opened, I walked out, and Nat looked up from her desk and eyed me over with her eyebrows raised to her hairline. "Uh Cora, you look..." She paused and grimaced.

I looked in the mirrored elevator doors and groaned. I placed my stuff on her desk, smoothed down my hair, and adjusted my dress to make sure it wasn't crooked across my chest anymore.

"I look like I just got railed in the CEO's office don't I?" I muttered, pissed off at myself.

"That's exactly what you look like, though if that had actually happened, I would have expected maybe a smile on your face or something to indicate you were at least pleasured from it."

"Ugh!" I groaned again and hung my head.

"Tell me everything."

"I just got railed in the CEO's office and I hate myself for it because I hate him."

"Mr. Jones? How could you hate him? He's the sexiest man in America and almost the richest man in the world and let's be honest, those alpha men are great in the sack." She was leaning forward on her elbows talking a mile a minute.

"I hate him because I know him from my childhood, and I didn't realize he was 'The Mr. Jones' and now I have to quit because he's demanding that I work upstairs with him and that will just end in disaster. Actually, everything will end in disaster regardless and I really wanted this job."

"Okay, we have a lot to go through here." She said with a smile. "Cocktails at a pub around the corner after work?"

"Sure." I said and rolled my eyes. "I could use some alcohol to burn him off of me from the inside out."

She laughed boisterously as I turned from her desk and headed back to mine.

I didn't want to quit Halo, I wanted this job to prove to myself I could do it. When I got to my desk I dropped everything and was pulling out my chair when Mr. Peterson poked his head out of his office. "Ah Cora! You're back, come on in and tell me how the meeting went."

I slapped a smile on my face and nodded, following after him into his office as he shut the door. I hated the way my inner thighs were wet from Maverick as I tried to focus on my boss.

"So how did the meeting go? Did he make the deal?" Mr. Peterson said, sitting on the desk as I sat in one of his chairs.

"Uh no, actually Mr. Jones threw them all out and is filing insider trading charges on them."

"Oh my goodness! What happened?" He asked, leaning forward like we were a couple of teenage girls gossiping and I laughed lightly at him.

"They sold their stocks when they walked in the room and tanked the value of the company, trying to sell a heap of trash to Mr. Jones.

I picked up that something was off and looked into it and caught it in time and he called the whole thing off. It got... really intense for a minute there. I thought punches were going to be thrown."

"Oh my lord!" He gasped and covered his chest with his hand. "Well, I assure you, there will never be that much excitement down here for your normal job as my assistant." He chuckled and walked around his desk.

"About that..." I started, grimacing. "I kind of quit while I was upstairs, and I don't know if it was accepted or not, or if I'm fired or transferred upstairs or what."

His eyes and his head shook back and forth as he tried to follow me. "Expand on that."

"I kind of know Mr. Jones, from my school-age years. He demanded I work upstairs with him after I caught the trick they were playing on him. I refused because I wanted to work here at this job, but he demanded I switch. So I quit. But I don't know where I stand currently."

"Oh." Was all he said as he slumped down into his desk.

"I'm so sorry Mr. Peterson, I really want to work here with you, I think there is so much for me to learn as your assistant. I'm just not sure if he'll let me."

"Well." He said and slapped his hand down on his desk, "It's nearly the end of the day already anyway and I haven't heard anything so let's just assume you are still Cora Valentine, Personal Assistant to me, and we will go from there. Why don't you go work on my schedule for tomorrow, familiarize yourself with it, and pick a place for lunch on our way back from our eleven o'clock meeting? And we'll hope that you get to join me for it tomorrow. Work for you?"

I smiled brightly up at him and stood, "That works perfectly for me."

"Good." He said, smiling.

I went out to my desk and did exactly all of that, but every time the phone rang, or my email pinged, I was afraid of seeing Maverick's name on the ID.

But it never happened; before I knew it, it was five o'clock.

"Okay, Cora, get out of here before he fires you and I'll see you bright and early tomorrow." Mr. Peterson stage whispered from his office door, and I nodded, grabbing my things, and sliding into my flats.

"Thank you, Mr. Peterson."

He winked at me and went back into his office.

As I got to the reception area, Nat was standing at her desk and looking for me. "So are we doing shooters of tequila for an hour until we're smashed or fruity sweet cocktails all night?" She asked, looping her arm in mine, and falling into step next to me.

"Shooters for sure. They're cheaper and quicker." I answered as we got in the elevator and started to go down to the lobby.

"I like your style girlfriend." She laughed.

She chatted on the way down with a few guys in the car and I tried to ignore the way they looked at me like I was fresh meat. There were already two alpha men that were fighting over me like a bone in a caveman's den and I didn't need to add any other knuckle-dragging testosterone to the mix.

Speaking of testosterone, when we walked out into the expansive downstairs lobby Reid stood talking to a security guard and when he saw me he headed towards us with a charming smile on his face.

"I'm surprised to see you still alive and in the building." He said when he got to us. He looked over at Nat and let his eyes travel over her appreciatively and then back to me.

"Yes well, for how long I'm allowed in the building is still a question," I said.

"Well, then I guess I'd better get you out to dinner while I still can." He said, holding his arm out for me to take.

"Uh, actually. I never agreed to dinner, and I already had plans with Nat here." I said. "Maybe another time."

"Or you can come with us, we're going to McCulley's to get black-out drunk on shooters of tequila to celebrate Cora's total shit show of a first day," Nat said, winking at Reid and dragging me towards the door. "Take it or leave it pretty boy." She called over her shoulder.

"Oh, I'm taking it, all day long." He said as he smirked and followed after us like he was preparing himself for a crazy evening.

"Ms. Valentine," A security guard called for me as we neared the door and I looked over at him as he spoke to me. "Mr. Jones would like you to wait for him here."

"Let's go!" Reid said, grabbing my other arm and running from the lobby with a laughing and cackling Nat and me in tow as we ran down the street like a couple of kids getting chased for lifting something from a five-and-dime store.

We made it around the corner before we stopped running and by then we were holding our sides and wiping tears from our eyes as we laughed wildly.

It felt good to laugh like that.

Luckily, McCulley's was literally on the corner, so we didn't have far to go before we ducked in off the street to hide.

We found a high-top table in the back and Nat and I each took a stool while Reid went to get our drinks.

"Hurry, tell me the dirty bits before he gets back!" Nat said, leaning forward.

"What dirty bits? It was hot as fuck, but I regret it now. And he was probably calling down to fire me in person so he could watch me cry." I said, laying my head down on my arms on the table.

She laughed and then snorted as she covered her face. Reid showed up with a tray full of shots, some beers, and a basket full of popcorn as we continued laughing at my ridiculous plight.

"Okay, cheers girls." He said, handing out shots with lime and salt. We each did a shot and chased them with beer and then did another one right away after.

We joked and chatted away for a while, taking shot after shot and shoving popcorn down our throats trying to absorb it. "Alright, now lay it all on me. How do you know Mav and how the fuck did you manage to get him so riled up from just being in the same room as him?"

"Oh jeez, where to start?" I said, taking another long drink of my beer.

"Start at the beginning," Reid said.

"Well, I took his virginity, for one."

Reid snorted on his next shot, and it came out of his nose as Natalie choked on a piece of popcorn, leaving the three of us in a heap of coughs and sputtering as the alcohol started making our filters fade and our friendships grow.

"Oh, please tell me all about Maverick Jones' first time." Reid finally said when he could breathe again. "Please tell me he was a two-pump chump and embarrassed himself entirely." He lay across the table with his hands clasped in front of him like he was praying to me.

I laughed and shook my head, "I'm not telling you that because I'd be telling you about my first time too and that's too personal. But he wasn't just my first, we'd been together since we were in second grade, and we dated all the way to two months before we were supposed to go to Duke together."

Reid's eyes widened, "No way! You're that girl!" He said in awe as he slumped down into his chair. "Oh, it all makes perfect sense now!"

"What? What makes sense?" Nat asked, looking between us as none of it made any sense to her obviously.

"He was miserable when he started freshman year at college. He didn't talk about life much outside of school, but he did say some bits and pieces about how the girl he was going to marry left him without a backward glance and how he had his whole life planned out with her before that. And you're telling me that girl was you!"

"Oh dear, you not only had Maverick Jones' body, but you also had his heart too." Nat quipped with a romantic look on her face.

"What happened to make you break up with him?" Reid asked, pushing another shot toward me.

I took it, loving the warmth that settled into my body from the alcohol. "I found him nailing my best friend into a wall at a party he wasn't even supposed to be at."

"Oh, ouch." Nat grimaced and Reid put his hand on my shoulder in support.

A menacing voice growled behind me. "I thought I told you to keep your fucking hands off of her." I whipped my head around to see Maverick standing behind me and I gracelessly fell off the other side of my stool as my alcohol cloudy brain refused to let my reflexes catch me.

Mav reached out with lightning-fast arms and caught me, sliding me back onto my stool with his large hands on each side of my hips. "Fuck." I groaned, holding my head.

"Are you drunk?" He snapped at me.

"And stupid." I agreed. "Among other things." As I refused to look up at him.

"Reid." He snapped out, "I told you to leave her alone."

I looked up at Reid who held his hands out in defeat, "I'm here with her sexy friend. Cora just couldn't take no for an answer and tagged along annoyingly." He winked at me, and I flipped him off.

"Oh no baby, don't put me in the middle of all that, I'm more likely to fuck Cora before I'd fuck you, you're too much of a man whore." Nat quipped, letting the alcohol loosen her lips and I groaned.

"No one is fucking me," I said to her, leveling her with my finger and what I hoped was a serious look.

Reid snorted, "From what I hear, Mav already had that luxury this afternoon."

"What!" I gasped, "Who did you hear that from?" I asked, completely ignoring the way Maverick stood with his chest pressed against my back or the way I leaned into his warmth even if I was as angry as a rooster with him. Reid raised his eyebrows at me and took a pull off his beer not answering. "Red riding bitch." I sneered and he laughed.

"Bingo."

I turned and glared at Maverick, letting my disdain for his red-headed bitch of an assistant ooze from my eyes. "I'll take care of it." He said, sliding his hands over my hips again as I leaned on my stool.

"Hmm." I quipped and turned back around.

He leaned down into my ear and whispered, "It's your fault for being so loud." He bit my ear lobe as he finished, and I tried but failed to suppress the moan it caused.

"I hate you," I said to him, not caring that Reid and Nat watched like we were fucking right here on the table in front of them.

"I know. I hate you back."

"Am I fired?" I asked, turning to look at him, but that was a mistake because that left his lips only inches from mine because he hadn't stood back up.

"Are you still insisting on working downstairs?"

"Yes."

"Then yes, you're fired."

"Shame." I quipped, turning forward again, and took another shot. I slid from my stool and leaned into him as I licked my lips. "I kind of enjoyed fucking the big boss in his office today. Can't do that if I'm unemployed."

He growled at me and slid his hands around my waist as I tried to scoot by him. "Don't tempt me, Cora." He leaned down and bit my ear again. "I know you're not wearing any panties and that your pussy is soaked with my come. I'm on the verge of picking you up and fucking you right here on this table. Hair-trigger close baby."

"Hmm, promises, promises," I replied and then pushed from his arms. "I have to pee."

Nat jumped down from her stool, "Me too." She slid her arm in mine again and pulled me away from the table and the brooding Mr. Jones, towards the ladies' room and the long line that accompanied it.

When we got in the hallway I sagged into the wall and wiped my brow. "Holy hell!"

"I know!" She squealed and leaned against the wall next to me as we waited. "I knew from looking at you when you got off the elevator that you two were hot for each other but seeing it in person... holy hell indeed girlfriend. Was it always that hot between you two?"

"I don't know, we were eighteen when we broke up, we'd been having sex for a few years at that point sure, but we were just kids. It was never as hot as it was today, that's for sure."

"I bet the whole distance makes the heart grow fonder thing had a hand to play in it."

"Yeah, distance." I mused. "That and the fact that he started the domino effect that ruined my entire life."

"What do you mean?" She asked, but I just shrugged her off, not meaning to open my mouth about my life back then.

"Nothing. I just can't think straight with all the alcohol in my system."

"Yeah, we did hit it pretty hard and fast thanks to Reid's fat wallet." She agreed and giggled as the line moved and it was our turn to go in.

When we weaved our way through the crowded bar towards our table, I stopped when I saw the groupie of women who were now hanging all over the two most eligible bachelors in all of New York City that we left at our table.

I stood ramrod straight as I watched a buxom brunette lean all over Maverick while he smiled down at her and I was instantly assaulted by images of him and Sarah from all those years ago. And every second of hurt I'd felt since then came back with them.

"Hey, you okay?" Nat asked, pulling me to the side of the bar against the wall.

"Yeah, I just..." I turned back to the table and watched as Mav tilted his head back and laughed at something she said before looking over her head towards the hallway to the bathroom. "I can't do this with him again. He'll destroy every little part of myself that I've gotten back over the last ten years. And what I have is already not enough to make me whole as it is."

"Oh girl," Nat said, pulling me into a hug. "I'm sorry he hurt you. I know exactly what that feels like and to know you were together for ten years beforehand, that's harder."

"Thanks," I said pulling back. This time when I looked over, Maverick's eyes were locked on mine over top of the brunette's head and I didn't try to hide the pain I knew he could see in my gaze. "I'm going to just go home and sleep this off and see how I feel in the morning."

She nodded and held my hand in support.

I took a deep breath and walked back towards the table, grabbed my purse and bag from underneath it, and then turned away towards the door.

"Where are you going?" Mav asked, stepping around not one but two women who tried to steal his attention on his way around the table.

"Home. You should stay and enjoy your evening." I said, nodding towards the table and a laughing Reid where he was surrounded by women who were eating up everything he said like catnip.

"I only came here for you." He said, looking down at me with annoyance in his eyes.

"Sure you did Mav. But there isn't anything here for you anymore. Today was a mistake. And now that I'm no longer employed with your company, it won't happen again."

"Stop." He bit out and took my arm, walking from the bar and dragging me with him. When we were on the sidewalk, the lights of the street were all on, burning away the sunset as he took a deep breath. "What is this about?"

I shook my head and looked him square in the eye. "I'll never get over what you did to me. I was having fun messing with you but seeing you so easily chat with other women just reminded me of that time when you so easily destroyed me, and I can't ever allow myself to be that girl again. Not even for you."

"What are you talking about? I was waiting for you. I came here for you. Why are you acting this way?" He asked angrily.

"Because you hurt me. Yes, it was years ago, but every single action you and I took back then has shaped my life into what it is now, and I can't just forget that. And I sure as hell can never forgive it."

"What about how you hurt me?" He snapped.

"Me?" I yelled, attracting the attention of people walking by. "What the fuck did I ever do to you except stand by your side and support you through everything you went through while you fucked around with God knows who behind my back."

"You left me!" His chest heaved inside of his expensive suit, and he put his hands on his hips as he leveled me with a menacing stare. "I was at my fucking lowest and at my first moment of weakness, you took off! Leaving me alone to figure it all out on my own."

"So I was supposed to stay with you while you broke my heart because you were grieving Luke?" I asked, my eyes watered as I thought back to how badly it had hurt to lose Mav's twin brother when we were all eighteen. "I was grieving him too!"

"You were supposed to give me a chance! You were supposed to let me make mistakes and give me the chance to fix them. That's what kids do! Instead, you took the easy way out and never looked back on it."

"I didn't take the *easy* way out Maverick!" I yelled, "You have no idea what that one decision did to impact the rest of my life! You don't know how hard the last ten years have been on me, don't you dare!"

"Right, it's been so hard on you to leave me high and dry and move on with your life. Sure, okay." He snapped bitterly. "You know what, keep your shitty job being Peterson's PA and go nowhere with your life. And don't worry about me bothering you because I won't make that mistake again. Because that's exactly what today was, a fucking mistake. I was stupid to think you would ever be capable of doing anything but think about yourself. So whatever, I'm done this time too Cora."

He turned and walked away from me and went back into the bar and back to the table filled with women ready to drop to their knees and suck his cock for his favor.

I sagged in defeat where he left me and rubbed my aching head as I tried to fight through the fog of alcohol and think clearly.

I walked away down the street to the subway entrance and waited for the train as I leaned against the pillar in a daze. I was replaying every word we had said to each other over and over in my head, trying to figure out if I made a mistake or not and I wasn't paying attention to my surroundings. I was distracted, and drunk and I knew better than to let those two things muddle my street smarts, but I was destined to make more mistakes as the hours of the day dwindled.

I leaned up off the pillar as the train rolled into the station and waited for the doors to open. But as I was about to walk on, a strong grip on my arm pulled me off balance and slammed me back into the pillar, bouncing my head off the hard surface. Stars danced in my vision as a hand clapped down over my mouth and a body dragged me backward away from the train. I kicked and screamed, fighting against the strong body, but I was no match in strength. A few scared glances from people waiting for the train fell on me, but quickly looked away, not wanting to get involved.

It wasn't happening. No! I screamed against the hand over my mouth, but it was muffled and quiet. The arms that were wrapped around me tightened and slammed me down onto the floor of the station as the train started to pull away, leaving the platform empty as I fought to get free. I bit the hand over my mouth and was rewarded with a punch to my side for it, sucking all of the air out of my lungs.

My shoe fell off as I kicked at my attacker wildly, and he fought me off while ripping my bags from my arms.

I grabbed my bags desperately as the man with a bandana over his face turned around and slammed his fist into my face twice before taking off up the stairs out of the subway.

I lay on the floor for a moment, in shock as I fought off the disorientation from the assault before I forced my body up off the ground.

I put my hand up to my face and winced as I felt blood dripping down my cheek and into my mouth. I walked over to where my shoe had been lost and put it back on in disbelief.

My mugger took everything. My ID, my work badges, my money, my cell phone, and even the good shoes I'd worn at work.

"No," I whispered as tears fell over my lashes.

The next train was supposed to be here in ten minutes, and I stood in disbelief as I waited for it, holding my sides, and trying desperately to wipe my bleeding face on my dress sleeve.

I made it home, in a daze of alcohol and shock as not a single person on the train or street stopped their day to ask if I was okay. Luckily my building's superintendent was a decent man with a sweet wife and kids, and he opened up my apartment for me and gave me a spare key to replace mine that had been stolen. None of my identification had been updated with my current address on it so I wasn't worried about someone showing up with my keys and using them to get into my apartment at least, but I still felt incredibly violated knowing someone had my belongings.

I forced my brain to shut off as I pulled my dirty and bloody clothes from my body and crawled into the shower, falling onto the floor, and sobbing as the water washed away the blood like it never happened. I knew the city was dangerous and I knew better than to let myself get distracted like that, I just had an off day and I got careless. And it was because I'd fallen back into Maverick Jones' life and lost my senses.

I sat on the floor of my shower until the water turned cold and then I forced myself from the tile and got out, wrapping myself up in a fluffy towel, careful not to disturb any of my wounds that ached and burned. When I wiped the steam from the mirror I gasped as I looked at my face.

There was a cut on the bridge of my nose, as well as my lip and cheek, and my left eye was already black and blue, and the white part of my eye was red and bloodshot. There was a knot the size of Texas on the back of my head and my ego was just as hurt.

I hated that someone got the best of me and left me feeling weak and helpless.

I left the bathroom and got dressed, before crawling into bed and calling my bank and turning off the two debit and credit cards I owned, thanking God that none of my money had been taken before I got to it. And then I called security at Hawthorn Tower to report the loss of my ID badges so they could turn them off as well.

The man who answered was nice enough and took down all of my information, asking if they were lost or stolen. I'd paused for a second before saying they were taken in a mugging but as soon as I said it, I regretted it. I didn't want that getting back to Maverick somehow.

When I was done speaking with him, I called Mr. Peterson's voicemail and left a message that I wouldn't be in tomorrow due to an unforeseeable circumstance and that I'd call him to speak with him directly tomorrow.

I could only imagine how smug Mav would feel if he knew I called out of work on my second day after our fight. He would probably gloat, thinking it was because of him.

Smug bastard.

I took a handful of Tylenol and brought my puke bucket with me to bed, in case the alcohol mixed with a concussion caused me to vomit in my sleep. I groaned as I lay in my bed, unable to get comfortable on either side because of my ribs and couldn't lay on my back because of my head.

Somehow, I managed to pass out, and it was well into the following day before I woke up, feeling even worse than when I went to sleep.

Chapter 5 – Maverick

I felt agitated and angry as I paced my office, which was not a familiar sensation for me. I had been that way since I left Cora outside the bar last night and I couldn't shake the feeling that I fucked things up even worse by walking away from her. I wanted to see her, but I forced myself to stay upstairs in my own office and away from hers.

Veronica walked into my office with a coffee and a smile, no doubt trying to sweeten me up. But even looking at her, got me more riled up. She set my coffee down as I glared at her and she paused, "Can I get you something else?" She purred.

"Perhaps you can give me an explanation as to why what I do in my office behind closed doors became any of your business yesterday. Or better yet, why you decided to open your mouth about what you heard and gossiped about it to others like it was any of *their* fucking business."

My tone and language put her on edge, and I reveled in the way her eyes widened a bit as she tightened her hands together in front of her.

"I'm not sure what you mean Sir–" She started but I cut her off.

"Do not ever let me hear rumors about myself or Cora Valentine leave your mouth again. Or I will fire you so fucking fast your hair will fall out on the elevator ride downstairs. Do you understand me?" I asked bitterly.

She straightened her spine and nodded her head. "Yes sir. I understand you."

"Good, now get the fuck out of my sight and do your best to avoid my wrath the rest of the day!"

She nodded again and scurried out of my office and shut the door behind her. She had gotten too used to having free reign around here because she was a damned good assistant but talking negatively about Cora was a sure-fire way to get fired.

I didn't care if I even liked Cora currently or not, but I would ensure that those in my life respected her regardless.

I owed her that much.

I cursed and drank down the steaming hot coffee, punishing myself for acting like a barbarian yesterday until I couldn't take it any longer.

I got up and stormed from my office and went down to Halo. I didn't know what I planned on saying or doing when I got to her desk, but I just knew I had to make sure she was okay.

When I got to the reception area, Cora's friend Nat sat at her desk, looking hungover as fuck and miserable. "Good morning Nat," I said loudly across the space, and she groaned at me.

"If I could flip you off and not get fired, I would." She said back plainly.

"That's fair." She drank far more than I thought was possible over the short time I stayed at the bar last night after I abandoned Cora.

I walked past her and headed down the small hallway towards Cora's desk. "Uh-" Nat started, suddenly finding energy. "If you're here for Cora, I don't think she's in today."

"What do you mean?" I stopped and turned back towards her.

"I don't know why, maybe the hangover was too strong, but she called off last night."

I clenched my jaw, looking down the hallway, and then nodded to her, "Thank you." I went back to the elevator and inwardly groaned when Sebastian stood inside the car, riding up to my floor when I stepped in.

"Good Morning Mr. Jones." He said with a particular smugness to his voice that I hated.

"Seb."

He went back to reading through his paperwork and then tsked his tongue. "That's interesting." He said, looking over at me.

I raised my eyebrow at him in question and he passed the paper to me. Pointing to a line on a security report.

ID Theft:

Picture ID and security badge for Cora Valentine were reported stolen at 9:57 pm.

The employee reported ID and badge were stolen in a mugging on the subway last evening.

"Mugging?" I snapped. "Fuck."

Seb grimaced as I threw the paper back at him. The doors opened and I flew out of them to my office. Reid was walking down the hallway and met me halfway. "Hey man, glad to see you standing straight this morning."

"Not now Reid." I bit out and walked into my office and straight to my desk.

"What is it?" He asked, cueing into my mood.

"Cora was mugged last night on the subway. She called off today too."

"What? Is she okay?" He asked, stepping around my desk to see what I was doing.

"I don't know, she didn't call me. Seb just showed me the security report from last night when she called in to report her badge being stolen."

I pulled up the database of employee information and typed in her name. Her picture popped up and I forced myself to look away from it when I wanted to just stare at her beauty forever.

I jotted down her phone number and her address and then stood up, walking away from Reid and my office.

"What are you doing?" He asked.

"Going to check on her." I answered as Veronica looked up from her computer, "Clear the rest of my day. I'll have my phone."

"But sir you have a meeting with –"

"I don't care, Veronica! I said to clear my fucking day."

"Yes sir." She said as I got into the elevator.

"Let me know if she's okay!" Reid yelled after me as the doors closed.

She was okay, she had to be. Because if she was hurt in the least, I'd never forgive myself for leaving her drunk and upset on the sidewalk outside of a bar last night when I should have been dragging her back to my penthouse instead.

That was what I'd been planning to do when I got to the bar, but then she wanted to spar with me, and I lost my cool.

When I got to the curb outside, my car and driver Franklin were waiting for me. He was in his forties and fit, ex-military but had a gentle look to his face that made him the perfect mix of bodyguard and chauffeur.

"Mr. Jones." He said, tipping his hat to me and getting in behind the wheel.

I gave him the address and told him to hurry as I dialed her number in my phone and pressed send.

It went straight to voicemail, and I groaned. "Fuck!"

It took me way too fucking long to get to her neighborhood and I hated the way the buildings got more run down and shitty as we neared her place.

Her building was no better, though it was cleaner than the others, but it was just as run down.

There was no doorman at the door and no security either and I ran up the stairs to her fourth-floor apartment.

I banged on the door, fighting to calm my breath as I clenched and unclenched my fists when more time passed without her answering the door.

"Cora!" I yelled, banging on the door again.

Still nothing.

"Can I help you?" A man stepped out of another apartment with a tool belt and a nametag on, wiping his hands on a rag.

"Carlos?" I asked, nodding his tag. He nodded back. "You work here?"

"I do. What do you need with Ms. Valentine?" He asked looking past me to her door.

"She was mugged last night, and now she's not answering. I'm afraid she was hurt."

"Who are you to her?" He asked, eyeing me up.

I pulled my wallet from my pocket and handed him my ID. "My name is Maverick Jones, I'm her boyfriend."

He eyed my ID and then eyed her door. "She's not answering?"

I shook my head no, banging on her door again. "Cora!"

"She was beat pretty good, my wife tried talking her into calling the police, but she wouldn't."

"She was beaten?" My blood boiled more as panic set in, "Can you open this door?" I asked, jiggling the handle.

He looked worried the longer she didn't answer, but behind me the lock slid in the door and then it cracked open.

"Hello?" Her hoarse voice called out.

"Cora! Open this door, right now!" I demanded. I couldn't see her through the crack and the chain was drawn still, but she pushed the door shut, unlocked it, and opened it. I turned and nodded to Carlos and then pushed the door open all the way and stepped in, shutting it behind me.

Her hair was a mess and she stood in a thin cotton nightgown, covering her eyes from the bright light of the hallway. Her apartment was dark, and I could hardly see her.

I stepped forward, pulled her hand down from her face, pushed her hair back, and growled when I saw the bruises and cuts to her face. "What the fuck happened to you, baby?" I asked, pulling her into my arms and she came to me willingly.

She sagged into my chest as I held her up against me. I slid one hand around the back of her head and felt a welt on her skull and grimaced, I tried to avoid touching it and causing her more harm. "Let's sit down," I said gently and walked her over to the kitchen chair only a few feet away.

She sank into the chair and looked at me through one eye, her other one was pretty swollen and puffy.

"What are you doing here Mav?" She asked and licked her dry lips. I stood up and opened the fridge, pulling a bottle of orange juice out and pouring it into a glass from a strainer on the counter. I handed it to her and helped her raise it to her lips and she hissed when it touched her split lip but drank it quickly. "I'm okay."

"No, you're not." I barely restrained my anger and rage as I looked at her bruised and beaten self. "What the hell happened?"

"I got mugged." She said, lifting her shoulder and cocking her head. "It happens all the time in New York."

"Why were you riding the subway to begin with?"

"How else am I supposed to get all the way across the city every day?"

"I don't understand why you live here," I said, shaking my head. "Why the fuck does your dad let you live in a place like this with no security in a shit-ass neighborhood, riding the subway for fucks sake, look at you." I snapped. She bristled at my anger and tried to stand up but swayed and fell back down into her seat. "I'm sorry." I rushed out and knelt at her feet, bringing her hands up to my face and taking a deep breath. "I'm sorry Cora, I'm just worked up, finding you like this. God, I've never been so worried in my life."

"I'm fine Mav." She said again, cupping the side of my face and leaning forward to rest her chin on my head. Even in a moment like this, she was trying to comfort me.

"You're not fine Cora, and I'll never forgive myself for leaving you alone on that sidewalk last night. I had no intention of leaving that bar without you, but then I let my anger get the best of me like I usually do with you. And I left you alone and unprotected and someone put their hands on you!"

"I'm fine. Please stop worrying like this. I'll be fine in a day or two, I just need to sleep it off."

She stood again and I rose with her to steady her and breathed her in as she leaned into me. "Did you go to the hospital?"

"No."

"Why the fuck not?"

"Because hospitals are expensive, and I don't have any identification or a way to pay for it right this second."

"Let's get you dressed, and then we're going to the hospital."

"What?" She said, looking up at me, "No. I don't want to go anywhere, I just need to rest."

"I don't care Cora; you probably have a concussion from that welt on your head and you need to be checked out! I'm not taking no for an answer so you can either pick out clothes to wear or I'll carry you over my shoulder dressed like that."

"I just want to sleep, please just let me sleep." She begged and sagged into me further.

"You can sleep once we're in the car baby." I led her to her bedroom and sat her down on the end of the bed. She stayed there pouting as I grabbed a bag from her closet and started throwing clothes in it. I walked into her bathroom and grabbed her toothbrush and hairbrush and then went back to her. She was putting her legs into a pair of yoga pants and struggling so I sank to my knees in front of her and helped her work them up to her thighs.

"Twice in two days, you've gotten on your knees for me Maverick Jones." She mused with a sad smile on her face.

"There isn't another person on this planet that I'd get on my knees for."

She watched me for a moment and then stood up and I pulled the pants up over her wide hips and tried to ignore the way her soft skin felt against my hands.

"For some reason, I don't believe that."

"Hmm." That was all I said as I pulled her gown up and over her arms, biting back a curse as I saw the bruises on her ribs under her perfect breasts and helped her into a sports bra and shirt before sliding a sweater over her arms and sneakers on her feet.

"I don't want to go anywhere, please Mav. Please just let me stay here."

"Shh," I said, pulling her up and picking her up into my arms against my chest, throwing her bag over my shoulder. "Let me take care of you."

She wrapped her arms around my neck and took a deep breath in at my skin, "You're ten years too late."

"I know baby."

God, did I fucking know.

I shook the hand of the doctor who had treated Cora and thanked him as I tucked her under my arm and walked out of the ER towards my waiting car.

She had a concussion and some contusions, but she would heal from them. I would never heal from the guilt though. "Take me home, Maverick." She said and I kissed the top of her head and pulled her along next to me. I didn't tell her that I intended on taking her to my home and she didn't specify either, so I nodded to Franklin and crawled in the back seat beside her.

She curled into a ball against the other door, but I needed to feel her against me. I dragged her across the seat and onto my lap as we worked through the mid-day traffic of New York's Upper East Side. "I'm sorry." She said, sighing into my chest.

"What are you possibly sorry for right now?" I asked, rubbing my hand over her back.

"For leaving you." She said firmly in a sad voice.

I clenched my teeth as emotions rolled through my system. I'd waited ten years to hear her say those words to me, but now that I had them I couldn't help but feel guilty instead of validated.

"I'm sorry for breaking your heart." I finally said and she snuggled into my chest further but remained quiet.

Franklin pulled into the private parking garage for my building and stopped at the elevator to my penthouse. Cora looked up and then scowled at me, "I meant my home."

"Shh." I chided her and stood from the car with her still in my arms, grabbing her bag and throwing it over my shoulder again. "Just give me this."

"Hmm." She mused but laid her head back down on my shoulder as we rode up to my apartment. I loved my home, but I'd never brought women home before and sure as hell didn't bring anyone here that I wanted to share the space with.

But as we walked into my modern penthouse, I found myself watching Cora's face as she looked around the space. "What do you think of it?' I asked, nervous and anxious for her to like it for some reason.

She smiled softly and slid from my arms and looked over at me. "It's very you Mav. I can tell you had a hand in designing it and that you take pride in it."

"I did."

"Why did you bring me here?"

"Because you should have been here all along Cora. You should have been by my side through every stage of life, and I'll never forgive myself for cheating you out of that."

She shook her head and held her hand up. "It's too much Mav. I can't –"

"Then just settle for letting me take care of you for now," I said and took her hand, pulling her behind me toward my bedroom. She looked over the room as I kept walking past the bed and closet and into the massive bathroom attached. "How does a bath sound?" I nodded towards the deep soaker tub.

Her eyebrows raised, "In that? Like heaven."

"Good." I turned the tap on and then poured a handful of salts in that I'd never bothered to open before but that my housekeeper insisted on stocking. She raised her eyebrows as I loosened my tie and pulled it free of my shirt and then took off my jacket, stalking towards her where she stood with her hip against the sink.

"Don't you have a company to dismantle or something?"

"I only want to dismantle your clothes," I smirked at her and she rolled her eyes at me as I slid my hands over her hips and kissed her forehead.

"Mav." She sighed. I slid her sweater off over her shoulders and down her arms and then carefully lifted her shirt off. "I don't know how to let you take care of me." She said, avoiding my eyes as she pulled my shirt from my slacks and worked the buttons loose.

"That's all my fault, Cora baby. One I plan on rectifying starting right now."

"What does that mean though? We just ran into each other yester-day and now you're saying things like you want me by your side and you want to take care of me, and I don't know how to just... let you."

I stripped my shirt off and groaned when her fingers slid behind my belt as she tilted her head back to finally look at me. "It means that I've only ever imagined myself marrying one woman before. You. And I know we just reconnected yesterday, and we have so much to discuss and figure out, but I want you, Cora. You hurt me when you left me and I have to deal with that the same way you have to deal with the pain I inflicted when I cheated on you, but I want to deal with that shit together and work on building something." I leaned down until my eyes were level with hers and I put one hand on each side of her face. "I want you. That has never changed for me. I spent ten years building something with you and another ten years regretting everything bad I ever did to you. Let's spend the next ten years living the life we should have been this whole time."

Tears pooled in her eyes as she took a deep breath.

"Okay." She whispered and I leaned forward and gently kissed her lips, running my tongue over the plump flesh I so badly wanted to devour but forced myself to keep it soft and light because of her injuries.

"Okay," I said back and then undid her bra and pushed it down her arms. "You're so incredibly sexy, I don't know if I told you that yesterday or not, but your body is maddeningly beautiful."

She chuckled softly and rolled her eyes as she undid my pants and held my stare as she pushed them down to the floor. She let her eyes flutter down to my bare cock and a grin pulled her lips up as she shook her head back and forth. "How did that fit inside of me?" She asked in wonder.

It was my turn to chuckle at her as I helped her step out of her remaining clothes and then led her to the tub. I sat down against the edge and held her hand as she gently slid into the hot water. She knelt between my legs, and I put my hands on her hips and guided her to lean back against my body.

I wrapped my arms around her stomach and held her for a long time, letting the hot water soothe us both.

"This is the first time I've seen you completely naked in ten years, and you're downright sinful." She said, running her fingers over the sensitive skin of my thighs under the water. "You've grown... everywhere."

I kissed her temple and hugged her tighter. "I became a man. In more than one way Cora."

"What do you mean?" She asked, looking over her shoulder.

"What I did to you... with Sarah." I started, hating the pain I knew this conversation was going to bring her.

"Stop." She said quickly and took a deep breath. "I want to hear what you have to say Mav, I want to know what happened and why you did what you did... but not right now." Her voice was soft and gentle, but I could feel the grief in it. "I just want to enjoy this moment, right here and now. For just a little while longer."

"Okay," I said, sighing as she clung to me. We lay in silence for a while longer again before she spoke again.

"When was the last time you soaked in a bubble bath in the middle of a Tuesday?" She asked, kissing my bicep where she rested her cheek against it.

"Never." I said quickly, "Well actually, there was that one time you had the flu, and you were miserable and sick and couldn't breathe at all, and I skipped school and snuck into your room and held you just like this in your tub while the vapor shit you put in the water burned my ass."

She snorted and laughed, "Your cheeks were red for two days from that stuff."

"It burned so bad. But I sat through it anyway for you, because you could finally breathe for the first time in days, and it was all worth it."

"I'd forgotten about that. We were what, juniors?"

"Yeah, I think so."

"Hmm." She said, thinking back to that time.

"That was the last time I sat in a bath before now too."

She turned to look at me over her shoulder, "You're trying to tell me no woman has been in this tub with you before now Jones?" She asked pensively.

"No woman has been in this apartment before, Valentine. None that I was romantically involved with anyway."

"But yet you brought me here?"

"I did," I answered easily. "And it feels right to me too."

She was quiet as the bubbles hissed around us from the salts. She ran her fingers up and down my arm where it wrapped around her body as she was lost in thought.

"Where have you been the last ten years?" I asked her finally, letting the need to know everything push through my need to care for her sore body.

"All over really." She answered, without actually giving me what I wanted.

"Tell me the truth, Cora. What happened? Why didn't you ever come to Duke?"

She sighed and turned in my arms to face me and then straddled me. "Duke was always your dream. Without you in my life anymore, it didn't hold the same appeal. Didn't you ask my parents anything over the years?"

"Yes, I asked about you every time I saw them for the first few years. But they were always vague or downright avoided the conversation and after a while, I just stopped trying."

Pain flared in her eyes, but she blinked it away, "Is your family still friends with them?"

"Not like they used to be, honestly. Your parents got so busy with Penelope and Jake's lives, that they really thrived through their weddings and then with becoming grandparents. It made my parents green with envy that they still don't have any grandkids to dote on like yours do." Her body tensed and something sad passed over her features. "Do you visit them often?"

She shook her head, not looking into my eyes. "No, I don't."

"Well, maybe we can change that," I said, but she slid off my lap and stood up, getting out of the tub abruptly.

"No. I don't want to change it Mav. And I don't want to talk about the past anymore." She grabbed a towel and wrapped it around her body and walked out of the bathroom, leaving me alone in the tub and confused as fuck.

"Wait a second." I snapped and got out, chasing after her. She stood in the bedroom, looking through the bag of clothes I packed for her, but I grabbed it and tossed it across the room, scattering her clothes across the floor.

"Maverick!" She growled and went to go get it, but I stopped her with a hand on each of her arms.

"Stop. Take a deep breath and just stop." I demanded and I watched as she desperately wanted to fight me but instead took a calming breath and relaxed. "Good girl," I said softly.

She rolled her eyes and squinted at me, "You're lucky I like you." She replied.

"I'm very lucky indeed," I said and pulled her towel loose and pushed it to the floor. She raised an eyebrow, but I silenced any retort she was going to throw at me by kissing her deeply. I was careful of how much pressure I put on her split lip, and I used my tongue to tease hers until she was clawing at my arms and neck, pressing her naked body against mine.

My cock was hard between our bodies, and she wrapped her hand around me and stroked me, making my hips jerk as pleasure built in my spine.

"Your cock is so sexy." She whispered against my lips as she wrapped both hands around me and stroked me from root to tip.

"*You* are sexy Cora." I pinched her nipple between my fingers and pulled on it, loving the way she arched her back, pressing her chest into my hand further. "I want you to ride my face and then I'm going to fuck you so good."

She moaned and licked her lips. "God yes."

I pulled her over to the bed and laid on my back and then pulled her up to straddle my face. She rested her hands on my stomach and leaned forward as I wrapped my hands around her thighs and spread them wide to lower her onto my waiting tongue. I flicked her clit before I sucked it into my mouth and rolled it between my lips. "Fuck, you taste so good, baby." I groaned.

She laid flat against my stomach, and I wrapped both arms around her waist and rubbed my face back and forth over her sensitive clit and wet pussy, letting my whiskers stimulate her. "Yes Mav, oh God. That feels so good."

Her hand wrapped around my cock where it lay heavily on my stomach, and I groaned loudly when her tongue licked up one side before swirling over the head of me. "Holy shit baby."

She chuckled and sucked my cock deep into her warm mouth as I tongue fucked her pussy. She moaned around me and shimmied her hips, rolling them back and forth over my face as she worked on taking more and more of me into her mouth. I wanted so badly to see her pretty lips spread wide around my cock for the first time in ten years, but I needed to taste her orgasm on my tongue even more.

I reached up and ran my fingers through her wetness and pushed two of them deep into her body as I continued to flick and suck her clit.

"Mav baby. I'm going to come. Oh God, I'm coming on your face." She moaned and her pussy clamped hard on my fingers as she fisted my cock and squeezed hard, stroking it quickly as she came. "Maverick. You feel so good." She moaned my name over and over again and I grunted.

"I'm going to come Cora." I bit out barely in enough time before the first shot of come exploded out of my cock and into her waiting mouth. She grabbed my balls in her other hand as she continued to stroke me and suck my come down her throat as the last of her orgasm rocked her body.

I threw my head back onto the bed and stared up at her sexy pussy that continued to throb as she laid her cheek on my thigh and gasped.

"Holy shit that was intense." She sighed and then squirmed when I bit the inside of her thigh and soothed it with my tongue. I slid from under her body and rolled us both over until I was on top of her body. She spread her thighs wide and pulled me into her arms and it felt like I was eighteen again and she was the only thing in the world that mattered.

"Hold on tight baby, I have ten years' worth of orgasms to push your body through," I said and she moaned.

"Yes sir."

Chapter 6 – Cora

He looked down into my eyes like he was a starving man, and I was his favorite meal. It made me feel so incredibly wanted and needed, just like how he made me feel when we were younger before everything went bad. "Fuck me Maverick. Please, baby." I purred and raised my hips to rub my pussy against the head of his cock where it lay between us.

"Well, because you asked so nicely." He replied as he leaned down and sucked on my neck in a way that made me writhe with pleasure beneath him.

He lined his cock up against me and pushed the head in, forcing a gasp from my lips at the invasion. "Your cock is so big Mav. You're stretching me so far." I rocked my hips back and forth to help him slide in. He pulled out and slid back in, pushing into me completely, and then ground his pubic bone against my clit.

I moaned and spread my legs wide, bringing them up his sides further, and forced my muscles to relax. "That's my good girl. Let me in." He purred and I moaned, biting his ear as he started thrusting in and out of me. "Fuck, your pussy is heaven." He slid his arm under my knee and hitched it high, using it as leverage against me as he fucked me good. "Is this okay, am I hurting your sides or your head?" He asked through clenched teeth as he fought to control himself.

"It will hurt me if you don't fuck me like you need me Maverick. Don't hold back on me. Show me that you've missed me like I've missed you."

That was his undoing. He widened his knees on the bed and fucked me like a man possessed. He sucked on my nipples and pinned my hands above my head as he pushed my body over the crest of an orgasm to rival all orgasms.

As I started coming on his cock his hips jerked spastically and he grunted, "That's it, milk my cock like a good girl. Take every drop I give you." He thrust hard and I felt him start coming inside of me and it shot me off into another spontaneous orgasm.

"Maverick!" I screamed and clawed at his back and arms, he kept pounding his hips into mine and pushing his come deeper into my body.

I went limp under him as I fought to catch my breath and his hips finally stilled. He let go of my wrists and then rolled until we were on our sides facing each other with his cock still inside of me. He twitched deep within me, and groaned, rubbing his nose up the side of my neck before biting my ear. "Tell me it feels as good for you as it does for me. Tell me no one else compares to what just happened."

I kissed his damp forehead and pushed his hair back, forcing his head to lean back to look at me. When his blue eyes were looking directly into mine I smiled at him. "No one has ever come close to comparing to what we used to have. And this, right now, knocks all of that out of the park baby. It couldn't possibly get any better for me."

"Good. Because I never want anyone else getting near you. You're mine." He said before kissing me deeply, teasing my tongue with his and caressing my body with his hands.

After a while, we stilled and laid on the pillows looking at each other. "I need a Plan B pill," I said. "And we need to start using condoms."

He shook his head as a serious look crossed his face. "I'm never putting anything between us ever again. My come will coat your insides for the rest of your life. Get used to it."

"And what about pregnancy?" I asked, leaning up on my elbow to look down at him.

"You wanted kids when we talked about our future before. Has that changed?" He said so nonchalantly.

"Well no, I still want kids. But not today."

"We're not getting any younger. And if we start having kids now, our oldest will be almost the same age as Penelope's baby. Don't you want them to be close to their cousins?"

I groaned and rolled away from him, forcing his cock to fall from my body and put my feet on the floor. He grabbed my arm and pulled me back onto the bed gently and quickly laid on top of me pinning me down with his large body.

"Stop running from me every time I talk about our families."

Pain erupted in my chest as I thought about everything I was kept from over the years. "If you want to talk about your family, go ahead, I'd love to hear about your mom and dad and anyone else you want to tell me about, but I can't talk about mine. And I don't want to hear about them either. Okay?" I snapped back.

"Why?"

"Because. Just drop it." My body shook as sadness overwhelmed me.

"No." He said, his eyebrows dropping over his eyes as he tried to read me. "Tell me why it upsets you so much."

"No Mav. Now get off of me."

"Not a chance. Tell me!" He demanded.

I yelled back as a sob ripped from my chest. "Because up until an hour ago I didn't even know I had nieces and nephews!"

Horror crossed his face as he watched me crack under him. I closed my eyes and felt the tears spill into my hair as he simply stared in shock. I covered my face with my hands and sobbed, letting tears I'd kept buried for years, free.

He got off of me and lifted me into his lap and held me as I cried. He leaned against the headboard and covered us up with the blankets as I fought to control my errant emotions. When I finally calmed down I wiped my eyes and buried my face in his neck.

"Tell. Me. Everything." He ordered calmly but with authority. "I need to know what's hurting you."

I took a couple of deep breaths and mulled it over in my head before finally just opening my mouth and saying the words I hadn't spoken to anyone ever before.

"They cut me off and kicked me out when I left you."

His body tensed under mine as my words hung between us. "What do you mean?"

"When I came home that night, I told my mom what happened. Stupidly expecting her to comfort me." I said with disdain and shook my head. He pulled back to look at me, but I kept my eyes down. "She ran right to my dad, and they both started screaming at me, demanding that I go find you and beg you to take me back. They told me over and over again how they had worked too hard to form a relationship with the Jones family for me to fuck it up for them with my stupid teenage dramatics."

"You have to be fucking kidding me." He growled. His arms were tight around me as rage coiled through his body.

I shook my head sadly. "When I refused, they gave me the ultimatum to get back with you or be cut off and kicked out of their lives forever. I thought they were kidding like they were playing some cruel joke on me. But half an hour later, I had a backpack worth of stuff and my cash savings of seven hundred dollars in my pocket and nothing else as they slammed their front door in my face. And I haven't spoken to them since." Maverick was silent but he threaded his fingers through my hair as he tried to contain his anger for me to continue. "I lost my college fund, my trust fund, my car, my cell phone, my future, and every picture or keepsake from our ten years together. I left with only a few things I managed to grab as I sobbed for them to let me stay. But it was nothing compared to what I had before I came looking for you that night."

"I'll fucking destroy them." He said in a voice so dark and menacing it made me shiver in his lap even as his skin warmed me. "I'll fucking make them rue the day they ever wronged you, Cora. I promise you I will."

"I don't want that. I don't want anything from them anymore. I've come too far, survived too much because of them, to go back now."

"How can you stand to be near me right now?" He asked, turning my head to look at him. "How can you look at me and not hate me for what they did to you because of me? Jesus fucking Christ Cora, why didn't you come to me?" He demanded, anger flooding from him the more he processed this. "Why didn't you let me help you?"

"Because that was what they wanted, they wanted me to come to you so they could continue to use the relationship they had with you and your family to their benefit. I don't know what they've gained from your name over the years but I'm sure it's extensive. That's why they never told you anything about me, because if they'd told you the truth you'd have destroyed them, and they knew it."

"How the fuck did you survive? Where did you go?"

I shrugged my shoulders and sighed. "I bounced around from couch to couch for a while and then made my way to the city and got three jobs and worked my ass off for years, living in shelters and shit ass apartments and refused to give up."

"Jake and Penelope didn't help you? Did they know what happened?" He slid out from under me and started pacing the floor in his naked glory.

I paused and shrugged my shoulders as I tried to handle this part delicately, "I don't know what they were told, but I didn't see them before I left, so they never heard my side either way."

He turned and looked at me with such disbelief on his perfect face. "Jesus Christ."

"I'm fine Mav. I survived without them." I knelt on the edge of the bed and grabbed him on one of his laps back and forth and pulled him to me. I pressed my forehead to his, buried my fingers in his hair, and held on to him when he tried to keep moving. "I'm right here, a stronger person than I was back then because of their evil ways. I'm right here, with you."

"You should have been with me the whole fucking time!" He snapped and growled through his clenched teeth as his restraint shattered. "I could have won you back if they wouldn't have thrown you out like fucking pieces of shit!" He wrapped his hands around my body and crushed his mouth to mine, kissing me roughly. It was angry and passionate, and I held onto him and took what he gave me. "They stole you from me for ten fucking years Cora. Admit it, if they hadn't forced your hand, you would have considered forgiving me. I would have gotten the help I so desperately needed to grieve properly, without hurting you. I would have earned your love the right way if you had still been around. You know we could have worked it out, don't you?"

I took a deep breath and admitted what I'd prohibited myself from even considering over the years. "Yes, I would have forgiven you with time. I would have figured out a way to work it out."

"I hated you for leaving me so easily and never even giving me the decency of talking to me about it afterward. I let my anger towards you fester the longer you didn't reach out to me, and it was all because of them. Not because of you at all." He cursed and pulled away, grabbed the lamp off the bedside table, and threw it against the wall where it shattered into a dozen pieces. He screamed at the top of his lungs as every muscle in his body went rigid with his anguish. He turned to me, and I slumped back on the bed in fear of the pure unapologetic rage in his eyes. "I will make them pay Cora. I promise you that."

"I just want you Mav," I whispered. I was trying to speak to the calm levelheaded part of him.

He walked back to the bed and took my hands in his, kissing each of them and placing them on his chest over his wildly beating heart. "You have me, Cora. I am yours. But I will get justice for what they did to you."

"How?" I whispered.

"By taking what they wanted so badly that they were willing to trade their child for it." He said and smiled down at me. "Their money and their power."

I shivered as I watched him make plans in his head, slipping into the role of the ruthless businessman he'd become over the years. I didn't regret telling him. If I wanted a real chance at us working out now after all this time, he needed to know the truth. But it didn't mean I wasn't scared to see what he did to the people who destroyed the one thing he loved most in this world at one point.

Me.

Chapter 7 – Maverick

I walked off the elevator on Wednesday morning and groaned out loud when I saw that Veronica, Reid, and Dexter were all waiting for me outside of my office.

"Go away," I ordered. But they all ignored me. Well, except Veronica, she sat back down at her desk and pretended to be busy, but Dexter and Reid followed me into my office and shut the door behind them.

"How is she?" Reid asked, and for the first time in the history of our friendship, he was not smiling or joking in some way.

I sighed and threw my briefcase down on my desk and sat in my chair. "Fucking beat to hell." I snapped. "But she'll heal physically. Fucker slammed her head off the wall so hard she has a concussion. Then he dragged her off into the darkness and punched her in the face and the sides before taking off with her bags. No one on the fucking platform did a thing either. They all just got on the train and let a man assault a woman in plain view and did nothing."

Anger vibrated off of me, but it wasn't just because of the mugging.

"She's tough, I'm sure she fought back the whole time," Dexter said, shaking his head.

"She never should have been on that fucking platform to begin with though. And that's my fault."

"How is it your fault?" Dexter asked, sitting down in a chair across from me as Reid took the other one.

"She's the only woman I've ever loved, and she's also the only woman that's ever hurt me. And I don't always think straight where she's concerned. We were at McCulley's, and she pissed me off and we argued, and I walked away from her, knowing she had been drinking. She wasn't paying attention on that platform because she was upset and drunk and I never should have let her leave like that."

"Mav," Reid said, shaking his head. "I was there too, I could have stopped her myself, but she was set on leaving. That's not your fault."

"It doesn't matter," I said, shaking it off. "It won't happen again. She's at my place now and I intend to keep her there. I have a lot to fix with her but I'm going to do it." I leveled Reid with a glare that made him wither a bit. "I'm only going to tell you this one time Reid. Cora is mine. I don't ever want to catch you hitting on her again or I won't think twice about destroying you for it."

He held his hands up and shook his head. "I hear you loud and clear Jones. I won't be anything but friendly to Cora from now on. I see how intense you get about her; I don't want that intensity aimed my way."

"Good," I said and leaned forward on my desk. "Because there's something I need both of your help with."

They looked at each other raised their eyebrows and then leaned forward, interested in what I needed from them. I tried to summarize it the best I could. "This stays between us for now but, Cora and I dated for a decade in grade school and when she broke up with me before we left for college, her family gave her an ultimatum, either get back with me or be cut off." I took a deep breath to fight the anger that swelled in my heart as I thought about everything Cora survived because of that decision. "They kicked her out with absolutely nothing at eighteen years old because they thought it would force her back into my arms. But she only resented me for it and refused and instead has been fighting to survive the last ten years on scraps when she should have had all of this." I said, raising my hands to the empire I sat over every day. "Her family valued their relationship with mine and what they gained from it, more than their own daughter's safety or happiness. And they've smiled in my face, making business deals, and socializing with my family ever since while she couldn't afford to eat."

"I think I can see where this is going," Reid said with a sly smile on his face.

"I'm going to reduce them to rubble for what they did to her. And in the end, she'll have the world and they'll be the ones struggling to survive."

"What's your first step?" Dexter asked.

"First, I need to meet with my father and tell him everything. I can't do this without his support because this empire was his dream first and I'll be severing a friendship with a family that he's had for decades. Then I'm going to approach Jake Valentine, Cora's brother. He's been trying to get my ear about a project in Manhattan he's been wanting to spearhead with me and I'm going to ask him about her. If he knew anything I'll be able to tell. And if he knew all along that she was cut off and didn't tell me, then I'll destroy more than just her parents."

"Sounds pretty cut and dry to me. Is she on board with it though?" Dexter asked, eyeing me closely.

"She'd rather just continue living like they don't exist in this world anymore. But if she's going to be by my side, then we're going to run into them from time to time. And I refuse to let her feel inferior even once to them from this moment on. So I need to be ahead of it first."

"Okay. Keep me updated and let me know what you need from me." Dexter said and stood, "And by the way the Shen Hu firm is dissolved, and so is every other business he had a hand in. He's nothing."

"Perfect," I said, standing and shaking his hand. "Thank you for taking care of that while I was AWOL yesterday."

He chuckled and so did Reid. "You know Jones, it was nice being able to actually do our jobs without you micromanaging us all day long. Believe it or not, you're allowed to stay at home with your sexy girlfriend from time to time without your empire collapsing." He said. "It's why you pay us the big bucks."

Reid interjected, "Yeah, you're just such a control freak you never let us off our leashes. It was nice."

I laughed and relaxed a bit in the company of my friends. "Well, chances are I'll be doing it more often in the future so be ready."

"On standby boss," Dexter saluted me and then left my office, laughing with Reid.

I shook my head and got busy. I set up a lunch with my dad for that afternoon and then called Cora's boss. She and I had argued at length last night about what she was going to do for work. She demanded that she be able to continue making her way in her career and didn't want me to have a hand in it. I, of course, demanded that she move up here with me and work at my side, helping me build what would grow to be hers too, but she locked down whenever I mentioned the future including us together and I reserved myself to just letting her kill some time at Halo while she adjusted to being in my world again. It wasn't like Halo was a bad place to work, I owned fifty-two percent of it in reality.

But what I didn't like was someone spending their time with her all day and that someone not being me. Since the moment I saw her in that conference room a few days ago, my body ached to be touching her in some way. Even when I was buried deep inside of her, which was exactly how I spent most of my time yesterday, last night, and again this morning, I still burned for more.

She was like a drug for me, and I couldn't get enough.

"Sir." Veronica stepped into my office and distracted me from my carnal thoughts of Cora naked and spread open in my bed this morning as I fucked her senseless before I left for work.

"Yes." I snapped.

"Your eight o'clock is here."

"Right," I said, relaxing my tone. "Give me two minutes and then show him in."

"Yes sir." She purred and then walked back out of my office, shaking her hips.

Had she always purred and openly tried to be seductive throughout the day? Or was I just noticing it now because Cora had made her distaste for her so apparent?

I shook my head and took out my phone and dialed Cora's new number. I'd gotten her a new phone yesterday to replace the one that was stolen.

Her sleepy voice answered, "Hmm, good morning Mr. Jones."

I groaned at how good her voice sounded saying my name like that. "Say it again."

She chuckled and cleared her throat. "What can I do for you, Mr. Jones?" She purred and it put anything Veronica ever said to shame.

Fuck I was hard again from just two seconds on the phone with her.

"You can come here so I can fuck you on my desk."

"You fucked me less than two hours ago Mav." She said.

"I have always had a giant appetite for you in case you forgot."

"I always thought it was just the needs of a teenage boy that left you constantly hard. You're telling me it hasn't gotten better with age?"

"Not where you're concerned baby. It's only gotten worse."

"Well, I suppose I can be used to satisfy your needs." She chuckled and then groaned.

"What's wrong?" I asked, worried.

"Nothing, I'm just sore." She sighed and I heard her shifting around in my bed and the urge to go home and crawl back into bed with her had never been higher before. Maybe Reid and Dexter were right, I was a control freak who never delegated until now and perhaps I should do it more often for times like this. Cora interrupted my thoughts of returning home though, "I'm leaving in a bit to go to the doctor." She said.

"For what?"

"To get started on some sort of contraceptive considering you refuse to wear a condom."

"We never finished that conversation last night." I reminded her.

"I know. And we're not going to agree on it anytime soon, so until we do, I need to protect myself."

"Fine," I growled. "But only because I'd rather come inside of you than on you, and I know you're not above making me pull out."

She laughed again and tsked her tongue at me. "Why does the idea of you covering my tits with your come turn me on so much right now?"

I groaned and palmed my hard-on. "You can't say things like that when I'm supposed to be having a meeting in a few minutes, Cora."

"Hmm. Well then I'd better get going, I've got a date with your hand-held shower head in five minutes, and I'd hate to keep it waiting."

"You minx." I was raging hard imagining her standing in my shower bringing herself to orgasm with my shower head.

"Only for you baby. I'll talk to you later."

"Franklin will drive you to your appointment," I said and she started to argue. "He drives you or I do."

She groaned and conceded. "Fine, I will let Franklin drive me even though I'm more than capable of getting there myself."

"Thank you."

"Hmm."

I lowered my voice in the way I knew she loved, "Think of me when you come."

She panted into the phone, "Always."

She hung up and I put my phone in my pocket as my door opened and my eight o'clock meeting walked in.

Alright, down to business I suppose.

I looked up as my father walked off the elevator a couple of hours later and smiled warmly at Veronica on his way into my office.

I stood up and rounded my desk when he walked in and hugged him tightly. He was dressed sharply in a suit and tie and looked great for his young age of fifty-five.

"You look particularly happy today," I said to him as we walked over to the seating area where our lunch was laid out. Veronica had ordered our favorites from the Italian place across the street and the scents had been teasing me for ten minutes.

He undid his suit jacket and tossed it over the chair before sitting down. "I am particularly happy today." He snickered and opened his lunch container. "I get Salvatore's for lunch with my son, what's not to be happy about?"

I laughed and sat down. "Be honest, it's the Salvatore's that got you here on such short notice wasn't it?"

"Well." He mused, conveniently not answering the question. "How are things, son?"

I took a bite of my meal and then sat back in my chair. "Things are... interesting," I said and he eyed me closely. He took a drink of his water and pushed his plate away.

"I should have known better than to ask before I got to eat my lunch." He raised his eyebrow at me and even though I was a billionaire and CEO of a company I'd built from the ground up; he was still my dad and he still made me feel like a kid when we talked like this. "Lay it on me."

"Cora Valentine started working for me a couple of days ago."

His eyebrows shot to his hairline, and he leaned forward in his chair. "Wow. How is she?"

I shook my head and couldn't help the stupid grin that pulled my lips. "She's breathtaking." He smiled at me and gone was the alpha CEO that he'd always been growing up, and in his place was just my dad.

"Tell me everything."

I sighed and the smile fell and so did his. "She took a job at Halo Optics downstairs and had no idea I was the CEO up here. Long story short she ended up translating a meeting with Shen Hu for me and caught some insider trading scheme they were trying to pull over my eyes and she saved me from making a nine hundred-million-dollar mistake."

"That's incredible." He praised.

"But then that night on her way home, she was mugged on the subway."

"Why on earth would Cora Valentine be riding the subway?" He snapped, scowling at me like it was my fault. I didn't have the heart to tell him it was.

"I had no clue, there were things that didn't line up with her story that drove me crazy. She lived on the west side, and took a job here as a PA." His brows knitted as I continued. "She rode the damn subway and every time I mentioned her family she clammed up and shut down."

"Something happened between them didn't it?"

"More than just something, dad," I said and bit back the anger that rose quickly.

My dad put his hand on my shoulder and squeezed. "What happened?"

"They cut her off." His hand slid off my arm as he tilted his head in confusion. "They kicked her out on her ass the day she left me after graduation. They demanded she beg me to take her back because they didn't want to lose the connection to the Jones family through our breakup, and when she wouldn't... she lost everything. She's been struggling to even survive for the last ten years while Dennis and Susan Valentine have benefited grossly from doing business with our family and socializing in our circle all these years."

"My God." He sighed and leaned back into his seat. "They've acted as though nothing was amiss for a decade while they shunned their daughter for a decision she made as a teenager." He shook his head as his anger surfaced, "Over a mistake *you* made as a teenager."

"I know and the worst part of it all, is we're still madly in love." I felt a zing of pain shoot through my heart as I said it out loud to my dad. I hadn't even told Cora I was still in love with her, and I didn't need to hear the words from her to know that she was still in love with me. I could feel it. "They stole ten years from me when they forced her out.

If they had left her alone, with a little time we could have worked it out and moved on. But instead, she had to fight to survive and refused to come to me because she lost everything because of me."

"Jesus Christ, Maverick. They need to answer for what they did to her."

"I agree. I plan to take everything they've gained from us away and leave them with nothing. Which is exactly what they deserve after destroying mine and Cora's life with their greed."

"You not only have my support Mav, but I'm going to help you." He said, back to business mode.

"Good. Because I want to do it in a way that is so catastrophic they never recover from it."

"It's exactly what they deserve. They'll regret the day they destroyed their perfect daughter, and they'll also regret the day they ever fucked with my son." His ruthless side rarely came out these days, now that he had retired and was enjoying the fun side of his businesses, but at that moment, he was full-on Christopher Jones, Billionaire CEO and father who would do anything for his children.

"Perfect," I said and leaned back into my seat, relaxing now that I had my dad's support in this. I would have done it without it, but I wanted it because I respected him and that meant something to me.

We ate our lunch, discussing the beautiful and captivating Cora Valentine the entire time and planning how we were going to destroy her parents. By the time he left, I was calm and settled in a way that I hadn't been all day.

I had two more meetings for the day and then I was off to go home to see the woman that consumed my every thought and desire.

My phone pinged while I was sitting at my desk in the middle of my last meeting, and I quickly read the message.

Cora: *Open when you're alone. And turn your volume down.*

There was a video attached to the message and my brain could focus on nothing other than knowing what was on that video. I forced myself to put my phone down and finish off my meeting and then even forced myself not to open the message as I gathered my things and walked down to my car.

Franklin was waiting for me at the curb, and I slid into the back seat. "Did you get Ms. Valentine to the doctor today?" I asked him.

"Yes sir. She's back at the penthouse now."

"Good. Thank you."

"Of course sir." He replied.

I took out my earbuds, no longer able to keep from watching this video that she sent to me, and put them in. I clicked on the video and watched in fascination as Cora's face lit up my screen. She looked at the phone and bit her lip and then backed up. She was completely naked and in my shower and she stepped back until I could see her entire body and I groaned, biting my knuckle. She was so fucking sexy.

She took the wand from the shower head on the wall and sprayed the water over her chest, letting it hit both of her nipples and then down further over her flat stomach and then lower still until it sprayed directly onto her pussy.

She moaned and spread her legs, putting her foot on the bench, and opening her legs wide so I could see her pussy lips as the water pulsed on her clit. She tilted her head back and slid one hand down her throat and to her tit, pinching her nipple as she went before reaching over and pulling at the other one.

"Maverick." She moaned and gasped as her hips rocked back and forth under the spray. "God, this feels so good."

My cock was rock fucking hard, and I palmed myself as I watched her hands roam over her body. Her chest rose and fell quickly as she worked herself towards her orgasm and the second it crashed over her body she moaned my name over and over as her back bowed and her legs shook.

"Oh my... yes... fuck I need you." She begged as she came. She dropped the handheld and sagged onto the bench as she caught her breath and looked over at the camera. "Hurry home baby." She purred and then shook her head as she walked back over to the camera and turned it off after blowing me a kiss.

She was going to drown in my come if she wasn't careful.

I pulled up the message and texted her.

Me: *I just watched your video, and now my cock is painfully hard, and I need to come. I'll be home in five minutes. Go lay in the center of our bed on your back, naked with your knees bent and your legs spread wide. When I walk in the door, I want to see you playing with your wet pussy, getting it nice and ready for my cock. I'm going to fuck you so good baby.*

Her response came almost instantly.

Cora: Can I come before you get home? Because I'm already close again.

Me: No. The next time your pussy comes it's going to be wrapped around my cock, milking it.

Cora: You'd better hurry then baby, I need to ride more than just my fingers.

Fuck.

Franklin pulled into the garage, and I bolted from the car waving to him. The ride up to my penthouse took forever. I shed my jacket and tie and was unbuttoning my shirt when I walked down the hallway to my bedroom. At the door, I took a deep breath undid the cuffs of my sleeves, and then slowly pushed the door open.

"Good girl." I praised as my hungry eyes devoured Cora where she laid so prettily in the center of the bed playing with her pussy.

Her back was arched, and her hand was in her hair as she writhed on the bed in need. "Please Mav. Don't make me wait any longer for you."

I toed off my shoes and then undid my belt and unclasped my pants, reaching down and freeing my cock from my briefs as I shoved them down my legs. Her eyes locked onto my cock, and she threw her head back as she buried two fingers deep into her pussy. She lowered her other hand around the bottom of her thigh and rubbed her asshole with her fingertips as she finger fucked herself.

I crawled up the bed and pulled her hands away from her body as I fell onto my stomach and buried my face between her thighs. She screamed and pumped her hips up into my mouth and I pinned them back down to the bed. I folded her thighs up to her stomach and lifted her ass off the bed and dropped my tongue to her asshole. She gasped and wiggled under me as I pushed my tongue into her and groaned.

I licked her good until she was nearly sobbing for me to fuck her. I pulled away and kissed her pussy again and then climbed back up her body. "Do you remember the first time I fucked your ass, Cora?" I asked her and she nodded her head quickly.

"Yes." She panted. "God, I was so scared and so fucking horny. We were arguing about something, and I screamed at you to just fuck my ass and you did."

"We were in the back seat of my car, and I'd already fucked your pussy raw, we'd fucked almost every hour that day and you still needed more. You were desperate for it."

Her eyes rolled as she remembered that night. "It was pitch black out where we parked and I dared you to fuck my ass because you'd been talking about doing it for months, but we never pulled the trigger."

"That's right, I'd fingered your ass almost every time I was fucking you around that time, and I tongued you every chance I got but we were both so nervous to do anal for the first time. We were just kids still; we had no business doing that shit."

"But you did." She smiled up at me as she rocked under me and slid the head of my cock through her pussy. "We were arguing about it, and I just rolled over onto my knees and screamed at you to just do it."

Her nails dug into my arms as I pushed the head of my cock into her pussy. "And I fucking did it. You had baby oil in your bag, and I lathered my cock up and slammed into you in one thrust. Fuck," I groaned remembering how good it had felt. "You screamed so loud as you pushed back onto me."

She dug her heels into my hips and pulled me into her pussy further, gasping as I filled her up. "I wanted to stop because it hurt so bad, and I was scared, but you told me no. You said I'd been daring you to do it for so long that you weren't going to stop once you were finally inside of me."

"That's right. I held you down and I fucked your ass so hard. You came... So. Many. Times." I bit out between each thrust as I started fucking her.

"You did it over and over again the rest of the night." She said and shook her head and moaned, "We parked on the side of that road for hours as you fucked my ass until I was bowlegged."

"And you loved every second of it because it was me doing it to you."

She looked straight into my eyes as she tightened around my cock and came, exploding around me, with her gasps and pleas filling the room. "Fuck my ass Mav. Make it hurt just like you did that night so long ago and claim it as yours once more."

Chapter 8 – Cora

"Roll over." He commanded, his whole body was still and tight over me as he fought to restrain his need. I knew I had him by the balls and he'd do anything I wanted him to right now. In the same way, I was so needy I'd do anything he commanded. It was always like that for us.

He slid out of my body and flipped me over roughly and I landed on my stomach. He pulled my hips down the bed until I laid flat on my stomach with my legs together between his knees.

He leaned down and bit my shoulder and then whispered in my ear. "Don't fucking move."

I watched as he walked away from the bed and into the bathroom, returning a moment later with a jar of Vaseline in his hands. He stood next to the bed, and I watched in fascination as he rubbed it over the length of his cock and slowly stroked himself, rubbing it in. He groaned and watched me closely as he worked himself over. "It's going to feel so fucking good sliding into your ass for the first time in ten years baby." He climbed back up on the bed and straddled my thighs. "Reach back and spread your cheeks apart so I can watch my cock disappear."

I reached back and pulled myself open for him and he pushed a slick finger into me. I bit my lip and held my breath when his cock pushed against my tight opening.

"Go slow," I hissed, as fear clawed at my throat.

"No." He said back and pushed the head of his cock into me. "I'm going to fuck you hard, just like you want me to. We don't do anything slow, love. We never have."

I hissed and buried my face in the blankets as he pushed his entire cock deep inside of me. "Oh my God." I groaned.

He grunted and leaned forward, grabbing the front of my throat, and pulled my head up as he lay against my back. He bit my ear as he pulled out and pushed back in. "This ass is mine."

"It's yours." I agreed as he slammed deep inside of me with the next thrust.

"Good girl."

"Yes, Mav." I panted and let go of my cheeks to put my elbows on the bed to arch my back more, pushing back into him with each thrust. "Just like that baby."

"You love to take my cock don't you?" He growled into my ear.

"You know I do. I've never wanted anything else from you but your cock."

"Liar." He bit out. "You need my cock as badly as you need my love." He fucked me hard, making my head loll to the side as he pushed me into that haze between pleasure and pain. "You've always been greedy when it comes to those two things. Which is why you're perfect for me Cora. Because I'm a greedy bastard when it comes to you too baby."

"Fuck Mav!" I screamed as I fell over the other side of an orgasm that stole my ability to see or hear until all I could do was feel. I felt how he claimed my body as his own over and over again through my orgasm, demanding more from me that I didn't know I had left to give until he took it.

"That's my girl. Come on my cock, your ass is so tight." He slammed his hips forward a couple more times and then stilled as his hot come branded my insides as he filled me. I gasped and fought to breathe with him on top of me and he rolled us until we were on our sides with him once again, still inside of me. He never liked pulling out of me before, and that seemingly hadn't changed as he got older either.

His cock softened inside of me but never really shrunk, keeping me filled and satisfied as his hands caressed every inch of my body. He whispered sweet words of praise into my ear as we relaxed in the late evening dusk.

"You're perfect." He said, speaking over and over affirming his feelings for me.

"I've been so lost without you."

"I'm never letting you go again."

"I'm still in love with you."

I opened my eyes when he whispered those last words and kissed my neck and shoulder. I heard him tell me that he loved me at least a million times over the ten years we were together but having gone so long since the last time left me doubting it and being afraid of it.

"You don't believe me, do you?" He whispered after a while.

"I hurt you when I left." That was all I could say back as the sadness of the lost years between us darkened my mood.

"I hurt you to make you leave me." He snuggled in even closer to me and wrapped his arms tight around my chest and body. "I love you, Cora. I never stopped."

I turned my head and looked at him, looking for any hint of reservation on his face but there wasn't even an ounce of uncertainty there. I offered my lips to him, and he hungrily took them in his. "I love you too Maverick. You're the only man I've ever loved."

"Good. Because I told my dad today that we were still in love. It'd be embarrassing if I had to retract that statement."

"You told your dad about me?" I asked, hating how the warmth in my heart spread as I thought about Christopher and Marsha Jones. They had always been so welcoming and loving towards me over the years of our relationship, and when I lost them the same night I lost Maverick, it was devastating.

"I did. I told him how much I loved you, how your parents stole ten years of our lives from us, and how I intended to make them pay." His voice was so strong and confident, and I felt myself shrinking into his arms and letting it blanket me. He always took care of me growing up, and he'd only been a boy back then. And now he was a powerful man and it seemed he could do so much more than before. And I wanted to let him.

"What did he say?" I whispered.

"That he couldn't wait to see you and make your parents pay for destroying you because of a mistake I made as a teenager. He's very protective of his family, you know that."

"I do." I smiled fondly, remembering the strong powerful father that had loved Maverick and Lucas endlessly and doted on Marsha affectionately. Their family was night and day different than mine, and I hadn't seen the differences in what they were back then. The Jones family had love and passion in their home. Whereas the Valentine house held only hunger for power and worry about their image.

I had been so blind back then.

"I'm meeting with your brother tomorrow." He said against my ear, biting it and using his hands to cup both of my breasts.

"Don't talk about him while your cock is still inside of me Maverick." I snapped a little meaner than I planned to.

He thrust his hips forward, sliding inside of me further, and pulled a hiss from my lips.

"Don't tell me what to do minx. I'm needy because of you."

I snorted at him. "Then fuck me and be dirty and demand things from my body that I've only ever given you. But don't do it while talking about my family."

He pulled from my body roughly and dragged me out of the bed aggressively. "Shower, now. I need to fuck your pussy next. Then we will finish our conversation about your family."

He carried me into the shower and scrubbed every inch of my body with his manly-smelling soap and expert hands before washing himself and then he leaned down and bit my neck, before soothing it with his tongue.

"I need to know who you've been with over the years." He said in a deep gravelly voice as he picked me up and wrapped my legs around his waist.

"I assure you, they were no one you would run into in your social circles," I answered back as he pressed his cock against my opening and slid inside of me. "Shit." I hissed at the invasion.

"How many?" He asked through clenched teeth

"That I fucked or dated?" I asked, trying to focus on his questions but was struggling as he thrust his hips and fucked into me.

"Both." He demanded.

"I don't know Mav..." I sighed and felt my eyes roll in the back of my head as he rolled his hips. "I dated a few guys casually but never bothered with them much, to be honest. I fucked a few more than that."

"Numbers Cora."

"I don't know!" I yelled in frustration. "Why does it matter? Are you going to tell me how many women you've fucked over the years?"

"I need to know." He leaned down and bit my shoulder as he pounded into me. "I need to know how many men you've let have you in my absence, so I know how many men I need to erase from your memory."

"They don't matter Mav. They were all casual and none of them compared to you. None of them made me feel like this." I said as I clawed at his shoulders and lifted my hips on and off of him as he thrust into me.

He grunted and slid his hand under my ass and pushed two fingers into my ass as he started fucking me wildly.

"Oh fuck." I panted as I pressed my head back into the tile and held on for dear life. "You drive me wild Maverick. You know my body like no one else ever has or ever will. And you're the only one my heart ever belonged to."

"That's fucking right." He groaned as my body clenched tight around him and my orgasm started rolling over me. "Good girl, come on my cock like a good fucking girl baby."

"Yes!" I screamed at the top of my lungs as he started coming inside of me and filling me with his hot come as he claimed my mouth with his, sucking on my tongue and absorbing my pleas.

His hips slowed, thrusting slowly into me from root to tip, pushing through his silky come. "I love you, Cora." He whispered, laying his forehead against mine. "I've never loved anyone but you."

There was an edge to the way he said it that caught my attention and pulled me out of my post-orgasm haze.

"How many women have you been with?" I asked and he opened his eyes and looked at me.

"Too many to count." He answered honestly.

"Ouch," I replied, dropping my legs, and sliding from his arms, removing his cock from me finally.

I grabbed the bottle of shampoo and busied my hands with lathering my hair up as he watched me.

"I never loved them."

"So you've said," I replied, keeping my eyes closed as I rinsed my hair. "How many have you dated?"

He didn't answer right away, and I cracked an eye at him, waiting for his answer, but he didn't give one. He just watched me as I poured conditioner into my hands and then worked it into my hair.

"Don't ask questions you won't answer yourself." I challenged.

He sighed and walked over to me and pushed his hands into my hair, tilting my head back to rinse the cream from my locks. I sighed as I held onto his biceps as his magic fingers worked into my scalp, careful of the bruise on the back of my head. "I dated three women exclusively."

"Do I know them?"

He paused and looked down at me as he moved his hands to my neck and shoulders, rubbing out the knots and tense muscles as he spoke. "One."

"Who?" I asked in a whisper.

"Cora, please." He whispered back and leaned down to kiss me, and I let him briefly and then pulled back.

"Just tell me who."

His eyes burned as he looked into mine. "Sarah."

The water froze on my skin as I looked up at him. "Sarah Washington? My old best friend Sarah Washington? The one you fucked to destroy us?" I yelled as panic started seeping into my veins.

"I'm sorry Cora, please know that being involved with her after that night you caught us was only ever out of bitterness. I was hurt that you took off without a backward glance like I meant nothing at all to you and so when the opportunity presented itself to hurt you back with her, I took it. And I regret every second of it."

I turned away from him and he grabbed me, but I swatted away his hands and sank onto the bench. I held my head in my hands as this new information swarmed in my brain. That had been my biggest fear over the years as I fought to stay away from him because of my stupid pride. I was afraid that he had gotten with Sarah and that they were senselessly happy together despite me and it had happened.

"My worst fear came true," I whispered into the silence.

Maverick sank to his knees in front of me and made me look at him, but I couldn't see through the tears that pooled in my eyes, so I closed them and closed him out.

"I'm so sorry Cora. You have to believe that I never would have done it if I'd known the truth about why you left. Please forgive me, Cora, I'm so sorry baby."

I shook my head as more tears fell. "She set us up that night and she got everything else that she wanted after it."

"What do you mean?" He asked, holding my face as he leaned his forehead against mine.

"She told me you were at that party. She knew I was looking for you and she told me you were there. And then an hour later I walked in on you nailing her. Do you really think that was a coincidence? And then you go and date her, publicly. Giving her every single thing she ever wanted."

"I had no idea." He whispered, haunted by it all.

"I know," I said, shaking my head. "I know you didn't know, and that's the only thing keeping me in your life right now when everything in me is screaming for me to run far, far away from you and all the hurt that will keep coming."

He moved so fast that I never had time to brace. He wrapped his arms around my waist, tore me off the bench, and pulled me into his arms, forcing my legs to straddle his hips. "Don't say that. Don't ever say you're going to run again." He threaded his fingers into my hair and held my face close to his as he struggled with his emotions. "I won't survive you running away from me again. I know that we both have baggage and hurt that we caused each other, I know you will always feel threatened by other women because of what I did to you, and I promise you this right here, right now, I will never hurt you that way again. I will never allow another woman to come between us like she did before. I promise you." He shuddered, his whole body shaking underneath mine. "But my trigger and my worst fear is you running away from me again, abandoning me like you did when I was at my fucking worst. I can't even explain to you how badly that destroyed my head and my heart the last time you did it. So I am begging you, Cora, if you've ever cared for me in the least before, don't ever run away and abandon me again." His hand was tight in my hair and his arm held me against his body almost painfully as he expressed the depth of his pain to me in a way that I had begged him to communicate with me when we were kids.

When Lucas died, a huge part of Mav died with him. I had tried to be everything he needed from me to help him grieve and process and cope with that loss, but he shut down and would never communicate what he needed from me. But here, once again on his knees for me, he was communicating and telling me exactly what hurt him the most, exposing himself to me and begging me to spare him that pain again. And I could never, even on my worst day, dare to use that against him.

"I won't," I said against his lips, wrapping my arms around his neck and clinging to him as tightly as he clung to me. "I won't leave you Mav. I'm not going anywhere. I love you."

His lips crashed against mine in a painful, ugly kiss that was all teeth and hurt as we cut our old wounds open and begged the other to help us put ourselves back together again. Seeing the man that had become so much, reduced to pain on his knees on his shower floor broke down the tallest part of the walls I'd constructed around my heart a decade ago and his love rushed in around the pieces to my damaged heart.

"I'm not going anywhere," I whispered again as I held onto him. He buried his face in my neck and clung to me just like that for a long, long time. I whispered over and over again, all of the things I had wanted to tell him over the years.

I told him how much he meant to me, how deeply I ached for him, how lost without him I had become. I promised him everything he asked from me and more and he promised it all back to me.

We weren't the same kids we had been when our lives were torn apart by pride and childish decisions. We were so much more than that now, and if we fought for it, nothing could ever tear us apart again. Because we had already overcome so much, we knew what our worst pains felt like and we both knew we were never willing to go back to that place again.

Chapter 9- Maverick

I stood in the doorway of my master closet and watched in awe as Cora dressed for the day. I was already dressed and ready to leave, and I stood with my coffee in my hand and watched as the love of my life slowly slid a pair of black stockings over her calf and knee, smoothing the fabric out as it ended at mid-thigh.

She dropped her leg off the bench where I put my shoes on each morning and placed her other bare foot on it to repeat the process and I couldn't keep my body still a moment longer. I walked into the large closet and placed my coffee down on the island in the middle and slid behind her lush body and wrapped my hands around her bare stomach. She wore a pair of black panties and matching bra and one black silk stocking, and I ached to drape her body in expensive lingerie of every color for the rest of her life.

"You smell divine." I said as I pressed my nose into the base of her neck behind her ear and took a deep breath.

She slid her hands over mine and leaned into me. "I smell like you. I need to shower at my own apartment tonight so I can smell like a woman again."

"Stay with me here." I said, kissing along her neck and shoulder before sliding my hand up further to palm her large breasts.

She moaned and laid her head against my shoulder. "You are insatiable, you know that."

"I'm addicted to you." I answered back, and it was the truth. After our breakthrough in the shower last night, I hadn't left her body until the sun was rising again this morning. And I'd taken her again only an hour ago when we woke up to get ready for work. And if I had it my way, I'd take her again before I walked into my office this morning. "I mean it though, stay here with me. Don't go back there."

"Maverick." She sighed and leaned down to put her other stocking on. "I can't just stay here and never go home."

"Why?"

"Because that would be living with you."

"And what's so wrong with that?" I asked as she looked over her shoulder at me and settled her thigh high on her leg.

"I've been alone for ten years, it's hard to imagine just giving up that independence in an instant."

"You would rather sleep alone at your own place instead of here with me?" I asked, trying to ignore the way that made my chest hurt.

She sighed again and put her hands on her hips, turning towards me. "When you put it that way, no."

"Then why do you want to go back there?"

"Honestly?" She paused and looked me in the eye as she chewed on her bottom lip. "Because a part of me is waiting for you to cast me aside again and the survivor instinct in me is telling me to keep my exit strategy in place so I won't be homeless again."

"We talked about this..." I started, handing her the dress she was reaching for around me as I fought to keep my frustration at bay.

"I know. But the way you're still afraid I'll leave, is the same way I'm still afraid you'll hurt me again and force me to leave. You don't understand what it's like not knowing where you're going to sleep every night. Or what it feels like to wake up in the morning at the homeless shelter and realize someone stole your only pair of shoes while you were asleep. Or how it feels to go three days straight without a single bite to eat." She said and sadness washed over her face. "I can't just give up my lifeline Mav. You're asking me to give up the only security I can trust right now."

"I hate this." I said plainly. "I hate that this is between us."

"I know." She said stepping into the black dress and turning for me to zip it up. "It's only week one, maybe with time I'll be able to let that part of me go."

I pulled the zipper up as she held her hair aside. "If you want to stay at your place, can I stay with you?" I asked.

She snorted and smiled at me. "You want to slum it with me in my run-down apartment?"

"I want to stay with you, period," I said forcefully.

She eyed me over her shoulder once again and shook her head. "I'll never turn down sleeping next to you Mav. If you want to stay at my place you can, but I think you're crazy to give up this heaven for my place."

"You're my heaven, Cora," I whispered and kissed her, backing her into the shelf behind her and deepening the kiss until she was clinging to me.

"We're going to be late for work." She purred but she rocked her hips against me.

"I think your boss will forgive you." I challenged as I slid my hand up the inside of her thigh towards the pretty black panties that I ached to tear off of her.

"You aren't my boss, and you know it." She hissed as my fingers rubbed her pussy over the silk.

"I'm your boss baby, in every sense of the word."

She moaned and spread her thighs wide as I slid my finger into her panties and over her wet clit.

My phone started ringing in my pocket and we both groaned, pulled away from our desire. She laughed and pushed me away and I reluctantly let her but not before bringing my finger to my lips and sucking it clean in my mouth, tasting her delicious arousal on my tongue. "I want you spread open on my desk for lunch today." I didn't let her reply, as I turned and grabbed my coffee from the island top behind me and took my phone from my pocket, "I'll meet you at the front door." I answered my phone, seeing Veronica's name on the screen, and walked from the closet as she sagged into the shelf with a horny look on her face.

Check mate.

Half an hour later we were pulling up outside of Hawthorn Tower in my Audi with Franklin driving. One of the front doormen opened the car door and I stepped out and turned to help Cora step out behind me. It was an incredible feeling, walking into work with Cora at my side, knowing we were finally building this company together now, even if it was ten years late.

"Mr. Jones." Parker the security guard said, nodding to me before he nodded to Cora at my side. She smiled at him.

"Morning Parker," I replied.

"Why did you name it Hawthorn Tower?" Cora asked me from my side as we went through the security turnstiles.

I paused and looked down at her and couldn't help the smirk that crossed my face as I thought about the story behind the name. "I was in the designing phase of the building, and my architect said that I needed to name the tower I climbed every day to command my empire from, and I stupidly thought back to the one thing I'd climbed almost every day growing up," I said as we paused in the center of the lobby. She shook her head, not figuring it out right away, so I tucked a strand of hair behind her ear and let her in on it. "The tree outside of your bedroom window, that I climbed up almost every night to sleep with you junior and senior year, was a Hawthorn tree."

Her eyebrows rose to her hairline and a gentle surprised smile kissed her lush lips.

"You named your empire after something to do with us?"

"Hmm." I agreed and shrugged my shoulders, "I guess even four years ago when I built this tower, I was still as obsessed with you as I was a boy, climbing up that fucking tree to get to you."

"Mav." She said with love twinkling in her eyes as she leaned up on her toes and kissed me gently. "I love you so much, and I'm still just as obsessed with you."

I turned us back towards the elevators to get out of the way of employees trying to get to work on time as I enjoyed her open display of affection. Reid came from the other side of the lobby, and I groaned at the shit-eating grin on his face as he walked up to us as we were stuck waiting for an elevator. The lobby was full of employees who feared me and hardly looked me in the eye, yet one of the only people in this building who would push every one of my buttons happened to join us at the same time.

"Ah if it isn't New York's most powerful couple," Reid said as he walked closer. Eyes from everyone around us looked at Cora and me, chasing that tidbit of information welcomed up by his big mouth.

"Reid," I warned in a deep voice. Cora rolled her eyes at him and smiled.

"Good morning, Reid." She said softly.

He leaned down and kissed her cheek in an overly familiar way that grated my nerves. "Watch it," I warned again but he brushed me off.

"How are you feeling Cora?" He asked, letting his smile fall from his face for the first time since he walked up.

I felt her spine stiffen a bit beneath my hand on the small of her back. "I'm well, thank you." She said firmly.

"I see that." He said back as the elevator door opened and we stepped in with a few other people.

When we started riding up Cora stayed silent at my side and Reid chatted on about everything in the world. I didn't listen though, I was too aware of the way Cora leaned into me, letting her fingers trace along the outside of my thigh as she nodded and smiled at the story Reid was telling her. When the three of us we were alone in the elevator on the way up to Cora's floor she turned to me.

"What time are you free for lunch today?" She asked, biting her lip devilishly.

"I'll make time whenever you are available."

"Noon then."

"Good, I'll have lunch delivered and ready at noon."

Reid interrupted ignoring my scowl. "Cool, what are we having?"

The elevator doors opened at Halo and Cora leaned up on her toes gave me a quick kiss and rolled her eyes.

She patted Reid on the chest as she walked past him "I'm the meal and you're not invited to partake or watch Reid." She threw over her shoulder as she walked out of the elevator and my eyes fell to the effortlessly feminine sway of her hips. Reid laughed and shook his head.

"Don't be late," I ordered as she walked away.

She looked over her shoulder at me and her eyes flashed before she winked. "Wouldn't dream of it."

The doors closed again as she rounded the corner towards her desk and then it was Reid and I in the elevator.

"So, her face is healing well." He said, "How are her ribs?"

I sighed and ran a hand over my face. "Healing. She fussed with her makeup for an hour this morning trying to cover up the mark on her nose and cheek. And I fucking hate that she has to worry about it at all."

The doors opened and we walked out. "I know man." He said, sounding almost sad. "You're meeting with Jake Valentine this morning right?" He asked as we got to my office.

"Yeah, at ten," I asked, anxious to get that meeting out of the way. Cora and I never circled back to this last night after our shower, so I hadn't gotten her feelings on how she wanted it handled.

"I'm free at ten if you want another set of ears in on it." He said, walking backward towards his own office.

"Thanks."

Veronica was waiting for me at her desk when I walked past.

"Good morning Mr. Jones." She said holding a coffee and a stack of papers.

"Thank you," I took the coffee from her hands and walked into my office setting my bag down on the desk and turning towards her. "What are those?"

She looked at the papers and then handed them to me. "Messages sir, from your mother."

Shit. She had called a few times last night, but I didn't answer them because I was busy emptying myself inside all three of Cora's holes all night, and I hadn't had a chance to call her yet this morning. "Thank you, Veronica." I took the stack and looked through them quickly, they all said the same things.

Call me.

Do not ignore me, young man.

Your father told me about Cora. Call me!

I chuckled and threw them on my desk. "Anything else?" I asked my assistant as she stood a few feet away staring at me.

She hesitated but then shook her head.

"Good. I have a lunch date from twelve to one, so block my schedule and get me the menu for that Chinese restaurant you order from for me, please." I turned and sat down in my chair.

"I can take care of your order, Mr. Jones. I know what you like." She said and the tone in which she said it caught my attention. I looked up at her and she stepped forward, getting closer to me and I watched as she ran her fingers across the button of her shirt that was struggling to contain her tits, looking like it was going to pop off at any moment.

I looked back up into her eyes and she smiled at me, almost like she was pleased I looked at her chest.

I scowled and looked away from her completely. "I'm not ordering just for myself Veronica. Ms. Valentine will be joining me. So just get me the menu and I will pick out what we want to eat."

She dropped her hands to her side and her spine stiffened in my peripheral vision as I woke up my computer. "If you insist sir." She said and then turned and walked out of my office.

I pressed the button under my desk closing the doors to my office and then mirrored the glass as I dialed my mother's number.

It rang only one time before she answered, sounding breathless and agitated.

"Maverick." She said. Her voice was smooth like honey, but it was laced with hurt.

"Mom. I'm sorry I missed your dozens of calls in the last twelve hours."

She tsked her tongue and I imagined her shaking her head at me in exasperation. "Tell me everything." She said simply.

"What did Dad tell you?"

"I don't trust what he told me, he has no flare for romantic notions, and you know it. I want to hear it from you Mav."

I smiled at her dramatics and settled into my chair. To be honest, she loved Cora like she was her very own daughter when we were kids, and she was devastated when our relationship ended as well. I just didn't know what she would think about this new information because we had refused to speak of Cora over the last five or six years as the time and hurt had spread on and on.

"She started working here at Hawthorn Tower on Monday, and I ran into her then," I said easily.

"Was she really cut off? Because of you?" She asked and I could hear her sadness through the phone.

"Yes." I sighed, feeling guilt fresh in my veins. "They pushed her out their front door that same night when she refused to beg me to take her back."

"My God Maverick. What did she do? Where did she go? Why didn't she at least reach out to your father or me for help? We would have taken care of her!" She was getting worked up and I sighed, hating telling her all of this over the phone. "She was devastated by what I did Mom. She was a kid and wasn't thinking straight and by the time she realized how bad the situation was, she was convinced she couldn't come home at all, to me or you guys. She instead, fought through homelessness, hunger, and God knows what else and clawed her way out of the streets and into the middle class."

"And now?"

"And now," I paused, considering how to lay this all out to my sensitive mother. "And now I'm trying to convince her to move in with me and then I'm going to try to convince her to marry me and then I'm going to try to convince her to spend the rest of her life as my wife and the mother to my children."

"Oh, Maverick." Mom sighed, "How does she feel towards you? How do you feel towards her? It's been so long since you've spoken to me about her. Not since you stupidly started dating Sarah."

"Mom." I interrupted her from bringing up any more painful reminders of what I'd done five years ago. "I'm madly in love with her still. And she is still in love with me. But the wounds that we inflicted on each other still ache and it's going to take time to heal those. She's spent the last few days with me and we're moving in the right direction."

"Your father said she was mugged on the subway, is she okay? You need to protect her; she can't be riding the subway now that she's going to be linked as Maverick Jones' girlfriend. Someone will no doubt victimize her for that connection alone."

"I know Mom, but you know Cora better than almost anyone else besides me. She's proud and headstrong and is unwilling to just allow me to consume her and her life simply because I insist on it. If I'm not careful here she's going to push back on principle alone. But don't worry, I'm going to make sure no one puts their hands on her ever again Mom, I promise."

She sighed and it sounded lighter than when the conversation first started. "When can we come see you two? I'm dying to hug her; I've missed her so much."

"I know, I'm working on something first and then we'll come out for a visit. Maybe early next week?"

"Working on something?" She asked, "Something involving the Valentines?"

I chuckled, "What did Dad say?"

She tsked her tongue again, "He basically came home demanding I find his suit of armor as he prepared for battle, that's what!" She barked. "He has been riled up since he returned home yesterday and understandably, so am I. I want to help you with this Maverick. I want to help Cora get the justice she deserves."

"It's not so cut and dry Mom. I'm not just going to get Cora justice. I am going to get revenge. They stole ten years from my life when they destroyed her. If they hadn't been so selfish and vile, I would have fixed the pain I caused her while simultaneously healing my trauma. I would have gone to therapy and done everything you and Dad had been begging of me for months before I hurt her and we would have gone on with our lives. We would have gone to college together as we planned, we would have been married and had kids by now, I'm sure. We would be celebrating anniversaries instead of trying to learn who each of us has become with this pain inside of us after all these years."

"I'm so sorry baby. I'm so sorry that they did this to both of you. And I don't care if it's justice, revenge, or a downright thirst for blood, I want to help."

My Mom had never spoken like this to me before. She was a gentle person and a perfect mother, but I was recognizing the mother bear in her that had come out when Luke and I were kids and my heart warmed knowing the wrongdoing to Cora called to that primal part of her.

An idea struck as I thought about it, "You want to help with the fall of the Valentine family?"

"I want to help pull the bricks out from under the foundation of their falsehoods." She said back instantly, firm, and strong.

"Then you make sure the Memorial for Luke is the biggest one yet. It's been ten years since he passed, and the event is the perfect place for me to introduce the world to my wife for the first time."

"The Memorial is in less than one month Maverick. Do you honestly believe she will be your wife by then?"

I chuckled, "If I had anything to say about it Mom, she would be my wife already. I plan on spending every spare minute showing her exactly how badly I want her."

She sighed almost dreamy-like. "I want you to get your happily ever after Mav, so badly."

"I'm going to Mom. And so is Cora."

"Good. It's about time."

I chatted for a minute longer and then ended my call with her and forced myself to get to work, knowing I was going to be meeting with Jake Valentine in a few hours and I needed to be on my game to spin a web to catch any deceit he may try to throw my way.

My intercom buzzed and Veronica's voice rang into my office. "Sir, Jake Valentine is here for your ten o'clock meeting."

I clicked the button, "I'll be with him in a few minutes."

I sat back in my chair and took a deep breath. This was the start of the end of his family and how he answered my questions in this meeting would decide which side of the fallout he found himself on.

I picked up my office phone, dialed Cora's desk, and listened to the tone of the ring.

"Mr. Peterson's office, this is Cora." Her sweet angelic voice rang into my heart and I growled at the buzz it lit in my veins. She sucked a breath in at the sound and then lowered her voice. "Mav."

"I love you," I said plainly.

I could hear the smile in her voice. "You told me that a few hours ago."

"I know. But I wanted to tell you again."

"I love you too Maverick Jones." Her voice was breathy, and I ached to hear her say my name like that again and again.

"Your brother is in my lobby."

"Ew." She replied flatly. "You really know how to be a buzz kill."

I chuckled, "I know, but I wanted you to know so that you didn't run into him on accident. Stay at Halo until I call you and tell you he's gone. Understood?"

"What if I'm told by my boss to go do something else?"

"Then you call me, and I will take care of it."

"I don't want to hide."

"I need to know if he knew what happened, or if he knew you were out there on your own."

A long pause filled the air and then she sighed. "I saw him two years after I left Mav. He knew."

I stilled and ice filled my veins. "Why didn't you tell me this before?"

She sighed again and I imagined her leaning back in her chair and crossing her legs in that sexy as-hell black dress, "Because I didn't know you intended on making good on this call for justice so soon." She paused and I knew she wanted to say more. "I didn't want to spend any more time in the past. We keep circling back to it and I hate the way it makes me feel."

"I need this Cora." I hardly recognized the pain in my voice as I left myself vulnerable to her judgments.

"I see that now Mav. I'm sorry I didn't tell you beforehand."

"What happened when you saw him?"

She sighed again. "I was working at a twenty-four-hour diner in lower Manhattan, and he came in with a bunch of friends. They were eating when I arrived for my shift and I approached him, stupidly happy to see him."

I could tell by the cold in her voice he didn't embrace her with open arms. "What did he do when he saw you?"

"He threw a glass of soda on me before I even got within five feet of him and told me to stop being pathetic and bothering him like I was some panhandler on the street. And then they all left and didn't pay their bill. I had to work for two weeks straight just to cover their tab out of my tips, forgoing paying my bills."

I growled again, imagining how good it would feel to push my fist through the center of Jake Valentine's face.

My office door opened, and my eyes followed Reid as he walked in, eyeing my murderous stare.

"I'll make sure he regrets it, baby," I said. "I love you, Cora."

"I know you do Mav. I love you too. But don't let the past consume you, it will just continue to darken your soul. Come into the light with me instead and leave it all behind."

"I'm going to burn their world to ash, and only then will I let your sunshine chase the shadows from my soul."

She sighed, "I support you in whatever you do, just know you don't have to do it."

"I know baby. I'll call you when he leaves."

"Okay."

She hung up and I gripped the receiver in my hand so tight the plastic creaked beneath my fingers before I hung it up.

"New development?" Reid asked, unbuttoning his jacket, and sitting down.

"Jake knew she was on her own out here. He threw a drink in her face and stiffed her with a bill she had to pay out of her tips as a waitress." With each word that crossed my lips, my blood thickened and heated up until it was molten lava.

"Son of a bitch." Reid said, shaking his head and running his fingers over the ridge of his lips. "What do you want to do?"

"I want to find out what this project is that he wants my partnership on, and then I'm going to go in and seal the deal before him and steal it."

"Genius." He said confidently. "Are you going to tell him you're back with Cora and know everything?"

"No. I have a much bigger plan in place for that. So I need to calm down before he comes in and somehow pretend I don't want to tear him to pieces."

"Okay, so keep the meeting short and I'll do most of the talking. Got it." Reid said, standing up and walking over to the bar, pouring bourbon in a glass, and handing it to me. I eyed him and he just nodded to it. "Believe me Maverick, you fucking need it. You look like the Hulk right now."

I took the glass and poured the drink back, swallowing it in one gulp, and then hit the intercom button, "Send him in."

"Yes sir," Veronica answered, and a moment later Jake Valentine strolled into my office with his hand in his pants pocket and a smug smile on his face.

I was going to enjoy ruining his fucking life.

Chapter 10 – Cora

I watched the clock obsessively and waited to hear from Mav that Jake was gone and out of the building. The longer that passed, the more worried I got.

Mr. Peterson popped his head out of his office, "Cora, can you go and grab the new campaign legalities from Dexter Chase up at Jones?"

"Uh…" I started, looking wide eyed up at my boss trying to figure out what to do.

"Is there a problem?" He said as he took his glasses off the ledge of his nose and looked at me.

"No." I said quickly, and stood up, "I was just trying to remember which one was Dexter, but I got it. Sorry." I said and smiled.

"Perfect, thank you."

I nodded and turned away and walked towards the elevators, racking my brain to come up with a plan.

I took my phone out of my pocket and quickly texted Mav.

Me: I have to come up to Dexter's office.

I got to the elevators and dragged my feet, silently praying for Mav to text me back. I couldn't get to Dexter's office without passing by Mav's and even if his walls were mirrored, my brother could look out of his office and see me pass by.

"What's up Cora?" Nat asked as she got back to her desk, eyeing me standing at the elevator bay hugging my phone.

"Nat!" I rushed over. "I need a favor!"

"Uh oh," She eyed me suspiciously.

"I have to go get the new campaign legalities for Mr. Peterson from Dexter Chase's office, but my brother is in Maverick's office right now and he can't know I work here yet."

"How are you going to get past then?" She asked, tilting her head to the side.

"I was hoping maybe you would be the one to get past the office..."

"You want me to go up to Dexter's office for you? Who's going to man my desk?"

"Me. It will take all of five minutes max, I can handle it."

"Are you sure? I don't even know what the legalities are to know what to get from him."

"Either do I!" I said hurriedly, "He will know. Just tell him it's for Mr. Peterson and he'll know, I hope."

"Cora..." She said, with wide eyes of uncertainty.

"Please! I'll buy your next two nights of drinking wherever we go! Please I'm desperate."

She sighed and looked at her watch. "Okay, I don't have any meetings coming up for another fifteen minutes or so, just answer the phone and take messages and I'll return them as soon as I get back."

"Oh my God, I owe you so much!" I gushed and pulled her in for a quick hug.

"Yeah, like thirty shots of top shelf tequila worth."

"Definitely." I agreed, shooing her towards the elevators and sitting down in her desk.

I opened my phone and texted Mav again.

Me: Nat is coming up to Dexter's office for me!

I cringed when her phone rang and I quickly answered it, trying to pay attention to the message while also watching the elevators like a hawk for her to return and trying to will a message back from Maverick into my phone.

As soon as I hung up the phone, it rang again, and I groaned. It went on like this for almost ten minutes before Nat finally returned with a large file in her hands and she blew out a large breath, blowing her bangs out of her face.

She ran to her desk and threw the file at me like it was a bomb and I caught it and stood. "Holy fuck!" She hissed and threw herself down into her chair.

"What?" I snapped. "What happened?" A cold sweat broke out over my entire body.

"Your brother is hot as fuck, that's what!" She gushed and fanned herself with her notebook.

"Ew!" I bit back quickly and grimaced. "You saw him?"

She nodded quickly and took a long drink of her water. "He was walking out of Mr. Jones' office when I was getting on the elevator. I panicked and slammed the button to close the doors in his face as he tried to walk in!"

I groaned and took a deep breath. "Thank you so much!" I said, squeezing her hand with mine and trying to express how much it meant to me.

"Drinks, tonight!" She said, leveling her finger at me.

"Deal. You pick the place, I'm there!" I said, holding my hands up, "No arguments here."

"Good. Now get, I have to answer these messages." She said, looking down at her notebook where I scribbled incoherent messages from the callers.

I grimaced and turned away, running down the hallway.

"Did you even try to make sense on here?" She called after me as I neared my desk.

"I owe you!"

I got to Mr. Peterson's office and handed him the file and he hardly paid any attention to me as he took them.

"Thanks Cora, I like the hustle."

"No problem!" I replied running back out of the office and collapsing into my chair.

My phone pinged and a message reply from Maverick came in.

Maverick: You handled that well. I'll be sure to reward you this evening.

I cringed and bit my lip. He wasn't going to like this.

Me: I owe her for helping me, her price was unlimited shots tonight after work. So you'll have to reward me some other time.

A second later my desk phone rang, and Maverick's name popped up on my screen.

Shit.

"Hello?" I said stupidly.

"No." His curt voice came through the phone.

"No, what?"

"No drinks, no shots, no Nat."

I looked around the office floor, to see if anyone was listening, "Mav." I sighed. "Those were the terms to our agreement, you of anyone should know I can't back out now."

"Do I need to remind you what happened the last time you went out after work for drinks with her?"

My hackles bristled at his tone, and I snapped back at him. "You mean when you showed up and ruined the evening?"

"I mean you being drunk and unaware of your surroundings and getting attacked on the subway!"

He was so angry, but I knew him well enough to know his anger didn't come from me directly, it came from his guilt.

"I'll drink water and I'll be safe on my way home."

"No." He said again.

"Maverick."

"No, damnit. No! I can't stomach the thought of you going out and being at the mercy of the world like that again Cora. No!"

"You don't get to decide what I can and cannot do Mav. And I cannot argue with you about it right now, I'm at work. I love you. I'll call you when I get home, okay?"

"Cora, don't you dare hang up right now, this conversation isn't over."

"I know it's not. I'm just pausing it. I love you." I said again, for added soothing of his alpha attitude. "I have to go."

I hung the phone up as he started to growl something at me and groaned. I hated this.

But I needed to keep some of my independence too, I just didn't know how to do that when bad things had happened last time.

"Cora." Mr. Peterson called, and I took a deep breath went into his office, and spent the rest of the day elbow-deep in paperwork and copyright law education.

I shot a text to Maverick to get a rain check on our lunch date when Mr. Peterson said we would be lucky to get done with everything by five if we worked through lunch. I didn't wait to see his reply to my message, because I knew he would be angry, and I didn't have it in me to disappoint him twice in a few hours.

Five o'clock came in a flash and I left my desk in a daze. My brain was numb from all of the information it had retained in the last few hours, and I nearly forgot my evening plans until I got to the reception area and Nat stood waiting for me.

"Are you ready to let your hair down!" She called loudly, shaking her short hair back and forth enthusiastically.

I smiled at her and let today's stress melt off my shoulders. "Yes, yes I am," I said back honestly. "Where are we off to tonight?"

"I was thinking we could go to Pandora's Patio, it's a block away but a little more upscale than McCulley's."

"Sounds... interesting. There are no boxes you're going to try to open while we're there right?" I asked, winking at her.

"No ma'am." She said shaking her head back and forth. "I will be on my best behavior."

I snorted and rolled my eyes. "Right."

We rode the elevator down to the main lobby and walked across the marble floor towards the front doors and as we passed through the doors held open by the doorman, my step faltered as I spotted a very intimidating Maverick leaning against the back of his SUV. He was the picture of perfection; his black suit was immaculate, and his dark hair lay perfectly atop his head matching his perfectly dark scowl as he stared at me as he posed with his ankles crossed and his hands in his pant pockets.

"Are you in trouble?" Nat whispered to me, halting next to me.

"Something you should probably know about me now Nat, is that I'm always going to be in trouble with that man."

She snorted and pulled me towards the brooding darkness of Maverick Jones. I was aware of his employees milling around us as we stood in a stare-down and was unsure of how to proceed. He answered for me though when he leaned up off the car and opened the back seat door. "Where are we off to tonight ladies?"

His voice was steady and calm, and to the untrained eye, he looked calm and unfazed. But I felt the power radiating off of him as he looked from me to Nat and back.

She stumbled over herself. "Oh, uh. Cora didn't tell me you were coming along." She said, elbowing me in the side and I groaned.

"She didn't know. But after what happened last time, there was no way I was allowing her to go without me. I'm sure you can understand." He said politely.

Nat melted next to me and looked at Mav with dreamy eyes. "Oh come on," I said, pulling her forward towards the car. I pushed her in ahead of me and slid in next to her as Maverick laid his hand on my ass, boosting me up.

His eyes were alight with mischief as he shut the door behind him. "So where are we going?" He asked as Franklin waited behind the wheel.

"Pandora's patio," Nat answered eagerly and adjusted herself in the seat.

"Good choice," Mav answered and laid his hand on my thigh. He let his fingers slide under the fabric of my skirt until his hand was under it, warming my skin.

I took a deep breath and pressed my thighs together, pulling a light chuckle from his chest. I looked over at him and he winked at me.

"You're in a better mood than I thought you would be," I said, ignoring the fact that my friend sat in the car with us.

He smirked at me, "All in good time dear."

His voice and demeanor were relaxed, but I heard the threat in his voice. And I felt it deep in my core as my panties soaked.

Luckily, Franklin pulled up outside of the bar we were going to at record speed, and Maverick stepped out, holding his hand out for me and then for Nat as we climbed out onto the sidewalk.

"Ah, what a surprise." A boisterous voice called from the doorway, and I looked up to see Reid and Dexter standing with two other men walking in the bar. They were quite the group to look at, all domineering and powerful in their expensive suits and stylish appearances.

But as we walked up to them, all of them paled in comparison to Maverick as he shook hands with the calendar-worthy men.

Mav was deliciously powerful and exuded a dominance that even other men fell under the spell of.

Reid spoke as he shook Mav's hand. "I thought you had plans of dragging Cora back to your cave by her hair?"

I elbowed Mav in the stomach, and he rolled his eyes at Reid. "You both are so dramatic." He murmured.

Reid laughed and leaned down to kiss first my cheek and then Nat's. "Ladies, this is Declan and Carter." He introduced the two men with them, and they nodded to us with attractive smiles. Maverick put his arm over my shoulders and pulled me against his side like we were sixteen again and not two almost thirty-year-olds in the middle of New York City. Dexter smirked as Reid asked, "So are we doing shooters again tonight ladies?"

Nat held her arms up in the air and wooed, "Yes! And Maverick is buying!" I laughed at her excitement and caught a smile on Mav's lips as he watched her silliness.

"Let's get inside before he changes his mind!" Reid whooped and we all filed inside the busy upscale bar.

The hostess looked at our group with wide eyes and I swear she saw dollar signs as she quickly grabbed the menus and led us to a large high-top table on the back patio under a sky of twinkly lights. The place was gorgeous, and it made me almost forget we were in the city, and it reminded me of home. Growing up in the suburbs of the city was something I had loved, being close to the hustle and bustle of the city but being able to see the stars at night at home made me happy.

"What's wrong?" Mav said, leaning in against me where he stood at my side.

I looked up at him and shook my head. "Nothing. This place is beautiful."

He looked around like it was the first time he paid attention to it and smiled. "Looks like your old back patio actually."

"Hmm," I said and grabbed the menu, trying not to get down.

"I'll build you one just like this if that's what you want." He sat down on the stool next to me and sat so close that his knees went around me, one against my back and one against my own, hugging me into his space.

I turned and looked at him and leaned in, kissing him slowly, not caring for anyone around us watching this PDA. It just felt right, and it was exactly what I needed after feeling on edge all day. "I missed you," I whispered against his lips.

His hands rested on my ass and my thigh as he leaned forward even more. "You missed our lunch date. I was looking forward to my meal." His voice was deep, and my body shivered at his words.

"I desperately wanted to be your meal." I purred back and he lowered his lips to mine again and took them in a hungry kiss, threading his fingers in my hair and holding me tightly where he wanted as he drank from my lips.

"Hey, you two, get a room," Reid called and the group snickered.

"I don't think I've ever seen Maverick Jones so enamored before," Declan said and I pulled back to see a wicked glint in Mav's eye as he licked his lips like he was savoring the taste of me.

I pushed my hair back off my shoulders and bit my lip as I tried to make the words on the menu make sense as the waitress came to the table and started taking orders.

Nat ordered shots and an array of other beverages I'd never heard of before and then the guys ordered some others with enough food to feed the entire restaurant. When she looked at me for my order Mav answered for me. "I'll have a Johnnie Walker, neat. And she'll have a glass of your top Cabernet. Thank you." He said, handing her the menus. "Put all of this on my tab please."

"Of course, Mr. Jones." The woman said, nearly drooling at his commands before running away to do his bidding.

He looked over at me and raised his eyebrow at me like he was waiting for me to argue with his decision to order for me but instead, I just leaned back in and kissed him softly. "Thank you," I said when I pulled back.

He watched me closely for a beat and then smiled. "You're welcome."

The guys pulled Maverick into a conversation about mergers and businesses that meant nothing to me, so I ended up chatting with Nat. Turns out she lived not too far away from here with two roommates and had been working at Halo for a year, hoping to climb the ladder and get out of the reception area.

She had applied for my job but didn't get it and I was glad she didn't hold that against me personally. By the time the waiter delivered our food, Nat and Reid were close to sloppy drunk, and Dexter was checking his watch like he wanted to be anywhere else but here. Nat and the other women, who had at some point captivated Declan and Carter, and were chatting with the like they were old-time friends.

Mav's phone went off and he looked at it before standing up and kissing my forehead. "I've got to take this. I'll be right over there." He said, nodding to the sidewalk outside of the patio, away from the noise of the restaurant and guests.

After he walked away another woman joined our group and hugged some of the women while looking over at Mav. She was our age, maybe a bit older but it was hard to tell thanks to her incredible Asian heritage. She had beautiful long black hair and exotic features and a killer body in a white silk shirt and pencil skirt. Her top was unbuttoned low, exposing her small chest but she flaunted it like she knew exactly how attractive she was.

She walked over and sat down in the seat that Maverick had vacated, picked up his drink, and took a sip. I felt myself balk at her boldness but refrained from making a scene about it until I knew more about the woman. I silently enjoyed my food, grabbed our waitress' arm as she passed, and ordered him a fresh one.

I caught a look from Reid as he looked between the two of us with a worried look on his face. He started to say something but the woman next to me interrupted him.

"How's our boy, Reid?" She asked, leaning forward, and shaking her hair over her shoulder.

Reid once again glanced from her to me and looked uncomfortable. Dexter, Declan, and Carter chose then to pay attention too and all three nearly recoiled when they saw us sitting next to each other. And that was when it clicked to me.

This woman was someone that Maverick dated.

One of the three.

"Uh- he's good. Really good actually." Reid said, passing me a tequila shot across the table.

Nat eyed me as the woman drank off Mav's drink again.

"Is that so?" She asked with a seductive voice, looking over to where Mav stood with his back against the railing, looking out over the street on the phone. "He looks good, that's for sure."

I downed the tequila, not even bothering with the salt or the lime, and then took another right after. It was about to get awkward as hell and I didn't want to get into it right now. I had been enjoying my night, but it was about to go down the drain. It was incredibly uncharted territory for me. We were never supposed to have other people in our lives, we were supposed to be each other's only, but fate had stolen that from us.

Reid smirked at me, knowing I had filled in the blanks, and decided to make things interesting. "Sue, have you met Cora?"

He said, nodding to me where I sat next to her. She flicked her eyes over to me, almost dismissively, and shook her head before sticking her limp, uninterested hand out in greeting. "Sue Lin."

I eyed her hand and chose to dismiss her right back, keeping my hands in my lap, and raised my eyebrow at her.

She dropped her hand as outrage quickly flooded her eyes while Reid snorted and Nat laughed out loud, nearly toppling off her stool and into Declan's waiting hands. He settled her and I took the tequila shot from her hands and passed it back to Reid.

"I think that's enough for tonight."

"Oh, I agree." Nat laughed. "I want to remember this tomorrow." She looked at me and Sue like we were her favorite reality TV show and she was hooked.

I sensed him without even seeing him, feeling his presence like a mist in the air fall on my skin, and a moment later Maverick walked back to our table. Sue stood up off her stool instantly to greet him, but he chose to walk the long way around the table and came up behind me, settling his hand on my neck and leaning down to kiss my cheek and whispering in my ear. "I love you."

"Maverick," Sue said, eyes flashing with jealousy as he ignored her for me. "How have you been?"

He stood against my back and put his hand on my hip as he reached for his drink. I put my hand on his arm, stopping him. "She drank off it, I ordered you another," I said.

His eyes flashed to Sue, and he scowled. "Interesting." But his manners forced him to acknowledge her. "I'm well Sue, how are you?"

"I'm good." She played with her necklace that dropped low into her cleavage and I groaned at the obvious ploy and took a sip of my wine. "I haven't seen you around lately, where have you been?"

"Been busy building my life with my future wife," Maverick said effortlessly and I choked on my wine.

Nat cackled and the others failed to hide their laughs as they watched on trying to look like they weren't hanging on every word of the conversation but instead looked in other directions drinking their cocktails.

"Future wife?" Sue snapped; anger burned in her eyes again as she dropped her hand from her tits to her hips. "You were single just a month ago."

"Cora and I spent ten years together Sue. The length of time we've been together this time means nothing."

She huffed and looked at me with tight eyes, "Hmm. Well, I suppose I'll see you next month at Luke's Memorial then." She said, trying to act like her connection to Mav was deeper than it was, using a connection to his parents to prove the point.

"Don't count on it," I said back, keeping my stare level and steady on hers as she smirked in challenge.

"I'll see you around Mav." She said and winked at him before turning on her heel and walking away, shaking her nonexistent ass like she was Shakira on her way out.

"Oh my God! Did you see the way she looked at you?" Reid raved as he fell onto his stool dramatically. "I thought we were going to have a catfight on our hands."

"I don't catfight Reid, I brawl," I said, enjoying the way his eyes flared excitedly. I slid from my stool, shaking Mav's hands off of my hips as I tossed another shooter back. I needed space and a minute to tamp down my anger. "I'll be right back," I said to him and started to walk away.

"Where are you going?" He asked, pulling me to a stop with a hand wrapped around my upper arm until we were nose to nose.

"To pee." I hissed. "Is that okay, *Mav*?" I said his name in a nasally condescending way to mimic the way she kept saying it.

His eyes flashed and his hand tightened around my arm. "Let's go."

He turned and dragged me through the restaurant towards the bathroom, but instead of turning down the hallway towards them, he went past them and into the kitchen.

"What are you doing?" I snapped, alarmed as fires and grills flamed up around us as chefs and cooks cleared out of his way through their domain. A man in a chef's hat and apron saw us and called out in a French accent. "Ah, Mr. Jones! What a pleasure to have you here with us this evening!"

"Francois, I need to use your office," Mav called back to him, without slowing his steps or waiting for a reply.

"Of course. Help yourself."

My face flamed as he walked deeper into the kitchen and then towards the very back of the building near the loading dock. A single door was closed in the hallway, and he opened it and pushed me through it before following me in and slamming the door shut. The room was dark and there were no windows in it, but it didn't matter.

He pushed me against the door in the pitch-black darkness until his body pinned mine to the wood and his mouth slammed over mine.

"Mav, stop." I panted as he pushed his thigh between mine and my hips rocked forward, rubbing my clit on his muscled upper leg.

"She doesn't mean anything to me." He ground out against my lips as he took both of my wrists in his hand and pinned them to the door above my head. "You're the only one I even see anymore."

"I know," I whispered, pushing my head back into the wood of the door. "I know, Mav."

"Then why are you mad at me?" His lips fell to my neck, and he bit and sucked on the skin, and I felt my panties dampen even more.

"I'm not mad at you."

"Bullshit." He snapped.

"I'm mad that she exists. I'm mad that there are women out there who know what it feels like to have you so consumed with them that they can't even think. I'm mad that there are women out there that love you."

"You're the only woman that loves me, Cora. And you're the only woman that knows me."

I scoffed at him and then moaned when he pinched my nipple through my dress. "I need to be fucked Mav. I need to calm down and that's the only way I'm going to do that right now."

He slid his hand up my dress and ripped my panties off of me in the next instant. "Take my cock out." He ordered as he bunched my dress up around my hips and ran his fingers through my pussy, pushing two fingers deep inside of me. "Fuck you're already soaked for me."

"I've been wet all day for you." I purred and pulled his cock out through his zipper. "Please fuck me, make me come on your cock, and make everyone else fade away."

He lifted me and pinned me to the door with his cock nestled against my entrance and then pushed himself into me with one brutal thrust. I gasped and moaned as he stretched me open. He grunted and panted as his large hands squeezed my ass cheeks where they held me up.

"Just like that baby," I begged. "Fuck me like you own me."

"I do own you, Cora." He snapped, slamming his cock into me over and over again, rattling the door in the frame. "I own your mind."

Thrust. "I own your heart." Thrust. "I own your body." Thrust. "I own your past." Thrust. "I own your future."

My frustration and anger snapped like a tight string inside of me and my orgasm ripped through my body, making every muscle cramp as they tightened around his body and his cock. "Maverick," I screamed.

"Take my cock baby. You're mine and I'm yours. You own me the same way I own you."

He slammed into me so hard I knew I'd wear bruises on my ass and hips from where he held me, but it made me burn for him even more. I ached to be engulfed in his flames and pain as he devoured me.

"I'm going to fill you up, Cora. Take every fucking drop I give you."

"I'm yours, give it to me baby." I panted.

I felt his cock swell and jerk inside of me and then the hot sensation that came with being filled with his come burned me from the inside out and I shot off into another orgasm, feeling it roll through me from my toes to my nose as he moaned my name over and over again. His hips finally stilled, and his cock stopped jerking as my pussy throbbed and my chest ached for air. We caught our breaths for a moment, the only noises in the room were our ragged breathing over the muffled sounds of the kitchen on the other side of the door. He pressed his forehead against mine and kissed me softly, leisurely tasting me and exploring my mouth until neither of us could deny that we needed to leave the confines of our dark privacy.

He slowly pulled his cock out of me and then set me down on my feet. He flipped the switch next to me on the wall and bathed the room in light as he helped me right my dress and smooth my hair.

"I don't want to go back out there," I said with a soft smile as I leaned into his chest.

"Let's go home then."

"I promised Nat I'd buy her drinks for helping me out today."

He snorted and put his cock away and fixed his tie. "I don't know if you noticed, but that girl is so far gone already, she'll never notice. I'll make sure Reid gets her home."

"I can't have Reid take her home, that's just asking for trouble."

"He took her home the other night."

"What? Why didn't I know that?"

"Because we've been dealing with a lot of other shit since then."

"Oh," I said, mulling that over in my head.

"Don't worry about her Cora. She's a big girl, and she's far from the type of girl that's going to let Reid Haskins take advantage of her."

I snorted and rolled my eyes. "I could imagine her chopping off his dick if he tried to push his luck."

Mav smiled and kissed my nose. "Don't ever think about doing that to me, okay?" He opened the door and walked back out through the kitchen. The staff in this high-end bar were trained perfectly, but not a single one of them looked at us as we walked through their domain, even though I'm sure they knew what we did in that office.

When we got back to the table Maverick told everyone we were leaving and made sure Reid would take Nat home, who was ready to go herself and we hugged goodbye.

We all walked to the sidewalk together and Franklin pulled up as soon as we stepped out of the restaurant and Maverick opened the door for me.

"How does he do that?" I asked as I slid in.

"Magic," Franklin said with a wink and a grin as I hooked my seat belt. I smiled at him in the mirror and then paused when I noticed the garment bag hanging in the back of the car.

"What is that?"

"My things for tomorrow, so I can stay at your place."

"You still want to stay with me?"

He pulled my legs up to cross over his knees and massaged my calves. "I don't plan on sleeping apart from you ever again if I can help it." He said so easily like there was no other answer. I smiled at him and shook my head.

"Okay, Mr. Jones. We'll see if you sing a different tune tomorrow morning after roughing it all night at my place."

Chapter 11 – Maverick

I was never staying at Cora's apartment again. I rolled my shoulders and they cracked and creaked as I groaned in agony. Not only was her bed the size of a shoebox, but it was hard and lumpy in the worst way possible. And her neighbors had a smoking habit that left them both coughing up their lungs all night long no matter how many times I banged on the wall.

She'd laughed at me this morning when I smacked my head on the metal bar over her shower as I tried to wash my hair under the spout that only came up to my fucking shoulders. And I'd tried my best to not snap and grump too much about how miserable I was given that it had been my stubbornness that made me insist on staying with her regardless of where she chose. But all was well because she'd tried to make up for it by falling to her knees in front of me in her bedroom and sucking my cock like a fucking dream until I came down her throat for all my troubles.

But it was the end of the day now and it was Friday and I wanted nothing more than to take her to my home and stay locked away until Monday morning. She'd brought a bag of clothes with her this morning when we left her apartment so I had a good feeling she would stay with me all weekend. And I had a couple of surprises for her too that I hoped she would be okay with.

"Here's Monday's schedule and your itinerary for our trip Monday Night sir," Veronica said, stepping into my office and pulling my attention from the view out my window.

"Huh?" I asked, scowling as she handed me the paperwork. She cocked her hip against my desk and crossed her arms over her chest as I read through the papers.

"You have four meetings Monday morning, and then we leave for the airport at two pm. Your jet is taking us directly to Atlanta and we'll go from the airport right to the building site to see the updates and approve new ones. Then we'll go to the hotel and have dinner there, I booked your favorite table at Le Crème and Tuesday we'll spend all day at the Potter building negotiating and dealing and return home on the jet that evening at seven pm." She explained, exactly like the paperwork said and acid burned in my stomach.

I'd forgotten about this trip and hated the idea of leaving Cora overnight already. I also knew she wasn't going to like that Veronica was coming with me for it.

"Thank you Veronica," I said, setting the papers down on my desk and rubbing my forehead.

"Do you have a headache? I can get you some medicine." She said softly, putting her hand on my shoulder and squeezing it like she was offering to massage it for me. Which to be honest, wouldn't be the first time she had done that, but her hand burned me where it touched. I shrugged it off and pushed my chair back and stood up.

"I'm fine thank you; I'm just going to get going for the day I think."

"Already? You've been leaving by five pm every day this week, you're usually the last one here. Is everything okay sir?"

"Everything is fine Veronica. I'm going to be leaving at five from now on, so make sure my schedule doesn't interfere with that."

"If you think that's best sir."

That made me pause, looking over at her. She wasn't usually so bold, and she was toeing a line she was dangerously close to crossing.

She sighed and leaned off my desk and stepped even closer to me. "I just would hate to see you lose your focus and let someone take your attention away from all of this." She held up her hands, highlighting my office and domain. "You've worked so hard to get here and you deserve so much Maverick, I just want to make sure you don't let someone take it all away from you."

I clenched my jaw, her message, while veiled was clear. I turned off my computer and shoved the paperwork in my briefcase and then leaned towards her, leveling her with my stare. Her eyes rounded and her lips parted as I moved closer to her at first I thought it was fear, but then a smile pulled her lips up on the edges and I saw her in a new light.

"Let me make a few things extremely clear to you Veronica. You will address me as Mr. Jones or nothing else. I've never permitted you to call me Maverick." Her smile fell and she took a quick breath in. "You will also never impose yourself into my personal life again. I know exactly how hard I've worked to get to where I am because I was the one fucking doing the work. I also know I've earned a bit of a break from the sixteen-hour days I've put in to get here." My hands clenched into fists, and I knew I needed to get her out of my office before I really let loose on her. "Consider this strike two for you, the first one was you gossiping about me fucking my girlfriend in my office the other day. If you get to three I'll fire you. I'm done giving you warnings Veronica."

"Sir, I didn't mean –"

"Yes, you did. And you've tried more times in the last week than I can count to get me to notice you sexually as well, and maybe you've always been so bold, and I've never paid attention or maybe you're just getting too comfortable here. Either way, it ends right here, right now." I snapped, loving the way her face crumbled as she shrunk back. "You're a damn good assistant but I can find another one who gives me less headache in an instant. Now get out of my office and go home!"

"Mr. Jones please –"

"Now!"

She turned and all but ran from my office and I watched as she gathered her things and scurried into the elevator, passing Dexter on her way.

He eyed her suspiciously and then walked directly into my office. "Something up with Red?"

"Yeah she got the notion she could flirt with me and that I'd take her up on it."

"Ooh."

"Keep your eye on her for me, would you? I don't need a lawsuit from her if I fire her for jealousy."

"I'll document it and have Sebastian put it in her file. She's most definitely the type of woman to go full vindictive crazy if things don't go her way."

I grunted and grabbed my stuff, looking at my watch to see it was now ten after five. "I'm out of here."

"Any big plans for this weekend with your new love life?" He asked with genuine curiosity in his eyes.

"Big ones, just none that are appropriate to share with friends," I said, winking at him and clapping him on the back as I passed him on my way to the elevator.

He laughed and nodded his head. "I remember those days. Enjoy."

"Will do, have a good weekend."

"You too."

The ride down to the lobby was short but I was anxious to get to Cora. When I got to the lobby I saw her standing next to my car, talking to Franklin, and watched her closely as I walked out the door. Her head tilted back as she laughed at something my guard said to her, causing my cock to stir to life. Fuck she was beautiful. She looked divine with her blonde hair in a stylish updo, wearing black dress pants, a red lace top, and a black blazer. I also knew she didn't have many outfits like it and that was part of my surprise for her that evening.

When I stepped outside into the loud chaos of the city, she turned to look at me approach her like she could sense me near. Her eyes twinkled and her smile blossomed into something far more sensual and primal.

I nodded to Franklin and handed him my case as I pulled Cora into my arms and kissed her deeply. She slid her hands under my suit jacket and wrapped her arms around my waist as I deepened the kiss.

"Baby." I sighed, finally pulling back. "Get in the car before I take you right here on the sidewalk."

She smirked at me but turned and climbed in the car and I followed after her. As soon as the door was closed behind me I pulled her across the seat to sit in my lap, straddling me. I unbuttoned her jacket pushed it off her shoulders and groaned when I saw how tight and low-cut her lace top was.

"Fuck, you are so sexy."

"Mav." She purred, running her nails over my scalp, and rocking her hips over my erection that ached to feel her skin. "We're outside of work."

"The windows are so tinted, no one can see anything."

"And Franklin?" She whispered.

"Is far too professional to watch," I said loud enough for him to hear. He pulled us out into traffic and started towards my penthouse as I kissed the tops of Cora's breasts through the v-cut of her top.

"I'm going to fuck these tits tonight." I groaned and groped them, pushing them together and playing with them before pinching her nipples through her bra.

"As long as you fuck my pussy, too."

"I'm taking all three of your holes, baby."

"Fuck, that's hot." She purred and ground her hips again. She got an evil glint in her eye and dropped her hands from my neck to my pants, pulled my zipper down and pushed her hand through the opening. "I need to taste you."

I groaned and my cock jerked when her hand pulled it out of my pants and stroked me in the open air of the car. "You want to suck my cock again, baby? You gave me such a good blow job just this morning."

"I know. I want more." She winked and slid off my lap to the floor between my knees and swirled her tongue over the top of my cock and then sucked the head into her mouth. I groaned loudly and laid my head back against the headrest as I unclipped her hair and ran my fingers through it. She bobbed her head up and down on my cock, pushing it into her throat and gagging over and over again.

"You're so fucking good at that." I praised, and she hummed, squeezing me tight with her hand that was chasing her lips.

"I want to swallow your come before we get home." She purred, looking up at me under her long lashes before diving back down onto me, going so far that her lips kissed the base of my cock and it jerked wildly in her throat.

"Be a good girl and swallow every drop. If you let a single drop fall from your lips I'm going to make it hurt when I take you."

She hummed and eagerly took me down her throat again. She loved this, knowing someone was hearing everything she was saying and doing and potentially watching, though I knew better because I could see him in the mirror and knew he hadn't looked back once. I wouldn't allow someone to get anything that was mine. And Cora, on her knees sucking my cock for the second time today, was all mine.

My balls were tight as she bobbed her head quickly and sucked me like a pro and I saw that we were getting close to my house. "Good girl. Suck me dry. I'm going to fill your throat up with come. Remember, not a drop falls from those sexy lips."

She bared her teeth and scraped them up my cock and I roared as my balls forced rope after rope of come up my cock and into her throat. My fingers tightened in her hair, and I held her head down on my cock as I felt her throat constricting around it. It felt so fucking good I was nearly cross-eyed with pleasure as she swallowed me down into her belly.

"Such a good girl." I moaned and let go of her head and she pulled up off of me and licked her lips with a hungry smile on her face. "Damn. I was looking forward to punishing you."

She climbed up onto my lap and kissed me, letting me taste myself on her tongue before she leaned over and whispered into my ear. "I need you to make it hurt baby. I want it."

"Fuck." I groaned, latching onto her neck, and biting as Franklin pulled into the garage and stopped outside the elevator. He got out of the car and stood with his back to us leaning against the hood, giving us privacy even though we clearly didn't require it. I put my still-hard dick back into my pants and zipped them up. "I'm going to fuck you so hard the second we're inside the door.

She opened the door to the car and jumped off my lap onto the ground. "Race you." And then she turned and ran to the open elevator and pushed the buttons. I grabbed her bag and mine and tore off after her, but the doors shut in my face, but not before I saw her lift her shirt off over her head and started undoing her pants. She was going to be naked before I even got upstairs.

"Fuck." I cursed and slammed the button repeatedly as my need for her swelled through my entire body. The car came back down and was empty when I stepped inside. I jammed the button for my penthouse and undid my tie and ripped my shirt open as I rode up.

When the doors opened I walked into my penthouse and cursed when I spotted her across the room, standing in the hallway to my bedroom in just her panties. She stared into my eyes as she pushed them down over her legs and then turned to run down the hallway, but I was already on my way to her.

She ran through the doorway to my room, and I caught her around the waist and picked her up. She screamed and fought against my hold, keyed up on the chase and I carried her to my bed and threw her onto it. She bounced and tried to scurry away from me, but I caught her ankles and pulled her back to me, and flipped her onto her back, spreading her legs wide and looking down at her soaked pussy.

"That pussy wants my cock so bad, doesn't it."

"I ache to feel you fill me up, Mav."

"Keep your legs spread wide, don't close them," I ordered as I let go of her ankles and ripped my jacket and shirt off, throwing them on the floor. I slowly slid my belt from my pants and arousal rushed through my body when her eyes flared as she eyed my belt as I folded it in my hands. "Someday, I'm going to cover your ass with red welts from this belt." Her head lolled back, and she ran a hand down to her pussy and rubbed her fingers over her clit in small quick circles and moaned.

I tossed the belt to the floor and shoved my pants and boxers down, kicking off my shoes to stand naked and hard between her spread legs. I stroked my cock as she played with her pussy and moaned when she took her fingers from her clit and pushed two of them inside of her.

"Fuck me Maverick. Fuck me so hard that there's no doubt in my mind who I belong to."

I pounced on her and pinned her hands above her head. "Do you doubt who you belong to right now?" I asked and bit her nipple, loving the sound of her scream in the air. "Do you not feel owned already?"

"No, I don't." She gasped and rocked her hips, rubbing her clit against my stomach. "I've been alone for so long."

"Not anymore." I snapped. "You'll never be alone again. And your body will never be empty of me again either." I pulled back and thrust into her, drawing another scream from her lips as she wrapped her legs around my waist and opened her pussy up for me. "Your body will always be filled, with either my cock," I bit her neck and sucked on it hard enough to leave a mark as she squirmed under me. "Or my come." I moved to the other side and left another mark on the top of her breast. I pulled back and stared into her eyes, "Or my babies." She moaned and started coming on my cock as I promised her over and over again that I was going to get her pregnant someday. I was obsessed with the idea of seeing her body grow with my child inside of it and by the way her pussy gushed around my cock, and she begged for more over and over again, she was too.

She fought against the idea of it the other day, but we both knew we had always planned on having kids together. And now that I had her back. I had a lot of lost time to make up for.

"Please Mav. Harder, fuck me harder baby. I need you; I need more."

"You have me, Cora. And I've got you, I'm right here." I rolled my hips and rubbed her clit with my pelvis. "I'm right here, deep inside of you. Deeper than anyone else has ever been."

I let go of her wrists, folded her knees toward her chest, and slammed into her over and over, sliding her body up the bed with each punishing thrust.

"Yes!" She screamed as she clawed at my arms. "Just like that." Her nails were drawing blood on my arms and my primal, animalistic need to consume her ignited something inside of me that I'd never felt before. I came unhinged, burying myself inside of her over and over again as she screamed and begged for it.

"Take it," I grunted; my orgasm was so close I could taste it. "Take every inch that I give you. Take it deep."

She shattered into another orgasm, and I rode her like it was my fucking life on the line until I couldn't hold it off any longer. I roared and felt my release coat her inner walls as they clamped down on me, milking more from me than I thought was possible.

When I finally stopped coming I collapsed on top of her and crushed her into the bed. She wrapped her arms and legs around me tightly and held on, panting as deeply as I was. "Oh my God Mav." She finally said. "I've never... that was..." She stopped again.

"Animalistic." I filled in the words for her.

"I feel so... fulfilled." She said and then laughed. "It sounds weird, but I feel like that was exactly what sex was designed for."

"Sex is designed for the purpose of breeding Cora, for procreation. The sole reason we were put on this earth is for breeding Cora, for procreation. And that was exactly what would have happened had you not started birth control." I growled at her, letting her know my distaste for the topic.

She groaned and pushed me, so I fell to her side, but I dragged her with me, refusing to pull out of her just yet.

She laid her head on my arm and looked at me with seriousness in her eyes. "How can you be so sure you want kids right now? With me."

I could tell this was an important conversation, and what I said now would reflect her opinion on the matter for a long time. So I made sure she was looking directly in my eye as I tried to convey to her how important it was to me. "You are the only woman I've ever imagined pregnant. Even when we were still in high school, there were times when I would think about the future and I could imagine you standing by my side with a growing belly, glowing and happily married to me. And that hasn't changed for me over the years. The primal, alpha part of me, needs to see you with our baby in your arms. It needs to take care of you and our kids for the rest of our lives. I ache to be fulfilled like that Cora."

She watched me closely and I saw when the tears filled her eyes before she closed them, and they fell down her temple.

"Talk to me," I whispered and kissed away her tears.

"I thought that dream of mine was gone forever when I lost you."

"I'm right here Cora. You have me, and you can have that dream back too."

She took a shuddering breath and then bit her lip. "I didn't start the contraceptive." She whispered.

"What?" I asked, not trusting my hearing over the roar in my ears at her admission.

"I got the prescription, but the entire time I was sitting there at the pharmacy waiting to pick it up, your words kept playing over and over in my head about how we're not getting any younger and how we've already lost out on ten years together. And I couldn't get it. And I couldn't get the morning-after pill either. I didn't know how to tell you though because I was afraid you would change your mind."

"Never!" I said forcefully, rolling her until she was on top of me, and I pulled her face to mine and kissed her sensually, drawing emotion all the way from my feet and putting it into this kiss. "Marry me, Cora. Let's make babies. Let's finally get everything we deserve."

She cried harder, closing her eyes as her tears fell onto my chest. "I'm scared."

"I know," I said sitting up and backing up against the headboard. She moaned as her hips rocked and I smirked, knowing my cock that never shrunk still impaled her because it was heaven inside. "To be honest, I'm scared too. We both have fears about this relationship. But I promise you, I'll never hurt you like I did before. And I'd never jeopardize our life and the happiness of our children like that either."

She sat in my lap for a long time, letting me run my hands over her entire body and kiss her deeply as our confessions sank in.

"Okay." She whispered against my lips after a while and I froze, hating the way my heart raced in my chest.

"Okay?"

She smiled and bit her lip. "Okay, yes. Let's do it. Let's do it all and get everything we've ever dreamed of."

"Fuck yes!" I yelled and she giggled at me as I hugged her close. "God, I fucking love you."

"I love you so much more, Mav."

"Not possible," I said and then rolled so she was underneath me again. "You know what this means right?" I asked as I slid my hard cock out of her body and pushed it back in again.

She gasped and her eyes rolled as she bit her lip. "Hmm?" She hummed.

"You thought I was insatiable before. But now you've given me the task of getting you pregnant, and that means I'm going to be fucking you senseless every single waking second of every single day until I get it done."

She moaned and dug her nails into my shoulders. "Wait a second…"

But the sound of the intercom ringing cut her off from the front desk. "Fuck." I groaned, dropping my forehead to hers as I remembered the surprise I'd planned for her.

"What's that?" She asked.

"A surprise I planned for you, that I now regret." I pulled out of her body reluctantly and kissed my way down her body until my lips landed on her lower stomach right beneath her belly button. I kissed the skin there gently and then looked up at her. "Our future is right here." Her eyes softened and she tilted her head happily as she watched me. I smirked and forced myself to get up. "Okay, get up. Get dressed in a bra and panties, put my robe on, and come out."

"What?" She asked, confused as I stood up and put my briefs and pants on.

"Just do it love. We've got a busy couple of days ahead of us."

She laughed and shook her head. "I'm so confused."

I laughed back at her and walked out to the front buzzer that went off again and answered it, telling the front desk to send them up.

A couple of minutes later I opened the front door to two women followed by two doormen with a large cart and a couple of large suitcases trailing behind them. Cora came out of the bedroom and raised her eyebrows as she eyed the chaos in our living room.

"Mr. Jones, I want to thank you again for trusting us with your pressing needs and I just want to reiterate that you will not be disappointed in our services." One of the women said as she stepped forward to shake my hand.

"I hope so." I replied, holding my hand out for Cora to join us, "My fiancé needs a brand-new wardrobe; everything." I said waving my hand up and down. "Outfits for business, evening wear, casual, as well as bathing suits, lingerie, shoes, accessories. *Everything*. Whatever she wants, she gets."

"Mav." Cora started to object from next to me.

"Let me spoil you. Finally. I'm long overdue."

"Doesn't mean you need to make up for it in one day babe."

"Give me this," I begged of her.

She eyed me for a moment and then conceded. "Okay." I smiled brightly at her and she chuckled shaking her head back and forth.

"You guys can get settled in the spare bedroom and I'll order us dinner. Okay?"

"Okay." She led the women to the opposite side of the apartment and into the spare bedroom while I went into my office and made an important phone call.

"Maverick," My mother's voice answered through the phone. "How are you dear?"

"I'm perfect Mom. I need a favor though." I poured a glass of bourbon from my bar and took a sip.

"Uh oh." She said wearily.

"Nothing bad, I promise."

"Okay, what is it?"

"I need the name of the jeweler that you use, preferably someone that will come to me tonight with a wide selection."

She paused for a moment. "A selection of what?"

"Engagement rings for Cora." I couldn't help the stupid schoolboy grin that pulled at my lips as I said it out loud.

"Oh." She gasped, "Are you going to propose?"

"I just did about twenty minutes ago and she said yes, and now I need to find the ring that she's dreamed of her whole life."

"Oh my God!" She screeched through the phone, "Chris! Mav and Cora are engaged! Oh my God!" she yelled again.

"Mom focus!" I laughed and waited for her to calm down.

"Okay, I'm sorry. I'm just so excited! And so happy, oh Mav! Okay, focus Marsha." I laughed again as she chided herself. "Uh well, the answer is easy, Ruby at Ruby and Son's. I can call him if you'd like. He's on the East Side so he's close and he'd come running for the opportunity to put the ring on the finger of the future Mrs. Maverick Jones."

"Okay, just text me the contact info and I'll call him. I have a specific style in mind and want to discuss it with him first."

"Okay, oh my God, Maverick I'm so excited. Tell me you're bringing her home for a visit this weekend, please! I'm dying to see her and now we need to celebrate."

"How about Sunday we come out and see you guys?"

"Perfect!" She gushed, "We can do a lunch out on the patio, it's supposed to be beautiful out."

"Okay, sounds good. I'll let you know what time we're coming out."

"I love you so much Maverick, and I'm so happy you're finally getting your happy ending."

"This is just the beginning Mom, we have so much living to do."

"Of course," She laughed, "I'll text you Ruby's number."

"Thanks, Mom. Talk to you soon."

I hung up with her and a moment later I got her text with the number for the jeweler and went to work arranging a selection of rings to be delivered tonight for Cora and me to pick out together.

The pieces of my life were falling into place, and I'd never felt more powerful.

Chapter 12 – Cora

I stood looking in the mirror of the walk-in closet in Mav's spare bedroom and admired my black strappy dress. It was sinful and elegant and sexy, and I felt all of those things in it.

My skin tingled with Mav's arrival to the room, and I looked over my shoulder to find him leaning against the doorframe, still wearing only his suit slacks, and holding a crystal glass of bourbon in his fingers. My god, he looked sexy.

And he was mine.

All fucking mine.

Sasha and Madeline, the two women Maverick had hired to be my shoppers, turned and looked at him as he watched me.

"That's a keeper." He said sexily, and my entire body shivered. He turned his attention to Madeline and nodded to the array of clothes spread out around the room. "Have you gotten what you need to make sure she's taken care of?"

"Yes sir." She said confidently. "We've got everything we need. We'll have an entire new closet delivered by tomorrow night."

"Perfect." He said, leaning off the door and looking back at me. I turned around to face him. "Leave that on." His gaze caressed my body from top to bottom as he walked into the room.

"Yes sir." I quipped sarcastically and his eyes flared.

"I'll pay you both extra to leave everything here and leave now."

"Of course Mr. Jones." Madeline and Sasha both quickly grabbed their personal items and scurried from the room. I shook my head at him as we listened to the front door open and close behind them as they walked out.

"Are you eager for something Mr. Jones?" I asked as I slowly walked towards him.

"Eager doesn't even begin to describe what I am when it comes to you."

I took the glass from his hand and tipped it to my lips, sipping the warming amber liquid and letting it settle into my belly. "Is dinner here yet?"

"Yes, it's in the warmer."

"Should we go eat then?" I asked, letting the fingers of my other hand tease the skin directly above his waistband.

"I plan on eating my first course soon, you'll have to wait a bit longer though." His eyes were dark and needy as he settled his hands onto my hips and picked me up, wrapping my legs around his waist. "My mouth is watering; I can almost taste it already."

I held onto him and took another sip of his drink as he walked us into the kitchen. He set me down on top of the marble countertop and took his drink from my fingers, pouring the rest of it back. "So what is this delicious meal you plan on indulging in without me?"

He ran his hands up my bare thighs and slid them under the short skirt of the dress, wrapping his fingers around the band of my panties before removing them completely. He pushed my knees open wide and then pulled my hips to the edge of the counter and laid my shoulders down on the counter.

"Mmh." He moaned as he ran his nose up my inner thigh. "You smell as good as you taste, love."

My back arched and I sighed as he teased me, blowing on my exposed pussy but not touching it.

"Do you always play with your food before you eat it?" I groaned and twisted my fingers into his hair, trying to pull his mouth onto my clit where I desperately needed him.

"Only when it's you baby."

"Fucking do it already," I complained. "Please!"

He chuckled and then flicked the tip of his tongue over my clit before sucking it into his mouth and pushing his tongue into my opening.

"Yes." I hissed and put my feet on his shoulders as he held me tightly and devoured me. "You're so good at that."

"Only for you baby." He growled and the vibrations against my clit made my body feel liquid and warm.

"I'm so close. You've got me so close, so soon."

"That's because I know your body like my own Cora. I've memorized it." He said, pushing two fingers into my body and curling them, rubbing on my g-spot.

"Oh my God." I cried, pulling his hair as I curled around him and his fingers curled inside of me. "Just like that, don't stop Mav," I begged as he sucked my clit and rocked me back and forth on his fingers. My orgasm ripped from my body as every muscle in my body cramped and tightened painfully through the agonizing bliss of my orgasm. I moaned and called his name over and over as he worked my body over.

I lay there gasping for my breath as he stood up, wiping his face with his hand and smiled at me with a predatory glean to his eye as he pulled me off the counter and walked over to the couch. He flipped me around until my knees were on the seat and my elbows laid on the back and he lined himself up with my entrance and slammed into me.

"Fuck, you feel like heaven." He growled as his hands gripped my hips and pulled me back onto his cock over and over again as he thrust into me. I dug my fingers into the cushions on the back of the couch and bit the pillow as he pushed my body towards another catastrophic orgasm. There was something about him that aroused me so much that all he had to do was look at me and I was on the precipice of an orgasm.

"You fuck me so good, Mav. No one has ever made me feel so good."

"I've never felt like this with anyone else either, Cora. You were the only one before and you're the only one now that can drive me wild like this. You turn me into an animal."

"Mine." I agreed and hissed as he spit on my ass and pushed his thumb into me. "God, yes Mav." I groaned, arching my back to give him better access.

He used the hand on my lower back with his thumb hooked in my ass to move me how he wanted, and I knew he was close. I could feel his restraint slipping as his hips jerked out of rhythm and his words became possessive and dominant.

"You're mine, Cora."

Thrust.

"You're going to be my wife."

Thrust.

"I'm going to keep you forever."

Thrust.

His hand landed on my ass cheek next, and I moaned as the fire lit through my spine. I rolled my hips basking in the burn. "Again." I gasped.

His hand landed on the same spot and more fire exploded through my nerves. His hand was so large and hot, branding me with the slaps.

These weren't gentle exploratory spanks; these were the spanks of a man who knew how to swing his hand to get the most pain from it.

"Beg for more." He hissed.

"More, please Mav. Spank me again." I cried, desperate for more of the fire.

He laid his hand on my ass again and again, kissing the skin expertly and my orgasm ripped from my core with a scream from my lips as my pussy and ass clamped down on his cock and thumb. "Just like that Cora, such a good girl taking everything I give you baby." He moaned and then his free hand squeezed my ass cheek painfully as he stilled his hips as his cock jerked and filled me.

I released my teeth from the pillow under my chest and laid my cheek against it as I felt his cock slowly pull out and push back into my body a few times as he prolonged his pleasure.

He pulled out of me completely and I looked over my shoulder at him as he dropped to his knees behind me and used his hands on each of my inner thighs to spread me open. "What are you doing?" I asked, feeling self-conscious.

"Looking at your swollen pussy covered in my come." He said with a smile in his voice. He ran his fingers through my folds and then pushed three thick fingers into me. "Don't want to waste a drop." He pushed his come back into me and the act was so taboo and so fucking hot. I clenched around his fingers, and he moaned, leaning in, and kissing the back of my thigh.

When he was done exploring he pulled me down onto the couch and covered me with his body. He wrapped himself all around me and held me close, kissing my hair and my forehead before pulling my hands up to his face and kissing each fingertip and then palm and inner wrist.

"You were never this affectionate when we were younger." I mused, enjoying his attention.

"I never loved you this deeply when we were younger. I never understood loss and pain back then, but now that I do, my love for you has developed into something... deeper."

"I know what you mean," I said quietly, feeling my love for him so intensely that it ached and hurt my heart in a way that made me feel alive and desperate for him.

"I don't want to, but we need to get dressed and eat." He said, sighing.

"Why can't we just stay like this forever?"

"Because my jeweler will be here in an hour with a case full of diamonds for us to pick out your engagement and wedding rings from."

My eyes widened and I looked up at him, "Just like that?" I asked.

He chuckled and nuzzled his nose against mine. "Turns out even the most prestigious jewelers would kill for an opportunity to say that my wife wears their stones on her body."

"Hmm, the life of the rich and famous." I mused.

"Life of me and you baby. And I plan on using every connection and benefit of my position in life to spoil you senseless. So get used to it, darling."

We got up, even though I grumped my way through it like a spoiled child. Luckily, Mav was charmed by it and not annoyed. We ate a Greek meal that he had delivered and by the time we were done, the intercom was ringing again. I looked at my watch and saw that it was nearly nine pm and I desperately just wanted to be in bed with Maverick wrapped around me inch for inch, but I would be lying if I said I wasn't excited to pick out my engagement ring either. It was something I thought I'd been robbed of forever, knowing I'd never marry a man that wasn't

Maverick but now that it was happening in his living room, I was breathless.

I ran my hands down the front of my black dress and Maverick watched me closely. He'd since changed into a pair of blue jeans and a black t-shirt, but he was still barefoot and sinfully delicious, and I wore my new designer dress like a coat of armor against my feeling of inadequacy.

"I love you." He promised as the front door opened and an older Italian man in a fancy Armani suit walked in with two younger men who couldn't be anyone other than his sons, carrying large cases in their beefy arms. The older man rushed forward to Maverick and shook his hand in both of his and looked up at my man in awe. "Ruby, thank you for coming on such short notice."

"Mr. Jones! What an honor to be allowed to adorn your beautiful future wife with the most important diamonds of her life." He gushed in a thick accent, and I instantly liked him. The man turned to me after Mav shook his hand and he took both of mine in his, kissing the backs of them affectionately in old Italian fashion. "My dear, I know I have just the set for you to wear with pride on the arm of such a man!"

I smiled at him warmly and he pulled back, ushering his sons forward and having them set the heavy cases on the kitchen island as Maverick pulled out a stool for me.

"Now we discussed briefly on the phone what you were looking for Mr. Jones, and I'm sure I brought a few different selections that will fit your requirements," Ruby said.

"What were your requirements?" I asked Mav as the sons started setting trays of rings and diamonds onto the marble.

"At least a five-carat solitaire stone center with a multi-diamond wedding band to match, I told him you used to like the vintage and dainty look and we needed to incorporate that if you wanted that still,"

Mav said, sliding a piece of my blond hair behind my ear as he looked down at me adoringly.

"Are you sure about this? About me?" I asked, forcing my eyes to stay locked on his instead of on the twinkling diamonds being laid out in front of me in case he was uncertain about this all. I didn't want to get my hopes up to have them pulled out from under me again.

"One hundred percent positive. I've never wanted anything more in my life Cora." He said, leaning down and I tilted my head back further and offered my lips to his, letting him kiss me.

When he finally pulled back I felt the blush on my cheeks and whispered against his lips. "Okay."

I looked down at the arrangement before me and took a deep breath, trying to stay grounded and sane as all the beauty tried to steal away my good sense. I chewed on my lip as I let my eyes rove over the twinkling options before me. "Holy moly, they are all giant."

Mav chuckled and Ruby smiled proudly.

I leaned forward and looked closer and quickly felt an overwhelming sense of anxiety crawl up my spine. "I can't," I said, leaning back and shaking my head. "They're all too much Mav."

"No, they're not." He said firmly. "They're not even close enough to being what you deserve after everything Cora. But I know there's not a chance you'd let me put anything bigger on your finger, so we'll compromise on these." He said, looking over the options and I watched him zero in on one that stole my attention just moments ago.

He reached forward and pulled a wedding band from the velvet cushion finger it laid on and looked at it closer before turning towards me and holding it out. "Do you remember the time I stole that ring from my mom's jewelry box when we were kids?" He said as the memory captivated us both. "We were what, twelve?" He asked and I snickered and nodded.

"My twelfth birthday." I agreed looking up at his face as he smiled.

"I brought it to your party and pulled you away from everyone and put it on your thumb because it was too fucking big to even come close to fitting on any other finger at that age." He laughed and shook his head. "It was ugly and gaudy as hell, but it was what I thought would impress you the most in my stupid pre-teen boy brain. My dad knew exactly where it had gone when my mom told him it was missing later that night."

"They grounded you for a month for taking it." I laughed and leaned into his side.

"I wanted to give you a real ring, considering we'd been engaged for years at that point already." He scoffed like it was no big deal to steal an emerald diamond ring from his mom's vaulted jewelry box. "My mom took me to Ruby's the next day and helped me pick out your promise ring and I gave it to you that night before they locked me away in solitary confinement for a month." He joked dramatically.

Ruby sighed and brought his hands to his chest. "I remember that!" He gushed on, "The spiral vintage infinity band." He recalled exactly the ring that Maverick had given to me two days after my twelfth birthday in a promise to me.

The band on the promise ring looked exactly like the band on the one he held, though this one had *far* more diamonds on it.

Maverick picked up my left hand and slid the twisted band on my ring finger and it glided effortlessly into place like it was meant for me. I held my breath as I looked down at the intricate wedding band of platinum and diamond around my finger that matched the ring I'd lost a decade ago.

"They kept my old one," I whispered as sadness tried to pull me out of this moment.

Mav's hand tightened around mine and I felt his entire body tense before I looked up into his eyes. "We'll get it back love, I promise."

I shook my head and took a deep breath. "I love this one," I said, looking down, admiring the new ring on my finger. "I don't need an engagement ring Mav, just this band is perfect."

He kissed my temple and slid his hands over my spine, chuckling into my hair. "Not a chance in hell." He said firmly. "But good try."

I rolled my eyes as he pulled back and we turned towards Ruby again who was watching closely with his sons on each side of him.

"I have the perfect match to that ring if you're interested in seeing it, dear," Ruby said and I nodded to him, eager to see the pair to the beautiful ring on my finger already. He reached into a case to his side, pulled the ring out, and handed it to Mav without letting me see it. Mav looked down at the gem in his hand and smiled over at me and I knew it was the one based solely on the twinkle in Mav's eye.

He took my hand and slid the engagement ring onto my finger, settling it next to the wedding band, and then kissed my palm before placing my hand on the countertop in front of me.

"My God." I gasped at how perfect the duo looked together on my finger. Tears burned the back of my eyes as I gazed lovingly at the giant ring he added.

"It's five carats." Ruby started, leaning forward to highlight the features of the diamond. "Round cut, with two more carats on each side down to the platinum band that twists into the infinity loops like the wedding band. Overall between the two bands, there is over nine carats."

I just stared down in awe at the set and then smiled up at Mav. "It's giant."

"It's perfect." He responded and then looked over at Ruby. "But I want an identical band to match the wedding band, so she has one on each side of the engagement ring."

"Why?" I asked, "These are more than enough."

"This one is for the past." He said, running his thumbnail over the twisted wedding band against my knuckle. "This one is for the present." He said, twisting the engagement ring slightly and then looking up at me. "And the other band will be for our future. I want to come full circle with you Cora. I want your engagement ring surrounded by me on both sides."

"Mav." I sighed, falling deeper in love with him at his sentiment. "You are so perfect."

Ruby sighed too as he watched us and I blushed again, feeling embarrassed by the open display of affection between Mav and I after so long without any sort of attachment to anyone in the world.

"I can have a matching band for you tomorrow," Ruby said. "The size is perfect for her hand, and you'll have a complete set."

"Perfect," Mav said, extending his hand to shake the older man's as the sons started loading the diamonds away. "That was far easier than I thought it would be. Though I should have known you'd make this as easy as possible on me."

"It's what we do." Ruby said, "I can't wait to tell the world that the future Mrs. Maverick Jones wears the diamonds from Ruby and Sons!" He cheered fanatically. "It's such an honor, my dear." He reached for my hand and kissed the back again, admiring the ring.

"I'll appreciate you holding off on spreading the word to the world just yet Ruby," Maverick said firmly. "You can cheer to the rafters that my fiancé is wearing your diamonds, but not a word more about who she is or about our past. If word gets out about Cora's return to my life, it will derail the plans that are in place."

Ruby's eyes widened and I watched both Mav and him closely through the exchange. "Oh of course!" The man agreed, "I love a good intrigue." He mimed zipping his lips, "The identity of your Mrs. is safe with me, Mr. Jones."

"Good, because I plan to adorn my wife in diamonds and jewels for the rest of her life and I will remain exclusively loyal to Ruby and Sons if you handle this correctly."

Ruby nodded quickly again with an excited smile on his face and then he gathered up the rest of his cases and the three of them left the penthouse in a flourish of dollar signs floating in the air between them.

When the door closed behind him I slid from my stool and walked after Mav who stood in the center of the living room, having led them out. I wrapped my arms around his waist and laid my cheek on his back, breathing in the scent of him, and kissed him through his tight black shirt. He laid his hands over mine on his stomach and lifted my left hand to twirl the rings on my finger.

"Promise me you'll never take these off." He said quietly and I felt the vulnerability in his voice as he asked for the reassurance that I wasn't going anywhere.

"You'll have to cut them off my cold dead fingers when I die if you want them back," I said firmly and he chuckled, pulling my hand up to kiss my fingertips. "Will you tell me what you're planning to do with my family? What are these big plans you talked about?"

He turned in my arms and placed his large warm hands on my hips, pulling my body flush to his as he looked down into my eyes. His blue eyes glowed against the dark features of his face, and I found myself mesmerized by his handsomeness even after all of this time. I could still see the carefree boy in his eyes, but that was the only place. The rest of him had grown and hardened into the powerful and dominating man standing before me now, and I couldn't decide which version of him I loved more.

"Are you sure you want to know? You've wanted to separate yourself as far as possible so far." He said gently, not judging me or avoiding the question, but making sure I wanted to really be a part of it before he divulged it to me.

I raised my diamond-encrusted hand to him and pointed to the new rings. "For better or worse darling," I said and he smiled before leaning in and kissing me deeply, tasting my lips and teasing my tongue.

"Till death do us part." He whispered against me and then pulled me over to an oversized armchair near the fireplace. He hit a button on the remote next to the chair and the fire roared to life and the lights dimmed around us as he settled down in the chair and pulled me into his lap, covering my body with his hands as he ran them up my bare legs and arms. "To start with, your brother has been bothering me for months about a deal he wanted my help making in Manhattan. I took the meeting with him to find out what the project was exactly and turns out, it's a very lucrative deal and if my gut is right, which it usually is in business, then something tells me he *needs* this deal more than he wants it."

"What do you mean?" I asked, playing with the fabric of his shirt against his chest.

"Your brother married a woman a few years ago, who, for a lack of better terms, is a gold-digging bitch." He said plainly and I snorted at his lack of tact.

"You don't say?"

He smirked and continued. "She has been running him up one side of the East Coast and down the other, spending his money like a bleeding artery. I think he needs this deal to go through in order to save not only his marriage but also his livelihood."

"Which is why he came to you." I mused.

"Yes." He agreed and then tilted my chin to look directly into his blue eyes as he continued. "Which is also going to be his fatal flaw, because I'm going to make this deal without him and steal his last grasp at saving himself from social suicide and bankruptcy." I shuddered at the intensity of his promise. "It's step one of my plan."

"Do I dare ask what step two is?" I whispered.

He leaned forward and pressed his warm lips against mine, melting my fear and anxiety of dealing with my family again. "Step two is marrying you next weekend and announcing it to the world at Luke's memorial fundraiser in front of your family, outing their despicable role in our demise in front of all of their colleagues and inner circle of friends. By then I should have a hand on every inflow of cash into the Valentine household and therefore have the ability to destroy them in one fell swoop. By the end of the fundraiser, the message to all of the guests will be clear, align themselves with the Valentine Family anymore, and they will fall alongside them. Cast them off like they did to you and remain in the good graces of the Jones family. Our family."

"Our family," I repeated tentatively.

"Ours." He affirmed, resting his hand on my stomach, and rubbing his thumb over the supple skin there under my dress. "The name our children will bear and carry on long after you and I are gone."

I groaned and leaned forward, kissing him deeply as his words turned me on wildly. He growled into my mouth threaded his fingers into my hair and pulled my head towards his roughly as he ignited the passion between us.

"Mav." I moaned when he wrapped his hand around my throat and pulled me over his body until I sat straddling his wide thighs.

"I'm going to fuck you in nothing but those diamonds until neither of us can remember our own names." He growled and bit my lip with his hand still firmly holding my throat. I wrapped my hands around his wrist and rocked my hips forward, rubbing myself on his growing erection under his soft jeans. "Cora." He moaned, letting his eyes flutter closed as I used his body shamelessly.

"Take me baby." I begged.

Chapter 13 – Maverick

Sunlight glowed through the windows of my bedroom, and my eyes adjusted to the bright intrusion. I never slept past sunrise because I was always at work, yet lately, I found it harder and harder to pry myself out of bed and away from Cora's adorable pouty lips that parted perfectly in her sleep when she tucked herself into my side.

As a teenager, I snuck into her room all the time, sleeping in bed next to her and waking with only enough time to scale back down the Hawthorn tree below her bedroom window before her parents got up. But this was different because instead of feeling like I was getting away with something, I felt like I was finally holding everything I deserved, and no one was going to come in and take that away from me.

Cora shifted in her sleep, rolling away from me and sighing into her side of the bed as she got comfortable again and I let her go, giving her space as I slid from bed to let her sleep. I'd kept her up well into the morning, using her body and intentionally trying to knock her up one orgasm at a time.

And God it was fucking intense each and every time I imagined finally getting the family with her that I so desperately desired. I shook my head, shaking away the shock that just a week ago I'd harbored so much anger towards her because of the way she left me before I'd known the truth. And now, she was my fiancé, and we were getting married next week.

Well, we were getting married next week if I could pull it off. And there was only one person in the world who could help me pull this off in a week. I walked out of the bedroom and into my office in a pair of sweatpants and looked out at the city below through the windows behind my desk for a while before sitting down in my chair and getting to work. I answered urgent emails and sent off some to my team, delegating duties, as Reid and Dexter had called it.

Hope they like being delegated to on a Saturday morning.

Fuckers.

"Ah hmm."

I looked up from my computer screen to the sexy as-sin woman standing in the doorway to my home office with a soft smile on her flawless face. She leaned against the door frame wearing my black shirt from last night, hanging off her shoulder and clinging to her flared hips where it ended right below her panties. Her hair was in a bun on top of her head and the bare toes of one foot ran up and down her other leg seductively.

"Well, good morning." I said, leaning back in my chair and rubbing my hand over the stubble on my chin. "God, you are breathtaking," I whispered in awe, feeling the tingles of desperation clenching my heart in my chest from how intense my feelings were for her.

She smiled shyly and rolled her eyes, chewing on her lip as she leaned off the doorway and tiptoed across the room to me. I pushed back in my chair and turned so my lap was open to her as she rounded my desk and pulled her down onto my thighs, letting her lush ass settle right onto the hardness of my insatiable dick that was fully alert now. My hands slid over the cotton barely containing her delicious curves and my body reacted to her instantly. She put both hands behind the back of my neck and slid her fingernails through the short hair at my nape as she leaned in and offered her pillowy lips to me.

"Good morning Mav." She purred and I felt the vibrations through her chest pressed to mine, sending bolts of electricity through us both. "I woke up alone." She pouted, sticking her bottom lip out and I leaned in and sucked it into my mouth and nibbled it.

"I didn't want to wake you up; I kept you up all night long as it was," I said, resting my palm on her bare thigh.

"I like what happens when we're both awake in bed though."

I chuckled and leaned back in the chair to look at her. "We have a lot to do before next weekend. I was just getting the ball rolling on it."

"The wedding you insist on having in seven days?" She asked with skepticism in her voice.

"The wedding I insist on having in seven days because it's ten years late as it is," I affirmed and she sighed.

"We don't have to rush this Mav. I'm not going anywhere."

"I know that Cora. But I also know what I want, and I want this." I said firmly, to show her I had zero hesitation. "Do you not want to be married to me right now?" I asked, the thought suddenly implanting itself in my brain. "Did I rush this for you? I didn't even ask you." I hurried on, panic starting to rush through my veins.

"Mav." She warned in a low but firm voice as she tilted her hips to pin me back in the chair as I started getting restless. "I'd marry you today if you asked me to. I'm not worried about it because of that. I'm just worried about..." She paused, letting her gaze fall from my eyes to my lips as she worked hers through her teeth.

"Tell me."

She sighed and looked back up at me, tilting her head in uncomfortableness. "I'm worried about what everyone will think. About me." Her voice was soft and quiet, and I could feel the vulnerability in it, so I tightened my arms around her waist and pulled her even closer.

"What do you imagine they will think?" I wanted to know what fears were in her head, so I knew in what ways I needed to reassure her.

"I'm afraid they'll think I trapped you. If I do get pregnant right away, everyone will think we got married because of that. And even if I don't get pregnant..." She faded off and sighed. "They'll still think I went after you for your money."

"Are you trapping me?" I asked her seriously, "Because last I checked, I was the one who kidnapped you from your apartment and hasn't left you alone since. I'm the one who is actively trying to knock you up every waking second and I'm also the one who fucked everything up years ago to lose you, to begin with." I leaned forward and kissed the side of her neck below her ear. "I want to talk about that, too."

She'd asked me not to get into it the other night, but I wanted to get it off my chest before we went any further in our relationship now because it was important to me.

"About that night?" She asked, and I could feel her hesitation in her spine.

"Yes. I need to confess to everything I did and explain to you why, so we have no secrets going into this marriage. I think it's best this way."

"Okay." She said gently but slid her legs off of mine and stood up, fighting against my tightening hold. "I just want some space when we talk about this so I can process it appropriately." She cut me off as I started protesting about her walking away from me and went and sat down in the chair across from me on the other side of my desk. She brought her knees up to her chest and stared at me with fear in her perfect turquoise eyes. "Tell me."

I leaned forward and rested my forearms on the desk, keeping my eyes on hers in reassurance. "I didn't cope after Luke's death. I distracted myself with you for weeks after he died, letting your presence calm me and soothe my hurt like a salve, but it never cured it. As soon as I was away from you or the moment you fell asleep and I was left with nothing but my thoughts, I was right back where I started."

"Which was where?"

"Angry."

She tilted her head and listened as I tried to explain my feelings from that time for the first time out loud.

"I was so angry at the jackass who drove drunk and hit him. I was so angry at the world for taking him away from me and leaving me here on this earth without him. I was so angry at myself for contemplating taking my own life to be with him again because what did that say about how I felt about you?" I asked hypothetically. "I was so grief-stricken that I couldn't even see how much pain you were in or how much pain I'd cause you if I ended everything to ease the burden that his loss left on me."

Tears pooled in her eyes as she watched me cut myself open like this. "I had no idea..." She whispered. "I didn't know you thought about suicide."

Her voice gutted me, but I had to keep going.

"I thought about it every single day, Cora. I can't describe to you what it felt like to have a physical piece of myself taken from me that night." I paused as realization dawned on me and I fell back into my chair in shock.

"What?" She asked, leaning forward, confused.

I shook my head and ran my hand over my face. "Holy fuck." I whispered in denial. "I never compared the two pains out loud before, but the night you left me standing in the middle of that street, the pain

I felt losing you was the same that I felt that night losing him." I shook my head again and took a deep breath. "I always likened the loss of my twin to losing a physical part of me, literally losing my DNA from this earth. But losing you that night was just the same because you took my heart with you in the same way."

The tears in her eyes spilled over her lashes and she wiped at them quickly but didn't say anything. I could tell she knew exactly what that pain felt like because I had inflicted it on her that same evening.

"That anger in me festered until it came to a boiling point a couple of weeks before that night, Cora. Do you remember what I'm talking about?" I asked, leaning forward again, and watching her face for remembrance.

"No." She shook her head and her brows dropped over her eyes. "What are you talking about?"

"That night in my parents' boat house," I said and rubbed at my chest as the shame rushed over me the same way it did every time I thought about that night. Which had been almost daily for ten years now.

Her eyebrows lifted as her eyes widened in surprise at the memory and her chest fell. "Mav…"

I cut her off, shaking my head. "It was a month after he was killed, and I was drunk, and you'd met me at the boathouse to drive my pathetic ass to your house to sleep it off since your parents hardly cared about me staying over at that point." Bile rose in my throat, and I couldn't hold her gaze any more. "You were trying to get me to leave, and I wanted to fuck, to let off some steam. But I'd been an ass to you for a few days straight and you refused me, but I let that anger and pain inside of me fester into rage and I –" I clenched my jaw and worked my anger back down to continue the conversation. "I forced myself on you."

I saw her move in my peripheral vision and looked up to see her covering her face, shaking her head back and forth.

"You said no… and I–" She shook her head faster and dropped her hands, but I pushed on. "I–"

"Don't!" She snapped.

"Cora." I tried again but she wouldn't meet my eyes.

"You didn't rape me Mav." She said firmly, "Don't you dare put yourself into that category."

"You said no," I repeated, not allowing her to let me off the hook on this.

"That wasn't the first time we'd struggled with power and consent, Mav. We fought often like that and one of us would coerce the other into sex to cool down. It was no different."

"It was completely different!" I roared, and she tilted her head at me as I stood up and leaned over the desk towards her. She stared up at me with tears in her eyes and her mouth open in disbelief. "I forced myself into your body, Cora! And you gave into me when you didn't want to because you thought you had to."

"I gave in to you because I loved you!" She yelled back, standing up and leaning over the desk to match my energy. "I let you because I wanted you just as much in that exact moment Maverick! I just knew it wasn't going to fix this!" She put her hand flat on my chest over my heart. "I just wanted to fix this for you, but I couldn't."

"I crossed a line," I admitted. "And as soon as I sobered up that next morning I made a vow to myself that I'd never touch you again if I wasn't sure I'd be able to control myself."

She dropped her hand from the bare skin of my chest and backed up with a confused look on her face as she processed my words.

A haunting look covered her face as pain filled her eyes. "You hardly touched me after that." She whispered in disbelief. "You only fucked me when I downright begged you to, and even then... my God." She gasped, covering her mouth. "You fucked Sarah because you wouldn't fuck me."

She stepped backward, dropping my gaze, and holding her head in her hands. "I fucked Sarah because I didn't care about her feelings or comfort, and I could use her body in the only way that made sense to me at that point in my life."

I walked around the desk to go to her, but she took a tentative step back from me as she processed what I was telling her.

"You fucked her rough. You fucked her how you needed to fuck, because I couldn't give you what you needed any more." She whispered as fresh tears fell over her dark lashes and stained her pale cheeks.

"No!" I bellowed, closing the distance between us, and tangled my fingers in her hair forcing her to look at me. "I was so angry, and I was terrified that I'd lose my temper with you again and destroy us."

"You did destroy us!" She shouted back with wide eyes as she pointed her finger at me. "You could have done anything you needed to do to me, Mav, and I could have taken it. I could have handled it, but you went elsewhere and refused to even kiss me. We went from having sex three to four times a day to not at all in weeks! Do you understand what that does to a girl's head at that age and beyond?" She was irate, and she fought against my grip on her hair, but I held steady, wrapping one hand around her slim waist, and pulling her flush to my body, ignoring her attempts to distance herself right now. "Do you have any idea how big of a hit my self-esteem took over the years thinking I was too thin, or too fat, or too blonde, or a million other things because you decided to fuck my best friend behind my back?"

"I'm sorry." I pleaded, leaning my forehead against hers and holding onto her as she clawed at me in anger. "I know how wrong it was Cora, I was so fucked in the head, baby. I made a mistake. I'm so sorry." I repeated over and over as she cried in my arms as the fight weakened her body and she ended up clinging to me. I picked her up and carried her back to bed and crawled in under the blankets with her, holding her as she cried for all of the things that happened during and since then because of that spiral in my life. I clung to her as fervently as she hung on to me as we grieved for the teenage kids who were so lost in life.

"I love you," I whispered after she went silent and still in my arms, praying it would be enough to heal that pain even if it was from a decade ago.

Knowledge was power in most situations. But right now, it was only pain.

Chapter 14 – Cora

I sat in the passenger seat of Maverick's sleek car and watched him drive through the city out of the corner of my eye. I squirmed in my seat as he weaved through traffic expertly in a commanding and controlling way that made me... fucking needy. I toyed with the hem of my elegant but simple sun dress where it fell at my mid-thigh while I fought to control my raging hormones.

I'd never been good at doing that around Mav when we were teenagers, and right now, I felt hornier than any teenage girl ever before.

Which wasn't good because he had been... gentle... since our conversation yesterday morning about why he had cheated on me all those years ago. I hadn't handled the revelation well.

Go figure.

But he had been soothing and kind and accommodating and, in turn, he had been...gentle.

Which was exactly how he had been a decade ago after that ill-fated night in the boathouse that had been the beginning of our end before I even knew it.

And I fucking hated it. He had given me time to come to terms with everything, the information about Sarah had been hard to hear, but honestly hadn't been super shocking to me when I looked at it all with a logical levelheaded brain.

Sarah had always been an easy type of girl, obviously because she had willingly fucked her best friend's boyfriend of ten years and set me up to find them. So I wasn't surprised to know he had given into her flirting and took what he wanted from her when he didn't know where else to turn while battling his inner demons.

But something we hadn't discussed because I was too raw with what information I'd already learned, was what happened with them in the years since that night after graduation.

And that was slowly eating away at me.

But what was eating away at me even faster than that, was how badly I wanted Mav to stop treating me like some delicate flower and fuck me the way he did when we were needy, lust-filled teenagers; like he had the first day in his office up against the door.

I needed him like that because that was the raw and unapologetic side of him that he had always saved for just me, but he was hiding from me again in an attempt to protect me, and I couldn't stand it.

He took a corner through a yellow light like the car was on rails and I slid across the soft buttery leather seat and moaned softly, biting my lip to stifle it the best I could as I watched his strong muscular arms handle the steering wheel with ease.

He looked over at me over the edge of his mirrored aviators and quirked an eyebrow at me as I smiled at him awkwardly, with a death grip on the door handle to keep myself from climbing over the center console and mounting him like a Sybian sex saddle.

He wore a short-sleeved white shirt and a pair of black jeans that screamed rich rockstar sex God and I was fantasizing about him nailing me in the center of a stage like a horny groupie.

"You okay over there?" He asked, and his deep voice melted over me like honey.

I nodded emphatically, and my voice broke, squeaking embarrassingly as I replied. "Perfect."

He eyed me closely again before turning his attention back to the road, but instead of just going back to driving, he reached his large hand across the car and laid it on my thigh. Pushing his fingers between my legs where I had them pressed together tightly, trying to ease the building ache there.

I turned my head to look out the window and put the backs of my fingers against my lips as I squeezed my eyes shut tight trying to control my reaction to his touch, but I'd made a critical error. With my eyes closed and the music playing loudly around us, my other senses picked up the slack and soon I could only focus on the roughness of his fingertips on the sensitive skin of my inner thigh, just inches below my panties.

My soaked panties.

"For fuck's sake Cora, what is wrong?" Mav asked, squeezing my thigh to get my attention back to him and drawing a breathy moan from my lips that he would have had to be deaf to miss. "Cora!"

"Pull over!" I gasped sitting upright in my seat.

"What?" He asked, looking over at me again. "Why?"

"There!" I nearly screamed, pointing to an underground parking garage for a shopping district we were currently driving through. "Right there, pull in."

He followed my direction and squealed the tires as he tore through the garage to a nearly empty lower level and parked against the concrete wall with no other cars near us.

"Cora Lynn, what the fuck is going on?" He demanded worriedly as he turned the car off.

I bit my lip as I looked at him and then decided to just go for it. I pulled my dress up quickly, pulled my panties down my legs and off over my heeled sandals, and then turned in my seat. "Fuck me."

His eyes widened as he looked down at my discarded panties and then back to my wild eyes as I reached behind me pulled the zipper of my dress down and pushed the airy sage green fabric down to my hips, revealing my swollen and heavy breasts to the cool air of the car. "What are you doing?" He barked, looking around the garage madly as I bared myself to him.

I spread my legs and slid my fingers against my swollen clit and moaned as I pinched one of my nipples, leaning back into the seat as he watched. "Take your cock out right now, Maverick Jones, and let me ride it or I'm going to get out of this car and find someone that will."

"Jesus fuck." He cursed but his jeans were straining to hold back his large erection as he watched me playing with my pussy in his front seat. A few seconds later he tore at the snap of his jeans and leaned his seat back all the way, giving me space to crawl across the center console and into his lap. "Fuck, Cora." He groaned when I fisted his cock and settled my legs on each side of his as my heavy breasts swung in his face.

He grabbed two big handfuls of them and looked down between our bodies where I coated the head of his cock with my wetness before sinking on it in one fast thrust.

"Maverick." I moaned and dug my nails into his shoulders as I rocked forward. His hands tightened on my breasts before dropping to my hips as he rolled his hips under me and rubbed my clit with his pelvic bone. He slid me back and forth on his lap, giving me incredible pleasure.

But none of the pain I craved.

"Mav, please," I begged, lifting myself and slamming down on his lap. "I need more."

"Easy, Cora." He hissed between clenched teeth as he rocked again.

"No." I cried, desperate and coming unhinged with my need. I slid my hand from his shoulder to his neck and squeezed my small hand over the wide muscles of his throat, forcing his head back into the seat so he had to look at me. His nostrils flared as his lips pulled back slightly to bare his teeth as he fought to remain in control. "I need you to fuck me like you did the other day in your office, Mav. Like you did when you took my ass the other night." I squeezed his throat slightly and slammed myself back down on his cock. "I want it raw; I want it to hurt," I begged.

"I can't." He growled, barely containing himself. He closed his eyes as I continued to ride him hard, and his hands dug into the thick flesh of my hips.

"Please!" I begged, tears springing to my eyes as I became manic, watching the perfect man in front of me battle himself for me. "I love you Mav. I trust you."

His resolve snapped as he shook my hand off his throat and wrapped his big hand around my neck, squeezing until I could feel the blood pooling in my head making me delirious and ecstatic.

"Yes." I groaned. "Fuck yes, Mav." He raised his hips up into me, impaling me on his cock punishingly over and over as he held me still, forcing me to take what he gave to me.

"This what you need?" He asked through clenched teeth, pinching my nipple, and leaning down to bite it and suck on it powerfully.

"Yes!" I screamed, feeling my orgasm crest over my spine and it sent delicious shivers down my limbs as he fucked me savagely. "Don't stop, just like that."

"Take it, baby." He growled. "Take my fucking cock, Angel. Come for me."

I came over and over again, letting it roll over my entire body as he kept fucking his cock up into my pussy, slamming his pelvis against my clit with each punishing thrust. I sagged into his arms as my body shook with fatigue after I finally found the release and pleasure I'd been so needy of all day.

"My turn." He hissed into my ear and opened the car door, jarring me out of my inebriated sense of bliss.

"What –" I started, but he just pulled my dress up over my breasts and stood from the car with me still wrapped in his arms as he kicked the door shut and walked to the hood. "Mav?" I gasped, looking around the garage, no longer feeling emboldened by my carnal lust after my earth-shattering orgasms.

He dropped me to my feet and turned me around to face the hood of the car, pushing a large hand between my shoulders and laying my chest against the warm hood. He tossed my skirt up over my hips and kicked my feet apart, spreading my legs before slamming his cock back into my body, pushing the air from my lungs as I took it.

"Fuck, yes." He growled, grabbing two large fistfuls of my hips and crashing into my body as he fucked me. I moaned at the sensation of being fucked openly in public on the hood of his car as he animalistically took me, exactly how I had begged him to. "You are mine." He bit out between clenched teeth before bringing his large hand down on the apple of my ass cheek painfully, eliciting a scream from my lips to echo the smack through the concrete garage.

"Yes." I hissed, pushing back into his body, begging for more. "Again."

He spanked me over and over again as he fucked me, and I pleaded for mercy and more at the same time.

"Take my fucking cock like the perfect little minx that you are, Angel." He leaned over my body, pressing my chest into the hood, and snaked his hand around the front of my throat to hold me still as he pumped into me.

"I'm coming." I gasped, clawing at the hood for purchase to push back against him more as the luscious waves of pleasure destroyed me.

"Good girl." He growled and then I felt his cock twitch inside of my tightened pussy as his orgasm ripped from his body with a roar from his lips. "Such a good fucking girl."

"Oh, my God." I gasped, fighting to catch my breath as my orgasm faded and I came back down to earth. Mav chuckled behind me, leaning over, and pressing kisses against my neck and shoulders briefly before pulling out of me and pulling my dress back down to cover my bare ass, tucking himself back into his jeans. "Did you just fuck me on the hood of your car?" I asked, turning around, and leaning into his waiting arms.

"Like a crazed maniac." He affirmed and chuckled into my hair as he pulled me over to my car door and helped me get back in before walking around to his side and climbing in. When we shut the doors and encapsulated ourselves back into the safety of our car, he turned to me with a pensive look on his face. "What was that about?" I looked down at my hands in my lap and took a deep breath, trying to decide what to say to him when he reached over and tilted my chin up with his finger, making me look into his eyes. "Talk to me, darling. Please." He pleaded, closing his eyes and expressing his need.

My lips moved before I even figured out how I wanted to answer him because his need called to me, "You've been treating me like you did after the boathouse again."

His brows dropped over his eyes as they flickered over my face, confused. "We've had sex nonstop since that conversation." He started, not understanding what I meant.

"And you haven't so much as held me tightly any of those times, though."

His shoulders deflated and his fingers fell from my chin to weave through mine in my lap, but he didn't respond.

"I don't want you to lessen yourself for me." I tried gently.

"I don't want to be too much for you either." He said instantly, in pain.

"Does it look like I can't take it?" I implored, waving my hand towards the hood, and he glared at me in frustration, so I gentled my voice and leaned towards him. "I like that side of you Mav, I always have. And when you hold back from me, I feel like you're hiding from me, and it leaves me feeling..." I scowled trying to figure out how to portray the feeling, "Empty. And alone." Pain washed over his face as he watched me intently. "I've spent ten years feeling empty and alone without you Mav. Don't make me feel that way when you're buried inside of me too." I begged.

"Cora." He gasped, closing the distance, and crushing his lips against mine. The kiss was anything but gentle or pretty, it was carnal and animalistic as he let himself show me how he was feeling, and I felt the tendrils of familiarity in the kiss from years past. "I'm so sorry."

I shook my head against his and kissed him again, "Don't ever kiss me any other way than how you just did Mav. Never again." I smiled, and I felt the whisper of a sigh from his lips as he came to terms with the internal battles raging on inside of his head.

"I don't want to mess this up again, Angel."

"I don't want to live half of a life either Mav. We've already done that. I want you, desperately. I need you. Every single part of you, every single second. Please don't hide from me."

"Okay." He said softly, breathing me in and nuzzling his nose into the skin behind my ear. "I love you Cora Lynn Valentine. I can't wait to make you my wife and make up for all this lost time exactly how you deserve."

"I love you, Mav. You're the only thing I've ever longed for without fail." I kissed him again and held onto him until we couldn't deny that we were officially late any longer. "We should go." I sighed and leaned back into my seat as he reached around me and buckled my seat belt for me in a way that just screamed *Mav*.

When he pulled back out onto the street and headed back towards our destination of Jones' Mansion, there was a calmness and comfort in the air between us that had been missing the last few days.

"Are you excited?" He asked, pulling through the impressive new front gate at his parent's estate as he held my hand in my lap.

I squeezed it and smiled at him as I bit my lip. "It feels like a mix of Christmas morning and going to a dentist appointment." I answered truthfully, as a laugh rolled out of his chest.

"Explain." He implored.

"I'm so happy and excited to see them, I've missed them both so much. That's the Christmas morning part." I said and took a deep calming breath as he put the car in park outside of the garage.

"And the dentist appointment part?" He turned in his seat towards me and gave me his full attention.

"Apprehension that I'm not enough anymore." I answered honestly. "That too much has happened, and it will never be the same with them."

He leaned forward and kissed my cheek, calming me with his touch. "There's only one way to find out how it feels to be back in our family, Cora." He said and pulled back, pushing a stray lock of hair behind my ear.

"I know." I turned and looked at the front door apprehensively before turning back to him. "Don't leave me alone until I tell you that I'm okay?" I asked, and his eyes softened even more at my request.

"Promise." He agreed whole heartedly.

"Okay." I said and nodded my head, watching as he climbed out of the car and walked around to my side, opening the door, and holding his hand out for me to take. We walked up the front steps and Mav opened the door, letting us in and I was catapulted back in time. Mav's childhood home had always felt more comforting to me than my own and walking in the front door again after so many years, felt like coming home for the first time in a decade. "I love you." I whispered to him as he squeezed my hand, watching my reactions and body language closely.

"Maverick?" His dad's voice rang out from the den at the back of the house, "Is that you?"

"Yeah Dad, we're here." Mav called out and pulled me into his side as we walked into the heart of the home.

"My God." Marsha gasped as she came running from the kitchen towards us walking down the hallway. She covered her mouth and stared at us with love in her eyes as she embraced me, pulling me from Mav's arms affectionately and hugging me tightly. She hadn't aged a day in ten years and yet somehow managed to look more elegant and timeless with her dark brown hair and warm brown eyes that were watery when she finally pulled back and ran her hands down both of my arms. "Cora dear," She said wistfully and shook her head. "We've missed you so much."

"I missed you both terribly as well." I said, as she pulled me into another hug. Christopher, Mav's dad lingered back and let Marsha fawn over me for a moment before stepping forward and pulling his wife back to hug me himself.

"You look incredible Cora; our son is a lucky man." Christopher said affectionately as he stepped back and Mav pulled me back into his arms, smiling down at me.

"I'm a very lucky bastard indeed." He said as I rolled my eyes at him. We followed his parents into the kitchen where Marsha was making her signature sangria and we all feel into a comfortable conversation and visit, like it hadn't been ten years since the last time we did this. When their chef announced that lunch was ready out on the patio, we all headed out to the beautiful oasis and settled around the table with an incredible spread laid out.

"You went way above and beyond with this lunch, Marsha." I said as Maverick passed me a tray with three different kinds of sandwiches on it, with three matching salads to pair them with."

"I know." She blushed, "It's not every day your daughter comes back home, though." She said, placing her hand on mine and squeezing it gently. Tears pricked the back of my eyes as she looked at me kindly. "I mean it when I say we've missed you so much over the years. And we have missed who our son was before you left, too. It feels like we're finally getting you both back."

I looked over at Mav where he sat back in his chair, letting his fingers play over the short whiskers of his short beard, and he smiled at me. "It's true. I've been... less than bearable at times." He admitted, and his dad scoffed.

"That's one way of putting it." Christopher joked as he took a large bite of his bacon club, before Marsha reached over and swatted his arm lovingly.

"How do you mean?" I asked Maverick, wanting to know more about the time we spent apart.

He laughed lightly and took a drink of his beer before answering. "Well, I've spent so much time working and building up my company that I've been absent from important moments in life. Like if I ignored them, they wouldn't pass without my two most favorite people in them."

I leaned over towards him, and he closed the distance, kissing my lips firmly and breathing me in before pulling back.

"I miss Luke too." I said, feeling the sadness of his absence filling the space.

"I can't believe it's been ten years this month." Marsha said, with a faraway look in her eye.

"Some days, it feels like yesterday, and then other days it feels like it's been a lifetime since I hugged him last." Christopher added.

"How is the fundraiser going Mom?" Maverick inquired.

"Beautifully. Other than last minute details, it's all ready." She said and the sadness passed from her eyes as she winked at Maverick, "It's set to be the event of the decade since people will be meeting the newest Mrs. Jones for the first time in public that night."

"I can't wait." Mav said, looking adoringly at me and I melted.

"Okay! Enough sappiness, I'm not used to this side of you." I said jokingly as I took a long sip of sangria to distract my heart from the butterflies swarming around.

"Have you two set any plans for the ceremony?" Christopher asked and Mav sat forward in his seat, ready to dive into details. It was such an out of body experience to see him in full business mode, especially when he was talking about our wedding or future.

It was... downright sensual.

I took another sip of sangria as I tried desperately to control my hormones; they had been running wild since our reconnection and I was near falling into a manic episode of need in front of his parents.

"We talked all day yesterday setting plans in motion." Mav said, "We're going to do it at my place in South Hampton next Saturday night. It's only going to be you two and a few friends. After the small dinner, we're going to kick you all out and continue trying to make some little Jones' so you two will stop hounding me for grandchildren."

I choked on my wine and sputtered as I tried to recover with wide eyes. Marsha and Christopher both laughed and smirked knowingly as I fought to get over the shock. "Mav." I warned. "That's not exactly dinner table conversation."

He laughed and shrugged his shoulders. "It's not something I'm trying to keep secret either, though."

I rolled my eyes at him as Marsha took pity on me and distracted me with talk about my wedding dress and flowers and such while Christopher preoccupied Mav with business. After a while I noticed a change in Mavericks demeanor from next to me and turned towards him to listen to what Christopher was saying in low tones.

"- Have Dexter get the paperwork ready for the take over and I'll get the PR team ready to release a statement by tomorrow afternoon."

"Take over?" I asked, politely cutting Marsha off as I shifted gears. Both Jones men looked over at me with their dark eyes, and I recognized the matching intensity in them. "What are you taking over?"

"Your brother's last-ditch effort to save his finances was on a new development plot of land set to make him hundreds of millions after the first five years." Maverick said plainly and I felt my eyebrows raise to my hair line. "I think he got wind that I wasn't going to go in on the deal with him to fund it, so he went and found another investor behind my back." I could sense the barely restrained rage in his voice even though he looked at ease as he spoke.

"So, how are you stopping him from getting the land?" I asked.

"I'm buying the company that is selling it for more than it's worth and steamrolling him right out of the deal. I'll be keeping the land and developing it myself."

"That doesn't sound like a good business deal if you're paying more than you'll gain." I speculated. "Don't make bad business decisions based on emotions, Maverick."

"I am buying the company for more than it's worth, but under my direction, I'll be able to develop and sell it for far more than he would have. Reid put together a plan to gross over a billion off the project in a five-year term."

My lips parted as I clutched my wine glass. "Oh."

My future husband smirked and winked at me. "Don't worry about my desire to destroy your family Cora, we're still going to make a pretty fucking penny off them to do it."

"Interesting." I mused and let that mull over in my head. "And you're executing it tomorrow?"

Christopher nodded, "The sale should be completed by noon tomorrow."

"And what do you expect Jake to do when he finds out about the loss of hundreds of millions in this deal?"

"I expect him to come to my office in a rage. So you'll be tucked away safe all day at least." He said so deadpanned as I scowled at him.

"You're going to let him in the building, knowing he's irate and unhinged?" I gasped.

"I want to see the look in his eyes as he realizes he's fucked."

"For your revenge?"

"For our revenge." He said.

I didn't reply, and I felt his parents' eyes on us as I processed everything.

"He will be safe, Cora." Marsha said softly, knowing without me even replying what was bothering me about it all. I gave her a small smile and pushed my food around on my plate, suddenly not hungry as Maverick and Christopher went back to making plans.

We spent the rest of the day with his parents, and after a few more glasses of sangria, I was able to relax and not stress about the impending explosion of my brother's brain in less than twenty-four hours.

By the time we left, it was well into the evening and nearing dusk. Maverick held my hand in my lap as he drove us back through the city towards his penthouse, but there was an edge to the air in the car.

"Talk to me." His voice rumbled across the space as I looked out the window. "Tell me what I did wrong."

I smiled softly at his openness and squeezed his hand. "I just worry about you."

"You think your brother is going to do something to harm me?" He scoffed.

I shrugged my shoulders, "My father has taught him everything he knows, and look what my father has done over the years to us."

He contemplated that for a minute before pulling his car into the garage of his building and helping me out. When I stood up, he pulled me into his arms and kissed me deeply, and when he pulled back I could see the softness in his eyes as he looked at me. "I'll make sure I'm safe, Cora."

"How?"

"I'll have security as well as Reid and Dexter in with me."

"And me?" I asked.

His eyes crinkled in confusion, "What do you mean? You'll be safe at Halo, just like the other day."

"You think I'll be able to do anything constructive knowing he's in the building, Mav?"

"What can I do to help you?" He asked genuinely, wanting to take the worry off my shoulders.

I leaned into his embrace further and looked him straight in the eye. "You can walk away from all the elaborate plans and scheming to destroy them. Just... live in the here and now with me."

"I can't do that, baby." He said with sincerity as he shook his head. "That's not how my brain works. I follow a code of honor, Cora, and they've destroyed that."

"So you'll destroy them."

"Yes." He said instantly, and I knew he wasn't moving on this topic.

I leaned up and kissed him, letting him deepen it as I clung to him before pulling back to look at him. "Then I guess distract me as best you can for the time being until this is all in the past."

A wicked gleam glinted in his eye as a predatory smile pulled his lips up, baring his perfect white teeth.

"Be careful what you ask for, Angel." He purred, "I'll claim your body to numb your mind anytime you need me to."

"Then claim me, Maverick." I begged.

And he spent the entire night doing just that.

Chapter 15 – Maverick

"Sir." Veronica's voice rang out through the intercom on my desk, "Dennis and Jake Valentine are at security downstairs, they're on their way up."

I sat back in my chair, running my fingers over my lips as I smiled like the fucking cat that ate the canary.

"You know what to do." I responded and then picked up my phone. The press release about the purchase of the development company being bought out by Jones Holding went out one hour ago. And it had ruffled enough feathers, my future father-in-law was joining his son to air his grievances with me.

I dialed Cora's number and her sweet breathy voice answered on the second ring. "Mr. Peterson's office."

"Darling," I growled, my body's reaction to her was almost instant.

"Well, hello." She purred back, and I leaned back in my chair.

"Your father and brother are on their way up to my office," I said firmly, hating the way the conversation turned from seductive to businesslike so quickly, but I didn't have much time to warn her.

"My father?" She gasped, and I could hear the fear in her voice.

"Nothing changed, baby. Just stay at Halo and I'll let you know when I throw them out on their asses."

"Why is my father here though? I thought he wasn't in on the deal?" She rapid-fired.

"He's probably just coming to try to convince me to keep Jake in on the deal, baby, he's a sniveling man on a good day, and today is not a good day for either of them. Don't worry."

"That's easy for you to say." She sighed. "Nat wanted to go out to eat for lunch, should I stay here instead?"

I looked at my watch, it was ten minutes to twelve, which meant she'd be leaving for lunch in a few and would be back long after Jake and Dennis were gone. "No, go out and have a nice lunch. If I haven't called you by the time you return, have Parker in security escort you two up to Halo, his security badge will override the elevator so no one else can stop the car on the way up or down."

"Okay." She said, but I still heard the trepidation in her voice.

"Everything will be fine darling, I promise you," I said as Reid and Dexter walked into my office, having gotten the S.O.S. call from Veronica moments ago. "I love you; I'll call you soon."

"I love you too, Maverick. More than I ever thought was possible." She replied and then hung up, leaving me reeling for a moment before my ruthless asshole persona slid into place as I dropped the phone into the receiver.

"That was fast," Reid said, walking over and helping himself to a glass of bourbon as Dexter leaned his back against the windowsill next to me, standing guard.

These two were my very best friends, second to Cora, and I had never paid attention to just how ready to rally they always were until recently. Their loyalty was unwavering.

"My future father-in-law is with him too," I answered.

Dexter's eyebrows rose as he pushed a hand through his blond hair. "Interesting." He was always a man of few words, something I never minded before, but now I wished I knew what he was thinking. But I'd have to wait until later to pick his brain because Dennis and Jake were stepping off the elevator, and one look at Jake's face said he was on a very short fuse.

"Oh, this is going to be fun," Reid smirked as he drained his glass, readying for battle.

Veronica opened my office door and let the two men in, who walked straight towards my desk as I stood up, buttoning my jacket. Jake was red in the face and clearly irate. He was two years older than Cora and me but had aged terribly and looked worn out on life already. No doubt thanks to his money-leaking wife. Dennis looked a bit more composed, but I could see the flare of superiority in his eyes as he made pleasantries.

"Maverick," Dennis said, reaching forward with his hand out for me to shake but Jake stepped forward and laid his fists on my desk angrily, interrupting any fake conversation Dennis hoped to have.

"What the fuck do you think you're doing?" Jake snapped, "I came to you to be an investor, and then you go and undermine me and steal the whole fucking thing out of my hands! I had a confirmed deal in place with the developer! Plans were already drawn up to start breaking ground!"

I raised my eyebrow at him challengingly and sat back down in my chair as Dexter still stood beside me and Reid stood at the window on my other side. "Plans to create small-minded, subsidiary properties that would tank the value of the entire neighborhood and fizzle out to nothing before you even started painting the exterior of the buildings." I debated.

"That wasn't your place to care!" Jake bellowed.

"It was my money you were trying to spend to do it." I snapped back. "Before you rolled over and went and found another investor, without even a courtesy call to me to tell me of the change in plans."

Jake clenched his teeth, unaware that I knew he'd procured other funds for his doomed endeavor. Insert daddy dearest to clean up his son's mess, though.

"Mav, Jake just got ahead of himself here. You remember how it was with your first real chance at a big payday. You didn't seem sold on it, so he wanted to pad a few more leads in case you decided against it. But it's not too late." He said, shrugging his shoulders like this was the most easy-going natural conversation in the world. When in fact the urge to not leap across my desk and strangle the son of a bitch that deserted Cora at eighteen was nearly more than I could handle. "Now that you are the primary owner of the development company, you can split a deal with Jake, take his already drawn-up plans make both of you some cash and just build a business relationship together as you go." He clapped his hands together like that was a done deal.

I looked from him to Jake, who began pacing around my office with his hands on his hips, and I raised an eyebrow at my future father-in-law. "Not interested."

Both of them stopped moving and stared me down in shock.

"What?" Dennis asked, laughing humorously as he shook his head like he somehow didn't understand what I'd said.

"What do you mean?" Jake snapped, starting to come unhinged.

"I'm not interested in going into business with you, Jake. Your plans don't meet my standards of class or revenue, therefore I'm going to build to suit myself and I'm vested to make far more money on the deal."

"Are you fucking kidding me!" Jake roared, jumping towards me, only to be caught by his lanky father just before he really regretted his entire life. I stood up slowly from my desk, as Dexter and Reid stepped forward to flank me as I eyed the two I was going to enjoy ruining the most out of the Valentine line.

"Let me make something explicitly clear to you both," I said, buttoning my suit jacket and leaning forward, the air of power surrounding me. "This is my empire you're standing in." Dennis' eyes squinted in challenge, the first sign of anger he allowed to show. "Jake came to me for help because everyone in this city knows he's forlorn in business sense, and that his gold-digging wife has bled him dry," I growled. "No one else will touch you or any deal you try to swing with a ten-foot pole because you're bad business." I stood back up pulled my jacket taught over my chest and licked my lips. "The only reason you're still standing and not flat on your back with a rearranged face is because of the relationship you built with my father, Dennis. But you have successfully drained that tit dry as well. You won't get another cent from my family as long as my bloodline runs this corporation, which let me assure you, is quickly growing to be a very long line." I tipped my hand and Dennis' eyes flared as he caught my intent. "Now respectfully, get the fuck out of my office before I slap your disgraced face all over page six with footage of you on your asses on the sidewalk outside."

Just then, right on cue, Parker and his security team walked in and stood dauntingly behind them ready to do just what I threatened.

"You're making a mistake boy," Dennis said, standing to his full height like he was going to intimidate me even though I physically towered over him in height and weight.

"Your mistake was thinking you brought any value to my business and that it was going to cushion your ride to my money." I nodded to security, and they stepped forward, indicating this meeting was over.

They left in a flare of curses and veiled threats but within minutes the lobby to my office was empty and quiet as the three of us stood silently, absorbing it all.

"Well, that went exactly like I had expected." Dexter deadpanned and pulled his phone from his pocket, scrolling through his email.

"Thanks for being here for it," I said, nodding to first him and then to Reid.

"Wouldn't dream of missing out on all the fun." Reid joked and swallowed down the rest of his liquor. "So your bloodline is growing, huh?" He asked with a mischievous grin on his face, which was enough to get Dexter out of his phone as I sat on the hook. "Does Cora know she's going to be a stepmom?"

"Fuck off," I grunted and grabbed the glass from his fingers and set it in the sink to be washed and grabbed one of my own. "What are you two doing this Saturday night?" I asked as I poured myself three fingers of my favorite bourbon and prepared myself for their inquisition.

"Preferably a brunette or two," Reid answered instantly without a drop of humor in his voice.

Dexter rolled his eyes at our friend's man-whore ways, something we'd all tried to force him to grow out of but were grossly unsuccessful. "I'm free." He said, pocketing his phone and putting his hands in his slacks, "What's on the agenda?"

"My wedding," I replied, tossing back half of my drink as they stared back, waiting for the punch line.

When they didn't get it, Reid stuttered, "Wait, seriously?"

"Seriously. I put my ring on Cora's finger, and we have scheduled the wedding for this Saturday at Ivy House"

"Wait, what?" Reid said, shaking his head again as his bachelor brain tried to process my words.

Dexter got a shit-eating grin on his face and stepped forward, shaking my hand, and pulling me into an aggressive man hug, slapping my back and congratulating me. "No fucking shit man, congrats!" He praised genuinely. "That's the best idea you've ever had."

I laughed and pushed him off of me and leveled my finger at him, "I'm tempted to agree with you if I wasn't sure you were trying to be an asshole about it in return."

He tilted his head back and laughed a full genuine laugh and I was struck by the fact that I didn't know the last time I'd seen Dexter Chase sincerely happy and laughing openly like this. It felt good to see one of my longest friends let the tension out of his shoulders for a moment. "I'm happy for you both. She seems amazing. Hell, the way she handled Sue at Pandora's Patio the other night, she's a force to be reckoned with. The perfect match for you."

"Wait!" Reid snapped out of his shock and waved his hands around wildly. "Married?" He asked, "You? How? Why?" His brain misfired.

"Well, Reid, when a man loves a woman..." Dexter joked, and Reid punched him in the arm before putting both hands on my shoulders.

"Are you sure?" He asked, "I mean you've only had her back for a... a fucking week." He shook his head again. "Don't you think it's rushing it? You don't even know her anymore. What if she's only interested in –"

"Watch it," I commanded in a voice I only used for my most serious business deals.

"I don't mean anything bad by it Mav, I like Cora. You know that. I just... married? This week?"

"And hopefully expecting a week or two after that," I affirmed.

"Jesus fuck." Reid gasped and clutched his chest dramatically.

Dexter snorted, "Careful Mav, you're liable to make his head pop clear off his shoulders at the mere thought of his bachelor buddy Maverick Jones becoming domesticated." I watched him as he joked with Reid but caught the way he spun his wedding ring with his thumb as he laughed and my heart wondered what he genuinely thought about the idea of me getting married, considering his own relationship status.

"I just... damn," Reid said and walked back over to the liquor cabinet and poured a full glass, slamming it back before pouring another one.

"I get it," I said, putting my hand on his shoulder. "I don't expect you to understand, and I get why it sounds abrupt to you, but that's only because you didn't know us together before. If you did, you wouldn't even blink about this."

"What do your parents think about it?" Dexter asked.

"They're fucking ecstatic. We were there yesterday, and it was like not a drop-in time passed between the three of them. They always loved her more than they loved me or Luke anyway because she never gave them any gray hair. She kept us out of trouble for the most part so they're over the moon to have her back."

"Good man, I'm glad. And count me in, I'll be there." He said, once again putting his hand out for me to shake and then nodding to Reid. "Jump on board, or he'll leave your ass behind for her. She's far prettier than you are, my man." He joked. Reid flipped him off and drank more. "Well, I'd love to stay and chat with you two girls about flower choices and dress colors, but I have work to do." With that he walked out, calling over his shoulder as he went. "Being the obvious choice for best man, I'll make sure your bachelor party is all set for Friday night, so make sure you're ready."

As soon as he was out my office door Reid turned on me with a scandalized look on his face, "He is not your best man! No fucking way! Over my dead fucking body." He roared.

I rolled my eyes and walked back to my desk. "I'm not having a best man, and I'm not having a bachelor party either."

"Blasphemy!" He scoffed. "If you're getting hitched, you're getting straight drunk the night before, it's my right!"

"Your right?" I laughed and sat down, grabbing my phone. "I didn't realize you were a part of this wedding."

"There won't be a wedding if I don't get to throw you a party first."

"Excuse me?" I laughed again, enjoying this obnoxious banter with my best friend. "Get out of my office so I can call Cora and tell her that her brother and dad are gone, and she doesn't have to hide anymore."

He turned around and huffed his way out towards the elevators. "Don't bother, I'm going down to talk to the bride right now. I'll tell her."

"Reid!" I warned, but he was already punching the button to the elevator and filliped me off again.

"Married." He scoffed to himself, drawing a peculiar look from Veronica as she looked back into my office, catching my stare before dropping hers back down to her desk as I hit the button to close my door.

I dialed Cora's number as I contemplated silently on what to do about Veronica as my Fiancé answered her cell phone on the second ring.

"Hello, handsome." She hummed and I growled.

"Come up to my office. I'm ravenous for you." I said in place of a greeting.

She chuckled and I heard the noise from the street around her as she said something to someone. "I can't. I'm out to lunch, asking Nat if she'll hold my wedding dress so I can pee Saturday night. It's quite a task for a new friend but I think she's up to it."

I leaned back in my seat and imagined her perfect face smiling as she talked to me. "I'll hold it for you." I offered.

"Not a chance."

"Why not? I've watched you pee before."

"Oh, I know. But then you'd get to see my special wedding night lingerie if you looked under my skirt, and we both know you'd peek given the chance."

"Special wedding night lingerie?" I asked, reaching down to palm my growing erection. "Do tell me more."

"Nope, I can't." She said cheekily, "It's a surprise. One I'm on my way to shop for as we speak so I have to let you go. Enjoy your less-than-fulfilling lunch and think of me. I'll see you after work." I heard Nat cackling next to her and imagined them walking down the street of New York City happy and joking and it warmed my heart, knowing not only did she have something worth laughing about, but that she had someone to do it with after spending so much of her life alone these last years.

"Fine. But I'm eating that delicious pussy on the car ride home tonight." I growled and she gasped. "Oh and by the way, Reid is on the hunt for you. He's appalled that I don't want a bachelor party and he thinks he gets to take it up with you."

"Oh great." She deadpanned and laughed. "Thanks for the heads up."

"I love you, Cora."

"I love you more, Mav."

I hung the phone up and couldn't wipe off the stupid grin on my face from feeling so overwhelmed with joy. But I forced myself to get my head back in the game and focus on destroying a handful of companies that funded the Valentine household and the joy spread through my system, but it was laced with something darker.

Something that felt a lot like revenge.

And boy was it fucking sweet.

Chapter 16 – Cora

"I can't believe you're getting married," Nat said as we walked down the busy sidewalk towards a store she was all but dragging me to. "You're living my biggest fantasy and I'm stuck watching from the sidelines." She fake pouted, but I knew better than to think for even one second she wanted anything to do with marriage.

"You just want the wild and crazy sex that comes with finding your soulmate." I teased and she shrugged her shoulders.

"Well, yeah." She snorted and pulled me along with her arm through mine. "Let's go get you something super sexy to shock him senseless for Saturday night."

She stopped at the front door of an incredibly high-end lingerie and dress shop that I wouldn't have even been able to think about affording two weeks ago, but today, with Mavericks platinum card in my purse, I contemplated it.

But only for a minute.

"I don't need to spend that kind of money to wow him," I said, nodding to the sexy-as-hell white set on a mannequin in the store.

"Need and want are two words you don't have to keep mutually exclusive anymore, Cora. Live it up a little." She bumped her hip against mine and opened the heavy glass door.

Maverick had insisted I take his credit card that had literally no limit on it while I waited for my own cards to be replaced from my mugging last week. Even though we carpooled to work and back every day, he didn't want me caught out on my own without access to money. And he had insisted that I use it leisurely as was my 'right' now as his future wife.

But it all still made me feel... icky. I'd never needed his money when we were growing up because I had my own from my own parents, who were all too happy to throw cash at me to keep up with the Joneses'.

Literally.

But as we walked into the shop, I felt out of place instantly. This place was exactly the kind of place my mother would shop and was exactly the kind of place I would have shopped at as Maverick's wife all this time, but I hadn't gotten that chance. And now, looking around at dresses that cost more than three months of rent at my apartment, I had trouble stomaching it.

My life had turned out differently than I'd planned, and it left me with a different mindset about all of this.

The women working at the counter wore clothes worth more than the ones I was wearing, and they were the nice ones that Maverick had bought me the other night with the personal shopper. Their eyes traveled up and down me and Nat as she walked around the store oblivious to the condemning stares of the employees and other shoppers. She flicked through various dresses and accessories as we worked deeper into the store towards the lingerie in the back.

"Nat, let's get out of here," I said quietly, trying to pull her attention from the satin and lace that she had her sights set on.

"Not a chance. We have twenty minutes before we need to head back from lunch, and we are going to find something to make that sexy man of yours drool."

A woman was standing a few feet away from us and I felt her eyes flick up and down my outfit before traveling over to where Nat stood wearing a black fitted Gucci dress, but it screamed knock off, even to me. And I'd been out of the game for far longer than this woman clearly had been.

"Ooh, look at this one," Nat said, pulling a baby pink set off a rack and holding it up to me. It was a plunging push-up bra with a harness-style strappy attachment that went from the neck like a collar, down past the bra and hooked to the panties and garter belt with rose gold accents.

It was incredibly beautiful, and I reached out to run my fingers over the fabric of it longingly.

"It will look divine on you with your flared hips and big knockers," Nat said, putting it over her arm as she walked around the display to look at something else.

The woman who had been standing a few feet away was even closer now and scoffed at Nat's lack of tact in describing my body and I glared at her. Suddenly feeling protective of my new friend against women who felt superior to everyone else based solely on their husband's bank accounts. I'd grown up around women like her, and I hated seeing my mother treat people like that regularly.

The woman was probably in her mid-thirties and wore her hair in a severe bun on the back of her head in a way most unflattering, but I knew without a doubt she did that because it accentuated her professionally sculpted cheekbones highlighted with filler. She wore a red fitted dress paired with gold jewelry and red bottom heels, but she looked overdone for a mid-day shopping trip.

If I had to guess, she was trying to seem better off than she was. At least that's what my spidey senses were trying to tell me, but they'd sat dormant for so long I could be a bit rusty.

"Here," Nat said, pulling my attention back to where she stood a dozen racks away with an arm full of options. "Go try these on." She pushed them towards me when I got close.

"These are way too many, I don't have the time," I said, scoffing at the half a dozen complicated sets in her hands.

"You're right." She paused, looking down at her options. "This one." She said surely, handing me the baby pink one and pushing me towards the dressing room. "Go on, but let me see before you take it off."

I ran into the curtained dressing room and started getting undressed out of my simple navy blue pants and white sailing top. I was just adjusting the straps of the bra harness when her phone rang, and I listened to her have a quick and curt conversation with someone on the other end.

"I have to go back." She said, in a voice like it pained her.

"What?" I gasped, half naked and unable to just leave. "Why?"

"Some fire at the office they can't put out without me, are you going to be okay to get back without me?"

"Well yeah," I said, pausing with my hands on my hips as I stood on the other side of the curtain.

"I'm sorry! I want to hear all about how it looks when you get back!"

"Okay, I'll see you in a few," I called back, shaking my head as I started taking off the outfit, knowing only wearing half of it, that it was the one. A few minutes after I was back in my top and walked out of my dressing room to buy my wedding night lingerie.

I walked through the store to cash out, but when I got closer I saw the woman who had been glaring at Nat and I standing at the counter with two female employees and a man who looked like a manager.

My step faltered when the first woman turned and glared at me again, staring down her nose at me.

"That's her." She said, and the employees turned towards me as more condemning glares flew my way.

"She came in with the woman that bolted out of here a few minutes ago." One of the employees said to the man and crossed her arms over her chest.

"Is there a problem?" I asked as trepidation crawled up my spine. The man stepped forward grabbed the pink lingerie out of my hands forcefully and tossed it on the counter.

"Where's the rest of it?" He snapped.

"The rest?" I asked, confused, looking between the four of them as other patrons stared on in morbid curiosity.

"The other items you took into the dressing room with you. Are you wearing them under your clothes?" The man asked as he pushed my hand away from my body where I had my arms crossed over my chest. His hand grazed my breast as he did before he grabbed for the strap of my purse.

"Don't touch me!" I snapped, backing up in shock as he reached forward again and tried to grab my purse.

"Give me the items you stole!" He yelled, attracting the attention of everyone else in the store.

Jesus fuck, it was so embarrassing. Shame and anger burned my face as my skin turned red with mortification.

"I didn't steal anything! I only took the one in the dressing room with me and came out with it two minutes later." He reached for me again, got his hand around the strap of my purse, and yanked it off my arm, ripping the neckline of my shirt with the force. "Hey!" I yelled and fought him for it. "You can't do that!"

"Shut up." He growled. "And riff-raff like you can't come in here and steal shit you have no means to pay for it. You were seen taking multiple sets into the dressing room and only came out with one. Where are the others?" He demanded as he opened my purse and dumped it onto the counter, looking for the mysteriously missing lingerie.

"I didn't take any others in there but that one!" I reached around him and grabbed for my stuff as he shoved me again, but not before I grabbed my phone off the counter as he tossed all of my things around like a size 36 DD bra was going to hide under my lipstick tube.

I opened my phone and hovered over Maverick's phone number for a moment before closing out my contacts dialing the main number for Jones Holding and stepping back as the man tried to grab my phone.

"Jones Holding, how may I direct your call." The head receptionist answered.

"Reid Haskins or Dexter Chase, please, it's urgent." I rushed on, begging that she would believe the urgency.

"One moment, please." There was a brief pause as I backed away again as the man scoffed, shoving my stuff off the counter in disarray.

"Hang up that phone right now!" He demanded, before turning to one of the employees who sneered at me, "Call the police."

The woman who had accused me of stealing crossed her arms over her chest and smirked at me like she was winning the biggest prize in the world as I was threatened with jail time. "Looks like she stole from a knockoff jewelry store too, judging by the size of that rock on her hand." She sneered. I clung to my phone and tried desperately to keep my breathing normal so I didn't fall into a full-blown panic attack.

"Dexter Chase." One of Maverick's best friends and Lawyer answered, and I gasped in relief.

"Dexter it's Cora, I need help."

"Hang that phone up right now!" The manager demanded again.

"Cora? What's going on? Where are you?" Dexter was stressed from the tone in my voice and the bellowing Neanderthal actively trying to rip the phone out of my hand.

"I'm at a store called Penelope Lace. They're accusing me of stealing and the manager keeps assaulting me, he ripped my purse off and threw all of my stuff all over, and now they're calling the police."

"Stay right there," Dexter demanded. "I'll be there in less than five minutes. I'll grab Mav on the way."

"No!" I begged. "He'll lose his damn mind if he comes here right now, Dexter."

"Fuck." He growled. "Okay, four minutes. I'll be right there."

"Thank you," I said right before the manager finally got ahold of my phone and ripped it from my hand, taking my earring with him, ripping open the hole in my ear painfully. "Ow, you son of a bitch! Oh my God!" I yelled before the man ended the call and tossed my phone on the counter with my pile of belongings. "I didn't steal anything!" I clutched at my ear, pulling my hand away to see blood smearing my finger. "Fuck."

"Mrs. Valentine is a very honorable woman and longtime customer here; she wouldn't make up a lie about a nobody like you." He sneered, and the employees nodded in agreement.

"Mrs. Valentine?" I asked, as my blood ran cold in disbelief.

The manager nodded to the woman who had accused me, and I searched her face for something familiar, but I had no idea who she was.

But then it clicked.

The trying to seem better off than she was, and the severe facial features.

"Jake's wife." I accused, and she scoffed at me. "How fitting."

"Do not say my husband's name like you're familiar with him." She cited, looking down her nose at me. "You're pathetic, coming into a place like this when you clearly couldn't afford anything and then having your cheap knockoff friend trying to distract everyone while you tried to steal lingerie like some common criminal."

The front door opened and in walked two uniformed police officers, assessing the scene of chaos in front of them. One was male and one was female, the male shook the hand of the manager and looked at me like he already assumed I was guilty, while the female police officer eyed the manager and Jake's wife speculatively.

"Thank you for coming so quickly." The manager said to the officers. "She called someone before I could get her phone from her." He said nodding to where my belongings lay. "She was seen taking multiple pieces of high-end lingerie into the dressing room and came out to pay for only one. I believe she's wearing them under her clothes."

"Ma'am, I'm going to need to see your ID." The male officer said, reaching over and digging through my things on the counter.

"I don't have one," I said bitterly. "It was stolen last week."

He cocked his head to look at me and then pursed his lips, "Convenient. I don't see a wallet here, how were you planning on paying for the items you tried on today if you didn't steal anything?"

"I have a credit card to use."

"Where?" He asked, looking down over my things again.

"In my phone case." And he grabbed my phone, fumbling with it to get the case open. "He assaulted me," I complained, pleading to the woman officer with my eyes to help me while also watching the front door, aching to see the familiar face of Dexter coming to help me. He was a lawyer; he'd know what to do.

"Did you rip her shirt and injure her ear?" The female officer asked the manager with a disapproving glare, stepping closer to see my injury better.

"She fought me when I tried to recover stolen merchandise, it was her fault." The middle-aged man shrugged like it was a ridiculous notion to even think about holding him accountable.

The front door opened, and I looked past the officers to see the two domineering and scary faces of Dexter and Reid as they walked to my side, staring everyone down until they all cowered a bit.

"I don't know about you, but that sounds a hell of a lot like admitting to assault. What do you think Dex? You're the high-paid lawyer." Reid said, and I sagged with relief as he put his arm around my shoulders, turning me to see my ear before handing me the square from his suit jacket to put on it so it would stop dripping down my neck. "What do you think you could get out of a woman beating piece of shit in a civil court case for this kind of injury?" He asked as the others looked on in shock.

They might not know who these men were by name, but they could tell they were important.

"For an average person," Dexter shrugged his shoulders as he slid his hands into his pants pockets, looking at ease even though I could feel the anger swelling inside of him. "A million, maybe two."

The manager scoffed as his eyes bugged out of his head. "Now wait just a minute. She's the thief here! I'm not paying her a dime!"

"That was for an average person." Dexter deadpanned, ignoring him. "But you fucked up because you didn't assault an average person, you decided to physically assault the fiancé of Maverick Jones. Six days before their wedding." He shook his head, kicking his toe across the ground and tsking his teeth. "Maybe you've heard of him, maybe you haven't." He shrugged. "Regardless though, you'll be lucky to be alive after Maverick finds out the love of his life was not only wrongly accused of stealing something he could afford to buy a thousand of every single minute of every single day, but that she was also illegally detained, her belongings were destroyed, and she was physically assaulted." He chuckled humorlessly, "No, you sir are a dead man walking. Mr. Jones will own this company and your entire life before the day is through, I promise you that."

Dexter's voice was cold and calculated in a way that made my spine shiver as I clung to Reid.

"Maverick Jon–." The manager stuttered as he looked at my brother's wife and then to the police and back. "I didn't... No, no, no." He shook his head back and forth. "This was all just a misunderstanding." He looked around wildly as he saw the danger he was in. "Tell them what you told me." He turned to my sister-in-law and demanded she tell her part in everything to save his own ass.

"Ah yes," Reid started, "Let's hear what the lovely Mrs. Valentine has to say about the future wife of the man who just bankrupted her already desolate husband not even thirty minutes ago. That's a credible source." Jake's wife paled at the news. He turned to the police. "We're leaving now. You can come to Hawthorn Tower to get her statement with her fiancé present. Because she will be pressing charges on both the shop and Mrs. Valentine." Then he turned to the shocked, stupid employees. "Put all of her things back in her purse, immediately."

The two women jumped at his order and started putting all of my belongings back in my purse before tentatively handing it to him as he led me past them all toward the door.

"You'll be hearing from me and my client." Dexter left in warning as we walked straight out of the front door and into the waiting SUV at the curb. Franklin closed the door behind us as we settled in the back seat, with me sandwiched between the two men.

When he pulled away from the curb I sank into the seat and held my head in my hands as complete shock vibrated through my system. "Thank you," I whispered before clearing my throat and saying it louder to both of them. "Thank you for coming to help me." I looked at Dexter and then at Reid. "I didn't know what else to do at the moment."

"Why didn't you call Mav?" Reid asked, looking at me curiously. "Why call Dexter?"

I scoffed and shuddered as I thought about how different the outcome would have been if I'd called my future husband during all of that. "He would have burned the world down if I'd called him like that."

Dexter chuckled lightly and shook his head. "He's going to do so much worse regardless when he finds out you didn't call him. But I understand your point."

I groaned and rubbed my temple and then looked down at my shirt. "I can't go into Hawthorn Tower looking like this."

"Don't worry, we've got you covered," Reid said but didn't elaborate as Franklin pulled the car around the back of the building to a service entrance. When we stopped, Nat stood on the loading dock, pacing back and forth with a sweater in her hands.

"Oh my fucking God." She gasped when I got out of the car, pulling me into a hug before turning her attention to Reid, "Tell me you beat the piece of shit that did this."

"Worse, I'm telling Maverick on them." He joked and headed towards the door. "Hurry along now, I'm going to go give him a heads up, but he won't wait long before he chases you down."

"Thank you, again," I said and smiled at him.

"Anytime darling."

I took the sweater from Nat and buttoned it up over my ripped and stained shirt and she pulled a makeup wipe from her pocket and ripped the packet open before cleaning up my neck and ear, which had stopped bleeding so we could check it out. It hadn't ripped the earring out completely, just snagged it and tore it a bit. But I wouldn't lose the piercing completely, which was good considering I was supposed to be getting married in six days and had planned on wearing some sort of earring to the ceremony.

"That's much better," Nat said with a sad look on her face. "Cora... I'm–"

"Stop." I held up my hand silencing her. "This isn't your fault."

"I dragged you there, knowing what kind of people work and shop there."

"Stop, they don't get off the hook because of their finances. They're shit people, period. Believe me, I know." I said.

Dexter nodded and smiled at me kindly, "Let's get you up to Mav before he comes looking for you. Because no one will be safe if he gets past Reid before he sees that you're alright."

I followed Dexter into the building and up the elevator to the top floor, feeling suspiciously like I was riding up to my own execution.

Chapter 17 – Maverick

"**S**ir, your jet is all set for takeoff at two." Veronica said, standing in front of my desk with a pile of files in her arms. "Everything is set for our arrival in Atlanta so it should all run smoothly."

"Thanks," I said, taking the file she held out for me, trying to ignore the way acid burned the back of my throat thinking about being stuck with her alone on a jet for three hours this afternoon.

And stuck with her in numerous meetings over the next twenty-four.

Fuck.

"Let me know if there's anything else you need Sir." She said and then walked out to her own desk.

I had told Cora about my trip Friday night after picking out her ring, and I had told her that Veronica was accompanying me to Atlanta. And I had to give her credit, because she responded better than I thought she would to that news, but it still churned my stomach knowing that she was going to worry about me cheating on her again regardless.

I'd implemented a new rule from here on out to alleviate any of this discomfort in the future.

No Veronica on my trips.

I just had to get through this one, and then I could change up my plans for the next ones.

I heard the elevators ping and looked up to see Reid walking towards me with an agitated look on his face and the hair on the back of my neck stood up. I dropped my pen and stood up, already knowing something was wrong.

"She's okay." He started, raising his hands to get me to settle before I'd even reacted.

"What do you mean?" I ground out through my teeth.

"Angela Valentine was at a shop with Cora and Nat. She accused Cora of stealing and things got... messy." He grimaced, and I erupted.

"Where is she?" I yelled as I walked around him to get down to Halo.

"She's on her way up." He said, blocking my path. "Dexter and Nat are with her."

"Dexter? What the fuck happened?" I roared, trying to piece together information as my brain short-circuited knowing that Cora was upset, and I knew she was upset because I could feel it in my blood.

"The manager got handsy, he shoved her around a bit and her earring got snagged, tearing her piercing open a bit, but other than that, she's fine, I promise."

"Why the fuck are you telling me this and not her!"

"She called Dexter for help."

"Why?" I shoved his hands off my shoulders and paced. "Why the fuck didn't she call me?"

"Because she knew you'd react this way, and she didn't want to cause any more of a scene in public." He said, looking at me uncomfortably. "She's mortified."

"What the fuck was Angela Valentine doing there at the same time? How did she know Cora was linked to me?" I shot out, trying to figure out how news spread that quickly after my meeting with Jake and

Dennis and how the Valentines had gotten the info that Cora and I were together.

"I don't think she did." He said, forcing me to stop walking and look at him. "I don't think Angela knew who she was at all, honestly. I think she's just that much of a vapid bitch that she started drama for the fun of it. But she fucked up because she fucked with you. And Dexter and I made that clear when we took Cora away from there."

"For fuck's sake." I cursed as my hands balled into fists and my skin tightened around my body. I loosened my tie and paced as it felt like my skin was strangling me. I imagined how embarrassed Cora had been. And it was all because of her sister-in-law.

The elevator bay pinged again, and I turned in anxiousness as I watched Cora and Dexter walk out of the car and towards my office. I was on her the second she cleared the doorway, tangling my hands into her honey-blond hair and pulling her into my fierce embrace.

"I'm okay." She said, but her voice broke, and she buried her face in my chest as I looked over her head at Dex and Reid in complete shock as I was, for once, speechless.

I pulled her back and ran my hands over her face, careful of her red and irritated ear, before running them down her arms to hold her hands in mine. "No, you're not," I said, taking in her pale complexion and watery eyes. "And it's all my fault."

"No, it's not." She argued, shaking her head, before laying it against my chest again. "She didn't know who I was, she was just being... a cunt." She said exasperatedly as frustration filled her body. "I was just so... I couldn't do anything. They didn't believe me because I'm a nobody!" She looked up into my eyes as her tears crested over her lashes. "How is it that those kinds of people still have the power to make me feel so insignificant, even after all of these years?" Her heart was breaking in my arms as her insecurities and triggers were being brought to life. "I hate them." She whispered. "I hate every single last one of them."

"I know," I whispered back, kissing her forehead, and holding her as her shoulders shook as I looked back at Dex and Reid. "What are we doing about this?"

Dex's eyes were burning bright with anger, and it struck me that twice in one day I'd seen strong emotions from him for the first time in years. Earlier was humor and mirth, and now was anger and determination. How long had I not noticed that he was just existing in a permanent state of blankness?

"Cora is filing assault and battery charges against the manager and defamation charges against Angela to start with. I'm also going to contact the owner of the store and threaten to wipe them off the face of the Earth for the way they treated her. If they're lucky, I'll let you let them stay open without shutting them down." He said, letting his anger out vocally in a way that was very un-Dexter-like.

Reid watched on in curiosity like me before turning to where I stood, still holding Cora tight in my arms. "I think it's time to reevaluate your plan of waiting to announce to the world that Cora is to be your wife."

"Why?" Cora asked, stepping back and wiping her eyes on the sleeve of her sweater.

"Because I can't stomach to see you like this again," I answered for him. "Twice in two weeks, someone has put their hands on you when I should have been there to protect you. If I can't be there physically, then I need to have the threat of me known to every man on Earth; no one touches you and just gets away with it."

"Mav..." She started, but I wasn't going to let her talk me out of it.

"He's right, Cora," Reid said with the still uncharacteristically serious look on his face. "You're stepping into a whole new world, it's different than it was ten years ago when you both were just kids. People will stop at nothing to get what they want, at least now they'll think twice about it if they know what kind of monsters are standing in your corner to protect you."

"Monsters?" She asked with her brows drawn together and Reid finally smirked at her with a one-sided dimple showing under his five o'clock shadow.

"Yeah, darling." He held his hands up to me and Dexter, "We're your monsters now. Hope you're not afraid of the dark because we're the biggest and baddest out there." He said and winked.

And I knew he was right. My two best friends had proven themselves today to not only me but Cora too. They would stop at nothing for her, just like they would for me. Just like I would in return for them.

"Then I guess it's time to tell the world." She said, with a slight shudder in her spine. I kissed her temple and smiled into her hair.

"I hope you're ready, future Mrs. Jones."

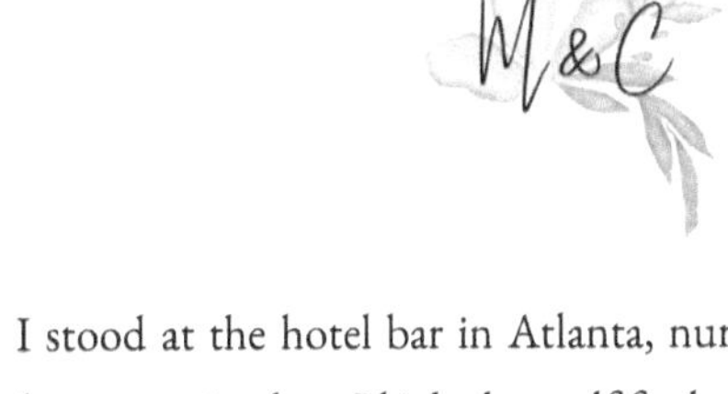

I stood at the hotel bar in Atlanta, nursing a top-shelf bourbon and a sour attitude as I kicked myself for leaving Cora this afternoon. I'd been ready to call off the whole trip after Cora's experience with Angela Valentine, but she had refused to let me stay home. She had contended that my staying home to stare at her was going to do nothing productive and that I needed to stick to my schedule. She hadn't gone back to work after leaving my office at least, instead, Franklin took her back to my penthouse and I'd called down to Jason Vogt, the CEO of Halo, and laid some boundaries down for Cora's employment with them. I owned the majority of the company, and should I get the inkling, I could dismember it from the inside out, so Vogt and Peterson, her direct boss, were going to have to deal with her having flexibility with her schedule until I could convince her to come work up at Jones with me.

But now, countless meetings down and thousands of miles apart from her, I was still barely containing my outrage and unbridled need to go home to her. I was supposed to be leaving for dinner in a few minutes, but my stomach rolled just thinking of eating right now.

God, I was a fucking mess.

"There you are." A seductive voice purred from behind me as a hand slid up my shoulder and I inwardly groaned, knowing this evening was not going to end well. I raised an eyebrow as Veronica slid up next to me at the bar, smiling a come-hither smile at me as the bartender stopped to get her order.

I slammed the rest of my bourbon and signaled for another before he walked away as I took my phone out of my pocket. "Veronica." I greeted her but tried to pay her no more attention than that.

Because she was crossing a dangerous fucking line dressed the way she was. She styled her red hair in a sleek updo and applied dark and sultry makeup to match the red satin dress she was wearing.

Well, *dress* was a stretch, to be honest.

It was a fucking piece of lingerie and acid burned the back of my throat again for the millionth time lately because I knew exactly what her intent was.

And I knew what the outcome was going to be.

And I was going to pay fucking dearly for it.

"Are you ready to go to dinner? My mouth is positively salivating, thinking about their Chesapeake Bay Chicken and that cranberry martini you turned me onto the last time we were here." Her voice was pure velvet, and I tried but failed to suppress the urge to bare my teeth at her disgustingly.

Fortunately, she faced the bar to retrieve her drink that the bartender just delivered and did not see my glare directed at her. I took my new drink and poured it back and then pulled cash from my money clip and laid it on the bar.

"For mine and hers," I said to the bartender as he turned to cash me out.

"Ooh, eager to get going are we?" She chuckled and took a sip of her drink before setting it down, turning towards me, and tilting her head up to look at me fully. "I'm so glad we were able to make time to unwind on this trip, the last one was so hectic I needed a deep tissue massage when we got home just to relax. I like getting the relaxed Maverick Jones all to myself."

"Veronica," I said with a dark warning tone to my voice, but she purposely brushed me off.

She slid closer to me until her breasts pressed flat against my chest and her hips brushed my groin. "Maverick, don't ruin it." She sighed and laid her hand flat on my chest before shimmying her hips against me. "Just for one night, don't try to hide behind that facade you use with everyone else. I know you better than that."

"You don't know me at all." I bit out and stepped back but she was anticipating that and she stepped forward at the same time, pushing me back into the wing-back barstool behind me before stepping between my legs and leaning in.

"Rumor has it you like to fuck hard, Maverick. That you are an absolute beast when you're buried deep in a woman's pussy. I know I can be exactly what you need to let some steam off, baby. Why don't we go up to your suite and I can take care of you like I know you desperately want me to?" She moved fast and closed the distance between us, sealing her bright red lips over mine, and the acid in my throat burned full force. I pushed her backward so fast that she stumbled and landed on her ass between a few other patron's feet and sputtered in shock.

"If the roles were reversed, and you pulled that shit as a man to a woman, you'd be facing a lawsuit and a sexual assault charge!" I bit out, wiping her taste off my mouth with the back of my hand, and spit onto the floor in disgust. "You're fucking fired, Veronica. And you'll be hearing from Dexter too."

"Are you fucking kidding me?" She gasped, as everyone in the crowded bar looked on. "For her? You're turning me down for that mousey little bitch?"

"Fuck off, Red," I swore, straightening my suit and walking off the raging anger building inside of me, leaving her sprawled out on the floor. I got to the elevators, stabbed the button to go up to my suite, and dialed one of my best friends, not even caring to look at the time of day, because I knew he'd answer.

"Mav," Dexter said. "This can't be good."

"I just fired Red."

"Shit." He cursed and I heard him moving around his house. "What'd she do?" He asked as I rode the elevator up to the executive suite I was in.

"Kissed me, and then talked shit about Cora." I mashed my teeth together at the unpleasant memory of her touching me. "She needs an economy plane ticket back to New York and I need a new assistant by Wednesday. A male."

"What you need is a Cora. Did you tell her yet?"

"Cora won't work with me, let alone for me. And no, I wanted to tell you first because I know Veronica is going to get salty and come for me on this. So you need to get ahead of it."

"Anyone see it happen that can cover your story?"

"The entire hotel bar watched me sprawl her out on her ass. I'm sure someone saw what happened before that."

"Good. I'll work on getting security footage and statements from employees on hand in case she tries to spin a different tale. But you need to call Cora. Now."

"On it. Thanks."

"Anytime brother." He said and hung up, onto the task of saving my reputation and marriage.

As soon as I walked into my suite, I cursed and ripped my tie from my shirt, pulling on the buttons and tearing my jacket off as I fought to stay in control.

Too much had fucking happened the last few days. My life had been one of order and predictability and now it was chaos, and I was losing my grip on it.

I dialed Cora's number and her sleepy voice answered on the third ring. "Hello, handsome." She called and I took a deep breath, letting the warmth in her voice move through my veins.

"Hello, Angel." I sighed, feeling tired and weighed down.

"I thought you were going off to dinner?" We'd spoken before I went down for a drink before dinner and she had been headed to bed, tired from her ordeal today.

"Change of plans. I'm staying in tonight."

"What happened?" She was in tune with me and caught my mood.

"Veronica made a pass at me." I said firmly, "I fired her and have Dex working on staying ahead of it."

"Ahead of it?" She asked, sounding much more awake now. "Ahead of what?"

"Of any tale, she tries to spin about what happened to get back at me for turning her down flat and firing her for it."

"Did you… did you touch her?"

"She kissed me," I answered her honestly, hating how that would hurt her. "And I pushed her on her ass in the middle of the bar for it."

She paused and took a deep breath, "Okay." She replied simply, but I could hear the wheels spinning in her head.

"Cora, I'm sorry. You know I was already working on eliminating having her travel with me and you know I wanted to stay the fuck home with you instead of being here. I should have just fucking stayed home." I ground out, cursing, and throwing a lamp across the room of the suite's living room.

"Maverick, stop." Her calm voice called through the phone. "I trust you. And I love you."

That stopped me short in the middle of my tirade and I froze with my hand wrapped around the neck of a matching lamp, ready to chuck it at the wall to match its twin. "You trust me?" I asked in disbelief. I was expecting anger, fear, and insecurity.

Not trust.

She sighed, and her sweet voice spoke to me. "I trust you Maverick. I know you didn't give her any reason to come onto you and that you didn't allow any of it to happen. I believe you."

"Okay," I said, in shock.

She chuckled a bit, and I relaxed, throwing myself into an armchair as I rubbed my hand over my face.

"So what are you going to do for tomorrow?" She asked, knowing I had a full day of meetings planned for tomorrow.

"Muddle through on my own until I can get home to you and bury myself in my favorite place on earth and forget about all of this. Dexter is going to start the process of getting me a new assistant, a male this time, and hopefully, I can make this transition smooth, but I doubt it will be. Training an assistant is one of the hardest things to do in my field. But it'll be worth it in the long run."

"Let me know if there's anything I can do for you from here, baby."

"You can go back to sleep and get the rest I know you so desperately need baby. I'm sorry I woke you up."

She chuckled and I imagined her stretching in the center of my king-size bed under the thick warm blankets wearing a sexy piece of satin and lace. "It's only eight pm Mav, it's hardly out of line for you to have called me. I just took a fantastic bath in your soaker tub and couldn't fight the fatigue any longer."

"Mmh, tell me more about this bath. Or about what color lace you're wearing all alone in my bed without me." I flirted, trying to let lust drag the anger from my bones.

"How about I show you instead?" She purred.

"Video chat?" I asked hopefully.

"No." She laughed, "That would get far too dirty for the energy I have right now, but how about I send you a little something?"

I laid my head back in the chair and relaxed fully. "I'll settle for that, Angel."

"Okay, then go have a drink and get some much-needed sleep, Mav. Don't stay up and dwell on this. I know how you are."

"I won't." I lied. "I love you, Cora darling."

I heard the smile in her voice. "I love you more."

I sat in the chair with my phone lying dormant in my lap for a few minutes and then an incoming message lit up the screen and I licked my lips in anticipation.

I opened the message to find a video of Cora standing in the mirror of our walk-in closet with the overhead lights out and just the low light from the sconces over the individual racks casting a warm glow over her tanned skin. She wore a deep magenta purple tank top and matching shorts with white lace scalloped edges and my body warmed watching as she looked into the phone screen, slid her hand through the top of her hair, turning her body to show me the way the back of the shorts cut at an angle, accentuating her sexy as hell ass and the fabric pulled across her large chest where her hard nipples showed. The video was on a loop, boomeranging back and forth as she did her little twist at the hips to show me her body while tilting her head sexily and I ached for her.

There was no sound with the video and I had to force myself to not call her back and demand to hear her voice while I stroked my aching cock. She did this to me with only a slight twist of her hips in satin pajamas, when other women had tried to get me hard for years without luck.

She was my soulmate, through and through. And I loved every single thing about her, which was why she could drive me positively crazy from ten states away with a simple four-second video.

I love it. I love you. Talk to you tomorrow.

I replied and then ordered room service and spent the next few hours losing myself in work to distract my body from the ache deep in my bones from missing Cora.

Chapter 18 – Cora

This was stupid.

I was stupid.

I paced back and forth down the long hallway, with an internal war going on in my brain as I tried not to let insecurity get the best of me.

"Just fucking knock." I whispered to myself and groaned at how stupid I was.

I walked back to the door I'd come all this way to get to and raised my hand pausing with it right above the lacquered surface for a moment and then laid it down hard a few times, rapping on it, jarring the silent air of the deserted hallway.

I listened intently for noises from the other side and fought to tamp down the anxiety as I waited longer and longer.

I had a key, but a part of me was telling me if I used it, I was going to walk in on something I shouldn't be seeing.

Because that's the kind of shit that happened to me. That was my type of luck.

But I pulled the sleek black key card from my pocket anyway shifted my bags in my hands swiped it across the sensor above the doorknob and pushed the door open.

The suite was dark and silent as I walked in, and I laid my bags on the table in the hallway before walking further in.

Maverick's suite.

It was a little after one am, and I'd fought with my conscience for a while after I got off the phone with him earlier and couldn't settle knowing he was upset and aching to be with me while he was stuck here for work.

And the longer I lay there in the center of our bed I knew I had no good reason to not come to Atlanta and be with him.

He needed me. I'd felt his need through the phone, and I was stupid to try to deny it. For ten years I'd had to ignore the way even his memory called to me and now that I had him back in my life, I wasn't going to let another moment like that pass between us.

So I'd called Dexter and had him help me get here to Atlanta without Mav knowing and now I was standing inside his silent hotel suite and second-guessing all of the decisions I'd made since our phone call earlier.

Like the one when I called Mr. Peterson and left an incredibly unprofessional voicemail telling him I couldn't work at Halo anymore, simply because I was being torn in so many different directions at once.

And Maverick had been right.

We should be building this empire together, with me at his side.

So that was what I was doing.

I was standing by my man's side and blindly trusting him to be everything he promised me he was.

I walked towards the bedroom and quietly pushed the door open to find the dark room illuminated by the bathroom light through the slightly ajar door. In the center of the bed, lay the man of my dreams.

I walked closer and stood at the end of the bed and silently watched him, in a moment so rare when he was unmoving and at ease. His dark hair was rumpled on his pillow where he lay with both of his arms up over his head, holding onto his pillow. His shirtless chest and abdomen were unobstructed above the white sheet where it pooled at his waist, and I licked my lips as I gazed at his muscles and strength on display like this.

I stripped myself bare before silently crawling up the bed next to him.

His eyelids fluttered as I pulled the sheet aside and slid my body in next to his, soaking in the warmth of his skin and feeling the flush of excitement burn through my system.

"Maverick." I moaned, leaning down and kissing his wide chest, trailing sensual kisses across the muscles to his nipple and sucking it into my mouth.

He groaned, and both arms came down off of the pillow as his eyes snapped open and he grabbed me in confusion.

"Cora?" His sleep-drunk voice questioned as I slipped my leg over his hip and between his own, feeling his naked cock stirring against my inner thigh when I slid on top of his body.

"Yeah, it's me, baby." I hummed, kissing down his chest and stomach as he tangled his fingers into my hair and pulled me back up his body to crash my lips down onto his. "Yes." I moaned as he consumed me through my mouth, using his entire body to kiss me.

"What are you doing here?" He asked, pulling his lips back far enough to press his forehead to mine and breathe me in with surprise in his voice

"I was wrong, I needed you." I bit his lip and sucked it into my mouth. "I should have been here with you to start with Mav. I'm sorry."

He rolled us over and pinned my naked body into the mattress with his, rocking his hard-on against my wet pussy as I spread my legs wide and wrapped my ankles around his back, pulling him against my body. "Cora." He groaned. "I don't deserve you."

"Shh." I hushed him and reached down between our bodies and dragged the head of his cock through my wetness, coating the tip of it and then pulling him into my body as he thrust forward, burying himself. "God, yes." I pushed my head back into the pillow as he started grinding his hips, filling me up and driving me wild.

He pinned both of my hands over my head and held me down as he worked my body into a frenzy of need and desire. "Come for me, Angel. Squeeze me tight and come for me." He commanded and rolled his hips in a way that drove me wild.

"Just like that, don't stop," I begged as I used his body for my pleasure. "Make love to me, Maverick."

"I've only ever made love to you, baby. Every single time I've touched your body since the day I met you, it's been with love."

"Yes." I moaned, feeling the bite of pleasure nipping at my spine. "I love you so much it aches deep in my soul."

"You're my fucking soulmate, Cora. You're the one woman that was made specifically for me in this entire world. We've proved that these last ten years apart. I was made for you, and you were made for me."

"Yes," I repeated as he pushed me over the edge of my orgasm and I leaned forward and bit his chest as it crashed over me, consuming me with primal need. "Maverick." I hissed as I felt his body tighten above mine as he thrust madly, bruising my wrists with his hands until he crested his own orgasm and fell off the other side, collapsing on top of me and burying his face in my neck.

"Holy fuck." He grunted and slowly thrust his spent cock in and out of me a few times, elongating his sensations before pulling out of me and rolling us until I laid at his side with my leg slung over his hip. "How did you get here?"

I chuckled against his chest and kissed it, "Dexter can be incredibly resourceful when he wants to be."

"Bastard." He grunted with good humor.

My impending news weighed heavily on my brain though as I lay in his arms, and I needed to rid myself of my secret.

"I did something tonight. After I talked to you on the phone." I said, holding my breath.

He turned and faced me, pulling me up until I was nose-to-nose with him. "Tell me."

I chewed my lip as his dark eyes stared into mine for a moment before I blurted out. "I quit my job."

I watched as the news processed through his head and a predatory smile pulled his lips up as his eyebrows slowly rose, "You quit your job?"

"Yes." I squeaked. And then swallowed down the vomit threatening to erupt from the nerves in my system. "And I think I want to get rid of my apartment."

His smile grew even bigger as he tightened his arms around me. "Why would you want to give up your security blanket, Cora?" He teased lightly, and I took a deep breath.

"Because I need to put all of my trust and faith in you, in order for this to work." I rushed on and groaned as he rolled us once again until I was straddling him with his back against the headboard and pulled my hips forward, pinning his cock between my wet lips as his come coated us both.

"And what are you going to do now?" He asked as he spread his fingers wide, covering my lower back with his large hands, rocking me forward against him.

"I thought I'd start by helping you out tomorrow in your meetings. And move into the penthouse with you when we get back. And go from there?"

He leaned forward and kissed me, sucking on my lower lip and then my tongue as he feasted on me like a dying man taking one last bite of life.

"I'm going to have you in my home and my empire darling. From sunup until sundown, you're with me."

I laughed and then groaned as he slid his cock through my drenched folds. "You'll tire of me. I'm telling you now, you'll get tired of me if you are stuck with me at home and work."

"Never." He answered instantly. "Not possible." He leaned forward and sucked on the skin beneath my ear, drawing a groan from his own chest as I slid my fingers up the back of his scalp, dragging my nails across the skin there. "I love you too much to ever tire of you, Angel."

"That's what you say now. But only time will tell."

"Time well spent, growing our business and our family." He lifted me and lowered me down on his cock again, letting his come lubricate the invasion until my clit pressed against his pubic bone, drawing a moan from my lips.

"Oh my God." I laid my hands on his chest and threw my head back as pleasure burned my soul.

"I'm your God, baby."

We were at a meeting with Keith Potter, CEO of a company that worked closely with Mavericks shipbuilding company and they were negotiating terms for a new military contract they were courting.

It was all Greek to me, to be completely honest, but I was taking notes and following along as best as I could.

I'd woken up with Mav and dressed the part of his dutiful assistant and went with him about his day as he conquered the world. When we'd walked into Potter's building, he'd introduced me as his fiancé and told them I was filling in for the day, nearly shocking their team senseless, because apparently, the world assumed Maverick Jones would be a bachelor forever.

Mr. Potter's assistant Lacy crouched next to me where I sat at the large conference table and whispered in my ear. "Ma'am, can you help me for a moment?"

"Sure," I replied, not sure what else to do at the moment, and quietly followed her out of the room while the two CEOs and their teams continued squabbling over things like shipyard rates, and engineer candidates.

"I'm sorry, I didn't know what else to do," Lacy said as she hurriedly walked next to me towards the front reception area.

"About what exactly?" I asked.

But the answer was given to me by the screeching voice I'd grown to loathe.

"About that," Lacy said, grimacing as we rounded the corner and saw one very irate and downright menacing little red-riding bitch, standing at the reception desk trying to get past.

"Get security here," I said firmly and then walked forward, drawing up every bit of head bitch in charge attitude I could muster, crossing my arms over my chest. "Veronica. What are you doing here?"

She turned on me and her eyes flashed as she looked me up and down. "What do you think I'm doing here?" She snapped. "I'm working."

"You were fired," I replied coldly and didn't waver, even as she stepped towards me with the staff of Potter and Associates looking on in shock and awe.

She sneered at me and flicked her eyes up and down my body again. "Did he tell you that he fucked me yesterday?" She accused and I fought the panic swelling in my heart. "The jet had hardly gotten in the sky before he had his face buried between my thighs, eating me out and getting me good and wet for that monstrous cock of his."

"Good try," I replied, trying to act like it didn't affect me to hear such blatant lies. "But everyone knows that he hasn't given you the time of day once over the last three years that you've worked for him, so why would he start now?" Her eyes squinted in anger at me as I kept going. "Now you need to leave. You no longer work for Jones Holding or any other company that Maverick owns, which means you are trespassing."

"He doesn't get to just fuck me and then fire me, Cora, I'll ruin him." I saw the moment she switched from bitter to desperate and knew without a doubt in my body, that she had been lying.

"He didn't fuck you at all, Veronica. And we both know if you try to spin a single lie past this point, you'll be the one turning tricks on the street to pay your rent by the end of the week if you aren't careful. He'll blacklist you, leaving you unemployable to any other person in the world for fucking with his life. So tread carefully here." I said, standing even taller and taking a step towards her until we were nearly touching, dropping my voice so only she could hear me. "And between you and me, it's not him you need to fear in this moment. Because I swear to God, if you do anything besides walk away with your tail tucked between your legs and move on with your life, I'll fucking destroy your entire world for trying to fuck with mine. I've lost too much in the past to just allow you to get away with something like this." She took a quick breath in, shocked by my change in demeanor. "Try me, cunt, and you'll regret it."

With that, I took a step back and raised my eyebrow at security who appeared behind her. "Please remove this woman from the building, she's no longer employed by Mr. Jones and is trespassing. Thank you." I didn't wait to see how her removal went, but instead turned on my heel and walked with my head held high back towards the boardroom and into the meeting. Maverick caught my eye as I sat back down in my seat and raised his brow at me questioningly, but I just gave him a small smile and went back to work, refusing to let that woman affect his day at all.

I got a power rush and a confidence boost from stepping into the role of Maverick's partner and rode the high the rest of the day as he concluded business in the early evening hours.

I could live this life, at his side, handling things like Veronica and taking some things off of his plate.

I could be an asset for this man if I let myself.

And I was going to.

Gone was the demure and silent girl who had run off into the night, letting others dictate my life and take everything from me. And in her place was a confident woman who was going to get what she deserved.

And I was going to start with becoming Maverick's wife, once and for all.

It was after eleven pm when we walked back into the penthouse in New York after our trip back from Atlanta, and I had to admit, I was bone weary.

But that was primarily because I'd kept Mav up until nearly three am last night in his hotel suite and then we'd been up and at the meeting with Potter by seven am.

"You look dead on your feet," Maverick said and I chuckled, walking ahead of him into the master bedroom.

"You are supposed to tell me I look fresh and beautiful, even when I look tired and haggard." I chided him as I slid out of my heels and headed for the shower. I desperately wanted to wash off the grime of travel and crawl into bed.

He caught me when I turned back from the shower after turning on the water and slid his hands around my hips, pulling me flush to his powerful body. "You are always beautiful, and you take my breath away." He said, before leaning in and whispering in my ear, "Even when you look dead on your feet." I felt his smile against my neck and laughed.

"Thanks, babe." I pulled away and turned my back to him holding my hair out of the way as he slowly undid the zipper at the back of my dress, sliding it down to my waist and pushing it off over my shoulders and then down my legs. I turned and stood before him in my panties and bra and watched as his pupils dilated and his nostrils flared. "Like what you see, big guy?" I asked, running my fingers down his tie to unbutton his suit jacket, and then pushing it over his arms.

"I love what I see. And you know it." He said, letting me slowly undress him, sliding his buttons free and exposing his powerful chest to me.

"I love your body." I cooed and leaned forward, kissing his chest while he undid his cufflinks and then dropped his shirt down to the floor. "My mouth waters every single time I see how muscular and strong you are." He groaned as I kissed my way down his washboard abs and to his belt buckle, opening it, pushing his pants open, and kissing the skin right above his boxer briefs. "You're my biggest fantasy come to life, Mav."

"I need you." He growled and tried to step back but I pulled his cock out of his briefs and looked up at him from my knees and licked the underside of him from root to tip. "Fuck."

"I want you to fuck my mouth Mav." I purred, tightening both of my fists around his impressive length, and stroking him. "You never let yourself go when you're in my mouth, but I want it."

"I can't." He pleaded, even as his fingers wove through my hair, pulling my head closer to his cock.

I smirked up at him and sucked the head of him deep into my mouth, keeping my eyes on him the whole time. I loved watching him come unhinged, and he rarely let me have free rein over him like this. "I need this." I bobbed up and down on him until my lips brushed the base of his cock and he moaned the most heavenly sound as he lost his grasp on his control.

"I fucking love it when you take me deep like that." He groaned, jerking his hips when I brought him back to just using my lips on his tip.

"Fuck my mouth," I said again, and I watched his abs tense as he contemplated it. "Mav, fuck my mouth." I implored, and his jaw clenched as I stuck my tongue out and waited.

"Angel." He fisted the base of his cock and slapped the head of it against my flat tongue a couple of times and then pushed deep into my mouth and pulled out. He groaned and did it again as he watched in rapture as I gagged on his thick cock. "My God you're beautiful like this." He let go of his cock and put both hands on my head and thrust hard, bottoming out in my throat, and then started a punishing rhythm, leaving me only able to take a breath every second or third thrust.

I dug my nails into his thighs and opened my mouth further, aiming it up so he could go even deeper.

"Good girl." He gasped. "Take it deep, just like that." His teeth were clenched together so hard I was worried he was going to crack his molars as he chased his pleasure. He reached down and wrapped his hand around my neck, feeling the bulge his cock made in the column with each thrust, and he squeezed his eyes shut tight as he got even closer to his finish. "Take off your bra. I want to come on your tits." He grunted. I reached behind me and tore it off as his entire body jerked and twitched before he pulled his cock free of my mouth and stroked himself.

"Cover me, baby." I cried and pushed my chest forward as he started coming, coating my tits and neck with his orgasm as he grunted and moaned.

When he was done, he stood above me with his delicious body heaving for breath as he looked down at the mess he made and the look on his face was pure... animal.

I slid one finger through a spot of come and wiped it up, before bringing it up to my mouth and sucking it clean as his eyes darkened even more than they already were. "Delicious." I moaned.

"Come here." He growled, pulling me up, slamming his lips down on mine, and kissing me roughly as my come-covered chest rubbed against his stomach. "You're so fucking perfect for me." He praised and grabbed big handfuls of my ass before sliding his fingers around my panties and ripping them off of my body and throwing them to the side. "I'm going to buy you a million pairs of those so I can rip every single one off of your delectable body."

He backed me up into the hot shower and directly up against the wall, where he continued to feast on my lips.

"I need you," I begged, grabbing handfuls of his hair and pulling his head back so I could plead for more. I lifted one leg, wrapping it around his hip and rubbing my aching pussy against the tip of his cock where it hung between his thick thighs. It twitched with each contact of my pussy as if it was searching for the opening. "Please." I almost screamed as he continued to hold me pinned against the wall under the water while he kissed his way down my neck and across my chest.

"Patience." He rasped, and I fought the hold he had on my hips, desperate for more. "Turn around." He said and spun me to face the wall and hit one of the lit-up controls on the wall and a second later, a jet of water shot out of the wall directly at my crotch and I hissed at the sensation. "Perfect height." He vibrated against my neck where he stood pressed to my back. He lifted my right leg and slung it over his forearm as he reached down with his long fingers and spread my pussy lips open. The water shot directly onto my clit, and I moaned in ecstasy at the intense pleasure. "Good girl." He praised.

I reached up behind me and wrapped my hand around the back of his neck for leverage, letting him hold my weight as I rocked my hips against the water. "Maverick, fuck that feels so good, baby."

"Do you have any idea how sexy you looked on your knees with my cock down this beautiful throat?" He asked as he wrapped his long fingers around my neck and squeezed. "Do you have any idea how close I was to losing my God damned mind and hurting you for my own pleasure?" He growled.

"I want you to make it hurt, Mav. I want you to give it to me exactly how you need to." I rolled my hips again and felt his cock swelling against my ass.

"I'm so conflicted." He admitted, holding me by my throat and my pussy as he forced me to take the pleasure he was giving. "I want to abandon every concern for your wellbeing and chase only my pleasure.

You push me so far towards the edge that I can't see reason when I'm buried inside of you."

"Do it," I begged. "I need to know I can give you what you need from me, Maverick."

"I love you too much to do that." He growled and squeezed my throat tighter and lifted me higher until my toes left the floor and pushed me against the jet completely.

"Maverick!" I screamed, clawing at his arms as I shot off like a bomb, exploding and falling to pieces on the floor at his feet. He moved me away from the wall and kissed my neck and shoulder as I rode out the shuddering waves of pleasure before he dropped me back to my feet and bent me over in front of him. I put my hands on the bench by my head and looked over my shoulder at him as he kicked my feet apart and crouched behind me, lining himself up and driving his cock in deep. "Oh, my God!" I bit my lip to keep from screaming at the way my body stretched to accommodate him, barely keeping it quiet as he pounded into me hard. I put one hand on the wall to push myself back against him and spread my legs wider to give him better access.

"I want to spank you." He growled. "I need it."

"Spank me." I gasped, so on edge I'd let him do anything. The other times, when he was buried deep inside of me like this, he had spanked me and it had been some of the best sex we had. I ached to feel him unrestrained within me.

His hand came down so fast I had no time to prepare as he propelled me forward towards the wall with the ferociousness of it.

"Yes!" I screamed in an animalistic cry. He kept pounding his cock deep into my pussy, stretching me and forcing himself into my body as his large hand covered my ass with welting slaps.

He growled and groaned as he colored my skin and I lost my grip on the wall as an orgasm ripped through me again, making my vision darken and my knees weak. He grabbed a fistful of my hair and pulled me back before I hit my face on the wall while wrapping his other arm around my waist. Hoisting me up, he sat down on the bench with me between his legs, facing away from him. I put my hands on his knees as my own closed and leaned forward, giving him the space he needed to keep fucking me. "You are so perfect. My perfect, perfect fantasy." He ground out between his clenched teeth. "I'm going to fill up your pussy until my come drips out of you. And then I'm going to do it again and again. Fuck, I need you covered in my come baby."

I moaned and mewed at him, unable to do anything else in the headspace between pleasure and unconsciousness as he used my body exactly how he needed it.

I was in bliss and purgatory at the same time. I needed more and less, and he somehow gave me both as he stopped thrusting and started grinding me back and forth on his cock, as he spread my legs over his knees, opening my pussy to him.

He rubbed my clit with his fingers, sliding them down on each side of his cock where he impaled me and rubbed us both as he prolonged our pleasures. "I need to feel inside of you while I'm fucking you." He growled into my ear.

"How?" I gasped, letting my head fall back onto his shoulder as he leaned back against the wall, leaving me sprawled out on his lap with my legs spread wide.

"Like this." He said as his thick fingers started rubbing the lips of my pussy right around my entrance before he pushed one in alongside his massive cock. "Holy fuck." We both groaned at the same time as he felt the inside of my pussy with his cock and his finger. "This pussy is mine."

"Yes." I moaned as he rubbed his finger against the front inside wall of my pussy, using his palm to rub my clit as he lazily fucked me.

"Maverick." I groaned as a new sensation filled my system. I felt him rubbing on my g-spot with his finger as he laid his other hand flat against my stomach and pushed his palm down.

It was like he was rubbing his fingertips with his palm through my body and then... lighting struck.

"Open your eyes and watch." He commanded as I gasped and clawed at him.

"Watch what?" I was so confused, hardly even conscious of what was happening, but I looked down my body to where his finger and his cock disappeared inside of me.

"I'm going to make you come, and when you do, you're going to squirt for me."

"Maverick." I moaned. "I don't know how." Shaking my head back and forth.

"Give it to me, Cora. I need it, baby." He pushed harder with his palm and the lightning coursed through my body again with each thrust.

Once.

Twice.

And on the third time, the lightning erupted from every nerve in my body and a cataclysmic orgasm ripped from my soul in the same moment as hot liquid branded my insides before rushing out around his cock.

He pulled his cock out and rubbed his fingers back and forth across my opening, spraying the shower floor with my release as I convulsed in his arms, thrashing around, and clinging to my sanity by just a thread. "Maverick Benjamin Jones!" I gasped in shock as he slid his cock back inside of me and lifted my used and exhausted body up and down onto it.

"I'm going to come." He grunted, "Going to fill that tight fucking pussy up with it."

I held on for dear life as I felt his cock swell to an unimaginable size seconds before he exploded, coating my insides with his come to mix with mine, leaving me completely spent and limp in his arms.

He held me like that for a long time, letting the warm water cover our bodies as we relaxed and recouped from the mind-blowing sex.

I finally stood up, letting his still semi-hard cock slowly slide out of me as he watched his come drip down my thighs as I turned around and held my hands out for him to take. This was the Maverick that I loved so painfully deep with every part of myself.

He washed my body, and I washed him before he dragged me to bed and wrapped himself around me from head to toe, taking a deep breath and breathing me in.

"Four days until you're mine." He whispered right before I fell asleep.

I kissed his arm that my head was lying on and smiled against his skin, "I'm already yours."

"Hmm." He agreed and drifted off to sleep.

"Wake up, sleepy head." Maverick's warm voice cascaded over me in my dream, and I reached out towards it. "Cora baby, you need to wake up, you have a big day ahead of you."

"Lies. It's all lies." I muttered and rolled over, burying my head under my pillow. Maverick's large hand came down on my bare ass cheek, sending a deliciously abrupt wake up call to my senses and I lurched up in bed. "Oof, what the hell?" I snapped, sitting on my heels, and rubbing my sore ass. "Spanking is only okay when your cock is buried inside of me, mister." I accused, pointing my finger at him with one eye cracked open.

He was standing in a three-piece suit looking completely put together and not at all groggy like I felt. "Noted." He smirked at me and leaned down to kiss me softly. "Now get up and get a robe on, my mother will be here in twenty minutes."

He turned on his heel and walked out of the bedroom leaving me dazed and confused as I stared after him. "Wait! What?" I called and crawled out of bed, grabbing my satin robe on the way, and cinching it closed around my waist as I walked out into the large open living space. "Why is your mom going to be here?" He stood at the counter pouring two cups of coffee and looking far too good for whatever ungodly hour it currently was after two super late nights in a row.

"Because she's bringing the designer that is going to hand sew your wedding dress together in three days." He said, looking at me out of the corner of his eye while I stood in surprise.

"Oh," I said. "Why didn't I even think about a wedding dress?" I asked, feeling a sudden rush of anxiety about all of the undiscussed details of the wedding. It was a super small affair, but there were still things that needed to be done even with only a dozen guests.

"Because I'm taking care of everything." He said confidently, handing me a cup of coffee, prepared perfectly before leading me over to the barstool at the island and forcing me to sit down as my brain continued misfiring.

"You're taking care of everything? When do you have time to plan a wedding? I've seen your schedule."

"Turns out I'm an incredible delegator, and my mother is an incredible event planner with an even better team."

"Huh." I wondered quizzically, and took a sip of my coffee. "What's my favorite flower?" I asked suddenly, trying to gauge just how on top of this he really was.

"Depends. If you're talking about a bouquet for the table or something, roses, and daisies. If you're talking about a formal flower for a bridal bouquet, you fell in love with my cousin Sasha's bouquet at her wedding when we were fifteen, so I chose white lilies and sunflowers to match yours." He said easily before looking completely confident. "Was I right?"

"Perfectly." I mused and took another sip of coffee. "What color scheme are we working with?"

"White, ivory, and sage green. You've always loved neutrals."

"How do you do that?" I asked, confused as to how he was so right and so at ease about it.

He chuckled, setting his coffee down and turning me on the stool before picking me up and setting my ass down on the cold marble countertop. "How do I do what?" He asked. He ran his hands up my legs from my ankles to my thighs, pushing apart my long satin robe in the process, and then spread my legs to step between them.

Desire shot through my body, but I forced my brain to focus on the task at hand here. "How do you know me so well, so confidently, even after all of these years?"

"I spent ten years memorizing you, Cora. Every day, even when we were in elementary school you fascinated me and I'd find myself simply watching you or committing anything you said to memory, to be sure I never forgot something important. I remember the way you picked pepperoni off your pizza but left the ham whenever we ordered pizza because you knew I loved the pepperoni. I remember the way you could never sleep during a thunderstorm because you're such a light sleeper." He ran his thumb over the apple of my cheek as darkness clouded his warm brown eyes. "I remember the way your cheeks get red and splotchy when you cry and the way you shake your head instead of saying yes or no because your parents always said you were too loud as a kid. I remember the way you told me someday you were going to fill a house with babies, so you'd always be wanted and needed because everyone else in the world has let you down at one point or another." My nose prickled as tears threatened to pool in my eyes at his heartfelt response. "But what I remember most is the way I thought of you every single day that you were gone from my life. Every single day I'd find myself staring off into the distance and remembering something about our life together and forcing myself to memorize every part of it, from the way your laugh sounded, or the smell of your perfume, or the feel of the soft skin behind your knee where I'd rest my hand when we sat together. I didn't want to forget a single thing about you, because once I started losing those memories, I'd start losing what little bit of you I had left. And that would be a fate worse than death Cora Lynn. I've never been able to be without you completely, not since the day I laid eyes on you."

"Maverick," I said, as tears slid free and down my cheeks. "Why did we let this go on so long? Why did we give them the power for so many years?" I cried.

"Because we didn't know Angel, but we do now. I messed up and they monopolized it. But we're going to be one unified front from now on, for the rest of our lives."

"God, I love you," I said, leaning forward and covering his lips with mine, loving the way his beard tickled my lips as he deepened the kiss, taking what he wanted from me in the early morning sunlight on his kitchen counter.

Our kitchen counter.

Someday that would start to stick.

The intercom buzzed and Maverick groaned into my mouth as his hands tightened on the bare skin above my thighs. "I have to go; I've been given strict instructions that I'm not allowed to be here for this part." He sighed.

I smiled against his lips. "Tradition would say anyway." I mused.

"I'll see you later." He kissed my forehead and then stepped back, answering the intercom, and taking the elevator down to the lobby. I jumped down off the counter and righted my appearance as best I could and a moment later, Marsha and a team of women with suitcases walked off the elevator and into the penthouse.

"Good morning darling," Marsha said sweetly, kissing me on the cheek. "Are you as excited as I am about this?" She asked.

"Well, Maverick only told me about it two minutes ago, so probably not." I laughed. "But I am excited."

She rolled her eyes and huffed, "He's known about this since Sunday. Men." She threw her hands up in the air and then laughed. "Where would you like our team to set up?"

I looked around the large open living space. "Here would probably be best right? It's the most open with the best lighting."

"Perfect." She said, giving direction to the team of women who were all dressed in sleek black outfits and hardly spoke. One woman was the actual designer, her name was Ellen Hu, and she was one of the sweetest and kindest people I'd ever met before. She had a giant sketchbook in her hand with blank pages and sat down on the couch next to me.

"What kind of look are you thinking about?" She asked and I chewed on my lip in hesitation. "Do you have a general shape you like, or color or fabric in mind?" She asked kindly.

I took a deep breath and opened my mouth, but nothing came out embarrassingly. I looked to Marsha who sat on the arm of the chair across from us with a gentle smile on her face, giving me time to figure it all out.

"I'm sorry," I said, closing my eyes and shaking my head. "I gave up on the dream of marrying Maverick ten years ago and have actively not thought about my future wedding during those years because I couldn't imagine ever marrying anyone but him. And then two weeks ago he swooped back into my life like a fairy tale, and I've been living with my head in the clouds for days now and this never crossed my mind." I apologized.

She put her hand on mine on top of my knee and squeezed, "Do not apologize to me about such things. It's my job to help you figure this all out, so that's exactly what I'm going to do." She smiled softly and I nodded and took a deep breath.

"Okay," I said.

Hours passed with a flurry of excitement as Ellen went through all of my options with me piece by piece and sketched out a spread of different ideas, putting different aspects that I liked together until we had a direction to go. Then I stood on a pedestal while she draped different fabrics across my body, pinning them together and taking measurements while Marsha chatted on and on, filling me in on more details of my wedding that Maverick had taken upon himself to decide, and I loved them all. I felt so secure in letting him take care of everything and it was... refreshing.

I'd missed having someone to lean on and had he been anyone else in the world, I probably would have fought him tooth and nail for control over these different aspects of my life. But I'd trusted him for a decade when we were growing up, and he'd proven himself over and over again in that time. Other than the way we ended, he had never broken my trust before, so I was willing to let go and let my trust in him flourish here and now.

It was fascinating watching this talented woman in front of me build a wedding dress piece by piece right on my body before taking all of those pieces off and perfecting it.

Before I realized it, dusk was falling on the city and Maverick still wasn't home. Ellen and her team packed up their supplies and left, with the promise that the dress would arrive Friday for a final fitting before we left the city for the wedding on Saturday. I had to trust her because that was what she did every day but, now that I'd heard about all of the plans and bits of wedding plans, I was nervous about them all lining up in time.

Before I'd talked to Mav this morning, and Marsha all day today, I'd just envisioned us standing in front of an officiant and saying vows, ending as man and wife.

But now my head was swarming with color palettes, hairstyles, flowers, vows, wine lists, menus, table décor, speeches, and honeymoons.

I sat down on the couch in one of Maverick's short-sleeved shirts and sweatpants, letting the incredibly oversized fabric swallow me up as I waited for him.

Magda, his housekeeper who I never saw except when she was feeding us like she was some ghost, had plated me a delicious dinner and now I settled in with a glass of his expensive red wine.

I heard the elevator ping in the hallway and a moment later Mav walked in the front door. He looked as disheveled as I've seen him in work mode before. His tie was loosened around his neck and his shirt sleeves were rolled up as he carried his briefcase and suit jacket. He tossed both into the chair by the door and closed the distance between us quickly as I stood up from the couch and set down my wine.

"Mine." He said gruffly before leaning down and kissing me deeply, wrapping his hands around the back of my neck and tilting my head to the side to kiss me seductively.

"Maverick." I moaned, pulling back to look at him. "What's wrong?" I asked, feeling how on edge he was, his body was nearly vibrating with it.

"I missed you." He whispered and sighed deeply like it was the first time all day he was able to let the burden of the day go. "This was the first time since I got you back that I've spent an entire day away from you. Twelve hours apart was torture."

I smiled against his lips, pulled his tie loose from his collar, and tossed it aside. "I know how to remedy your pain." I kissed up the side of his neck as he leaned down to let me.

"Yes, fucking please." He growled.

Chapter 19 – Maverick

I ran my fingertips up and down Cora's arm leisurely under the steaming water of our bubble bath as she leaned back against my chest. I'd fucked her like a man possessed when I got home, laying her out on the dining room table like a feast and pounding her body into the unforgiving wood top before taking her into our bedroom and laying on my back, letting her ride me unhurriedly for hours until both of our bodies gave out after an obscene number of orgasms.

And now we were resting in the bath and finally talking about our day. It had floored me to see her eyes light up as she told me about her day with the designer and my mom. She was passionate and excited about the wedding now that it was only a few days away and I loved to hear her tell me all about it all.

"Tell me why you looked so rumpled when you got home." She insisted as she kissed my bicep where her cheek leaned against it. My arm was draped over her chest with my hand resting on her stomach and I was tracing circles of the skin that would hopefully soon tighten as her belly grew with our babies inside of her.

"I told you, I missed you." I kissed her temple.

"There's more to it than just that." She said firmly and I smiled against her hair.

"How do you know that?"

"Because I know you." She said instantly, so sure of herself.

I tightened my hold on her and breathed her in before diving into the hell my day had been.

"I got a call from the chief editor of a tabloid magazine today. Veronica sold them the story about the other night at the hotel."

She stiffened in my arms slightly before leaning further into me. "What did her story have to say?"

"Everything that she spun to you at the meeting with Potter." She'd finally told me about Veronica's visit to Potter's building after we were on the jet home last night and while I was mad that Veronica had lied to her and caused a scene; I was proud of Cora for stepping in and handling it like a boss.

"That you fucked her." She bit out.

"Yes. And then assaulted her and fired her publicly to cover for it." I growled.

"She's such a cunt." She swore, and I chuckled lightly behind her at her choice of swear word.

"Yes, yes, she is." I agreed. "They agreed to add the security footage of her coming onto me with the testimonies of the multiple people there that night that heard what she'd said to me to debunk her story before she could spin it her way, in exchange for an exclusive about our wedding."

She cringed in my arms, "I hate that we have to give them an exclusive into our personal moment just so they'll tell the truth to the world."

"I know." I said, rubbing my hand across her stomach. "That's just part of my world though. My PR team also released a statement today about you and I getting married this weekend."

She turned in my arms and looked at me with fear in her eyes. "Everyone knows that we're together now. And getting married in three days?"

"Yes. We were photographed leaving Hawthorn Tower together Friday and it was a really good photo, so we used it for the article."

"Wow. I've been locked away in here all day, I had no idea the news was out there already." She thought on it for a moment, "Has there been any... communication from my family about it?"

I tensed. I'd known what her question would be before she asked it and had tried to steel my reaction to it but there was some things I couldn't control. And my growing hate for her parents and brother was one of them.

"Yes, your family released a statement this afternoon in response."

She was quiet and then shook her head. "They gained from it didn't they?" She accused.

I kissed her temple again and turned her head, so she was relaxed into me again before I answered her. "They said that they were over-joyed about our families joining together finally after all these years and that they look forward to our happiness for years to come."

"Oh, come on." She snapped and huffed in indignation.

"I know baby. Don't worry because we'll be bringing to light the truth about their involvement in our wedding exclusive piece."

"Ugh," She cringed. "I hate them."

"Me too Angel. Veronica's story will air tomorrow morning." I said and I held her as she processed everything. Because there was nothing else I could do in that moment. I couldn't fix this for her right this second, and I was doing everything else I could in this moment to make it better for her, so I just had to hold her and support her this way. "Can I ask you a question?" I asked.

She laughed lightly and nodded her head.

"When will we know if you got pregnant or not this cycle?"

She snorted and laughed again, "That was not the question I was expecting from you, I won't lie."

"I know."

She hummed for a moment and then turned to me. "I'm due to get my period in a week or so. Which means…" She tilted her head to the side, "I ovulated sometime in the last few days."

"So the chance to get you pregnant is passed?"

She turned and sat between my thighs facing me. "I don't know the exact moment I ovulated, and they say there's like a seventy-two-hour window before and after ovulation for the egg to be fertilized. But yes, I'd guess I ovulated early last week based on when I'm due to get my period again, which would mean there's no chance of getting pregnant now if I'm not already."

I nodded and ran my finger over my lips in wonder. "When can you test?"

"Anxious?" She joked, raising her eyebrow at me in jest.

"Incredibly." I answered honestly.

She tilted her head and got a dreamy look in her clear blue eyes and ran her hands up my arms. "I don't know, I've never had to test before. I think they say it's best to wait until your missed period, but some tests can tell a few days before that, but I think they're less accurate."

"Okay." I let all of that process in my head as I tried to be patient. "I know it's only been two weeks; I've just waited ten years for you and can't help my anxiousness."

"I know, baby." She said, crawling up onto my lap and laying her head on my shoulder. "I know exactly what you mean."

"What exactly do you expect me to do with my day?" Cora huffed from the doorway as I walked out to the elevator the next morning. She leaned her shoulder against the doorjamb wearing a sexy-as-hell silk nightgown in the same shade as her blue eyes. Her hair piled on top of her head, and she didn't have a stitch of makeup on.

She was positively breathtaking.

"I expect you to relax until the stylists get here for your hair and makeup trial run," I said, before pushing the elevator button.

"I want to work Mav. I thought that was your end goal anyway." She replied, leaning up off the doorway and walking out to me. "Get me to quit Halo and work with you, *building our empire*." She imitated my voice and I laughed at her and closed the last few feet of distance between us.

"That is my goal Cora, but we get married in two days, so my goal for right now is to make sure you have the most memorable experience possible up until that moment you walk down the aisle to me. Pamper yourself and relax, embrace the experience baby. You can come to work with me when we get back from the honeymoon."

She scoffed and turned her cheek to me when I went to kiss her, "By then I'll be pregnant, and you'll lock me away in some macho man display of protectiveness."

I smiled and turned her face to meet mine and kissed her, lingering, and letting my tongue soothe her bad attitude for a while before pulling back. "I promise Angel, you'll be at my side soon enough."

She pursed her lips but didn't rebuke that, because she knew it was true, and I knew she was just being difficult about it because she didn't know what to do with idle time anymore. But that was going to change soon because she was going to be my wife and she deserved to relax now that she didn't have to fight to simply survive anymore.

"I love you," I said softly, kissing her once more. "I'll see you for dinner."

"I love you too." She replied as I walked into the waiting elevator and stared at her beauty until the last second when the door shut between us.

On the ride to work, Franklin interrupted my normal email perusal. "Sir, there's a... bit of chaos outside of Hawthorn Tower this morning."

I put my phone down and looked at him in the mirror. "What do you mean?"

"A crowd of paparazzi has formed, waiting for you and Ms. Valentine. There's a mix of fans in the crowd too."

"Fans?"

"Yes, sir." He replied with a grimace, "A sort of Maverick and Cora fan club has formed. They have signs and everything."

"Good lord." I sighed and rubbed my forehead.

"Can I be frank with you sir?" Franklin asked uncharacteristically.

"Always."

"I think you could use the positive interaction with people before the scandal breaks in an hour."

Of course, Franklin knew about Veronica's bullshit, he knew everything.

"I hear you," I replied, adjusting my tie, and pocketing my phone as we neared the tower. Chaos was a good word to describe what was happening outside the front door to the tower. Crowds of people swarmed the entire sidewalk and fire lane, impeding foot traffic and the flow of cars. "Jesus Christ."

"I agree, sir," Franklin said as he parked next to the curb where police were helping to keep things as orderly as possible. He walked around and opened my door after police pushed people back enough to create a walkway into the tower and I was assaulted with the camera flashes of the paparazzi and the shouts of everyone to look their way. I smiled and gave a little wave as I walked out into the crowd.

"Mr. Jones!"

"Is it true you and Ms. Valentine were high school sweethearts for ten years?"

"Why the rush for the wedding?"

"Is Ms. Valentine pregnant?"

"You were photographed last month with Sue Lin, were you and Ms. Valentine together then?"

I listened to the barrage of questions and could tell I had one chance to get ahead of Veronica and paint the truth for the people curious and took it.

I held my hands up to get everyone to quiet down for a moment and spoke out loudly over the crowd. "Ms. Valentine and I started dating in kindergarten, it's true. She was the best part of me, my better half if you will. But we fell apart before college thanks to some circumstances out of our control, alongside my own teenage stupidity. But we've reconnected recently and decided we've lost enough time together, so we're not wasting a second more. Cora and I will be married this weekend and I will spend the rest of my life wooing and earning that woman's love because I am so incredibly unworthy of her grace and forgiveness from past mistakes. But I assure you, there is nothing in this entire world that would keep me from her again, and no one will ever compare." The crowd erupted with more questions and shouts of excitement as I raised my hands again to calm them. "I don't care if you've somehow deemed me worthy of your time and want to spend it camped outside of my building for fleeting glances of me coming and going," I laughed softly, "I assure you though, I'm not very exciting or entertaining." The crowd laughed good-heartedly, and I continued. "I do however ask a few things of you all. I ask that you don't make all of my dedicated employees late to work as they try to come and go, and I also ask that if you're going to wait around for Cora, that you are respectful to her and her space." I let my smile fade from my face as I embodied the powerful CEO I really was, "Because I will not tolerate her being hackled or disrupted discourteously for one second. And believe me, you do not want to see what I'm capable of when that woman's happiness is at risk." The crowd fell silent but looks of pure delight crossed the faces of everyone gathered. I nodded and gave a small smile to them again, "Thank you for your time, now I have some businesses to run."

I walked away through the front door, leaving the crowd's shouts for more behind me, and rode the elevator upstairs to my office where Reid and Dexter were both waiting for me.

"What?" I snapped as they watched me closely.

"Her story broke five minutes ago, but she sold it to a different publication," Dexter said with a grimace.

"One without the rest of the information with it," Reid said.

"Fuck." I growled, shoving open my office door throwing down my briefcase, and turning on the multiple TV monitors on the media wall. Sure enough, Veronica's story was plastered across the headline of an hourly gossip stream.

Billionaire Playboy Maverick Jones caught cheating with his assistant Veronica Meyers a week before his wedding. Is his

almost wife Cora Valentine going to stick by his side through yet another cheating scandal?

"I'm really starting to hate that cunt." Dexter said from behind me, and I grunted in agreement. I grabbed my phone and dialed the editor that I had worked with yesterday and she answered on the first ring.

"Mr. Jones, I know why you're calling, and I just want to assure you that we are on it." She said in place of a greeting.

"On it how?" I bit out.

"Your story will go live any second now, my team is working tirelessly to push it out on every single platform we have as well as flooding it with traction from every employee and asset we have. Our story will be pushed hard and therefore should be the one that is seen most. It has the most information with it, which is what people crave." Someone spoke to her in the background, and she came back to me. "It's live. Our story with the security footage and statements is live, it would help to have your own team push it as well."

"On it," I said, and I turned to find Dexter and Reid already on it, both on their phones giving orders. "Didn't she violate her contract with you by selling it twice?"

"She did, my guess is she got word somehow that we sold out on her and she took her chances somewhere else."

"Get me what information you can on that, please," I said.

"Will do Mr. Jones. We'll work this diligently to make sure it ends favorably for you."

"See that it does or the deal on the wedding exclusive is off." I bit out and hung up, tossing my phone on my desk, and then rubbing my temples. "Fuck." I cursed again, agitation running up my spine, knowing this was going to negatively affect Cora and there wasn't a single thing I could do about it.

I dove headfirst into work on shutting Veronica down and destroying her, putting all of my other work on the back burner and before I realized it, the lunch hour was nearly upon us. I had commandeered Reid's assistant for a few projects where she could be spared because I had yet to get another one hired.

It turned out, that hiring a male personal assistant was harder than expected, most candidates were either underqualified or not a good fit for the role here at Jones.

Tanya, Reid's assistant opened my office door and walked in, carrying a large take-out order, and set it down on the table as I eyed her curiously. "I didn't order anything," I said, standing up and walking towards the delicious-smelling lunch she was laying out. She paused, confused and unsure of what to do as she eyed the containers.

She asked, with an almost fearful tone, "If you didn't order it, then who did? It's as if the food could be poisoned."

"I did."

I turned, and in the doorway to my office stood an angel.

My angel.

"I wanted to make sure you ate today because I know how you get, and I knew you'd forget with everything going on," Cora said as she walked into my office looking regal and poised in a royal blue dress with gold jewelry to accent it. Tanya smiled sweetly at Cora and excused herself, closing the door behind her as I closed the distance between the two of us and wrapped her up in my arms.

"What are you doing here?" I asked against her neck where I all but clung to her.

"I already told you, feeding you." She pulled back and ran her hands down the sides of my face, looking deep into my eyes. "Are you okay?" Her voice was soft and gentle, and it was nearly my undoing.

"Not even close," I answered honestly as I felt my hard exterior crumbling around me in her arms. "I need you," I said and lifted her into my arms, carrying her over to my desk, and set her down on the cold top before pushing her thighs apart and stepping in against her body. "I fucking *need* you," I repeated as I dove and sucked on the swell of her breast above the modest neckline of her dress.

"Lock the door and take me, then." She purred, reaching behind her to pull her zipper down.

I smashed the button to lock the doors and tore her dress down her body, exposing her bare breasts to my hungry mouth. "No bra today?" I asked as I sucked on her perfect nipple until it was rock hard in my mouth and then I moved to the other one, repeating the process.

She threw her head back as her fingernails dug into the back of my neck. "I wanted to shorten the process of getting you inside of me, so I left a few layers off." She panted.

I growled at her and pushed her dress up the rest of the way and stepped back to look down her body to see her perfect bare and wet pussy spread open for me. "You're fucking perfect for me." I slid her off the desk and pushed her dress down over her hips and onto the floor before picking it up and draping it over the back of my chair. I couldn't have my perfect future wife looking rumpled when she left. She palmed my erection through my slacks, and I groaned as she fisted me with the exact amount of pressure I loved before undoing my slacks and pulling me free.

"Take me, Mav. Right here on your desk like I'm the most important thing on your agenda today." She purred and lifted herself onto the desk again and laid back. I raised her legs and pushed them together against her chest, kissing her ankles and calves as her sexy pussy opened to me between the thickness of her thighs the further I pushed them back.

"These heels stay on while I fuck you," I ordered, and she wrapped her arms around the backs of her knees and turned onto her side a bit so I could see her past her legs.

"Whatever you say, Sir." She purred, and I smacked the head of my cock against her exposed opening.

"That's fucking right." I lined up and pushed the bulbous head of my cock into her pussy, growling at the way it looked disappearing between her swollen lips in this position before pulling it out all the way and pushing it in again. "You take my cock like an angel," I said as I pushed deeper until I was buried completely inside of her. She gasped and laid her head flat on my desk as she took me. I grabbed both of her ankles where they hung between us and held onto them as I started thrusting hard into her welcoming body.

"Just like that." She gasped, letting her eyes roll. "Use my pussy to milk your cock, baby."

"Fucking hell Cora," I growled as her dirty talk spurred me on, I was already impossibly close to coming from just today's frustration alone, but I needed to make her come.

"Slam into me, don't stop." She begged, unaware of how much pleasure it was giving me at the same moment.

"I can't," I growled, slowing down my thrusts and opening her legs to rub on her clit.

"Yes, you can, Maverick. I want you to use me for your pleasure. Don't hold back." She gasped, tightening her legs together again and grabbing a hold of my shirt, pulling me forward into her again.

"Fuck." I grunted, throwing my head back and giving in to the urge to slam into her body until I filled her up.

"Yes." She cried, reaching over her head to grip the edge of the desk, holding on as I used her body how she wanted.

"Such a good little pussy." I cursed, "Milking my cock." Fighting for control, yet one look in her clear blue eyes as she challenged me to come, was my undoing. I let go of her ankles, wrapped both hands over the tops of her shoulders at the base of her neck, and jack hammered into her over and over, rocking my desk with my powerful thrusts as she cried out. I exploded, feeling my orgasm in every single nerve in my body. Filling up her body with my orgasm, and she took every fucking drop just like she was supposed to until my body was locked up tight with cramps and I fell backward into my chair. "Holy fuck." I gasped, loosening my tie, and fighting to remain conscious after such an orgasm.

She let go of her legs and went to drop them to sit up, but my hands shot out and palmed the back of her thighs, pressing them against her chest again and spreading them open. "Don't you dare move." I ordered as I rolled my chair forward and looked up at her naked body as she raised her eyebrow at me. "I haven't come without getting you off since we were newbie teenagers, Cora," I said embarrassingly.

"I wanted it like that, Mav, this was for you." She said sweetly as I ran the pads of my thumbs over the outer lips of her pussy and pushed them open to see where my come pooled inside of her pussy. I slid one thumb up to her clit and used the silky come I'd left behind and rubbed it over the bud of nerves that was swollen and aching to be pleasured, even if her words said otherwise. "Mmh." She moaned, laying her head back on the desk. I used two fingers at her entrance, pushing them into her pussy, collecting as much of my come as I could, and pushed it back inside of her body like it was going to make a difference at this point.

She'd told me she couldn't get pregnant anymore this month, but I wasn't going to stop trying.

I needed to breed her like a fucking broodmare.

It was instinct, a desire I couldn't calm or reason with.

And on instinct, I leaned forward and sucked her clit into my mouth while I finger fucked her used pussy. She gasped at the sudden attack on her sensitive nub and curled up around my head, but I put my other hand around her throat and pushed her back down onto my desk as I tasted my orgasm on her skin.

I'd never been one to come inside of a woman without a condom on, my pull-out game had always been spectacular too. So I'd surely never tasted my come inside of a woman's pussy before, but with Cora, it was becoming another new addiction of mine.

But I'd never done it when my come was freshly left inside of her. Usually, it was only the remnant taste of it when I'd eat her out later.

But this...

This was primal and straight animal instinct as I devoured her taste and scent of her arousal mixed with my own. "Fuck, you taste good like this," I growled at her as she mewed and cried out for more. "I need you to come, Cora. I need your orgasm more than I need my next breath."

I rubbed my pinky against her ass as I thrust my two fingers into her pussy in a punishing rhythm and then pushed it into her tight entrance as I sucked hard on her clit, causing her to snap beneath my mouth as her orgasm tore her body wide open.

The door to my office rattled and I looked up Cora's body to see Dexter standing on the other side of the mirrored glass, trying to open it, confused by the denied access and I smiled against her pussy as I added another finger to her ass.

Two in her pussy, two in her ass with my teeth pinching her clit.

It was the perfect combination of pleasure and pain to send her into another catastrophic orgasm headfirst.

"Maverick!" She screamed, uncaring who heard her as I gave her everything she deserved and more. "Yes!" She moaned, riding my face with her fingers buried in my hair in a death grip.

Dexter paused and then backed away from the door, rubbing a hand over his jaw as he finally figured out what was happening on this side of the glass. It spurred me on even more knowing he knew my fiancé was getting railed hard in my office right now while he listened.

And a part of me wanted him to know exactly what I was doing to her in an exhibitionist way.

I pulled my hands free of her body and flipped her over roughly, so her heeled feet landed on the floor with her tits pressed flat against my desktop. I slapped her ass hard, the noise echoing around the room seconds before her loud moan. "Beg me to fuck you." I hissed in her ear as I lined my cock up with her pussy.

"Fuck me. Please, please, please! I need you." She said and I slammed my cock deep into her in one rough thrust. "Yes!" She screamed again. The entire time I watched as Dexter still loitered outside of my office door, listening, even though he knew I could see him standing there.

It wasn't the first time he'd been involved in my sex life, more than once we'd tag-teamed a woman from a bar in our younger days. But it had been years since he'd shown any interest. Years since he'd married Hope and became a boring married man anyway.

Yet there he stood, with one hand in his pocket and one hand on his jaw as he listened to Cora beg for more.

And I knew the second she finally opened her eyes and saw him standing out there too, because she gasped and froze as I fucked her. "Mav..." She paused.

"He's been there for a while, listening to us," I grunted, horny as fuck from our little voyeur friend. "I bet he's jealous of everything I'm doing to you right now."

"He's married!" She gasped, but it ended on a moan when I reached around her body and flicked her clit.

"He's still a man Cora. And you're hands down the sexiest woman on this earth, he'd have to be dead not to get aroused listening to you getting fucked."

"Oh my God." She shook her head and put her forehead against the desk while I worked her over. "You feel so good."

"You feel even better baby. I'm going to come again until I'm dripping out of your pussy all day long."

"Yes." She begged, lifting her head, and looking back out the door again. "Please." She purred a little louder.

I snickered against her ear and bottomed out hard. "Such a good little cock slut."

"Mmh." She moaned, rocking her hips at my degradation.

"My cock slut."

"Yes, yours. I'm yours Mav." I watched as her back tensed up and seconds later her pussy clamped down tight on my cock as she moaned long and loudly, signaling her orgasm and I couldn't fight it off anymore. I came with a roar, filling her up and slamming her against my desk as I fought to control my need for her. "Oh my goodness." She mused with a chuckle as she lay under me.

"Yeah, I'd say." I agreed, kissing her shoulder, and then stood up and pulled out of her. I noticed the lobby was empty outside of my office and wondered when Dex had walked away but moved on from it to help Cora get cleaned up and dressed.

When we finally settled down at the table to eat our lunch, we were both calmer and relaxed. "How did you know I needed this?" I asked her as I dug into the meal she chose for me. But she knew I meant more than just the food.

"Because I knew you were no doubt unraveling from not having control over the situation with Veronica. But I wanted you to know that we're solid."

"Have you seen the video?" I asked tentatively.

She stilled, chewing her food before wiping her mouth. "Yes. I watched it this morning."

"I'm sorry." I could tell without her even bringing it up that it had affected her.

"I knew everything that had happened in the video, you'd told me word for word what went on. But seeing it..." She said, before shuddering. "I hate knowing that she even touched you. That she'll always have that memory to go back on. Disgusts me." She said honestly.

"I'm sorry," I said again, not having any words to make it better at that exact moment. She reached over and put her hand on mine.

"I know that Maverick. I only feel enraged *for* you baby. Not because of you." I took a deep breath and nodded my head to her. "I don't think..." She started, "I don't think I want to go out to eat tonight."

"We can't hide because of this." I reminded her.

"I know, but I also don't want to ever feel like we're putting on a show either. I don't want to act a certain way with you because someone else dictated it. That feels ingenuine and I don't want to ever get to a point in our life where we do that Mav. My parents did that my whole life, always acting like they had strings pulling them around, making them dance for other's entertainment because they cared what others thought of them more than they respected themselves. And look where that has gotten them through the years."

I leaned back in my seat and watched her open up a small part of her past for me, something that she didn't like to do often. "Okay. We'll stay in tonight. We leave the city tomorrow anyway, so it'll be nice to have tonight with just you."

"Just me." She said with a smile. "Think of all the trouble you could get into with just little old me." She hinted.

"Oh darling, if you only knew." I joked and felt at peace with the world for the moment.

Cora was my peace and my haven.

I just had to protect her from all of the world's darkness, so she had peace as well.

Cora stood next to me on the elevator the next morning, riding up to my office wearing a sweet baby pink pantsuit with a white lace top underneath and a breathtaking smile. Today was our last day before we got married, and both of us could feel the excitement in the air.

She had refused to let me keep her at home yet again today, after her hair and makeup appointment yesterday morning before her surprise lunch date visit to my office. I had scheduled a massage and nail appointment at our penthouse today but she had gone behind my back and rescheduled it for tomorrow morning at our home in South Hampton so she could come to Hawthorn Tower today and help me button up some loose ends before our week off next week.

And it made me love this woman even fucking more than I already did.

When we walked off the elevator, she kissed me on the cheek and went to walk off away from me.

"Where are you going?" I asked her quizzically.

"I'm setting up in the board room down the hall." She replied with a raised eyebrow.

"You're working in my office with me today." I said flatly.

"No, I'd get zero work done if I was locked away in your office all day today, and you know it." She deadpanned and took another step backwards towards the secondary conference room between Reid and Dexter's offices.

"Cora." I warned, unmoving from the lobby area of my own office. "I want you close."

"And I want to be productive." She said with a shrug of her shoulders before blowing me a kiss and walking away. I stood rooted in place and watched the gentle sway of her hips in that stupidly sweet pink outfit and groaned, to which she laughed melodically as she disappeared around the corner.

"Women." I muttered in time for Dexter to get off the elevator and see me staring off after her.

"Hmm." He mused, with a clap on my back as he walked off after her towards his own office. He'd been avoiding me since his little peep show yesterday and I was allowing him to until now. Now he needed to come clean.

"Dex, a minute." I said and walked into my office, not standing around any longer to make sure he followed. I knew he would.

Even if he didn't want to.

He walked in after me and shut the door behind him before stopping in the middle of my office with his hand in his pants pocket like he had been done yesterday outside of my door.

He didn't say anything as I dropped off my stuff and then turned to face him.

"Did you enjoy yourself yesterday?" I asked him plainly, fighting the urge to smile like the smug bastard I was. Finally, I gave up the fight and smiled wolfishly at him.

"I should be asking you the same thing." He lobbed back.

"I had a ball-emptying good time."

He smirked and looked at the ground. "I had no intention of interrupting. To be honest, it took me way longer than it should have to realize what I was hearing. And then I was a little... frozen." He said, "I guess I'm a bit out of practice."

My smile fell a bit at the first mention of his love life in years. "You haven't... since..." I said, feeling surprised by his statement.

He rubbed a hand on the back of his neck and looked away. "No."

"Damn," I said, falling into my seat. "It's been four years, Dex."

"I know." He huffed and then sighed. "Believe me, man, *I know.*" He threw himself down in the chair across from my desk that he always sat in and crossed his ankle over his knee. "I just can't seem to make myself do it."

"She really fucked you over didn't she," I asked, toeing a line that Dexter never allowed usually, but he had shared a bit so far.

"Yeah, you could say that."

"Dex..." I started, but to be honest, I didn't know what to say. Cora was better at this than I was, but I knew there wasn't a chance in hell Dex would talk to her about it. I had been his best friend for the better part of eight years at this point, and this was the first time he had dared to speak of his wife since everything went to shit.

"Don't worry about it." He said suddenly, standing up and clearing his throat as he adjusted his tie. "I got to go. Sorry, I was a weird fuck and listened to you screw your wife." He turned away and I could see the self-loathing radiating off of him.

"Dexter." I snapped in anger at hearing him put himself down. "Don't walk away."

"I'll see you at ten for the quarterly meeting." He said without turning around and walked right out of my door without a second hesitation.

"Fuck." I muttered and sighed. I needed to find a way to get him to open up about whatever the fuck had been going on in his life, and I knew exactly who could help me crack the complex code that was Dexter Chase.

Reid.

Because that man could annoy a mime enough to get him to talk, eventually. Luckily for me, the two of them would be trapped with us in the Hamptons for the next two days, and the situation was perfect to let Reid loose on him.

I also had another task to get started if there was even a prayer of getting it done in time for my return to the office in a week.

I dialed the head of maintenance and construction for the tower and had him meet me in my office a few minutes later. Steve was a middle-aged man that had worked in high-rise construction his whole life and his knack for small details was invaluable in this business. He helped me build Hawthorn Tower from the ground up basically, and I knew if anyone could get this done, it was him.

"Mr. Jones, I hear congratulations are in order, Sir." He said as he walked into my office with his tablet and notebook under his arm. I stood and shook his hand, walking over to the doorway of the conference room along the edge of my office, and motioned for him to follow along.

    A.M. MCCOY

"Thanks, Steve, that's what I need to talk to you about." I hinted and stood along the wall of windows overlooking the city that mirrored my own. "I need you to renovate this conference room into an office for Cora, my soon-to-be wife."

He raised his eyebrows at me and looked around the space. It was a large boardroom-style space, with a large twenty-person table in the center and extra seating space along the walls. "You want this to be an office?" He asked, looking around before nodding his head. "Okay, that shouldn't be a problem."

"Not just any office, though. I want Cora's space to be as equal to mine as possible. Obviously, my office is nearly four times the size of this space, but she won't need as many different use spaces in here because she will be able to use mine for anything extra that she needs." I turned and walked around the room as I talked. "She needs her own restroom for sure. Then I was thinking desk over here along the exterior wall and then we can put a couch over here by the wall to my office and a small conference table opposite on the hallway wall. I also want her to have the same mirrored glass and door mechanisms that I have. And it needs to be feminine yet powerful."

He eyed me closely with a knowing smile on his face as I went into detail about the color scheme I was envisioning for her and her future assistant's space outside of her office. When I got it all out, I got down to the part that was going to make him twitchy.

"I want it done by the Monday after next," I said firmly, as his eyebrows shot to his hairline once again.

"Ten days?" He specified.

"Exactly. Money is no consideration here Steve, hire thirty new carpenters if you need them and pay them double to work around the clock, I don't care. Work with Sasha from Lading Designs for the design and décor of the space and get it done as close to Monday as possible. We'll be coming back from our mini honeymoon, and she wants to get right into work, I want to surprise her with this. She's working in the boardroom between Reid and Dex right now and I can't have my wife in those kinds of volatile conditions."

He chuckled, knowing exactly what kind of brute Dex was and what kind of shameless flirt and gossip that Reid was. "I'll get the team on it right away." He said, shaking my hand and taking a few pictures of the space before leaving with his task while I went back to my own office, feeling excited to get this done for her to surprise her.

Chapter 20 – Cora

I sat at my makeshift desk in the board room between Reid and Dexter's office staring out of the window while I tapped my pen against my notebook obsessively. The door to the boardroom opened on Reid's side and he walked towards me with a shit eating grin on his face.

"One of two things is going to happen having you working here so close to me." He said, as I looked up. Pulling myself out of my conundrum of a daydream. "I'm either A," he said holding out his finger, "going to get absolutely no work done at all ever, because I'll be too busy standing in here distracted and having fun with you." He ticked off his other finger. "Or B, you're going to find some way to become my boss and make me your slave, in which case I'll be the most productive person in the world because I can already tell you run a tight ship."

I rolled my eyes at him, and he laughed, standing over my shoulder and looking down at my blank notebook page.

"Or maybe you're the one with a distraction and productivity problem." He joked, as I elbowed him in the stomach. He sat down in the chair next to me and leaned back. "What's on your mind?"

I chewed on my lip and looked at him, but still didn't say anything. I'd worked diligently for the first few hours of the day, clearing task after task off Maverick's plate, even sitting in on an interview with HR for a new assistant.

Whom I positively loved.

Because he was overqualified and incredibly professional.

He was also, a he.

Win for me!

But since lunch, as I watched the clock get closer and closer to the end of the day and the time that we left for our wedding, I was painfully aware that I needed help. Yet I had no idea who or where to get it from.

"Cora!" Reid said, snapping his fingers in front of my face. "What's with you? You're acting strange."

I chewed my lip again and looked down at my empty notebook page. "I need your help," I said to him quickly, closing my book with a resounding thud.

"Uh." He backpedaled, "No offense, Cora, but I get into trouble when I help you." He said, and I deflated a bit before a wide, devilish grin crossed his rugged pretty boy face. "Who am I kidding, I love your kind of trouble." He said, leaning forward again and clapping his hands. "How are we making Maverick raging mad today?"

His eyes gleamed with mischief, and I laughed, feeling a bit of stress leave my shoulders.

The other door to the boardroom opened and Dexter strolled in from his office, looking at ease. And I couldn't help the shiver of embarrassment that coursed through my system, remembering the look of lust on his face as he stood outside of Maverick's mirrored door yesterday, listening to us have sex.

He looked at me, and for the briefest of seconds, I thought I could see the look of trepidation in his eyes as he walked further into the room, but his cool, composed mask slid into place so quickly, that I couldn't be sure.

"Are you going to sit in here and bother her every day?" Dexter asked Reid, who flipped him off.

"Like you weren't coming in to do exactly the same thing." Reid deadpanned.

Dexter nonchalantly shrugged his shoulders, and I relaxed a bit into my chair, if he could act like it wasn't weird, so could I.

"Actually," Reid started, "Cora here was just asking for my help in making Maverick pissing mad again, and of course, I agreed. You in?" He asked his friend.

Dexter's eyebrows raised to his hairline, and he looked at me with question, "You want to make Maverick mad and you're enlisting Reid's help to do it?" He asked, holding my stare in a way that I'd learned was his signature intimidation move. "I'm a bit offended you didn't come to me first, considering how close of friends we've become."

I rolled my eyes and threw one of my extra pens at him as he sat down on the other side of me and leaned forward on his elbows. I could have laughed had I not been so plagued with concern over my current conundrum. I had two of the most powerful and eligible men in New York City boxing me in, the very center of their attention, like they were willing to do anything for me at that moment.

"Spill it. What are we doing?" Dexter asked, serious now.

I fought the doubt in my head and then just spit it out. "I want a prenup."

Reid choked and coughed into his hand in shock, and Dexter stared at me without blinking.

When Reid could finally breathe again, he shook his head back and forth as he stared at me in wonder. "Oh, he's going to be so much more than just raging mad at you."

I hit his arm and turned my attention to Dexter, who still hadn't blinked. "You want a prenup?" He asked, and I nodded my head. "To one of Forbes' richest men in the world?" He asked, and I once again nodded. He cocked his head to the side and leaned towards me on his elbows and looked like he was struggling to say his next sentence. "You know, they typically protect the party that comes into the marriage with more, and not the one who comes into the marriage with... nothing." He said. And while I appreciated his attempt at delicacy, I still rolled my eyes at him.

"Believe it or not, Dex, I was top of my graduating class and earned my full ride to Duke on academic grounds, but the only reason I chose to go there was because it was Maverick's dream school. I also earned scholarships to other schools like Berkley, NYU, and Columbia even if my fucked-up family took away my chance to go. I'm a very smart person, so yes, I do know that in our situation, a prenup would normally be requested by Maverick to protect him from me taking any of his money if we divorced." I kind of snapped, but that was because I was already on edge about the topic. "And protecting Maverick is exactly why I want one."

Both men looked downright guilty for their shitty reactions to my plea for help and stayed quiet while I worked through my feelings on it. "I don't want anyone to ever be able to say I'm anything like my family. I don't want to benefit from this marriage financially, that's never been an interest of mine and I want to be able to prove that to the world if I need to."

"He'll never sign it," Dexter said finally, looking compassionate to my cause. "He'd give you his entire empire today if you asked it of him,

Cora, he's never going to allow you to cast yourself out. He's already redrafted his will and trusts to leave you everything in the case of his death, there's no way he'd go and sign a prenup."

"Yeah Cora, I appreciate what you're trying to do here, honestly it's fucking refreshing to see someone be selfless in this dog-eat-dog world that we live in, but even if Dexter wrote one up, Mav would never sign it," Reid said, laying his hand on my arm.

"I know he won't sign it, guys. I know Maverick better than anyone else, and I'm not going to force him to either, because it would take me threatening to not even marry him to get him to do it, and I won't leverage our marriage and union against him like an ultimatum. But if I sign it, if I know that he's protected, it will make me feel better."

"You want to sign a piece of paper that basically says if you and him divorce for any reason, then you'll walk away with nothing you didn't gain together through marriage? Correct?" Dexter asked.

"Kind of correct." I said, grimacing, "If he cheats in any way, I'm taking that fucker for every fucking dime and draining him dry. After I cut off his dick and shove it down his throat, of course."

Reid snorted and Dexter smiled knowingly. "I don't know if I've told you this or not Cora Valentine," Dex said, "But I'm quite a fan of yours, and I'm glad to have you joining our ring of friends."

I smiled and leaned back in my chair, feeling lighter and more at ease, though I still knew Maverick was going to cause an earthquake in New York when I gave him the prenup.

"If you don't shut the hell up, I'm going to puke in your suitcase." I cursed at Reid as he sang Frank Sinatra on his way out of the living room of Maverick's beautiful vacation home on the morning of my wedding, like the asshole I was learning he could be.

I was sitting on the couch with Dexter, my legs stretched out across his lap and a pillow over my head as I waited for the obscene amount of ibuprofen I'd taken to start working so I could start feeling human again.

"Seriously though, who knew Maverick and Reid could drink so much and be so unaffected?" Nat groaned from where she lay on the floor across the room. She'd been lying on the couch when I came out to the living room, but at some point, she'd fallen off.

"It's fucking rude, really." Dexter chirped from next to me and I poked his side with my toe.

"Shouldn't your tolerance be the same as theirs with as often as the three of you go off and get into trouble?" I asked, my voice muffled under my pillow. He reached over and pulled it off my face, letting the sunlight assault my eyes, and hugged it to his chest.

I was glad to see he'd traded his puke bin for a pillow finally. It had been touch and go there for a while.

"Someone has to stay sober around those two hooligans." He said, and I smiled for the first time all morning.

"Remind me to be that person next time, would you?"

"Not a chance darling, I call dibs for the rest of eternity." He groaned, scooting down further on the couch, and putting my pillow over his face. "Ooh, this is heaven." He moaned, and I tried to snatch it back with my toes, but he grabbed both of my ankles and held them captive to keep me from succeeding.

"I thought you were my favorite Dex, but I'm second-guessing that now." I lied.

"You don't get to take that title back now, missy. Not after the four rounds of karaoke I won for you last night."

I scoffed, sitting up quickly and then groaning and holding my head as I fought the nausea to scold him for his bold-faced lie. "You sounded like a dying cat during Dancing Queen and who knew you could get even worse for Shania Twain in the next round."

I could just make out the smile on his face under the edge of the pillow and cursed him for baiting me. He knew he sucked, but by the time the karaoke started last night at the bar we were at, he and I were both way too drunk to care. We put on one hell of a show from what I could remember, before Maverick dragged us off the stage and back to the house. Which was good, because Nat and I had a puking competition on the walk back up the beach and it would have been embarrassing as hell to do that in the middle of the bar.

"God, can you believe you're getting married today?" He asked from his dark cave, and I felt a smile pull my lips as I thought about it.

"Let's just hope Mav goes through with it before he realizes he's marrying way, way down with me." I mused, playing with my engagement ring, and turning to sit with my back against the cushion next to Dexter.

He'd always been so quiet that I had a hard time getting a read on him before, but since I called him during my little shoplifting legal battle, he'd been a perfect ally and I found myself drawn to his quiet friendship. It was quite the contrast to Reid's boisterous and outgoing nature and yet somehow I fell right in between the two formidable men my almost-husband called his very best friends, and they'd accepted me into their pack.

"Did you know every time you say some self-deprecating bullshit like that, Maverick intentionally starves two underprivileged kids in a third-world country?" Dexter asked flatly from next to me and I elbowed him roughly, causing him to groan and lift his head, dislodging his pillow cave.

"Why would you say something like that?" I gasped in shock as he laughed at me.

"Because that's what he used to say to me when I did that shit." He lifted one eyelid to look at me and shrugged his shoulders. I looked over across the room to where Nat lay face down on the carpet and I was pretty sure she was passed back out because she hadn't moved or spoken in the last few minutes.

"So..." I said quietly, waiting for Dexter to open his eye again that he'd just closed before continuing. "I was surprised when Mav told me there would be no plus one needed for you this weekend." I tapped his ring finger on top of the pillow on his lap that was encircled by a gold band. "Considering."

He looked from the end of my finger to my face and then over to Nat before he closed his eyes again and stayed silent. I thought perhaps that he was going to straight up ignore me, but after a while, he sighed and swallowed. I watched in fascination as the long column of his neck muscles worked under the tight skin there in his reclined position. I'd been wrong when I'd met Dexter for the first time thinking that his blonde hair and blue eyes made him look like the boy next door type. Because last night when he'd finally let loose a bit and relaxed, I saw a different side of him, and he was anything but mediocre.

He was downright hot with a brooding, quiet mystery to him that I knew, for a fact, would have sexually intrigued me if I wasn't so consumed with Maverick and his dark looks and moods.

"I'm..." He started, and paused, swallowing again as I waited for him. "It's..." He faded off again and sighed. "I'm more attached to my ring than my marriage at this point."

I raised my eyebrows at him, "That leaves me with more questions than answers, you know that right?"

He smirked an almost sad one-sided smile, "You and me both Cora."

I was about to ask him more, but the front door opened, and Maverick stalked in, wearing a pair of low-hanging athletic shorts and sneakers, dripping with sweat fresh from a run and my brain short-circuited.

"Damn, I'm a lucky woman." I mused and nudged Dex with my elbow. "He's sinfully sexy, right? It's not just my beer goggles?"

Dexter groaned next to me and put his head back down on the cushion, covering it with my pillow once again. "I see better every time I look in the mirror."

Mav raised an eyebrow at us where we sat all buddy-buddy as he wiped his discarded t-shirt over his face and chest. "You two look cozy." He said and I could hear the bit of a challenge in his voice.

I smiled sexily up at him, where he stood ten feet away, laid my head on Dexter's shoulder, and shrugged. "I needed someone to distract me from these cold feet." I lifted my bare feet into the air and wiggled them at him as he scowled deeper. I dropped my feet and smile at his dark look. "I was just kidding."

When he turned and stomped towards the master bedroom without a backward glance, I really started to worry I'd pushed too far.

"Hey! Wait a second," I said, leaping off the couch and running after him. Monkeys with cymbals played inside of my head and my stomach was being tilted like a carnival ride, but I finally caught up to him as he headed into the master bathroom.

His house on the water was magnificent, in a way that everything Maverick touched was. But my favorite part by far was his master bathroom, and I planned on spending an hour every single day of our short honeymoon soaking in the giant tub overlooking the ocean.

But I had to worry about that later because I wasn't sure I was going to be getting a honeymoon, judging by the tight muscles covering Mav's back as he slammed the shower handle open and turned on the water.

"I was kidding Maverick." I tried again, standing still in the center of the bathroom. The alcohol and hangover were clouding my brain, and I was dumbfounded about what led us here. "Maverick!" I snapped, letting my fear morph into anger. "Fucking say something or I'm leaving."

He turned on me like a predator, sweeping his hand out lightning fast, wrapping it around my throat, and pushing me back against the glass shower wall. My eyes rounded, and I grabbed his wrist in surprise as he pressed his body against mine. "You'll leave?" He hissed, "Are you trying to make me a psychopath, Cora? Threatening to leave me is a sure fucking way to do that."

His hand was tight around my throat, not pressing on my windpipe, but I still felt the power behind his grip.

"I meant leave the room. What the hell is wrong with you?" I snapped, trying to stiffen my spine and hold my head high, which was almost impossible with his large hand wrapped tightly around my entire neck from chin to sternum.

"Is something going on with you and Dexter? My best man?" He growled and for the first time in the last five minutes, I saw the vulnerability there.

"Dex?" I asked confused, "Because I was sitting next to him on the couch?" I shoved at his chest, suddenly getting pissed. "Fuck you."

His eyes flared and his body tensed, "He knows what your moans sound like. He knows what noises you make when you take my cock, and then you snuggle up with him on the couch. Of my house!"

"*Your* house?" I yelled, "Get off of me!" I pushed and shoved at him, slapping his arms and hands where they still held me in a vise grip. "You're the one that let him listen to us, Maverick! You fucked me even harder, making me get louder when you saw him there. Don't you dare throw that in my face like it was my doing!"

He fought the barrage of my hits like they hardly stung, while never letting go of my throat. "You. Are. Mine." He growled.

"I never argued that fact, you Neanderthal!" I screamed back at him.

He growled again and crashed his lips down onto mine, stealing my breath and consuming me as I fought against him, biting his lips, and shoving at his chest. He reached up with his free hand and ripped my shirt open straight down the front, exposing my bra-covered breasts to him as he hungrily took a handful of one, pinching my nipple through the padding.

"Bastard!" I screeched, but I grabbed his shorts and shoved them down over his hips in the same second. He kicked them off and pressed his body flush to mine, rubbing his cock against my bare stomach and groaning.

"You. Are. Mine." He repeated, and it sounded like a threat.

"I've never acted like anything but yours Maverick, you were the one that forgot who you belonged to long ago." I threw at him. It was a low blow and the first time I'd vocalized a dig at him for his infidelity a decade ago. "You're the one who stepped out, not me." My voice dropped quietly, the hurt audible in it and I regretted opening that wound the second I did.

His eyes cleared, the anger dissipating as regret flooded them. "Cora." He sighed, but I covered his mouth with my hand.

"Don't." I commanded. "Not today." I shook my head. "But don't you dare ever act like I'm the threat in this relationship. Because I've never wanted anyone else but you, Maverick."

"I know." He said, releasing his hand from my throat and standing up, putting space between us. "I know, baby."

I swallowed and took a deep breath, feeling a calm fill my veins. "I shouldn't have joked about cold feet. I'm sorry."

He shook his head sadly and pushed a lock of hair behind my ear, letting his fingers trail over the sensitive skin beneath the shell of it. "I never should have touched you like this." His eyes fell to my neck where he ran the pad of his thumb over the artery in my neck thumping below the surface. "I'm sorry."

"Please don't." I said, "Don't retract back into that shell of half living with me again. I can't stand it when you go there." I closed my eyes and shook my head.

"I need to control my... need for you. It consumes me sometimes."

I stepped forward and closed the space between us, sliding a fist up his thick cock swinging between us. "Does it look like I shy away from it?"

His eyes fluttered closed as his jaw clenched as I worked my fist up and down him. The air was thick with steam from the shower, and I pushed him backwards with my grip on him until he stepped into the shower. I let go of him and stepped away when he reached for me with a smirk on my face. His glare darkened as he realized I meant to leave him alone. "You're going to leave me high and dry like this?" He reached down and stroked himself and I watched in fascination.

"Your mom and her beauty team will be here soon." I said, pulling my eyes away from his cock and taking my ripped shirt off, throwing it in the trash. "We weren't even supposed to see each other at all today, anyway."

"I want you." He growled and pouted comically, letting the darkness that had plagued him a moment ago fade.

"I want you too. But I want the next time that you're inside of me to be as your wife."

He groaned and his eyes drooped as he continued to stroke himself to my words.

"Wife." He repeated and a small smile crossed his face.

"Mmh." I hummed in agreement. "I should go." I took a step back but couldn't help giving his cock one last longing look.

"Okay." He agreed, smirking when he saw my hesitation.

I bit my lip and then forced my feet to step backwards again, and again until I was at the doorway to the bathroom. "I love you." I sighed and then smiled. "I'll see you at the altar."

He smirked and nodded to me. "I'll be there with bells on Cora Lynn."

I turned and ran from the bathroom, grabbing my bag of things I needed for today, pulling on a new shirt, and left the bedroom.

"Holy cow." I groaned, fanning myself as I entered the living room. Marsha and her team were standing there with an amused look on their faces as Dexter, Reid and Nat smirked at me knowingly. I froze in the middle of the room as all eyes were on me, embarrassingly.

"Nothing like a little hate sex on the morning of your wedding day to start the festivities off with a bang, huh?" Dexter quipped with a devilish grin on his face.

Apparently, we'd been louder than I'd thought.

"Shut it, troublemaker." I growled at him, and then turned to my future mother-in-law with what I hoped was an angelic look on my face. "Ready?"

"Oh darling, I've waited for this day my whole life." She hummed with her honey voice and took my hand, pulling me out towards the large pool house in the back where we would be spending the day getting pampered and ready for my wedding.

My wedding.

GAH!

Chapter 21 – Maverick

The sun was setting over the horizon as I stood next to Reid and Dexter beneath an arbor of wood and flowers in our tuxes. We stood with our backs overlooking the ocean, with the gentle breeze and occasional saltwater spray spritzing through the air.

Reid laid his hand on my shoulder as the violinist started playing the melodic tune that Cora had chosen to walk down the aisle to. My mother stood next to the aisle of white rose petals and smiled at me with tears in her eyes before turning to look at the antique double doors set up to act as a barrier for Cora to start her walk down to me. Nat stood on the other side of the altar in a wine-colored dress and an edgy smile as she winked at me.

I took a deep breath and focused on the doors as they opened, revealing the most breathtaking sight I'd ever seen before.

"Angel," I whispered to myself, and Reid's hand patted my shoulder in agreement before sliding off.

Cora was magnificent as she stepped through the doors with her hand lying on my father's arm. He had offered to walk her down the aisle in place of her father, and she had broken down in tears of joy at his offer. She had always been loved dearly by my parents and I adored that she had them today standing for her as much as for me.

Her honey-blonde hair was swept back in an arrangement of curls and braids with simple white flowers adorning the diamond hairpiece my mother had given her. The dress she wore not only looked made perfectly for her, which I knew it was, but it looked like something that no one else in the world would have been able to wear because it was perfect for my Cora.

It was pristine white satin that draped over her curves like a second skin. It had thin straps holding up the low-cut v-neckline that settled between her breasts tastefully. The fabric hugged her flared hips and then opened into a thigh-high slit adorned with lace before pooling out into a train.

She smiled up at me nervously as my father stopped in front of me, letting the officiant say his part. She took my hand, handing her bouquet to Nat, and stood there with me, while everyone else faded away.

"God, you are exquisite," I said, ignoring whatever the man overseeing the ceremony was saying.

Cora smiled shyly and blushed fourteen shades of red as everyone else laughed.

"Sorry, please continue." I nodded to the man, who did just that.

He spoke his spiel and then it was time to say our vows. I was up first and surprised her when I didn't take a piece of paper out to read off of because everything that I needed to say had been brewing in my heart for nearly three decades.

"Angel," I said as tears already began to pool in her eyes. Everyone else disappeared from around us as I stared into her beautiful blue eyes and saw my destiny. "We were barely old enough to tie our shoes the first time I laid eyes on you, and I had no idea what it meant to love someone romantically then, but I knew what it meant to feel purpose and meaning. And that is what I felt towards you from that very first moment on." She wiped away a tear and took a shuddering breath as I went on. "I never thought twice about my feelings for you over the years, following along with what my heart and my body told me to do, from first asking you to be my girlfriend, then my wife while we were still in elementary school." She chuckled as did my parents. "To asking you to prom and making plans with you for college and life beyond.

"I made terrible mistakes while trying to traverse the grief in my heart over losing Luke and I jeopardized everything because of it. But now, ten years later, with you back in my life and back by my side, I make this promise to you. You will never wonder if you are loved from this moment on. You will never fear loneliness or uncertainty. You will have a steady hand to lead you through life, a strong back to burden the pain and worry of the world for you, and a home full of little feet to fulfill you and love you back in the purest way known to man." Her shoulders shook as she cried, listening to my promises to her. "But most of all, you will never endure pain like you have these last ten years while we were apart because I vow to you here and now, I was made to be yours and I'm never going anywhere. I love you."

She dropped her head and kissed my knuckles, where her little hands held tightly to them between us and took a couple of calming breaths and wiped away her tears before clearing her throat and looking up at me with such love in her eyes.

"Maverick." She started, also not using paper to portray her feelings to me. "From the little boy that protected me on the playground in elementary school, to the jock that would still hold my hand around his friends regardless of the hackling he got. To now, the honorable man standing in front of me promising me every single thing I could ever dream of; it has always been you. I've envisioned this day, regularly throughout my life, and the only thing that has managed to stay the same as my dreams changed was that the man standing here with me was you." She shook her head slowly as I tightened my hands around hers. "It will always be you." My nose burned as tears of my own fought against the iron mask I wore most days.

"I have lived with you and, regrettably, without you. And I know as well as I know the deepest, darkest part of my soul, that I am nothing without you. My very purpose in life is to be the partner and wife that you deserve, so here and now, my vow to you is that I will never leave. You will never fear loneliness like you've known before, because this is it, baby." She smiled through her tears and tilted her head to the side, "You're stuck with me. From now until forever. I love you, Maverick Benjamin Jones, with my entire being."

I stepped forward, canceling what little space was between us, to begin with, and slid a hand around the back of her neck and the other around her hip to land on the small of her back. Her eyes widened in surprise before they fluttered closed as I laid my lips against hers, feeling her smile melt as an unapologetic emotion and love took its place.

The officiant cleared his throat and our family and friends laughed and cheered as I jumped the gun and threw tradition to the wind, kissing my wife for the first time without waiting for anyone to tell me that I could.

"I now pronounce you husband and wife, Maverick, you may continue to kiss your bride." The man said behind us as I did exactly that. I kissed Cora, dipping her back romantically until neither of us could breathe, and finally pulled back, only far enough to press my forehead against hers and breathe her in.

"Hi, husband," Cora whispered whimsically, with a peaceful smile on her face.

"Hi, wife." I responded, "God, what I plan to do to you as my wife." She laughed and leaned into me as we finally pulled back to look at our family, before walking down the aisle hand in hand and stopping on the deck of our home to grab a flute of champagne from the coordinator.

We spent the rest of the evening dancing with our friends and my parents and enjoying the wedded bliss we both so longed for until I noticed the aching longing in Cora's eyes when she looked up at me.

She looked over at me across the expansive deck under the string of lights above us as she stood next to my mother and listened to something she said. But her eyes never left mine, and I could read her like a well-loved book as she beckoned me with those pretty blue irises.

I turned to Reid, who stood next to me where we watched Dexter twirl Nat around the dancefloor expertly and held my hand out for him to shake. He eyed me for a moment before a knowing grin spread across his pretty boy face.

"So that's it, huh? Kicking us all out?" He joked, shaking my hand and pulling me into a one-handed hug, slapping my back and sighing as he held on. "Congratulations Maverick. There's not a better man out there to deserve a woman like Cora. She's incredible, and I'm thrilled for you." He said.

I pulled back, keeping ahold of his hand, and laying one on his shoulder as I looked him in the eyes. "I think that's the most emotional and romantic thing you've ever said before." I joked, to which he scoffed and pulled away.

"That's because you're not a woman I'm trying to seduce." He took a long drink of his bourbon and winked, but the damage had been done.

I'd seen a bit of longing in his eyes as he said those things to me. Maybe Reid was seeing that marriage to a woman like Cora wouldn't have to be an end to anything like he usually whined.

An end to fun.

An end to privacy.

An end to independence.

"You just have to meet the right woman, Reid," I said seriously, waiting for him to look me in the eye. "Then you can find this kind of happiness with it." He didn't reply, but just nodded his head and pulled away as Nat and Dexter came up to us. Nat was twirling in her dress, a good buzz clear in her smile as she pulled me into a warm hug. I hugged her back as Reid left to go hug Cora, signaling to my parents that the reception was over. Nat followed him and I stood side by side with Dexter.

Quiet and pensive Dexter.

Although, tonight, there had been a bit less scowl on his face and more brief unguarded smiles. But right now there was that wise look on his face that only someone that had done this before could have. "Take care of her and your marriage above everything else." He said, looking at me from the corner of his eye. "Don't let small things fester or become more than they are." He continued as I turned to face him and give him my full attention. "And for the love of God, knock her up before she smartens up and realizes that she is the one who married down, not you."

I laughed out loud, gaining the attention of our small party as I shook Dexter's hand, pulling him into a hug as well. "Thank you for being by my side today," I said honestly.

He shrugged his shoulders, fixing his sleeve as he refused to meet my eyes. "I couldn't let Reid have all the fun." He nodded to Cora as she walked up to me and wrapped her arms around my middle as I put my arm around her and kissed the top of her head. "Take care of him for us, will you?" He asked her and pulled her from my arms as she willingly went into his and hugged him tightly. He took a deep breath as she held onto him, and I knew what he was feeling at that moment because Cora gave the best hugs.

He was feeling like the most important person in the world and feeling valued.

Which was something he'd lacked for years now. Thanks to that poor excuse of a wife that he still allowed to tear him down.

"We'll see you next week, Dex. Don't forget to have your mess cleaned off the conference table before I get in there this time. Or I'm dumping it all in the trash." She said, winking at him in jest as he looked over her head at me.

"Don't you worry, darling; your desk will be fresh and clean when you get there." He teased, he was in on the plans for her office renovation but luckily she didn't look too deep into his joke as he pulled away and took off with Reid and Nat in tow, headed back to the city to leave us alone in peace in our home for our honeymoon.

My parents walked up as Cora tucked herself back into my side. And they mirrored our stance, still very much in love even after a marriage of over thirty years.

"Thank you both so much for your help to pull this off in a week," Cora said sweetly.

"It was an honor to be a part of tonight, dear." My dad said, patting her on the shoulder before reaching over to shake my hand. "We're both so happy for you two."

"Thanks, Dad, we appreciate everything you've done for us over the years," I said affectionately, leaning down to kiss my mom on the cheek without letting go of Cora.

My mom patted me on the cheek and then leveled me with a serious look. "Make sure you give her all of your attention this week. Don't let work distract you from a time you'll never get back. Life will never be this simplistic again, trust me." She said knowingly and then turned to leave, not offering us the chance to waste any more time entertaining them.

Chapter 22 – Cora

My wedding night.

I was dead on my feet from such a long day of prep and a crappy night of sleep the night before thanks to all the alcohol I'd drank at our last night of freedom party.

Or at least that's what Reid had called it.

But standing in the center of the patio, under the twinkling lights with my brand-new husband, a current of electricity burned through me as his eyes roved over my body.

Maverick took my hand in his, slowly bringing it to his lips and gently kissing the center of my new wedding ring set before placing my hand on the flat of his chest, on top of his muscled peck.

"Do you feel my heart racing like a teenager's right now?" He asked, smiling down at me in the magical moonlight.

"Matches mine," I replied, lifting his own hand to lie flat over my breast. "Feels like the first time all over again."

"Because it is, Cora. This is the rebirth of us, the fresh start we never thought we'd need." He stepped closer and ran the pad of his thumb over my bottom lip as his eyes lay transfixed there, following the movement of his thumb. "I love you more than the very breath I need to fill my lungs with. I never imagined the way I felt about you could grow. I used to think when we were young with the whole world laid out ahead of us, that I loved you more than anything else, and yet it still grows. Every. Single. Day." He lowered his mouth to mine, seducing me with the rhythmic motion of his lips as I opened mine to him.

His tongue slowly slid in against mine and I tasted him like he was a part of me. "It's too much," I said softly, tangling my fingers in the hair at the back of his head.

"What is?" He asked, his brows pinched together in confusion.

"This ache inside of me for more of you." I stood up on my toes and pressed my body flush against his from nose to toe. "It burns me from the inside out."

"Then let me soothe it, from the inside out." He whispered against my mouth and lifted me, carrying me in a bridal carry across the porch and into our home. He didn't stop or slow until he laid me down in the center of our massive bed. The windows and shades were still open, letting the cool spring air in and with it the moonlight, bathing the bed in its glow.

I memorized every inch of his body as he stood at the end of the bed and slowly pushed each button of his shirt through their hole before dragging his belt free of his slacks. He was teasing me, and usually, I'd be crawling up his body, begging for him to hurry to me and aching to be filled.

But tonight was different.

When he finally stood bare at the end of the bed, he pulled my ankles to him, sliding my sandals from my feet, and then kissed his way up the inside of my thigh until his beard tickled the skin right below my panties.

"Yes." I moaned, raising my arms above my head, and running them back and forth over the cool duvet as I focused on every sensation of the moment.

"Promise me something, Angel." He whispered, pushing my gown up my legs until my thin lace panties were visible to his hungry eyes.

"Anything," I promised as I watched his strong fingers slide under the band of my panties and pull them down my legs. "Whatever you want, it's yours."

"Promise me that in the future, when you are angry with me, and doubt what we have when I inevitably make mistakes, that you'll look back on this moment and remember how desperately I love you. Look back at this moment and feel the thickness of the surrounding air, heavy with my devotion to you."

"Maverick." I cried, "I promise, but only if you do the same when you doubt my dedication to this marriage and fear that I'll leave. Look back and feel this, right now, and trust in us."

"I promise." He sighed and dropped his mouth onto my aching clit, slowly and gently swirling his tongue over the swollen button and dragging out a long, pained moan of pleasure and torture.

"Oh, baby." I buried my fingers in his hair and rocked my hips against his talented mouth as goose bumps coated my entire body.

"You taste divine." He hummed against my clit as his thick fingers rubbed up and down around my entrance.

"Yes." I hissed and clawed at his neck, pressing my pussy into his face more as I chased the promise of pleasure.

He brought one hand up my body and his fingers toyed with the hard peak of my nipple through the silk of my gown, pinching it and then twirling his fingers around it as he mirrored the sensation against my clit. "Come for me, wife. Come on my face so your pussy gets nice and wet for my cock."

"Ah," I cried as he pushed his fingers into me and sucked hard on my clit, pushing me over the edge of my orgasm and careening down the other side. He hummed, moaned, and growled against my clit as I thrashed beneath him until he could take it no longer, finally pulling his face off of my pussy and crawling his naked body up mine to settle between my soaked thighs.

He crashed his lips against mine and drank eagerly from them as he rocked his hips forward and back, rubbing the underside of his cock through my wetness.

"Off." I begged, clutching at the straps of my wedding gown, "Help me take it off."

He slid his hands under my body and pulled the zipper down as I shimmied my arms out of it and then he knelt between my legs, pulled the slinky fabric over my wide hips, and tossed it on the bench at the end of the bed. He stayed knelt between my spread thighs and wrapped his giant fist around his thick cock, stroking himself as he looked down at my naked body before him.

My eyes fluttered closed as my arousal pulsed through my body. I slid my fingertips over my nipples, pulling them into hard peaks again, and then palmed both breasts, playing with them while my husband of a few hours watched like it was the sexiest thing he had ever seen.

"Use your left hand and rub your clit." He ordered as he continued to stroke his cock.

I slid my left hand down my body as his eyes followed its movement to my spread thighs and I ran the pads of my fingers over the swollen flesh of my pussy, circling them around my clit as my back bowed.

"Do you have any idea how sexy it is to watch you play with your pussy with my rings weighing down your finger; claiming you as you pleasure yourself." He growled, tilting his head slightly and biting his bottom lip as his nostrils flared. "So fucking beautiful, Wife."

I leaned forward enough to grab his left hand, newly weighed down with my ring on his finger, and brought it up to my breast, squeezing it under mine as he pinched my nipple. "Touch me Mav. I need you." I whimpered as I continued to play with myself and reached for his cock, squeezing my fist around the bulbous head of him that was nearly purple with need. "Make love to me," I begged, willing him to move over me with my eyes.

He gave in to me and laid down on top of me, letting his weight settle me into the mattress once again, and kissed me deeply, tasting my lips and then my neck and chest as I reached between our bodies and led the head of his cock against my soaked opening and arched my hips to take him. "Tell me how badly you want this." He demanded and rolled his hips to rub himself against me, but withdrew before he pushed in. "Tell me you ache for me like I do for you."

"Yes!" I moaned and leaned up to kiss his neck and shoulder. "I tremble with need Maverick, please don't make me suffer any longer. Make me your wife in body and soul."

He growled and thrust forward, filling my body with his in one achingly slow yet powerful movement. "Fuck." He hissed and cracked his neck like the effort it took to stay slow was a whole-body decision.

I lifted my legs, locking my ankles behind the small of his back as he started a leisurely slow and passionate rhythm that was perfect. We usually fucked hard and quick, and when he was slow or gentle with me it was because he was withdrawing into himself in doubt and self-loathing. But at that moment, in our bedroom on the night of our new marriage, it was perfect.

I clawed up and down his back and arms as he rode me, and he kissed my neck and breasts, working me up into a frenzy of deep, erotic thrusts. Each time he bottomed out, he rolled his hips, rubbing my clit with his body and pushing me further towards my orgasm as he called out to his own.

"So good." I panted, "You feel so good."

"Remember this moment Cora." He said, stilling to take both of my hands in his and entwining our fingers where he pushed them down next to my head on the bed, anchoring us together.

"Maverick." I moaned, turning my head from side to side as my orgasm broke over me like a tidal wave. It started at my core and washed out to my limbs, rolling over and over through my body.

"Open your eyes, baby. Look at me when I make you come like this." Maverick demanded, and I opened my eyes to stare into his bright blue ones that glowed in the moonlight as he watched me shatter around him. His nostrils flared and his pupils dilated and then a moment later his spine straightened as he buried himself inside of me as deep as he could get and moaned my name over and over as he came, finding his bliss in my body.

"Holy fuck." I whispered and Maverick chuckled, leaning down to bury his face in my neck before rolling off of me and pulling me against his side.

"Hmm." He agreed and ran his fingers up and down my spine. "That was otherworldly indeed, Wife."

I nibbled on the flesh of his peck, "Are you forgoing calling me Cora or Angel anymore for the word wife?"

"It has a delightful ring to it, don't you think?"

"Yes, but I like the other names too."

He rolled to face me and pulled my body flush to his front, his heavy cock laying between us against my stomach. "Then I will simply add it to my list of pet names for you, Angel." He said with a devilish smile on his face before leaning forward and kissing me so deeply I lost sense of time and place as we made out like a couple of teenagers again.

"Somehow you've made an honest woman out of me while making me feel like a teenager and kid at heart all over again, Maverick. And I never want to feel anything else when I'm in your arms."

"Your wish is my command."

"I need to go home in time to get a dress for Luke's memorial Saturday," I said from my perch on the couch in Maverick's office. He sat at his desk doing a bit of work, and I was laying out reading a book I found in the library.

A whole-ass library.

In my home.

I pinched myself occasionally to remind myself that this was real, and it was mine.

Maverick was mine.

And my God, he looked so damn good being mine, too.

It was Wednesday, we'd been on our honeymoon for four days and I'd be lying if I said the idea of going back to the city and back to normal life didn't sadden me a bit. He looked up from his computer and peered at me a moment before standing up and walking around his desk. He wore a pair of black athletic shorts and nothing else and he looked... edible.

His tan muscular chest rippled as he prowled across the room towards me and I bit my lip, lying in wait to be consumed as prey.

"Let's go shopping here, we can get you a dress and then we can go back to the city in time for the event Saturday night. I'm in no rush to give up my alone time with you just yet." He said, sitting down on the edge of the couch and putting a hand on the back cushion, leaning over me, and pinning me in.

"I'm in no rush to go back. I quite like this side of you." I said, raising my palm to lie flat against the side of his face, running the pad of my thumb over the faint lines at the edge of his eye.

"What side of me is that?" He asked, turning his face to kiss my palm. I slid it down his neck and pulled him down to me, kissing him gently and then pushing him back a bit.

"The side of you that's calm, relaxed, and utterly obsessed with me." I joked, loving the way the lines next to his eyes deepened when he smiled. He was aging so gracefully, he looked mature and powerful, but now and then I'd get a glimpse of that teenage boy under it all and I'd melt completely for him all over again.

"I don't think my obsession with you is ever going to fade, love, regardless of where we are spending our time."

"Maybe not." I tsked, "But here you have the time to devote to acting on that obsession without other responsibilities." A serious look passed over his face and his smile lines faded as frown lines over his eyebrows deepened. "What?" I asked, suddenly worried about being too needy.

"Say the word and we'll walk away from all of it."

"What?" I asked again, sitting up against the arm of the couch as he leaned in closer, canceling the space I'd put between us to focus. "Away from what?"

"Everything." He said so easily. "Work. Responsibilities that don't revolve around you and our family. I'll walk away from it all. Just say the word."

"Stop it." I gasped and shook my head. "That's not what I was saying," I said hurriedly, because I could *feel* how serious he was about it. He'd walk away from it all for me if I asked him to. "I was just saying there's a difference in you between the two worlds, Mav. But that's not a bad thing, baby. I don't want you to change."

"I'm serious though, Cora." He said. "We have more than enough money to live this same comfortable lifestyle for the next four generations of our family. I don't *need* to go to work every day."

"I know you don't need to, Mav, but it's a giant part of you. And I knew that before we were even out of high school. I knew this was your future, and I still chose to be by your side for it."

He didn't look necessarily convinced, but he didn't look like he was going to jump off the edge and liquidate Jones Holding either. At least not in the next ten minutes.

"I don't want to wake up one day and realize that I waited to live my life until I was too old to enjoy it. I've seen too many men in this lifestyle do that, and I don't want that. And I don't want to miss out on any of the important moments in life with you or our kids."

"You won't Mav, look at your dad. He's in his fifties and he retired years ago to let you take over things. He benefits financially and gets to do whatever the hell he wants to do with his days. You can do the same thing, however, whenever you want to baby. Don't worry about me, I'll tell you if I need more of you. Or if you're smothering me and I need less of you." I added cheekily, and he growled at me.

"Never. You are never getting less of me." He said, leaning in and kissing me again. "I can't possibly give less of myself to you when I feel like I can't exist without you engrained in every part of me."

"Oh, Mav." I sighed dreamily and kissed him. "You're so romantic."

He smiled down at me with a predatory glean in his eyes. "Now go get naked so I can fuck your ass before I take you to town and fuck you in some high-end boutique's dressing room to scandalize the stuck-up patrons." He growled and I could tell he was serious.

I snorted and shook my head. "And there is the Maverick I know and love."

Chapter 23 – Maverick

I held my hand out to my wife, helping her step out of the car and onto the sidewalk outside the boutique in town. She took my breath away, wearing a simple wrap-style lavender summer dress and white strappy sandals. Her long blonde hair was twisted up on the back of her head and I was finding it hard to focus when the slender slope of the back of her neck was calling out for my attention.

Her asshole was still currently filled with my come from when I fucked her an hour ago in the center of our bed, yet the back of her feminine neck was getting my dick hard again.

I was a fucking goner.

"You look exquisite, darling," I told her, loving the way her eyes twinkled with love as she looked up at me.

I held her hand and kissed her softly before walking us up the front steps and opening the door. When we stepped inside, the high-end perfume smell of the place assaulted me, but I gritted my teeth to deal with it for Cora's sake. It was why I loved having a personal shopper for both myself and her, we could avoid these types of places all together.

And especially since the terrible experience Cora had at a shop in the city. She was tense next to me, and I knew she was remembering the shame and mortification those bitches cast down on her, but no one and I mean no one, was going to so much as look in Cora's direction with anything but respect and kindness with me by her side.

I'd make sure of it.

I kissed her temple as a woman looked over to greet us, nearly swallowing her tongue when she saw us standing in her doorway. "Mr. Jones!" She gasped, rushing around the counter. Other women and employees in the store turned quickly at her shocked salutation and were all watching in shocked curiosity.

The press buzz had not died down from the scandal of Veronica's lies last week and word spread quickly about our wedding last weekend, leaving us the most talked about couple in all of New York. Cora posted one candid photo of us dancing after the ceremony to her Instagram and it had gone viral, leaving her inundated with hundreds of thousands of new followers and messages alike. Everyone wanted to know the new Mrs. Jones.

"What an honor to have you both here at Oliva Grace's. Whatever you want or need while you're here, I'll be more than happy to provide for you immediately, Mr. and Mrs. Jones." She said, nodding at Cora but giving me the primary amount of attention. And it seemed that Cora was fine with that as she tucked herself in against my side more. "My name is Aurora and I'm the manager here."

"My wife requires an evening gown for a very important event this Saturday," I said firmly. "We're spending the week at our home on the beach and hope to avoid going back into the city early to get her a dress that meets her needs," I said, leaving it open-ended.

"Of course!" The woman rushed on, turning her attention to Cora. "I'm positive we have exactly what you're looking for. Come with me, and I'll get you both settled in a private dressing room, and we can start showing you dresses." She turned and led the way to the back of the store. I held my hand on the small of Cora's back and walked with her past the other women who, to their credit, did their best to hide their shock and cell phones as they tried to snap pictures of us.

This was the first time we'd been out in public as Mr. and Mrs., and I knew it was likely to draw attention.

Aurora led us into a large room with mirrors, a platform in the center, and a velvet chair directly behind it as her team fluttered in around us wordlessly. I settled myself in the chair, crossing my ankle off my knee, and sat back to watch the process unfold as Cora was doted on. Champagne and snacks were brought into the room as the team of women measured Cora and listened to her tell them what she was looking for.

Of course, Cora, not one to make a fuss of anything kept her description simple in needing a gown that was fitted and not overly statement-making, but Aurora was a professional and listened intently before discreetly turning to me before leaving the room to get started.

"She looks divine in a plunging neckline," I said easily, letting my fingers run over my lips as I stared intently at my wife standing on the platform in front of me. "I'm thinking a rich tone, perhaps royal blue." I mused, envisioning the deep blue against her skin. "Yes, blue." I nodded. "Let's start there." I pulled my eyes away from her flushed cheeks from being in the center of the spotlight and turned to her shopper. "She'll also need matching lingerie and heels. I'll take care of the jewels. I'll help her get undressed, so please don't return until I open the curtain to tell you she's ready."

Aurora nearly sagged to the floor in awe before composing herself, nodding quickly to me and running from the room to do my bidding. When I looked back at Cora, there was a dreamy look in her eyes to match the flush crawling up her chest and face. I stood up and walked towards her, slowly, letting the chase build for the capture.

Her eyes widened, but she stayed rooted as I brought my hand up to the bow at her hip and dragged it undone. She took a deep breath and watched my eyes intently, not dropping them to what my hands were doing as I pulled her dress open, exposing her pretty white matching lingerie before pushing her dress over her arms and tossing it into the chair I vacated. "You are divinity," I said, letting my wonder in her out into the atmosphere. Even on the platform she was shorter than me, but she was almost eye height and I liked that she didn't look up into my eyes right now.

She was regal and so much more than I'd ever encompass into words.

I put both hands on her hips, spreading my fingers wide to cover her ribs above her waist before sliding them around to her back to undo her bra. I'd only just fastened it onto her body an hour ago, yet my mouth watered to bare her skin to my needy eyes already.

She watched me with a lust-filled stare as I unclasped it and pulled it forward and over her arms, tossing it into the chair with her dress. "You bewitch me." I groaned as I palmed her large breasts in both of my hands, tweaking her nipples and drawing a breathy moan from her lips. I knew she was holding back because only a heavy velvet curtain shielded us from the busy store on the other side, but I'd made my intent clear earlier. I was going to scandalize the entire store by fucking my wife in the dressing room.

"Maverick." She whispered as I lowered my lips to her nipple, sucking it into my mouth powerfully and flicking my tongue over it as her eyelids fluttered. "Please wait."

"You're so pretty when you beg," I said, pulling my mouth off her nipple but using my fingers to pinch and pull on them in its place. "Why do you want me to wait," I asked. I dropped my hands down her feminine stomach I ached to see filled with my growing baby and pushed my fingers into the band of her panties. Her breath hitched in her throat as I pushed them down and then helped her step from them, falling to my knees in front of her and looking up at her body. "Why don't you want them all to know who you belong to?"

I leaned forward and pressed my tongue between the lips of her pussy, directly onto her clit and flicked it. Her head fell back as she gripped two handfuls of my hair to keep her balance. I lifted one of her legs over my shoulder and tilted my head, deepening my assault on her pussy as she covered her mouth and moaned. I sucked her clit into my mouth as I held her up with both hands on her ass, devouring her mouthwatering pussy.

"Stop." She panted. "Please." She begged, but she rocked her hips forward, pressing her clit into my mouth further. I smiled against her flesh, knowing she was mine regardless of what she said.

"Come on my face, and then I'll let you free," I told her, rolling my tongue over the sensitive bud, and then pushed it deep into her opening, groaning loudly as I got a full taste of her arousal. "Come for me Wife. Now." I demanded firmly and spanked her ass, loving that she was going to wear that mark in front of the women who were about to dress her.

She gasped and moaned loudly as her clit twitched and pulsed in my mouth, pushing her orgasm over her senses. She rocked her hips, both hands still buried in my hair as she came on and on, and I never relented on the suction of her clit while she did, drawing it out until she was shaking in my arms.

Only then did I let her free of my mouth, gently kissing my way up her stomach and chest, paying attention to both of her swollen nipples and then to her lips, pushing my tongue deep into her mouth as she sucked on it seductively. "Oh, God." She moaned and rested her forehead on my shoulder as I held her up. "You're incredibly talented at that, husband." She mused, a sated smile on her face.

"Do you know why I did that, here and now?" I asked her as I pulled the satin-changing robe they left for her over her shoulders and tied it around her slim waist.

"Why?" She asked.

"Because I wanted you relaxed and sure of yourself while you allow these women to help you. I wanted them all to know I was so over-whelmed with you that I took you here, privacy be damned because that's how badly I *need* you." I growled. "No one will dare to treat you with anything less than you deserve ever again. Not if I have anything to say about it."

She melted in my arms, and I wrapped them around her tightly. "I love you so much, Maverick. I can't believe I got my fairytale ending back."

I chuckled into her hair and stepped back from her. "This is far from the end darling, I have so much of the world to show you."

She stayed standing on the pedestal and I walked over to the curtain, throwing it back and revealing a blushing Aurora and four others standing awkwardly with arms laden down, waiting to come back in. "Thank you for your patience," I said, running the pad of my thumb over my bottom lip dramatically and reveling in the way the women's eyes widened and they blushed even more as a groan of embarrassment sounded from behind me.

I sat back down and supervised the staff of the shop fussing over Cora like she was the Queen of England herself.

The first gown they put on Cora was the one, I knew it instantly. But I indulged the experience and let them fawn over my beautiful wife, donning dress after dress on her delectable body until she was sure which dress she loved the most.

"The first one." She said firmly, before looking over her shoulder at me for my opinion and I smiled wolfishly at her.

"It was my favorite." It was a deep royal blue in satin, the tiny straps led to a deep V-neck that ended directly under Cora's voluptuous breasts. The bodice cinched in tight at her waist and then flared out dramatically into a full satin skirt over her wide hips.

She looked divine, and I knew instantly what type of jewels I needed to adorn her with for the event.

Aurora checked us out at the counter, gazing longingly at my black Centurion credit card as she slid it through the machine. I'm sure she worked on commission and was set to make a hefty cut of the designer dress, but I wanted to reward her more for her kindness to Cora. I pulled my money clip out, handed her a bundle of hundreds and nodded to her, "For your kindness and professionalism."

Her eyes rounded as she took the money and slid it into her pocket. "Of course Mr. Jones." She said and turned to Cora. "It was a pleasure to have you in our store today, Ma'am. Please come back anytime you need anything else and we'll make sure to see to your every need."

"Thank you Aurora, it's been a wonderful experience," Cora replied sweetly, and I took her hand, leading her from the store with her heavy garment bag over my arm. I walked to the car laid it out across the back seat and went to open her door for her, but she paused and stepped back.

"I want to run across the street for some snacks." She said, nodding to the convenience store and looked downright devilish.

"You do love your snacks, don't you?" I mused. "I have to make a phone call, anyway."

"I'll run over and be right back then." She stood up on her toes and kissed me sweetly. "And I'll be sure to grab you some peanut butter cups because we both know if I don't get you your own, you'll eat all of mine." She said and winked as she pulled back.

"Hurry back," I called after her as she crossed the busy street at the crosswalk. I found myself rooted right in place, watching her graceful legs as she gently jogged out of the way of traffic and into the store. But I shook myself out of it and picked up my phone, dialing the man I needed to help me finish her look for Saturday night.

"Ruby, it's Maverick Jones. It seems I need your assistance on another time-sensitive project for my wife." I said when the older man answered.

"Oh, Mr. Jones! What an honor to be a part of another project for the lovely Cora, what can I help you with?"

"We have the charity event for my brother's memorial this Saturday, and we've just picked out Cora's dress, a satin sapphire gown, and I want to drape her with diamonds and jewels to match. Can you help me?"

"Ooh Mr. Jones, I can help you for sure!" He said, and I laughed at the giddy mirth in his voice. We talked for a few more minutes about the ideas I had and then hung up, with the man on the mission to get me pictures within the hour and the jewels delivered to our penthouse, ready for Saturday night after I picked out the final set.

I turned towards the shop across the street in time to see Cora step out of the front door with a bag filled to the brim with her loot and chuckled. She met my eyes over the roof of the car and smiled guiltily at the amount of snacks she got. She paused at the crosswalk, waiting for the light to change so she could cross, and then she stepped out onto the street.

A shiver crawled up my spine and moved down my arms as I watched her elegantly walk across the street, but it wasn't out of admiration this time. Something was wrong.

A second later I heard it, the rev of an engine coming from the other end of the block, and my gut sank as I whipped my head towards the sound.

A black truck weaved around traffic as it raced towards the intersection like it was intentionally trying to break the law.

I whipped my head back towards the intersection as the truck neared and screamed for my wife. "Cora!" But she was already turning her head towards the noise of the truck barreling down on her. I dropped my phone from my hands and took off at a sprint towards her as she whipped her body around towards the other sidewalk and tried desperately to get out of the truck's way in time. "Cora!" I screamed again.

People were frozen all around us as they watched the horrific scene unfold. The truck blasted through the intersection, swerving right towards Cora and it blocked my view of her as my heart sank. I couldn't see where she was, I couldn't see if she got out of the way in time as my legs pumped powerfully, carrying me towards the scene.

The truck sideswiped a car parked on the side of the street before the crosswalk, and it clicked in my brain that it was trying to run Cora down.

Chaos broke out, multiple people screamed as the truck collided with multiple other cars before racing off down the street, away from the scene.

But I couldn't pay it any more attention as I finally got across the street to where Cora lay on the ground. "Cora, baby!" I wrapped my hands around her arms as she bolted upright, trying to scramble the rest of the way out of the street and my heart finally started beating again as I realized she hadn't been hit. "Shh," I said, "You're okay."

She was hysterical, her eyes were wide, and she was as white as a ghost as she clung to me. "Mav! He... he aimed..." She stuttered in shock. I ran my hands up and down her arms, checking for injuries there and on her head and face, but all was clear.

Her knee was scraped open from falling on the ground, and her dress was ripped along her thigh, but other than that, she was fine. "Oh, my God." I gasped and crushed her to me. "Holy fuck." She clung to me, gripping my shirt in her tiny hands as she tried to calm down too. "You're okay baby, it's alright."

People gathered all around us, watching in horror as multiple people called 9-1-1 and relayed information about the truck to the operators.

"I want to get up." She said, looking around at all the people and cellphones aimed in her direction. "Mav, get me out of here."

"Shh." I said, picking her up, cradling her against my chest, and looking around, trying to find a gap away from everyone.

"Is she okay?"

"I called 9-1-1."

"Was she hit?"

"That truck ran her down!"

Everyone was yelling out in shock and dismay, and Cora shook in my arms. I needed to get her out of here. Traffic was completely stopped all around, thanks to the multiple cars that had been pushed out into traffic after the truck hit them, so I crossed through the wreckage towards my car across the street.

I opened the passenger door and gently sat Cora down on the seat, taking her face in my hands and kissing her deeply. I felt her shakes become more violent as the adrenalin wore off and I ran my hands back down her body. "Does anything hurt? Is anything broken?" I asked.

"No." She gasped, shaking her head. "I just tripped and fell. It didn't hit me."

"Okay," I said again and took a deep breath. "Let's get you out of here."

"Cora, are you okay?" A woman asked from behind me, and I turned to find Aurora standing outside her store with a ghost-like look on her face.

"I'm taking her home. Can you do me a favor, Aurora?" I asked her, and she nodded quickly.

"Of course. Anything."

"When the police get here, tell them the truck tried to run her down and that I took her home to get her away from the crowd forming. And give them our address, they can come there for a statement." I said, telling her our address, though most everyone in this elite neighborhood knew where I lived anyway.

"Absolutely." She said, taking the card I handed to her and giving Cora a small smile. "I'll take care of it."

"Thanks," I said, putting my hand on her shoulder before shutting Cora's door and hurrying around the car, pulling out and weaving around the stopped cars on the way to our home.

I picked her hand up from her lap, gently trying to avoid the few scrapes on the palm, and kissed it, needing to touch her to assure myself that she was really okay. She had a death grip on my hand the whole way home, refusing to let go.

And I was all too happy to indulge her.

Chapter 24 – Cora

I t was Friday night, and we were due to leave for the city in the morning so we could get ready for the memorial fundraiser at the penthouse. We'd finished dinner and were lying on the couch watching a movie, but my mind was elsewhere.

Someone had tried to kill me.

That's what Maverick had said after we spoke with the police on Wednesday. Two days ago, someone tried to run me down on the street and kill me. And I couldn't... wrap my head around it.

I was a nobody.

No one.

Inconsequential.

Sure, I was married to a powerful man. But it didn't feel like an attack on him through me. But what the hell did I know about it, I'd thankfully avoided assassination attempts up until this point in my life.

When we'd gotten home from town, Maverick had been... deranged. He had withdrawn from the present reality and sank into a dark, dark hole inside of himself as he processed everything. He'd been doting and affectionate and caring for me hand and foot, but I'd seen the darkness in his eyes. Someone had tried to take me from him.

And he was going to move heaven and hell to find them and make them pay.

Cellphone footage of the attempt had quickly made its way into the biggest tabloids in the country, and with it came a barrage of different stories about the who, or the why someone would try to kill me. And according to police, they had no leads.

But Maverick was not a man to sit idly and let something like that just…go. He'd hired guards upon guards to literally just stand around the house and follow us around when we left to go home tomorrow. I was informed that I would have a personal guard with me at all times that I was outside of our home, from that moment on. And he had also informed me that I wasn't allowed to leave the house, without him.

To be honest, I was absolutely fine with that, because I had no ambition to go somewhere so there could be a repeat performance of the truck fiasco. But I also knew, in the back of my head, that I couldn't stay a prisoner in my own home for the rest of my life.

"What are you thinking about?" Maverick asked, from where he lay with his back pressed into the corner of the sectional couch in the den, holding me with my back pressed to his chest.

"How do you know I'm thinking about anything? We're watching a movie." I said, trying to take the melancholy out of my voice. I didn't want to ruin our last evening as honeymooners with thoughts about something I had no control over currently.

"Because I can feel your brain spinning from here." He said easily, tightening his arms around my waist and laying his chin on my shoulder. "Talk to me. You've been quiet." He whispered gently against my ear.

I sighed, hit pause on the movie that was playing, and relaxed into his arms. "Who would want to hurt me?" I asked. "I don't understand it, Mav. I'm a nobody."

"You're wrong." He said firmly. "You're the very center of my universe." I scoffed at him. But he didn't relent. "I mean it Cora; someone may have tried to hurt me by taking you away from me. And unfortunately, the list of people that I've angered over the years is… daunting."

I could hear the remorse in his voice, and I ached to soothe it for him, but I couldn't. Because he was right.

Someone was trying to hurt him through me, and neither of us knew who it was. And that made me feel vulnerable.

"So what do we do?" I asked him.

"*We* don't do anything." He said resolutely. "I have hundreds of people contracted right now to find who did this. So right now, you just have to be patient with me while I figure this all out. And in the meantime, I want you to just stay calm and try really hard to not let it scare you too much." I snorted in disbelief, and he chuckled in my ear. "Just think of it this way, baby. You're stuck with me now, even more than before. Where you go, I go. What you do, I do. You've got yourself a new shadow." He joked.

"I don't mind having you attached to my hip, Mav, I just don't want to do it out of fear," I said sadly. "I'm tired of living my life based on someone else's actions."

"I know." He said. "I know, baby."

We lay there like that for quite a while in silence. Both of our heads were spinning with unanswered questions and concerns, and I finally just needed a break.

"I'm getting more snacks," I said, pulling myself from Maverick's arms. "Want another peanut butter cup?" I asked him with a sly smile on my face.

He laid his head back on the pillow and smirked. "I ate all of mine."

"Good thing I knew you would and got you more than I told you." I kissed his nose and walked back into the kitchen where the bag of snacks, that I'd somehow managed to keep locked in my clutches while I ran for my life, lay on the counter.

Apparently, I value a few things in my life, and snacks are one of them.

I dug around in the bag, looking for but not finding what I wanted, so I tipped it over and dumped all of the candy and snacks out onto the counter. Among the pile of goodies was a small box that I had forgotten I bought in the convenience store that day.

A pregnancy test.

I'd picked it up, figuring it'd be good to have on hand if my period turned out to be late but hadn't thought about it again since everything happened.

As I stood at the counter, I was suddenly torn about what I wanted in terms of pregnancy. I'd been so happy and excited to try to get pregnant before, but now, knowing someone had tried to kill me, the prospect of carrying a little defenseless life inside of me, terrified me.

If I couldn't even protect myself, how was I going to protect an unborn baby?

I hated that someone was able to taint the joy we'd been living off of while trying to get pregnant, and it left me... angry.

"Maverick," I called, staring down at the box on the counter. "Come here for a second, please."

A moment later my husband walked into the kitchen, looking perfectly content to be summoned by me, and wrapped his hands around my stomach to hold me. "What is it?"

I held the pregnancy test up and showed it to him, looking over my shoulder. "I forgot I'd bought this the other day, with all the snacks."

He took the box from my hand, like looking at it closer would give him the answers he wanted to know. "Your period is due tomorrow, right?" We'd talked about it so much lately he was paying attention to my cycle.

"Yeah."

"Do you want to take one now?" He asked, and I couldn't miss the excitement in his voice, and it broke my heart. I dropped my head into my hands and shook my head back and forth as I lost hold of my emotions. I hadn't cried about the attempt on my life, I'd compartmentalized it like if I didn't think about the pain of it, then it wouldn't hurt.

But now that dam had broken free, and tears poured out of my eyes.

"Hey," Maverick said softly, throwing the box onto the counter and picking me up, turning me around to sit on the counter as he stepped between my legs and pulled me into his arms. "Hey, don't cry, baby. Please don't cry." He begged, squeezing me tight as my cries turned to sobs.

"I'm sorry," I said, hiccupping and holding onto him tighter.

"Shh." He said lovingly, running his hands up my back and soothing me until I was able to control the sobs and calm down. "Talk to me."

"I'm terrified that if I'm pregnant, something bad will happen to the baby because of whatever that person was doing when they tried to hurt me. What if something happens to our baby because of us?" I asked, looking up into his strong and steady eyes like he'd have all the answers for me.

"I can't promise you that something won't happen, Cora. I wish I could." He said, closing his eyes as it pained him to admit that he didn't have control of the world. "But I can promise you that we'll do our very best to protect our family. I'll protect you."

I shook my head. "I was so excited to take a test, but now I'm just... afraid."

"I know." He said, validating my feelings. "Me too. But I'm still excited if I'm being honest." He leaned down, so I had to look at him and he had a small smile on his face, and it warmed my heart. "Tell me you still want to have a baby with me."

"I still want to have your baby, Mav," I said instantly, not hesitating out of fear or anything else. "I do."

"Then let's go take the test, and we'll figure the rest out as we go." He was so strong and sure I found myself leaning into him and nodding my head, letting his excitement pull my own out as he led me down the hallway toward the master suite with the little box in his hands. "How do we do this?" He asked, tearing the box open and pulling out the pamphlet that looked to be twenty pages long.

I chuckled at him, grabbing one stick from him and a paper cup from under the sink. "You stay here while I go pee and dip the stick in it. Then we wait." I said, nodding to the pamphlet, "Read how long we wait after we dip."

I went into the toilet room and peed in the cup, dipping the stick into it afterward and then wrapping it back up in the wrapper.

When I came out and washed my hands, we both stared at the wrapper-covered test on the counter between us like we'd be able to see the results through it or something.

"How long?" I asked him, walking into his open arms as I dried my hands and let his warm embrace calm my nerves.

"Three minutes." He said and sighed. "Three minutes to find out if my come is as strong as I think it is."

I snorted into his chest and then laughed. It felt good to laugh after all the fear over the last few minutes. He held me like that until the three minutes had come and gone, yet neither of us made any move for the test until it was almost rude not to look at it.

Maverick kissed the top of my hair and reached for it, taking a deep breath before pulling the wrapper off of it.

Pregnant.

"Oh, my God." I gasped, covering my mouth, and staring in shock.

"Hell yes!" Mav roared, tossing the test down on the counter and picking me up, swinging me around the bathroom in his arms and cheering boisterously. "We're going to be parents!"

I laughed, wrapped my legs around his waist, and held onto him as cheer and unapologetic joy filled our souls.

We had wanted this so badly. We'd waited ten years for this without even realizing it. We deserved this.

And as my husband twirled me around the bathroom some more, cheering and celebrating, I vowed to never second guess it or worry if now was the right time again because I wouldn't regret or second guess this baby again, not once.

It was amazing how quickly you could love something that even five minutes ago you didn't know existed.

But I did.

I was indisputably in love with our teeny tiny baby growing inside of me. And I was going to embrace it.

"Mav, baby." I moaned, arching my back and spreading my legs wide around his shoulders. "Mmh." I'd been sleeping thirty seconds ago, and the electric feel of Mav's tongue had woken me up, running over my clit.

What a hell of a way to wake up.

"You taste so fucking good." He hummed against my pussy before sucking my clit into his mouth.

I looked down at my body in the dark bedroom and watched my Adonis of a husband sprawled out on the bed feasting on me and moaned. "God, yes." I stretched my arms above my head and shivered in pleasure.

Maverick's usual insatiable sexual appetite has only been heightened since finding out that we're pregnant. He fucked me on the bathroom counter after reading the tests, in the shower, in bed, and on the couch.

And judging by the lack of light coming through the blinds, that was still only a few hours ago.

"I need you." He groaned against my body. "I'm fucking obsessed."

"I'm not complaining." I joked and reached down my body to pull him up to me. He crawled up and laid between my legs and I moaned when I felt his hard cock press against my wet pussy. "I'm going to need you to wake me up like this every morning for the rest of my life." I joked and his smile was breathtaking.

"That could be arranged." He said as he leaned down and kissed my neck, sucking on the skin.

"Careful mister! No hickeys for the fundraiser tomorrow."

"What about if I gave you one right... here?" He asked, dropping his lips to the swell of my breast.

"Thanks to the plunging neckline you requested, that would be visible, too."

"Hmm." He said, moving to the other breast, suckling on it, and then moving back up my neck to nibble my ear. He rocked his hips, running the underside of his cock through my wet lips, coating it. "I want your ass." He said and pulled back to kneel between my legs. "Roll over."

He put his hands on my hips, twisted me over onto my stomach, and pulled my hips up into the air. I chuckled at him as I braced my elbows on the bed and spread my legs to open myself to him. "Eager?"

"For you, always." He said, leaning down and licking my ass, pushing his tongue in deep before pulling away and getting lube from the end table next to the bed. But he didn't just come back with the lube, in his other hand, he had a purple vibrator that was thick and bulbous.

"Feeling frisky Mr. Jones?" I asked, raising my head up to look over my shoulder as he crawled back up behind my exposed ass.

"For you, always." He repeated and leaned back down to lick my ass again. "Did you know you're the only woman I've ever done anal with?"

I felt my jaw go slack as I looked back at him in surprise. "Seriously? Why?" Not that I was complaining. I liked having something of his that was only for me.

He shrugged his shoulders as he opened up the lube and poured it onto the top of the dildo, watching in fascination as it slid down the purple surface. "Because no other woman has ever aroused me so badly that I needed to possess her there. Not like you."

"Where are you planning on putting that?" I asked, eyeing the thick toy. It was smaller than his cock, but more grooved and bumpier.

"I'm going to put it in both of your holes before we're done." He answered so nonchalantly. "But I'm going to start with it in your pussy. Lean forward and arch your ass more, baby."

I groaned, leaning down on my chest, and tilting my ass up how he liked. He pressed the end of the purple vibrator against my pussy opening and pushed it in, letting the lube spread up the shaft as he pushed it deeper. The head of the toy was angled slightly, and it rubbed against that magic spot inside of me. "Mmh." I moaned, spreading my legs out further underneath me.

"That's my good girl." He thrust it in and out a few times before he clicked the button on the end, and it started vibrating inside of me. I mewed and purred as he kept up the thrusting and then turned up the vibrating, making me cry out with need. "Oh, that's so good."

I heard the lid of the lube open again and seconds later, the cold liquid hit my exposed ass and then Mav's hard cock was pressing against the tight muscles. "Holy fuck." He groaned, letting go of the vibrator to wrap both hands around my hips and pull me backward onto his cock fully. He hissed and his cock twitched inside of me. "I can feel the vibrator against my cock." He moaned again and pulled out and pushed back in. "The entire length of it, holy fuck. That feels incredible."

He was on edge, barely hanging on by a thread, and I couldn't help the smile that pulled my lips back as I tightened on his cock and the toy. A slew of curses came from him and I moved my hips to pull me off his cock and then pushed back into him. "Cora." He warned, his hands holding my hips in a bruising hold. "I'm fucking close already."

"If you don't fuck me, I'm going to kick you off and fuck myself with that amazing vibrator." I challenged him and reached under my body to grab the handle of the vibrator that he'd abandoned in his own need. I pulled it out and pushed it back in, and he groaned again. I could feel the vibrator rubbing against his cock through my body in such a weird and foreign way, but I fucking loved it. I pushed the vibrator in until it was pressed against my G-spot and held it there, angling the head against it to get the most pleasure from it. "Oh, God." I moaned and Maverick lost his hold on his sanity and slammed his cock back into my ass all the way and started fucking me.

"I want you to squirt when you come." He said through clenched teeth. "I want you to fucking cover me with it."

"Mav, I don't know how." I gasped. "You made me do it last time, I don't know how."

"Come here." He said, tightening his hands around my arms right above my elbows and pulling me up until my back was against his chest. His cock was stretching my ass at this angle, and it hurt, but it was short-lived because he reached around and grabbed the head of the vibrator from my hands, and pressed his other hand flat against my stomach. "I fucking want it." He growled in my ear as he crouched down lower behind me to slam his cock deep.

"Holy shit." I gasped and put my hands on my thighs to brace myself.

"Feels. So. Fucking. Good." He bit out and I knew he was on the edge of his own orgasm, but he was forcing himself to hold off until he got me there. There were so many sensations going on at the same time, and I closed my eyes to shut out everything else.

"Yes." I gasped, the vibrator was pushed straight onto my g-spot with his hand on the outside of my stomach pressing it in even harder, his cock was thrusting in and out of my ass and I reached up and pinched my nipples as the dam broke, and I fell headfirst into a giant orgasm.

"Come, baby," Mav demanded. "Fucking come on my cock. Give me what I want." He said, and he leaned down and bit down on the top of my shoulder along my neck painfully as his restraint snapped. He started coming as my ass clenched down hard on his cock and then that liquid fire spread through my clit and then coated my thighs as I started squirting around the vibrator. "Fuck yes." He roared, pulling out the toy and rubbing his hand back and forth over my clit, elongating the powerful orgasm. "That's my fucking slut."

"Fuck!" I screamed, falling forward on my hands as he drove his cock in powerfully, shoving me forward onto the bed as he fucked me through both of our orgasms. "Holy shit." I gasped, pushing the pillows out from under my head as I fought to catch my breath. "Oh, my fucking—"

He chuckled against my back, leaning over me to kiss the mark on my shoulder from his teeth before kissing down my spine. "Again."

"What?" I gasped as he quickly pulled his cock out of my ass and held my cheeks open to look into my gaping ass that was filled to the brim with his come.

"Fuck that's sexy." He said, but then hurried on, flipping me over onto my back and pulling me around the side of the bed so that my hips hung off the end right above the bench. He knelt on the bench and pushed my legs wide.

"Maverick Jones, there's no way you could possibly be able to—" But I didn't get another word out as he fisted his still rock-hard cock and slammed it deep into my pussy. "Oh, my God!" I gasped and dug my nails into his stomach as he fucked me deep and hard.

"That's right baby, I am your God." He said with a devilish smile on his face. "I control your body." He said and reached down. "This cunt." He rubbed his thumb over my clit. "This ass." He reached under me with his other hand and pushed two fingers deep inside my used hole. "I own it all."

"Oh, my God." I panted again on repeat as I clung to him while he savagely fucked my body like a lifeless toy. "It's all yours."

"Damn right it is. And right now, I want my pussy to squirt again." He said and took his hand from behind me and laid it flat on my stomach, pressing gently into that magic spot. "I won't be able to do this once our baby grows. So I'm going to drain every drop from you while I can."

"You're an animal." I gasped, rolling my nipples through my fingers. They were so sensitive, and it heightened every other sensation.

"I'm an animal because you draw it out of me. It's your fault." He said with a vicious smile on his face.

"Hmm." I mused, incapable of saying anything else as he worked my body back to its boiling point.

"That's it, baby." He praised me when I started clawing at him, chasing euphoria. "There's my dirty little slut, always ready for more, aren't you?" He asked, rubbing harder on my clit and forcing my orgasm to crescendo, drawing that branding heat out of my core, covering his cock and my thighs.

"Maverick!" I screamed overcome by it all.

"That's a good girl. Fuck, that's so sexy Angel." He growled and thrust harder and then roared his own release into the dark room around us.

He pulled out of me and leaned forward on his arms, gasping for his breath.

I ran my fingertips over the side of his face where he hovered above me. "Well Mr. Jones, I think that was one hell of a way to end a honeymoon." I smiled up at him as his face split into a breathtaking smile.

He slid his hands around my waist and stood up, taking me with him. I wrapped my legs around him and held on.

"Oh honey, we've got almost six more hours before we need to head back to the city, I'm far from done with you."

"Mr. Jones." I squeaked scandalously as he carried me down the hallway. "Where are we going?"

"To the spare bedroom, since you made such a mess in ours." He said cheekily, and I slapped his chest with a glare.

"Not my fault."

"No." He laughed and held me closer. "No, it wasn't baby. But I'm going to let you sleep for a few more hours before I wake you up and wreck the spare room too before we go home."

"Jeeze Louise," I murmured but I would be lying if I said I wasn't completely on board with being used sexually by my husband like this.

Chapter 25- Maverick

I stood in the doorway of our master closet and admired the beauty standing in front of the mirror, twirling side to side to see her reflection in her sapphire blue dress.

"You take my breath away," I said and watched her crystal blue eyes snap up to mine in the mirror as she looked at me over her shoulder. "I mean it Cora; I've never met a woman so capable of knocking me off my feet without even trying."

She dropped my gaze and smiled as a blush colored her cheeks. She was never particularly good at taking compliments, and she hadn't gotten any better over the years.

"Thank you." She whispered, looking back up at me as I walked into the room and wrapped my hands around her stomach, settling them on the flat surface that was growing our baby even as we spoke. She leaned back into my touch and took a deep, calming breath as I kissed the skin between her shoulder and neck.

Her hair was swept up again, exposing her neck, and I was just as wild about it as I was that day at the boutique.

The day that someone had tried to kill her.

My body tensed as I thought about it again, for the millionth time just today. We still had no leads.

The private detectives I'd hired had found the truck that was used in the assault, but it had been stolen and there were no leads as to who was driving it when it tried to run her down. And now the stakes were even higher to find who was behind this with Cora's pregnancy.

We decided not to tell anyone about it right away until we knew where the threat was coming from in hopes of not escalating anything with the news. But I ached to keep her and our baby safe, and I hated feeling helpless.

"What's that?" She asked, noticing the way I had my hand behind my back.

"What is this?" I asked, pulling my arm around and holding out the velvet jewelry box to her with a smile on my hand. "I told you I'd take care of the jewels."

She smiled brightly up at me and shook her head, "I'm sure Ruby was excited to hear from you again so soon."

"He was most accommodating," I replied and then reached around to the front of the box and slowly lifted the lid.

I watched her eyes as she looked in on the diamond and sapphire set lying on the satin cushion, waiting to adorn her sexy body. Her eyes widened and her cupid bow lips parted briefly before her smile widened. "Oh, Maverick."

"Here, let me help you," Setting the box down on the island, taking the wide cuff bracelet out, and undoing the clasp. It was diamonds and sapphires circling a wide platinum cuff the width of three inches and, as soon as I slid it onto her dainty right wrist it slid into place perfectly.

"Wow." She mused, turning her wrist back and forth to admire the glint of the jewels in the overhead light.

"Now these," I said, sliding the large matching earrings out of the box and handing them to her to put in. They were flower-shaped and hung from the bottom of her ear lobe accentuating her delicate neck and jawline perfectly. "Stunning."

She smiled again and turned to look back in the mirror and admired the finished look. "I love you, Maverick Jones." She mused, leaning back against my chest as I stepped forward again to wrap my hands around her waist, holding her and our baby.

"Not nearly as much as I love you both," I said, running my fingers back and forth over her stomach.

She shook her head and turned, "We'd better get going, or we'll be late."

"I suppose you're right," I said, releasing her reluctantly and holding her hand as we walked out to the foyer. When we walked off the elevator in our private garage, Franklin waited with my Audi and our new guards. Seven men with various military backgrounds stood flanking the two matching black Audis that would be used as cover vehicles on our drive across the city. I nodded to the lead guard, Gunner, and shook his outstretched hand.

Cora tucked herself into my side as she eyed the giant men speculatively, uncomfortable with their new presence around us but understanding of their necessity.

"Mr. Jones. Mrs. Jones." Gunner said, addressing us both as he was instructed to do. He was from a branch of the military that went bump in the night, leaving him highly qualified for the position, but he was intimidating as fuck, even to me. He and his team all wore black suits, but the bulge of weapons was evident under their jackets, in a way that screamed they weren't trying to hide that they were armed and ready. Which was exactly what we wanted people to see because I wasn't going to let anything happen to my wife. "We're all set for the trip, Franklin has planned the route and we've run the drills. At the event, we'll be around, never far from you both should you need us."

"Thank you. Let's be on our way then." Franklin opened the back door to our car, and I helped Cora inside before walking around to my side and getting in. Gunner sat in the front passenger seat and Franklin drove us out of the garage and across the city to my parent's home where the fundraiser was held each year.

"I'm nervous," Cora said, resting her hand over her stomach and taking a deep breath as she looked over at me. I raised our linked hands to my lips and kissed her knuckles.

"You're going to do great love," I reassured her and she smiled softly up at me.

She was nervous about her first event as Mrs. Jones knowing that all of the people from our past lives would be there mingling with the people from our new life together, but I knew she would fall into the role of my wife and partner effortlessly.

Before long, our convoy was pulling through the gate to the valet drop off and I leaned over, capturing Cora's light pink lips against mine. "If you want to leave, just say the words and we'll go. Okay?" I told her firmly and she nodded in understanding before Gunner opened her door and helped her slide from the seat.

I got out and walked around to her side taking her hand back in mine as the media that was lined up along the red carpet started going wild. The photographers screamed our names and called out to us, trying to get us to look at them for the money shot as we walked down the backdrop of sponsors to the center of the long carpet, stopping in front of the Jones Holding logo directly under the logo for the Luke Jones Memorial Fundraiser.

I pulled Cora into my side, keeping my hand on the small of her back, and looked out at the flashing lights as she did the same. I felt immense pride standing with her at my side as my partner and wife in front of the world. I looked down at her and slid my finger under her chin, tipping her head back to look up at me. Her eyes rounded slightly in surprise before fluttering closed as I lowered my lips to hers gently, savoring the taste of her on my lips long after I pulled back a fraction of an inch.

"I love you," I said over the roar of the paparazzi.

She smiled up at me, looking more relaxed and sated after a bit of physical touch from me. "I love you too Maverick."

"Let's go kick this party off," I said, pulling her from the carpet, ignoring the screams for more looks as we walked into the event which was much more muted thankfully.

"Wow," Cora said wistfully as we walked down the lighted pathway to the expansive backyard where the fundraiser was in full swing. Gold and black tablecloths lined hundreds of round tables under arches of twinkling lights and chandeliers. A giant round dancefloor sat in the center of the space and a large stage was affixed to the lower patio portion of the back of the house, lifting it up above the crowd that milled around.

"Jones." A voice called from the edge of the tables and I turned to see Reid and Dexter walking towards us with drinks in their hands.

"Wow, you look positively breathtaking tonight, Cora," Reid said, leaning down to kiss her cheek and hand her a flute of rose-colored champagne that she awkwardly took from him and held in her hands.

Dexter pushed Reid aside and kissed her on the cheek as well and gently took the glass from her hands with a small smile on his face. "You're positively *glowing* tonight." He said with a wink and tossed her drink back himself before setting it on a passing waiter's tray.

"That was rude," Reid said, appalled that Dex stole her drink. But Dex just knowingly rolled his eyes and winked at her again before turning to me to shake my hand.

He pulled me in for a one-handed hug and said softly, "Congratulations, Dad."

I smirked at him, unable to hold back the joy that had been running through my body for the last twenty-four hours from the news. "How'd you guess?" I asked him quietly, as Reid obliviously chatted Cora's ear off about something.

Dexter just shrugged his shoulders and smirked again. "Call it a hunch."

"Hmm." I hummed at him, taking a drink off a passing waiter's tray and taking a sip to calm my nerves.

"There you all are." My mother's voice called from behind us and I turned Cora as my parents pulled us both into hugs. My mother looked elegant in a white lace dress that offset her dark features timelessly and my father, like myself, Reid, and Dexter, wore a black tux that never went out of style.

My mother fawned over Cora for a while, keeping her close between us as people came up to introduce themselves to her, vying to fall in the good graces of our family's newest addition like it would benefit them somehow. Little did they know, she had zero cares in the world for connections and social circles but humored them all politely regardless.

People who ran in the same circle as her family growing up came up to her and warmly addressed her like they were trying to pretend that she hadn't been missing from all of our lives for the last decade.

The attack on her life had rattled my parents and best friends almost as much as it had us, leaving them angry and upset alike. And I could feel their intense protectiveness over her, even without looking at the half circle of people surrounding her, keeping my beautiful wife closed in on each side.

I was listening to something a business associate of mine was saying to my mother and Cora when Reid nudged me in the side. "Incoming." He said and nodded towards the crowd as four people moved towards where we had congregated.

"Cora," I said, leaning down to my wife's ear and gaining her attention. "Your family is coming this way."

Her spine stiffened, and I slid my arm back around her body to pull her close again, shielding her with my own. The Valentines stepped forward and the crowd that had been standing around us cleared for my in-laws, unaware of the rift that swelled between us.

"Cora, darling." Her mother said, looking at her with what she was trying to pass off as warm affection when even I could see the fear and apprehension in her gaze. "You look lovely, I always told you blue was your color." She said, trying to take credit for the beauty that her daughter was.

"Maverick picked it out, and I doubt he's ever considered or cared for your opinion on anything in his life," Cora said stiffly, unwilling to allow the woman to gain anything in front of the crowd. I smirked evilly at my wife's claws and the power she wielded as the crowd watched ravenously. And that was the plan all along, let the Valentine's peers see their despicable nature firsthand and distance themselves from it on their own.

Susan Valentine bristled instantly but quickly covered the dig, laughing it off, as did her sniveling husband as they pretended to miss it completely.

Dennis changed tactics and turned his attention to my father, who stood on the other side of my mother, with a look of disdain on his face to match my own. Dexter stood at his side, and I smirked at the formidable wall of allies that Cora had in this moment. "Chris, I heard you had an impressive day down at the club the other day. I heard you shot par, which we both know isn't something you do often." He said, laughing by himself for a moment before Jake and Susan joined in, once again trying to force the narrative.

I couldn't stand it for another moment, given the way the crowd had tightened around us. Curious eyes were flitting between us and them, trying to figure out why on earth two families that had been linked for years were suddenly acting so out of sorts, especially considering the recent news of our marriage breaking.

"Let's cut the bullshit," I said firmly, lifting my drink to them and making sure my voice was loud enough that at least the next three rows of spectators would hear me. "You four have a lot of nerve showing up tonight at all, much less showing up and pretending to have any sort of relationship with any of us anymore. Your biggest vice always has been and always will be your pride and hunger for power, and you made that painfully obvious when you cast your daughter out at eighteen because she refused to be your puppet any longer. Do either of you have any fucking clue what her life was like, alone and desolate in the world, without a single person in her corner?" I asked, raising my eyebrows as Dennis scoffed like I was exaggerating.

"That's a dramatic retelling of a situation that you weren't present for Maverick. It's been grossly inflated through the eyes of a teenage girl." He dismissed his own daughter, and everyone saw him for the real piece of shit that he was. Reid's body next to mine nearly vibrated with anger, much like my own.

"Cora dear, you always did have a flare for the dramatics," Susan said with a flip of her hand.

"Fuck you." I hissed at her menacingly. "Don't you dare step on Jones property and say anything false about one of us. Because that's exactly what Cora is now, she's a Jones." I said, stepping forward as her tiny hand gripped my tux jacket to hold me back. "She should have been a Jones years ago, and she would have been if you two pathetic excuses for parents hadn't cut her off and thrown her out when you realized you could no longer control her. You stole ten years from us and mark my words here and now, I've made it my sole purpose in life to destroy every single thing that you hold near and dear for it." I turned my intense glare away from the two of them to Jake, where he stood next to his cunt of a wife. "I've already ruined your son and his disgusting uncultured swine of a wife," The surrounding crowd gasped as my anger truly burned bright. "And before long, it will be you two who are left with absolutely nothing while Cora lives the life of the queen that she truly is."

"You listen here," Dennis said angrily, stepping forward like he was going to do something, and I stepped forward, matching him and exceeding him inch for inch as I stared down at him.

"No, you listen," My father stepped in between us as he looked down on Dennis as well, "You destroyed your daughter for your selfish gains and in turn, you destroyed my son. *My son!*" He said firmly. "And if that boy of mine wasn't on the mission to take everything from you in revenge, I'd do it myself, and we both know I know more than enough of your secrets that you've tried to keep hidden over the years to do it without even lifting a finger. So you're going to keep your whimpering useless self as far away as possible from my son and daughter, or I'll do just that." He turned his back to them and motioned over my shoulder as my team of guards and his own stepped forward, flanking our group on all sides. "Get them the fuck out of my home."

I wasn't used to hearing my father swear anymore, but I couldn't feel anything but immense pride as I watched him seamlessly fall into that role that I'd watched him embody my entire childhood. He was my biggest role model growing up, and even as a powerful man myself,

I was still in awe of him. The guards stepped between people and grabbed Dennis and Jake by the arms and started dragging them away as Susan and Angela looked around, mortified of being thrown out on their asses.

"You'll pay for this, Cora! I'll make you pay!" Dennis screamed over the crowd as he was dragged away, and I wrapped a quaking Cora in my arms and stepped between her and the path that they had taken to shield her from it as much as I could. The crowd was in shock as my mother turned to them and directed them all.

"As you can see, we've allowed the guards to take the trash out this evening, and we're ready to get on with a good time. Are good folks all ready for an amazing evening?" She asked loudly, and the crowd cheered boisterously as they snapped out of their shock and thrived on a good scandal.

Everyone dispersed as the emcee took the stage and started directing everyone to their seats for the events to begin.

"Are you okay?" I asked Cora where she still clung to me as we walked towards our table.

"I don't know, honestly." She said and took a deep breath. "But thank you for standing up for me." She said, looking up at me and smiling softly.

"Anytime, Cora. Anytime, anyplace," I said reassuringly as I pulled her seat out. She sat between me, and Dexter and I watched her start to relax as the attention fell off of her and me and went to the entertainment.

We were sitting through the dinner auction, where various sponsors had donated things like box seats to events, or weeklong getaways at vacation properties, when Cora leaned over to my ear.

"I love you endlessly. Do you know that?" She asked, and I looked away from the stage to where she sat as the picture of perfection next to me. Her crystal blue eyes looked up at me lovingly, and I leaned down to kiss her hungrily. She kissed me, but pulled back and smirked at me. "I have to pee, again." She deadpanned and I couldn't help but grin at her. We'd found her first pregnancy symptom, the constant need to pee.

"I'll come with you," I said and started to stand with her, but she put her hand on my arm.

"I can make my way there and back, besides we both know Gunsmoke is going to follow after me anyway."

"Gunner." I chastised. Messing up his name turned out to be her passive-aggressive way of dealing with his constant presence.

"That's what I said." She hissed at me and stood up as I pulled her chair back before kissing me on the forehead and walking off towards the bathrooms.

Chapter 26 – Cora

I stepped out of the bathroom stall to wash my hands and felt the hairs on the back of my neck prickle and stand on edge as I looked around the crowded room.

Cruel green eyes found mine in the mirror, and my blood ran cold.

"Penelope." I said, slowly turning from the sink to look at my baby sister where she stood by the door, staring at me with anger and contempt in her eyes.

"I'm going to need to ask you ladies to leave." She said loudly, drawing confused looks from the other women in the room as they froze in place, unsure of what to do. Anger flashed in my sister's eyes momentarily before she reached into the pocket of her sleek, full skirt and pulled out a gun. "What part of that did you dumbasses misunderstand?" She roared and the women in the room sprung into action, running over each other to get out the door. As the last woman ran out the door, she briefly looking over her shoulder at me with scared eyes. Penelope locked the deadbolt on the door and took a menacing step towards me. "Finally. A moment alone with the precious and pompous Mrs. Jones." She sneered.

"Pompous?" I grit out between my teeth, "That's rich coming from you." I said, refusing to show an ounce of fear as she took another step towards me. The rational part of my brain told me that Gunner was right outside the door and would soon be breaking it down to get to me after the alarming way those women ran from the room. But with each second that passed, the doorway was suspiciously empty.

"You just couldn't leave well enough alone, could you?" She said, taking another step as she waved the gun in my direction. I tried desperately to remain calm and strong but my skin crawled being this close to a gun and I ached to cover my stomach with my hands but didn't want to tip her off to my condition.

"What do you mean?" I asked, stalling.

"You got what you wanted, you got Maverick Jones. Did you have to take down our entire family in the process? I never did anything to you, yet you've set out to destroy me just as easily as you will them."

"I haven't set out to destroy anyone Pen!" I rushed out, "Maverick wants his revenge against our parents and Jake for the lies they've spun to him over the years, but he's never spoken ill of you, not once. He doesn't intend to come after you."

"Even if he doesn't directly ruin me, he's ruined the Valentine name! We didn't all marry billionaire playboys Cora! My family won't weather this storm unscathed."

"So, what are you going to do?" I asked her, once again eyeing the gun as she waved it around in her agitation. "Shoot me? Kill me? Will any of that make it any better for you? What about your kids?"

"Don't you dare talk about my kids!" She screamed and rushed forward, jamming the gun into my chest as she grabbed a handful of my hair to hold me still. I grabbed her arm as I tried to find something, anything at all, familiar in her eyes to prove to me she was the same girl I'd sang to every time there was a storm or let have all of my popcorn at every movie theater because it was her favorite treat. But I saw nothing but my father looking back at me. "My kids will never get a fair chance at life thanks to their dear Aunt Cora."

"You're wrong!" I rushed on, trying desperately to speak to the compassion in her as my skull burned from her grip in my hair. "You're the one ruining their futures. Doing this right now. Pen, please just put the gun down and we can work this out, you and me. I know for a fact that you weren't treated right over the years by them, anymore than I was. If they were evil to me, they were evil to you too. We can find common ground here!"

"Shut up." She snapped and pushed me backwards until my hips bent backwards over the porcelain sink. "Shut the fuck up. The money from the insurance policy will protect my kids from your husband's wrath, I don't need anything else from you."

"What policy?" I asked angrily, feeling my blood start to boil at the absurdity of this. "What are you talking about?"

Where was Gunner?

Or Maverick?

"The life insurance policy Mom and Dad have on you. They took it out years ago, and all you had to do was walk the fuck out into traffic like a good fucking girl, and we never would have had to resort to this." She sneered, jamming the gun up under my chin and pressing my head back further. "But you couldn't even die like you were supposed to, big shocker there. You were never capable of doing anything right, not even keeping a lovesick boyfriend that had already committed ten years to you. You went and fucked that up, too."

"Fuck you." I bit out, shoving at her, but she was bigger than I was, and had better leverage over me leaving me unable to dislodge the gun from under my chin. "You hired the truck to mow me down?" I accused and sneered at her. "You say I fuck everything up, but you couldn't get that right, could you?"

I didn't see it coming, but she swung the gun out wide and back towards my face, whipping me with the butt of it and pain reverberate off my skull and left me dazed and staggering. I brushed my fingers over the spot where she'd hit me in my hairline and felt the gooey warmth of my blood spilling. Nausea rolled through my system, and I fought back the urge to throw up and tried to focus on her face and, more importantly, the gun. My vision was blurry and distorted as I blinked, trying to see clearly.

"They were so right about you, you know?" She sneered, leaning forward until her face was right against mine with her hand still locked in my hair and the gun pressed back under my chin. "Selfish doesn't even begin to describe you. This world will be better off when I rid it of you." She said and pulled the hammer back on the gun menacingly as I tried to push her arm away, but my head was swimming still and making it hard to connect. "Any last words you want me to tell your doting husband after I make him a widow?"

"Yeah." I gasped and blinked again, swallowing down the bile in my throat. She paused as I tried to focus again, and I knew this was my chance. "Tell him you're as big of a cunt as our sister-in-law," I growled and shoved her with all of my strength, dislodging the gun from my chin a second before it went off.

The bullet ricocheted off the wall behind me, shattering the mirror and raining glass shards down on us. The noise was catastrophic, and my right ear exploded in vibrating pain, but I couldn't focus on that at the moment. We each had both of our hands wrapped around the gun, fighting over it where she held it pointed directly at the ceiling. It went off again as we struggled, the bullet shooting out the light above us, but neither of us would let go.

I knew I was going to run out of stamina and strength before she did, thanks to the size difference between us and that I needed to make moves quickly. I brought my knee up hard against her stomach, and she groaned and doubled over in pain. "Bitch." She spit and head-butted me, sending more stars forward to dance in my vision as my arms lost their leverage against her. The barrel of the gun was pointed directly at my face as I shoved her again.

"Cora!" Maverick screamed from the other side of the door as a loud crashing noise vibrated through it like he threw himself against it, trying to get it open. The sound of his voice empowered me, and I screamed as I pushed her hands away from my face with all of my strength. Four more shots rang out from the gun as we battled, peppering the stalls and mirrors around us as she slammed me into the wall and tried to get her foot against my stomach to kick off of me. "Cora!"

Maverick screamed again as he repeatedly slammed himself into the door, I looked at it out of the corner of my eye and noticed it barely budged with each hit.

Fucking thing was steel, and I was running out of time.

"Get off me," I growled, reaching forward with my mouth and latching my teeth into her arm, biting down hard until I felt them sink through her flesh as blood spilled into my mouth.

The nausea rolled through me again at the metallic taste, but I didn't let go, even as she screamed in agony and tried to shake me off. "I'm going to fucking kill you." She sneered and threw me onto the ground, straddling my waist as she leaned her chest against the back of the gun and pushed my arms down until the barrel was aimed directly at my chest. She laughed maniacally as the door behind her exploded open and then gunfire rang out through the room again, shot after shot echoing around me as I waited for the pain to come.

But it didn't.

My sister's eyes widened before her arms went limp and she fell forward, covering my body with hers and pinning the gun between us as I gasped under her weight. "Help!"

"Cora." Maverick swore as he ran to me and lifted Penelope's body off of mine, throwing her across the room in a heap before lowering himself down next to me, "Oh God." He gasped and I clawed at him, desperate to get off the floor and into his arms.

"Maverick." I sobbed, clinging to him as he lifted me into his lap and ran his hands over my face and chest, looking for gunshot wounds. "I'm okay." I wheezed, "I'm okay." I was covered in blood, but it wasn't all mine.

"Call an ambulance now!" Maverick bellowed over his shoulder, and I looked over to where Gunner holstered his gun and pulled his cell phone out. He had a giant wound to the back of his head, blood poured down the back of his neck and he looked angry. Really fucking angry.

Dexter took the gun from where it was still clutched in Penelope's hands, emptied it of its remaining bullets, and slid it into the back of his belt before reaching down and checking her for a pulse.

He pulled his fingers away and looked over at me, and it was then that I noticed the pool of blood spilling out underneath of her. "Is she..." I whispered, looking back up at Dex as he stood over her.

"Yeah, she's dead." He said with a grimace, and I buried my head in the crook of Maverick's neck to block out the sight of my dead sister. Regardless if she had tried to kill me or not, it was the first time I'd seen a dead body, and the blood that ran through my veins was also pooling across the floor beneath her.

"Get me out of this room," I begged Mav. "Please get me away from her body."

"Come on." He said, standing up with me in his arms, stepping over her body and through the door. Reid stood in the hallway and squeezed my arm in silent support as he ran next to Mav, who jogged down the corridor towards the mansion. I looked out over the event space and every single table was empty, with many of the chairs turned over and decorations spilled.

"What happened to everyone?" I gasped as Reid opened the door to the brightly lit kitchen and Mav carried me in before setting me down on the counter.

Maverick grabbed a towel out of the drawer and ran it under cold water before pressing it against the wound on my forehead. I grimaced and tried to pull away, but he laced his fingers around the back of my neck and held me still as he probed the wound.

"Maverick." I tried again. "Where is everyone?"

"It doesn't matter. None of it fucking matters." He gritted out between clenched teeth, and it was then that I noticed the cut on his knuckles and the split in his lip.

"Stop," I said, grabbing his hand and forcefully pulling it down away from my head. "Talk to me." I tried desperately to get him to meet my eyes, but he wouldn't. His body was locked tight in anger, and he was hanging by a thread. I turned to his best friend, who stood at my side. "Reid." He had the starting of a black eye and his tie was hanging crookedly off his neck. "What the fuck happened?"

"They planned an attack on you." He said.

"Reid." Maverick bit out as I looked back and forth between them rapidly.

"She deserves to know." Reid bit back and looked at me. "They blocked off the entrance to the restroom building, that's why we didn't get to you faster. The women that had been in the bathroom came out screaming, but there was a group of men waiting for us and it took a few minutes to get through them and to the bathroom."

"That's why Gunner didn't come right in," I said, piecing it all together.

"They blitzed him, knocking him out, when he came to, he attacked them from the back, and we were able to get past them."

"Who were they?" I asked, "Where are your parents? Are they safe? Did anyone else get hurt?" I asked in a panic.

"Shh," Maverick said, putting his hands on both sides of my face and turning me back to him. "Calm down Cora. My parents are safe." He said, and I took a deep breath, feeling my body shudder on the exhale. "Good girl. Now tell me what happened in that bathroom." He ordered.

I shook my head, remembering the fear and adrenaline coursing through my body the whole time. "I was washing my hands when I saw her, she was standing by the door, and she told everyone to get out." I shuddered again. "When no one listened to her, she pulled the gun out of her pocket and waved it around and then locked the door behind them." I closed my eyes, shutting out the realization that my sister was going to murder me tonight. "They hired the truck. My parents and her, maybe Jake, too." I guessed. "I don't know exactly."

"What was her plan tonight?" Maverick asked me, running his thumbs back and forth over my cheeks.

"Shoot and kill me so my parents could collect on a life insurance policy they had on me." Maverick ground his teeth together, but remained silent. "She said they took it out a few years ago, they must have forged it, who knows."

"They were going to collect on it because I bankrupted them." Maverick assumed, and I could feel his guilt as clear as my own.

"Don't," I ordered, snapping at him, and shaking my face free of his hands. "They were going to do it one way or another, you know that."

"But I egged them on." He spit out and dropped his hands from my body completely, stepping backward, creating space between us. He looked... gutted.

"Stop it!" I demanded. "Don't you dare do that right now, Maverick."

But he was retreating further and further with a haunted look on his face. "It's my fault. My need for revenge nearly cost you your life." He said as he scrubbed his hands over his face. "Everything bad that's ever happened to you has been because of me."

"Maverick," I yelled and slid off of the counter, barely keeping myself from crumpling to the floor as the weight of everything left me weak and tired.

"I can't." He said, looking up at me once more. "I can't be the reason something happens to you or the baby. I'm sorry, but I can't." He said and then turned and walked away from me through the house. "I love you too fucking much to be the reason for your death, Cora. Forgive me." His body trembled, but he kept walking away from me.

"Maverick," I screamed. My legs gave out as I tried to chase after him, and I collapsed as Reid caught me milliseconds before I hit the floor. "No!" I sobbed as he disappeared, walking away from me. "Don't leave me," I begged.

But he didn't turn around.

He left me.

"I can't survive like that again." I gasped and tore at my throat like something was choking me as Reid held me to his chest. "Not again." I sobbed into his chest. "Please, not again."

I sat at my dingy kitchen table and stared out the dirty window, unseeing. The piece of toast in front of me was left untouched and forgotten as I was lost in yet another daydream.

A dream of the man I longed after and ached for but hadn't seen or talked to in months.

Two miserably long months without Maverick and I wondered if I'd survive it again this time. How had I survived it for ten years last time?

I was withering away physically and mentally and didn't know how much longer I could hold out for him. He had walked away from me the night of Luke's memorial and never looked back. He tried to take care of me from afar, making sure I had access to his penthouse and his beach home where we'd been married, but I couldn't force myself to go to either of those places. The memories of the love we'd shared in those places felt suffocating to even think about now. So instead I'd crawled back into the hole that I'd survived in for ten years and hadn't come out since.

He wired money into my accounts, but I left it all untouched. He sent Franklin and Gunner to sit outside of my apartment building every single day in case I needed to go somewhere, but I never left while he was there waiting for me. I hardly left at all.

He sent his mom and dad, Reid, Dexter, and Nat, to check up on me, but I didn't answer the door when they knocked or called.

I was just a shell of the person I'd been, and I didn't want to let them see me like that.

The worst part of it all was that I understood why he walked away from me. I understood his fear and his pain, and I knew he was trying to do what was right for me and our baby, but it didn't make it any easier to stomach.

Our baby was growing rapidly, I was now in the second trimester and finally almost free of the terrible morning sickness that had plagued me every waking minute for the first few months. My baby bump had officially popped, and nothing I owned fit anymore, but I couldn't bring myself to go shopping for maternity clothes. If I did, I'd have to acknowledge that this pregnancy was happening, and that Maverick was missing it.

He'd been so excited to be a dad, but he didn't even contact me to make sure the baby was okay, and that hurt.

I was supposed to go to an ultrasound appointment, but the idea of seeing the baby without him felt wrong, and I struggled to find the joy I was supposed to feel.

I'd been able to put it off so far, my OB had been willing to wait on an ultrasound until the second trimester, but she wouldn't wait any longer. She said it was imperative to make sure there were no defects or worrisome problems and that she couldn't in good conscience wait any longer. I had to face reality because no one else could do it.

A knock sounded on my door, and I turned to glance at it. I stared for so long before finally making my way toward it.

My chest ached, hoping that it was Mav, but my brain knew it wouldn't be. I silently looked through the peephole and saw his best friend Dexter standing in the hallway, staring at the peephole like he could see me looking through it. "Open the door, Cora." He said softly, like he was tired.

He wore a suit like usual but looked... drained.

I stepped back from the door and stood in the kitchen, waiting for him to leave, like he always did after a while.

"You forced my hand, remember that." He said from the other side of the wood before I heard a key turn in the lock, and I watched in shock as the deadbolt turned and the door started to open. It opened a few inches before the chain hung up, but it was the closest I'd been to Dex since the day after the fundraiser when I was discharged from the hospital, alone. "Stand back, Cora." He said gently again, and he forced the door open, ripping my chain off the wall.

He pushed the door open, stood on the threshold, and looked at me with a sorry expression on his face. "What the hell, Dex?" I gasped.

As he moved forward, his hand reached for the doorknob, twisting it shut and securing the deadbolt with a decisive turn. Finally, he turned his attention back to me. His eyes dropped from my eyes to where my belly stretched my shirt before he looked around my unkempt apartment. "Come here." He whispered in a barely audible voice, before closing the distance between us, wrapping his large arms around my shoulders, and hugging me.

It was the first time anyone had touched me besides my doctor, and I didn't realize how starved I was for physical contact until that moment. I wrapped my arms around his waist and hugged him back like my life depended on it, telling myself I'd allow it for only a few seconds more, and then I'd kick him out.

I just needed a few more seconds of comfort.

I'd end it any second now.

But I didn't. I couldn't.

"How are you?" He asked me, smoothing his hand over my messy hair as he held me tight. "We've all been so fucking worried about you."

I shook my head, burying it further into his chest. "Not everyone," I said pathetically, and then pulled away, wiping at the tears that escaped my lashes embarrassingly.

"Come, sit down." He said and led me over to the couch and made me sit down as he took his jacket off and sat down at the other end, turned to face me. "Talk to me, tell me how you and the baby are."

My hand instinctively went to my growing belly, and I looked across the room to stare at the wall. "We're alive."

"Barely." He grunted, and I glared at him.

"Leave," I said firmly, standing up and pointing to the door. "If you came here to point out how pathetic I am, just leave Dex. I have no problem recognizing that on my own. I don't need your help."

He scoffed at me and pulled me back down to the couch. "I'm sorry, that's not what I meant." He said, and I glared at him. "You're skin and bones, Cora. Are you eating?"

"Eating is kind of hard when you have an alien inside of you that makes you throw it all back up, Dex. I don't know if you know how growing a human works or not, but it's actually a miserable process."

"I know it is." He said sadly and then, "I was a dad once."

The air instantly blew out of my sails, and I wilted into the cushions of the couch. "What does that mean, exactly?"

He sighed, rubbing a hand over his face, and undid his tie, tossing it over his discarded jacket. "I was married to a woman that I loved… far more than she loved me. A year into our marriage she got pregnant, and I was elated to grow our family. Ecstatic really. I was there for every step along the way."

I turned on the couch to face him, "So what happened?"

"Turned out the baby wasn't mine; she'd cheated on me and knew the whole time that it wasn't mine. But let me think it was until she decided she wanted to be with the other guy." He sighed as his eyes glassed over. "She left with my son when he was eight months old, and I never got to see him again."

"Oh my God," I said, covering my mouth as tears burned the back of my eyes for him. "I can't imagine having a baby for eight months and then losing him like that. I'm so sorry, Dex."

He nodded and continued, "I waited around, hoping she'd come back to me." He looked down at his ring finger where his wedding ring still circled his finger. "I guess a part of me still waits."

"God," I whispered and took his hand. "I'm so sorry." My attention fell to my own wedding ring on my finger that I had contemplated taking off a million times lately.

He shook his head and took a deep breath, "I appreciate that, but that's not why I came here."

"Why did you come?"

"To make sure that you were taking care of yourself and that little one. Because I know how hard the first few months of pregnancy are on a woman."

"Thanks, but I'll be... fine," I said, giving him a sad smile. "I have to be right?"

"Right." He agreed, but it lacked conviction.

The alarm on my phone rang loudly out into the room and I got up to grab it off the table next to my forgotten-about breakfast.

"What's that for?" He asked, watching me as I turned it off.

"To remind me to leave," I said and then looked over at him, unsure of how much information I should tell him. We hadn't discussed Maverick, and I didn't know if he was going to tell Mav what he had found out today. I was too proud to let my husband keep tabs on me without doing it himself.

"Leave for what?" He asked, leaning forward to rest his elbows on his knees.

"Have you talked to him?" I asked, unable to hold back any longer.

He held my stare for a moment and sighed. "I have. A few times."

I clenched my jaw and processed that as anger coursed through my veins. I was glad to hear he was still alive, but I hated that his radio silence was only directed at me. "Got it," I said and walked into my bedroom and shut the door behind me. "Well, this visit has been great, Dex, but I need you to leave now."

I said and took my shirt off, searching for something a little looser to wear to the doctor to see my baby for the first time. Maybe the visit with Dex was for the best, because I had a renewed sense of anger in my veins, and it made me want to make sure this baby was okay, if for no other reason than to prove to Maverick that I didn't need him if he didn't need me.

I came back out to the living room to find Dex standing with his jacket back on and his tie hanging from his pants pocket where his hands rested.

"What are you waiting for?" I asked him.

"You; turns out I have the rest of the day off. So I figured I could buy you lunch after whatever it is that you have to do this morning."

"Turns out, huh?" I asked him sarcastically as I grabbed my purse. "Well, you're not invited to tag along, so get lost."

He smiled at my fire, and I fought the urge to punch him in the gut for it.

"Good try, Jones." He said, using my new last name, which sounded bitter in my ears. "But you're going to have to deal with me tagging along."

"You can't tag along, Dex."

"Well, where are you going?"

"Why does it matter?" I huffed, annoyed.

"Why is it a secret?" He countered, and I rolled my eyes at him and opened my door, flicking my now useless chain out of the way.

"You're going to have that fixed by the time I go to bed tonight, by the way," I said and walked out into the hallway with him following like a puppy.

"I can do that." He said easily. "Or you could just do what you should do and go home where you're safe and protected by security and you wouldn't need a flimsy chain that I broke with hardly any effort."

"I am home, Dex. This is my home."

"This was your home before you married Maverick, Cora." He said angrily and I rolled my eyes at him, locking my deadbolt and walking down the hallway, not bothering to see if he followed or not.

I knew I wasn't going to get rid of him that easily.

"Well, the son of a bitch abandoned me, Dex. I don't have anywhere else to go anymore."

"Cora." He said sadly as I stepped into the elevator, but he didn't follow it up with anything else. There wasn't anything else to say about it. We rode in silence for a minute before he sighed. "He's a wreck without you."

I forced my face to remain impassive as pain exploded inside of my chest at the mention of Maverick being a mess. I shouldn't care. It was his fault, after all, but I couldn't turn it off just because I wanted to.

I couldn't just stop loving him.

"Good," I said firmly and walked out of the elevator, leaving him standing there as I headed towards the back door of my complex and away from the black Audi that I knew would be idling at the curb.

"Where are you going?"

"Anywhere that you aren't." I fired back and huffed as he reached around in front of me to open the door to the back parking lot and groaned when I saw his sleek sports car parked there. I glared at him as he smirked at me.

He held up the fob, and the car chirped as he unlocked the door. "Don't act like you haven't missed me as much as I missed you, dancing queen." He said affectionately, and I was catapulted back to our night out on the town before our wedding when Dex sang karaoke with me. I gritted my teeth together as he opened the car door and waited for me to get in. And to be honest, I really didn't want to ride the subway to the hospital anyway, so I gruffly sank into the low car as he smirked at me.

"Can it, Chase," I ordered, and he mimed zipping his lips as he walked around the car and got in the driver's seat.

"So, where are we headed?" He asked as he started the car.

"Wilson Hospital," I said, and ignored the way he looked at me.

"Is everything... okay?" He asked, looking down at my belly before looking back at me.

"I have an ultrasound," I said quietly and then sighed. "My first ultrasound."

Dexter reached over and squeezed my hand before shifting his car into reverse and pulling out of the parking lot towards the hospital. "I can't wait to see if my niece or nephew looks like me." He said with genuine excitement in his voice and I couldn't even pretend that I didn't welcome his presence in the room with me. I had dreaded doing this alone, and having a friend, even the male best friend of my dead-beat husband, was better than nothing.

"Cora Jones." The nurse stood at the doorway and called my name, but I was frozen in my chair. "Mrs. Jones." She said again, looking right at me. It was hard to pretend I wasn't who she was looking for when my face and name had been plastered all over every news outlet for months following the attack at the fundraiser.

"Sorry," I said and stood up as Dex held the door open for us both. When we got into the ultrasound room, the nurse eyed up the tall handsome man next to me that obviously wasn't my husband; Maverick Jones was more of a household name than Cora Jones was. And Dexter was definitely not my husband. "Uh, he's filling in today," I answered her unspoken question, but she just nodded, seemingly unaffected by the awkwardness.

I was sure she had seen her fair share of baby daddy drama in her years here.

"Okay, Mrs. Jones, please have a seat on the table and the doctor will be in shortly." She said and left me to sit on the crinkly paper-covered table as Dexter walked around the room, looking at the equipment with a peculiar look on his face.

"Are you okay... with this?" I asked him, trying to be sensitive to his own loss. "You could have stayed in the car, you know."

He rolled his eyes at me grabbed the ultrasound wand from the stand and swung it around. "As if I'd miss this."

I didn't have time to rebuke his statement about it not being his place to be here, that it was Mavericks. Because the doctor walked in and caught Dex mid sword thrust with the internal dildo looking wand and suddenly there were far more embarrassing things to talk about.

"Mrs. Jones." My doctor said, eyeing Dexter as he sulked back to his chair next to me guiltily. "Are you ready to finally see this little one?" She asked, and I took a deep breath.

"As I'll ever be." I said and laid back on the table as she lifted my shirt to bare my stomach and covered it with warm gel.

"Here we go." She said and placed the wand against my skin, moving it around until a teeny tiny little baby showed up in black and white and I was transported through time.

We're going to be parents!

The primal, alpha part of me, needs to see you with our baby in your arms.

A home full of little feet to fulfill you and love you back in the purest way known to man.

Those were the things that Maverick had promised me before he walked out of my life in the exact way he vowed he'd never do.

Dexter grabbed my hand, clenched it in his and brought me back to the present as I watched my baby wiggle on the screen and a cheerful smile crested my lips.

"Wow," I whispered, and my doctor looked down at me with a smile on her own face before turning back to the monitor.

"You're measuring right on time, based on your last period. Baby here has a strong heartbeat." She said before pulling it up and a second later the noise of its heart filled the room and tears ran down the sides of my face into my hair. "Everything looks perfect." She said, printing off an arm's length of pictures and handing them to me. I stared in awe at them as Dexter said something to the doctor and a moment later, she handed him another strip of pictures.

I pulled my eyes away from my baby to eye him suspiciously, "Why do you get pictures of my baby?" I questioned.

"Because I can't be their favorite uncle if I don't start my brag board now."

"Brag board?" I asked, snorting at his ridiculousness. "What the heck is brag board?"

But he just shushed me as the doctor went through more information about my baby and what to expect in the coming weeks.

The rest of the day passed in a blur of actual unrecognizable joy as I thought about my baby growing big and strong inside of my belly. Dex took me to lunch and spent the rest of the day with me in my shitty apartment, eating all sorts of take-out that he ordered, conveniently leaving it all in my fridge when he left, and watching trashy reality tv with me until well past ten pm.

As I crawled into bed, I had a sense of purpose pumping through my veins when I laid my head down on my pillow and pressed my hands to my belly. "I love you, little one, and I'm going to find a way to do this right for you. With or without your daddy." I whispered into the darkened silence of my apartment.

Chapter 27 – Maverick

I sat in the dark of my hotel suite living room, holding a glass of bourbon in my fingers and staring into the fireplace as the liquor numbed my thoughts and feelings.

It was the only constant in my life lately.

I went to work when I needed to, which had been less than a dozen times in the last two months. I ate when the pain in my stomach got so bad I was left with no choice. And I drank almost constantly.

It was the only thing that made living without Cora bearable.

Because walking away from her that night in my parent's kitchen had been the single most painful thing I'd ever done before.

And I'd done some fucked up shit in my day.

But that took the cake.

I thought I had been doing the right thing at first, trying to distance myself from Cora so she would stop being hurt because of me. And I'd held true to that belief for a while, a few weeks at least.

But then the resolve had started to fade and the ache I'd buried deep in my chest burned painfully bright, leaving me second-guessing everything.

However, the passage of time had been substantial, and I found myself uncertain of how to convince her that I deserved her trust, especially when I no longer trusted myself.

So instead of going to her and trying to beg her for forgiveness, I sat alone in my hotel suite and drank myself into an early grave.

Cora's family was arrested the night of the fundraiser on conspiracy to commit murder charges, as well as fraud and a laundry list of other crimes that would hopefully put them behind bars for a very long time. Her brother Jake turned on everyone else, his wife included, and struck a deal with the DA to save his ass. As long as they all paid for what they did to her, I didn't care. I couldn't care about anything else anymore.

Reid showed up at my suite some nights, silently sitting with me and drinking with me before he'd get up and wordlessly walk back out until the next night he'd show up. It was like he didn't know what to say or do, and decided to at least physically be at my side, even if he didn't have anything else to offer me at the moment.

And I let him, because being alone fucking sucked.

Dexter avoided me mostly, and the few times I'd spoken to him or seen him at the office, his anger was apparent, even if he tried to contain it.

And given his experience with marriage and kids, I understood where it came from, and I couldn't blame him.

So I weathered his glares and radio silence at face value of what they were; exactly what I deserved.

Tonight was one of those nights that Reid had joined me hours ago, and sat silently on the couch as he poured himself drink after drink, refilling mine as he went.

Misery did love company, after all.

Just as the silent misery seemed unbearable, the front door to the suite swung open, creating a loud bang as it collided with the wall. The sudden burst of light from the newly illuminated room blinded both Reid and me, momentarily stealing our focus.

"What the fuck, man?" Reid swore, staring up at where Dexter stood with his hands in his pockets as he looked at us.

"You two are pathetic, you know that?" Dexter said angrily, nearly sneering at us as he walked over to my bourbon collection and picked up the only remaining bottle of it. He held it in his hand for a moment, reading the label before pursing his lips and hauling back and chucking it against the wall on the other side of the room.

"Jesus fuck." Reid snapped, ducking as liquor, and glass rained down on him where he sat on the couch.

I didn't flinch, though, and I didn't lash out at my friend. I could order more bourbon with the press of a button on the hotel phone, after all.

Dexter turned towards me and pointed his finger at me as anger vibrated off of him. "Do you really have nothing to say for yourself?"

I just stared at him, feeling the alcohol burning off and lifting the haze of numbness the longer I sat in his presence.

He was such a fucking buzz kill when he wanted to be.

He scoffed and turned away from me, shaking his head and running his hand through his hair. "Do you have any idea how I've spent my day, Mr. Billionaire washout?" He asked. "Besides putting out fires for you, and saving your career and reputation that you've left in the hands of a man who can't sober up any longer than you can." He said, throwing a hand towards Reid who at least had the decency to look guilty, I couldn't even manage that right now. "No? No guesses even?" He mocked.

"Why don't you tell me?" I finally said, getting my tongue to un-stick itself from the roof of my mouth and form a coherent sentence for the man who was in reality keeping my business afloat.

"I'll tell you." He said, shaking his head at me, "I'll fucking tell you." He bit out. "I spent my fucking day taking care of your wife because

God knows you haven't cared to see to her well-being while you've drunk yourself stupid. And she's so grief-stricken that she can't see to it herself!" He yelled.

The mention of Cora pulled me out of the last bit of haze, and I leaned forward on my knees. "What do you mean?"

He clenched his teeth and shook his head angrily. "She's been sick! Morning sickness has kicked her ass. Hard. She's a fucking bag of skin and bones and I wouldn't have known that had I not broken into her apartment and forced her to let me help her! Because you've gone and fucked her up in the head so badly, she won't let any of us be near her!"

I stood up, pitching forward and barely catching myself before falling face-first into the carpet. "Sick?" I tried to wrap my head around it.

"Yes, Mav, fucking puking her brains out every time she tries to eat, sick. You know, from that baby, you insisted on putting inside of her, even after she told you she wanted to wait to protect herself. But you just couldn't wrap your fucking dick up and think about anyone else besides yourself, could you?" He roared, "Nope, Maverick Jones, Mr. Entitled forced the situation on her and then walked the fuck out, leaving her to deal with the consequences like some dead-beat piece of shit."

He laid into me hard, and I knew I deserved it. But my brain was short-circuiting as I imagined Cora suffering without me there to help her. "Dex," Reid said, trying to calm him down, but Dex brushed him off.

"Don't you even care if your child is healthy or not? If it's growing at the right rate or showing any signs of malformations or deformities? Don't you care about any of that shit?" He roared. "You know what? I'd give anything to have my son back and you're sitting here pissing away your own chance at fatherhood with a damn good woman who has been so desolate, she wouldn't even allow the doctor to do an ultrasound on her because she kept holding out hope that you'd show the fuck back up in her life and experience seeing your child for the first time with her. That maybe you'd be by her side like you vowed to fucking be at your wedding!"

He marched forward and grabbed the glass out of my hand that I'd forgotten about and chucked it against the wall to shatter alongside the bottle of booze before turning back to look at me.

"You're pathetic and you're losing her while you sit here and try to grow the balls to win her back. But it's going to be too late if you wait any longer, Mav." He said and his eyes burned with pain as he implored me to ease my own. "Go to her Maverick, before you lose her for good, man."

"I—" I said, trying to come up with the excuses I'd been using up until this point.

She's better off without me.

I'm no good for her.

She deserves better.

"Oh, and in case you were wondering." He said, reaching into his pocket, grabbing a wad of black and white photos, and throwing them at my chest, which I just narrowly managed to catch before they fell to the ground. "Your innocent baby is perfect, growing right along like it should be. No thanks to you, of course." He finished and threw himself down in a chair by the fireplace and watched me as I opened the pictures.

"My God," I whispered, collapsing back into the chair behind me as my world imploded around me.

My baby.

I was looking at pictures of my teeny tiny baby growing inside of Cora's belly and Dexter was right. It was fucking perfect.

I could make out its little head and body and wiggly legs in the various pictures and my heart broke to know I'd missed this in person.

I looked up at Dexter and Reid, where they stared at me, waiting for me to do something. "I have to go to her," I said quietly, before clearing my throat and saying it again with more force behind it. "I have to go to her." I stood up and started to walk towards the front door when Dexter grabbed me by the arm.

"Not a chance, am I letting you go to her in your condition right now, you'll fuck up the one chance you have at this. And make no mistake Maverick, you have one chance at this." He said before turning and snapping his fingers at Reid. "Make coffee, strong and black. And drink a pot's worth of it yourself while you're at it." He said and looked back at me. "Go fucking shower, you stink. And put yourself back together into the man that she deserves. Don't you dare go to her as anything less."

Well fuck me running, Dexter was bossy when he was right.

The door opened easily with the key that Dexter had given me, and I silently slipped into the small apartment I'd vowed to never step foot in again. It looked the same, but it also looked... lifeless.

Much like I'd felt these past few months.

I took my shoes and jacket off and walked silently through the apartment towards the bedroom in the back as nerves raced through my entire body. Every cell in my body was keyed up and anxious as I entered Cora's immediate space. My body could sense her before I even made out her tiny body in the center of the bed. She was lying on her side, hugging a pillow to her chest as she slept peacefully, and my heart ached from laying eyes on her finally.

I didn't dare wake her up, knowing from what Dexter told me as he pumped me full of coffee and sobered me up, that Cora was in the part of pregnancy that left her drained and exhausted, but that it would be getting better soon. So I pulled a pile of discarded clothes from her closet out of the chair in the corner of her bedroom and sat down, resolved to simply watch her as she slept.

I already felt a sense of calm filling my senses from simply being near her that I hadn't felt since I'd left.

She rolled over in her sleep, kicking the blankets down off her legs, and laid on her back. She wore a tank top and panties, and so much skin exposed itself to my eyes. Letting go of the pillow she stretched her arms over her head and I was finally able to see her swollen belly, growing my baby deep inside and it was like seeing the sunlight for the first time in my life. I was propelled out of the darkness and self-doubt that I'd been drowning in without her and stood in the light of day after so long. And it was life-changing.

My body stirred as I let my eyes rove over her changed body, and I fought back the growl that wanted to rip its way out of my chest.

I also fought the urge to crawl into bed next to her, knowing it was selfish to just assume she'd welcome me back after so long.

"Mav." She sighed in her sleep and reached out across the bed to the side that I slept on usually, like she was searching for me. "Hmm." She hummed, turning on her side again as she rocked back and forth.

I leaned forward on my elbows and was so close to her that I could have reached out and touched her bare leg if I wanted to.

She was restless all of a sudden, tossing and turning and rocking back and forth in her sleep. I watched her closely for what felt like hours, trying to tell what was plaguing her in her dreams to decide if I should wake her up or not.

She moaned and spoke incoherently for a while before reaching up in her sleep and she palmed her breast through the thin fabric of her tank top and moaned again. "Yes, Maverick."

My blood roared in my ears as I realized my sinful wife was having a sex dream.

About me.

I palmed my erection through my pants and watched as she lazily played with her tits. "Please." She begged prettily and then panted. "Hot. I'm so hot." She rolled and tore her top off completely, tossed it off the end of the bed, and laid on her back, spreading her legs wide as she kept playing with her gorgeous breasts. They were bigger than normal; my guess was pregnancy had contributed to that, and I bit down on my knuckle as I watched her play with her rock-hard nipples.

She was panting and kicking her legs around in the bed. "Fuck me, please make it stop hurting." She cried and ran her fingers over her panties, rubbing them over the wet spot that had formed over her pussy, and I was unable to stay still any longer. I stood up quickly and walked to the side of her bed, ready to lie down next to her.

But Dexter's words rang loudly in my head, and I froze, standing next to her, staring down and watching her like a voyeur.

You only have one chance at this.

Something told me she would freak out if she woke up to find me in bed with her, but I also wanted to ease the need she so clearly ached for.

Before I could decide, one way or another, though, her eyes snapped open and then blinked rapidly as she looked around the space before looking up at me, looming over her in the dark like a fucking creep.

"Maverick?" She asked, tilting her head to see me better before she realized she lay there naked except for a thin pair of drenched panties. She looked down at her body and then back at me, and I expected her to fly into a fit of rage, but she just relaxed back into the mattress and watched me. "I smelled you, in my dream." She said softly. "You still smell the same."

I smiled and leaned down over her, gently pushing a strand of hair back off her damp forehead. "You were begging for me to fuck you while you played with yourself," I said honestly, as I let my eyes drop to where her lush tits heaved.

"Then why didn't you?" She asked with a challenge in her eyes.

"Cora." I growled, teetering on the edge of sanity. "You have no idea how hard it was to stay still and watch you as you begged for it."

She tilted her head again and then lifted her hips, slid her fingers under the band of her panties, and pushed them down. I didn't even bother trying to hide the way I watched her remove the last stitch of fabric from her delectable body.

I stood up to my full height over her and watched as she slid her fingers through her wet lips, rubbing her clit quickly while staring up at me. "Take the pain away, Mav." She whispered. "Prove to me that we're going to be okay, even if we aren't right this second. Please."

I couldn't deny her when she asked so nicely like that. I reached behind my neck and pulled the collar of my shirt over my head and tossed it onto the floor next to her panties as her hungry eyes roamed over my chest and abs. "Are you sure?" I asked her, giving her one last chance to back out as I dropped my hands to my jeans and paused.

"Make love to me Maverick, I'm begging you." She said firmly, and I tore the denim off until I stood naked next to her bed. I fisted my cock where it stood standing at attention and her blue eyes fluttered closed as she watched, while she continued to rub herself. I slid my hand over the soft skin of her inner thigh, parting them further, and knelt between them.

Feeling her skin against mine nearly had me panting, for it was something I'd taken for granted before. I leaned over her body, holding my weight up above her baby bump, and stared deep into her eyes for a breath.

"I'm so sorry you were hurt because of me," I said, feeling the grief wash over me again. *"By me.* I never should have left you. I never should have abandoned you and our baby. I can't stand how you've suffered over and over again because of me. I thought leaving you would protect you from me and the dangers swarming me." I sighed, "But I think I was wrong."

"I know, baby." She said. "I'm sorry you blame yourself, because even now, I don't." She brushed her fingers over my cheek tenderly. "And I don't blame you for walking away to try to protect me. But it hasn't been easy on me either."

"I know," I said, laying my forehead against hers. "I'm done wallowing in self-pity, if you'll have me. I want to come back." I whispered. "I need to come back Cora, I can't exist without you and this baby any longer." I laid my hand on her stomach and was amazed at how firm it was under my large palm. She covered my hand with hers and tears pooled in her eyes. "By the time I realized leaving wasn't the answer, too much time had passed. I didn't know how to come home to you."

"We'll have you, Mav." She sniffled and pulled my head down to kiss me, and it felt like coming home. I savored her taste as she deepened the kiss until we were both desperate for more. "Take me, baby." She whispered. "Make me forget the pain and heal in the passion."

"Your wish is my command, Angel," I said back and then kissed my way down her neck and chest as she sighed and stretched out under me. I paused at her voluptuous tits and grabbed both in my hands, pinching her nipples and sucking them into my mouth.

"Careful, Mav, I'll come from that alone if you're not careful. They're so sensitive and it feels so good when I play with them."

"You play with them often, do you?" I asked her with a smirk on my face as I sucked one into my mouth, flicking it with my tongue as she writhed underneath me.

"Every chance I get." She panted, "Just like that Mav, oh God. That feels so good."

It was now a personal mission to get her to come like this because she was right; she was nearly coming unhinged from the sensation and it was magnificent to watch. I switched to her other hard nipple and twirled my tongue around it as I watched her. She looked so fucking sexy with her blonde hair fanned out across her pillow, her eyes closed, and her lush lips swollen and puffy from my kisses, parted on a sigh as she moaned under me.

"Suck on it." She panted, and I pulled the bud into my mouth and sucked hard as I pinched the other one. I slid my thigh between her spread legs and hitched it up, pressing against her bare wet pussy, once, twice... "Oh my God!" She cried and the next second she shattered beneath me as I continued to suck on her perfect tits. "Yes, baby! That feels so good."

When she came down from her orgasm, I watched as the red flush crawled across her chest and neck, proving she had enjoyed herself. But I was far from done with her. I kissed my way down past her breasts, hating the way her ribs showed through her skin as I went. "You're too skinny, Cora," I said, and she rolled her eyes.

"Your child has made eating difficult. But it's gotten better the last week or so." She said, running her fingers over my cheeks again affectionately. "Don't worry about us, Mav, we're going to be just fine."

I kissed her palm and then lowered myself further until my lips hovered right next to her belly button, I pressed a kiss gently to the taut skin there. "Hey little one, it's your daddy," I said softly and Cora ran her fingers through my hair as she watched. "I'm sorry I haven't been around for a while, but that's not going to keep happening anymore. I promise." I said, kissing her skin again. "But I need a favor from you, well two actually. I'm going to need you to stop making your mama sick because she needs to give you all the nutrients possible so you can grow up big and strong like your daddy."

"Are you assuming it's a boy?" She asked tenderly.

"Hmm." I looked back down at her belly, "Or maybe you'll be dainty and graceful like your mama, who knows." She smiled back down at me as I continued my little conversation with our baby. "But the second favor I'm going to need from you, regardless if you're a boy or girl, is I'm going to need you to plug your ears and close your eyes and pretend your mama is on a boat because I'm going to do some really obscene things to her right now that will scandalize your innocent virtue for the rest of forever."

"Oh my God, Maverick." She laughed and swatted me, as I chuckled against her belly.

"So do that for me, and I'll make sure you get ice cream for a snack every day for the rest of your life, got it?" I said and then nodded my head like the baby responded. "Good, go team."

"You're ridiculous." She groaned but didn't complain any further because my lips dropped further down her body to her exposed pussy and the mood in the air shifted from tender mirth to electric chemistry. "Maverick." She sighed as I pushed her legs back towards her chest, wide of her belly, and opened her to me.

"Yes, darling?" I asked, my mouth poised right over her clit and her scent was making me dizzy with need.

"I need you; I don't need any more foreplay." She begged.

"I need this," I responded and leaned down to run the tip of my tongue over her swollen clit before sucking it into my mouth like I had her nipples.

"Oh, God." She said and fell back onto the bed. "Hurry up if you must, but I need your cock." I smirked at her and pushed two fingers deep inside of her, scissoring them to open her up as she thrashed around on the bed.

"Good girl." I praised as I felt her hips rock back and forth, trying to find the rhythm needed to come again. "Come on my face baby."

Her back bowed and seconds later she screamed my name as her fingers dug into my hair and pulled. Her thighs squeezed my head and I grabbed them, pushing them open again as I continued to tease her.

"Now!" She gasped, "That was the deal, give me your cock right now."

I smirked and crawled up her body, pressing her thighs wide around my hips as my thick cock searched for her opening. "I've missed you," I growled against her neck as I ran the head of my cock through her wet folds. "I've really fucking missed you."

"Show me how much." She purred, scraping her nails over my scalp.

I pushed forward, thrusting into her until my balls laid against her ass. "Fuck." I groaned, kissing her deeply as my hips took up the rhythm we both loved.

"Maverick." She clawed at my back as I fucked her with long and deep thrusts, from root to tip and back again. "I thought of this, the entire time you were gone." She panted, "Of our wedding night when you told me to memorize at that moment how much you loved me. That's what I've held onto these last two months, Mav."

"Good girl." I circled my hips, already feeling the delicious tingles of my orgasm nipping up my spine, threatening to end this before she got off again. "You're so perfect."

She mewed and pulled her legs back wider, switching the angle that I was hitting inside of her, and her eyes rolled when I found her g spot. "Yes." She groaned.

The muscles in her neck tightened as she pushed her head back into the pillows further, and then her body stiffened beneath mine. Her pussy clamped down on my cock and started pulsating around it as her orgasm pushed her into bliss.

"Good girl." I gasped, pulling back to watch her face as she drew my own orgasm from my body and took my come deep inside of her. "So fucking tight." I panted and dropped my head into her shoulder as my cock twitched inside of her for a moment before I rolled off of her and pulled her to lay on her side facing me.

I ran my fingertips up and down her spine as we both came down from the euphoria coursing through our bodies.

"We're going to be okay, Cora darling," I whispered into the darkness as she snuggled into me deeper. "But we cannot stay here for another minute and I'm burning this lumpy ass mattress to put it out of its misery."

She snickered against my chest and shook her head. "Good, because I miss our bed so much."

"Let's go home, Angel."

"Let's."

Epilogue – Cora

I stood in the elevator, wearing a dark wine-colored dress that hugged my obnoxious belly and reminded me of the dress I'd worn on my very first day walking into Hawthorn Tower. It was hard to believe that had only been a few months ago.

This time, however, I didn't ride up to my floor with a handsome CFO trying to get my name as he flirted with me shamelessly. I rode up with my husband on both of our first days back to work since the Friday we'd left for our wedding.

The night that Maverick had shown up in my apartment, breaking the stretch of loneliness for both of us, had been the first day in healing the damage that the time apart had done. He made good on his vow to burn my mattress if we didn't leave my apartment right then and there, and we left to go back home to the penthouse together for the first time.

That was four weeks ago, and we'd stayed pretty secluded in the time since as we made up for lost time. Maverick worked from home, diving headfirst back into his role as CEO and micromanaging boss. Much to Dexter's approval.

While he worked tirelessly in the office in our penthouse, he was never more than a few steps away from me as he helped nurse me back to a healthier version of myself while I fell into the honeymoon phase of pregnancy with open arms. Each day we'd spend time together, enjoying the quiet silence around us and making memories through the pregnancy.

Like afternoon bubble baths in our soaker tub where Maverick would hold me against his chest and run his hands over my belly, talking to our baby, or reading a book from the library he was building up to match the one in the beach house.

After we would get out of the tub he would sit me down on the bed and help me rub lotion on my belly and tell our baby all of the things he thought they should know about the world they were coming into.

And I fell helplessly in love with him as not only my husband but as a father.

And standing in the elevator, getting ready to walk into the corporate world he had built with his bare hands, he was the picture of perfection.

The doors to the lobby of Jones Holding opened up and Mav led me out, holding my hand as we passed Peter the main receptionist on our way down the hall to his office.

"I have a surprise for you," Maverick said in a rumbly low voice at my ear as he pulled me towards the conference room next to his office.

"Oh, lord." I droned in feigned annoyance. He'd been surprising me with things from the moment we got back together, and he outdid the last one each time.

He smirked down at me and paused outside the mirrored door, and it was then that I realized the glass was set to match Mavericks, so there was one long continuous wall of mirror along the entire lobby. "Close your eyes." He said and I did, to humor him as he pushed both doors open. "Open them, baby." He said with a smile in his voice, and I tentatively did as he commanded.

And my breath was completely whisked away at the sight before me.

"Mav." I gasped, letting my eyes roam around a brand-new office built for a queen. I walked into the room and looked around in awe at the massive desk along the windows overlooking the city below and the comfy-looking couch and armchairs along the wall, and then at a small conference table in the corner. "What is all of this?" I asked him, turning around to find him leaning on the doorjamb with a sinfully sexy smile on his face.

"Your new office, Mrs. Jones."

"My–" I stuttered and shook my head, looking back over the beautiful feminine office around me. "I don't understand." I said, "I thought I was just going to sit in the boardroom, I don't need a whole office, Mav."

"Yes, you do." He said firmly and stepped forward. "Because my mom wants you to help takeover, the Luke Jones Charity and you're going to need a professional space to take that on. And besides," He said, sliding his hands over my hips and pulling me into him. "I've been clear about wanting you at my side here since day one, Angel, and this office, literally attached to mine, is exactly where you belong. We're building a legacy not just for ourselves anymore, Cora, but for our kids to take over someday. And I want to be able to hand them something that has as much of their mother in it as their father when we do."

I took a deep calming breath and looked up into his eyes, forcing myself to trust that he wanted me here alongside him and let the excitement that was trying to take over my entire system through and danced from foot to foot as he smiled widely down at me.

"I love it, Mav." I purred and offered my lips to him, and he hungrily accepted, kissing me deeply. "You're perfect Mr. Jones."

He chuckled against my lips and tsked his tongue, "I'd like to be able to say this was an incredibly selfless decision that I only thought about your happiness when I made it, but to be completely honest with you there was one selfish motive paving the way when I started this project before our wedding."

"Oh, yeah?" I asked, biting my lip. "What was that?"

"I won't have to do anything more than carry you across the threshold between our offices each day when I'm ready to spread you out on my desk to eat my lunch." He said with a wickedly naughty glint in his eye.

I scoffed at him and swatted his arm. "Want to break in my new desk before I sit down at it for the first time?" I countered and he growled deeply in his chest before stepping over to a panel on the wall.

"Why Mrs. Jones, how did you know that was the very first thing I have written on my agenda for the day?" He asked as the doors swung shut and locked, and we were completely encapsulated in a mirrored box with naughty depraved things on our minds.

The End

Ready for the next King of Hawthorn's story?

Have a nibble to hold you over for now.

Indulging His Desire

Want a snippet of another King of Hawthorn Tower's Story?

I've lived as half the man I used to be for the last four years.

I just simply... existed. I didn't feel anything, I didn't indulge in anything I enjoyed, I didn't even hardly smile or laugh anymore.

Or at least I had until a new neighbor moved into my building and captured my attention, drawing me in like a moth to a flame. For the first time in four years, something... stirred deep inside me.

I was obsessed from day one, unable to keep my eyes away from the apartment's bedroom window directly across from my own like a fucking voyeur. The shades were never closed and my view into the mysterious bedroom was never obstructed.

And therefore, the object of my most recent desire was always on display for me, and the more times I watched the show put on, the surer I became that the curtains were left open on purpose for me.

So I found myself staring, waiting, and hoping to catch glimpses of the tanned skin colored with bright tattoos, or the dark brown hair that looked like silk, or the sexy as hell piercing green eyes that would stare back at me as I watched.

The problem though?

The object of my desire, the very thing I'd become obsessed with sexually... was a man.

And I was... straight.

Or at least I had been.

Dexter Chase's story is ready to download today and dive in!

https://a.co/d/cU5QnNE

Stalk Me

Want to stay up to date with all of my shenanigans and upcoming news? Pretty Please?

Check out my website: www.ammccoybooks.com

How about TikTok, are you there? https://www.tiktok.com/@ammccoy_author?is_from_webapp=1&sender_device=pc

Facebook? I've got a readers group there! Twisted After Dark: A .M. McCoy's Reader Group is mostly unhinged and full of exclusive news! https://www.facebook.com/share/g/b41rkBMkSurWz43i/

IG? https://www.instagram.com/ammccoy_author/

Amazon? https://www.amazon.com/stores/A.-M.-McCoy/author/B07QNRJMLB?ref=ap_rdr&isDramIntegrated=true&shoppingPortalEnabled=true

I think that's all for now!